W9-BNW-134

MAN OF THE HOUR

ALSO BY PETER BLAUNER

Slow Motion Riot

Casino Moon

The Intruder

MAN OF THE HOUR

A NOVEL BY

PETER BLAUNER

LITTLE, BROWN AND COMPANY

Boston New York London

Copyright © 1999 by Peter Blauner

All rights reserved. No part of this book may be reproduced in any form or by any electronic or mechanical means, including information storage and retrieval systems, without permission in writing from the publisher, except by a reviewer who may quote brief passages in a review.

First Edition

The characters and events in this book are fictitious. Any similarity to real persons, living or dead, is coincidental and not intended by the author.

Library of Congress Cataloging-in-Publication Data
Blauner, Peter.
Man of the hour : a novel / Peter Blauner. — 1st ed.
p. cm.
ISBN 0-316-03817-2
I. Title.
PS3552.L3936M36 1999
813'.54 — dc21 98-31801

10 9 8 7 6 5 4 3 2 1

MV-NY

Printed in the United States of America

To my beautiful and talented wife, Peggy

Woe to him who seeks to pour oil on the waters when God has brewed them into a gale! Woe to him who seeks to appease rather than appal! Woe to him whose good name is more to him than goodness!

— HERMAN MELVILLE

MAN OF THE HOUR

Prologue

The students withdrew from the classroom like a tide pulling away from the shore, leaving just one boy stranded in a chair at the back.

He looked at the clock, glanced at the floor, stared out the window at the ruins of Dreamland Amusement Park over by the Coney Island boardwalk. Anything to avoid the watchful eye of his teacher, Mr. Fitzgerald, who sat at his desk, studying him.

"Do you know why I asked you to stay, Nasser?" he asked the boy.

The boy shrugged, refusing to look at him. He was eighteen and already expert in a certain kind of resistance.

"I read the journal you gave me," the teacher said, holding up a sheet covered on both sides with an emphatic red scrawl.

"Then okay," the boy mumbled. His accent turned the *th* sound into a buzzing *z*.

"Thirty-five times you wrote, 'I hate America.' "

The boy started to smile and then stopped himself.

"You know, there's only one *m* in America." The teacher came over with the page and sat beside the boy, showing him where the misspelling was. Even in a chair, he towered over the student.

"Ya habela," the boy said. *"Coosa mach."*

"Okay," said the teacher, not understanding the specific words, but getting the general sentiment. "If that's the way you feel, that's all right. I was kind of an angry kid myself." He edged his chair a little closer. "But listen, as long as you're here in school, you might as well get something out of the place."

The boy ignored him and started humming to himself.

"Look, there's more eloquent ways to make your point." The teacher pulled out a slim booklet and began reading aloud from Allen Ginsberg's *Howl.* "I saw the best minds of my generation destroyed by madness . . ."

The poem was a kind of last-ditch effort to hook kids who couldn't be reached any other way. It could either take the top of their heads off or make them recoil in horror and revulsion. But one way or the other, it never failed to engage them.

Fitzgerald was aware of Nasser rocking slightly in his chair as he kept reading. But when he got to the part about "angelheaded hipsters" seeing "Mohammedan angels staggering on tenement roofs," the boy put his hands over his ears and shut his eyes.

"Stop it!" he said. "This is the blasphemy!"

"All right, all right." The teacher closed the book, realizing he might have gone too far. He always avoided the more graphic parts of the poem, but he'd forgotten that line was in there too. "We don't have to read the whole thing."

Tell me I didn't lose him already, he thought.

The boy slowly lowered his hands and looked at him. "I don't know why they let anyone write this," he said in a wounded voice.

"I'm just trying to show you that you're not alone," Fitzgerald told him. "You don't have to go around like a scream looking for a mouth. You know? There's a hundred thousand other ways to go."

For the briefest of seconds, the words caught the boy's interest. There was a spark behind the eyes. He started to turn in his chair. Is he going to open up? The teacher leaned forward. But then the movement stopped. The boy had reached the edge of something and couldn't make himself go any farther.

"You can't understand." He shut his eyes. "In a million years, you could never understand."

Fitzgerald decided to give it one last try. "Look," he said. "I can tell you're a bright, sensitive kid. But you're obviously miserable here. Nothing's getting through. Tell me how to get inside your head."

"I don't want you in my head!"

"All right. Then tell me how to help you. How's that?"

But he could feel the boy disengaging, closing down on him. You never knew what baggage these kids were bringing into the classroom. Some of them walked straight in from war zones and prisons. Others were just naturally antisocial.

"Just leave me alone," Nasser said, turning his chair away.

"Okay." The teacher thought of putting a hand on the boy's shoulder but then decided against it. "But you know, Nasser, I can't pass you with the kind of work you're doing. If you're willing to put in a little extra time, though, I think I can help you. I can maybe even help you graduate. Then you can spend the rest of your life hating America and it won't be my problem anymore." But that didn't even rate a small smile from the kid. "So come on. We're not in a war yet, are we?"

The boy listened to the words, shivered a little, and then got up and walked out of the room without looking back.

1

By midnight, Church Avenue in Brooklyn was almost a dead artery. An old Chevy dragged its muffler down the middle of the street, and the sound echoed like tin cans falling in a canyon. Sodium streetlights shone down on corrugated iron gates in front of a liquor store, a nail salon, and a shop specializing in wigs made from "Real 100% Human Hair." Only a check-cashing place was still open, with blue neon in the window and a giant dollar bill on the sign out front.

Across the street, two men sat in a bruised red '88 Plymouth, watching the door and the movement behind the window.

"*Aynu hoa*," said the one behind the wheel, a big bear of a man with an onion-dome bald head, a heavy graying beard, and tinted aviator glasses. "Where is this guy? My ass is getting asleep."

"That's not how you say this, is it?" said Nasser, sitting beside him.

"Sure it is," said his friend Youssef, switching back to Arabic. "It means you're tired of waiting."

They looked like father and son, sitting there. Youssef was muscular but going to flab. A long crimson scar was visible through the buttons at the top of his shirt, and the tails were out over the gun in his waistband. Nasser, who was now twenty-two, had grown up thin and tense, with liquid brown eyes, soft prim-looking lips, and an accidental hint of Elvis Presley in his pompadour. Thus far in his life, he hadn't been able to grow more than a weedy little beard to make himself look devout, so he'd just decided to stay clean-shaven. A rusty key dangled from a chain around his neck.

"Maybe we should go," he said.

"We're not going anywhere," said Youssef, the Great Bear. "Remember what this is about. This is about *jihad*."

"Yes, I know about *jihad*." Nasser chewed his fingernails. "This is a Holy War. But I don't see why this is a Holy War *here*. This just seems like stealing."

"Everything is *jihad*." Youssef nudged him with his elbow. "Everything you do from when you get up in the morning. If you have a cup of Turkish coffee, instead of the instant American kind, this is *jihad*. If you tell a brother about the Holy Book, this is *jihad*. If you turn off a television, this is *jihad* in the mind. But the greatest thing you can do for *jihad* is to fight. Remember, one hour on the battlefield is worth a hundred years of prayer."

"I know."

"What we're doing here is like the caravan raids from the olden days, after the *hijra*. The Prophet himself allowed this."

Nasser took his fingers from his mouth. He wondered if this was wise, what they were about to do. Yes, Youssef could cite verses, whole *suras*, to support it, but words could be twisted and turned to mean anything.

"I still don't know. Can't we raise the funds another way? Isn't this *haram?*"

"Of course it's not *haram*." Youssef started to shrug but then suddenly grabbed Nasser's arm. "Okay, it's him," he said in a low, heated voice. "This is the one we follow."

He leaned across Nasser's lap and pointed out a tall, thin Rastafarian in a camouflage jacket and a green knit cap, shambling up the street. The man walked with a loping rhythm, as if there were music only he could hear.

"He always comes late, this one," said Youssef. "I've been watching. It's because he smokes the marijuana. I am sure of this. That's why he's never on time to relieve the one behind the counter. He's a pig, I tell you, this one. I've seen the way he eats. The jerk chicken and the jerk pork. *Uch*. I tell you it makes me sick just to think about it."

Nasser sat there, watching the Rastaman a moment, trying to hear the music. Then trying to imagine the man eating pork and smoking marijuana. Trying to work up some hatred for him.

The Rastaman went into the check-cashing store.

"Come on, let's go." The Great Bear reached for the door handle. "Remember what you're supposed to do and nobody gets hurt. When he opens the door to go behind the counter, we go in after him."

A passing livery cab almost sideswiped Youssef as he got out and put on a baseball cap with an *X* on it. Nasser put on his own *X* cap and climbed out on the passenger side, squeezing between two car bumpers to get to the curb. The .22-caliber pistol felt like a brick in the pocket of his maroon vinyl windbreaker.

He watched the glass door open and saw Youssef follow the Rastaman into the check-cashing place, the bear pursuing a hound dog. Nasser hesitated for just a moment on the sidewalk, the humidity of the night enfolding him. He wondered how many blocks it was to the nearest subway station. His nerve. Where was his nerve? He saw the cracked glass door swing shut behind the Great Bear. Then he reached inside his shirt and fingered the key hanging from the chain around his neck, knowing he had no choice.

With blood pounding in his ears, he moved quickly across the pavement, pulled the door open, and stepped inside.

The check-cashing place was little more than a twelve-by-twenty room with scuffed black-and-white linoleum floors, scrappy wood-paneled walls, and a little stall in the corner for local jewelry makers and incense sellers to peddle their wares. A bald-headed black man in shirtsleeves counted money behind a smudged bulletproof glass partition. There was a tinge of ammonia and marijuana in the air and a radio was playing a raucous reggae song with a deep-voiced hectoring singer, a walrus of sound.

The Rastaman in the green knit cap was knocking on the chipped wooden door next to the glass partition, ready to go in and relieve the man behind the counter. Nasser prepared to reach for his gun. But then the door behind him opened and a stout young woman in a red beret entered the storefront, pushing a little boy in a stroller—no more than two years old, wearing tiny black Nikes and a sheriff's badge made from tinfoil. Nasser froze, looking at the woman and the child. What were they doing here so late? The place was supposed to be empty at this hour. He looked over at Youssef, expecting a signal to change their plan, but Youssef was standing at a tall side table a few feet away, studiously ignoring him and pretending to sign a check.

"So I tried your remedy and I feel much better now." The woman approached the Rastaman. "But that aloe vera, it's disgusting."

"What did you do, child? Swallow it?" The Rastaman parted his hands.

"You mean, I was supposed to rub it on?"

The Rastaman laughed and knocked again on the door next to the partition.

And then everything changed. Time seemed to expand and contract simultaneously. The chipped door opened. The woman with the stroller bent down to tie the baby's Nikes. Nasser saw Youssef pull back his shirttails and reach for his gun. He had to remind himself to breathe. Youssef was charging at the Rastaman and pushing him through the partly opened door some ten feet away, shouting: "Open the cash drawer or someone will get hurt!"

Back in the main room, Nasser took out his gun and pointed it at the woman reluctantly, tentatively, as if they both knew he had no intention of using it. He thought of saying something to reassure her, but decided against it—Youssef would be too angry. Instead, he stared at the little boy's tinfoil badge, with its five points, wondering how long it had taken the woman to make it.

Then he heard the shot in the room behind the glass. A ferocious little sound like a balloon bursting. Part of him shriveled inside, hearing it. The room suddenly became warmer. The air closed in around his ears. The woman with the baby started to scream, knowing someone was dead. Nasser tried to say something to comfort her, but then the gun in the other room went off again.

He moved quickly into the doorway and saw the Rastaman splayed across the floor like a rag doll, arms and legs tossed around him, head turned, blood staining the front of his camouflage jacket and puddling on the floor next to him. Youssef was pulling the bills out of the cash drawer and stuffing them into the little blue laundry bag he'd had folded up in his back pocket. He didn't see the bald black man in shirtsleeves rising up behind him, his face covered in blood, pulling out a small silver handgun.

Nasser saw his own hand rise with the .22, as if floating up through water. The impulse to squeeze the trigger came from somewhere besides his brain. The gun jumped and bucked in his hand and the noise bit into the air. A small part of the bald black man's head flew off as he wobbled, fell against a stool, and slid down to the floor, still holding his gun. An angry black-red splatter remained on the wall panel behind him, with long spindly lines dripping down.

The woman in the other room scrambled, trying to get out the front door with the baby in the stroller. Nothing in her life had prepared her for this moment. Whereas everything had prepared Nasser. It was his destiny to be here and to do the things that would come afterward. So why did he still find himself paralyzed?

Youssef finished with the money, passed Nasser in the doorway, and came back into the main room. The woman turned away, not daring to face him. She understood that looking at either of them meant death. But it was too late. Youssef stepped up calmly and shot her in the side of the head.

She fell away from life, without even a chance to look back at her baby. And for a moment, this struck Nasser as unutterably sad, not at all part of the natural order. He knew these people were infidels and deserved to die, but he couldn't help himself. When Youssef turned the gun toward the boy, who was screaming in his stroller, Nasser gently nudged him from behind.

"Come on, sheik, we have to go," he said.

Two minutes later, as the car sped down Flatbush Avenue, Nasser still kept feeling the kick and burn of the gun in his hand. Slowly he tried to get back into the proper flow of time again. He fingered the key on the chain around his neck as headlights washed over the windshield and police sirens sounded from far away.

"Don't worry, my friend, they are not following us," said Youssef, one hand on the wheel, the other fumbling for the little amber bottle of nitroglycerin pills in his shirt pocket. "We are going home."

"What happened?"

"What do you mean 'happened'? We were successful. I am so excited, I think I'm going to throw up. I don't have a chance to count yet, but I'm sure we have enough to finance the next stage."

Nasser realized he was still trembling from the force of events. "Sheik," he said, using the word the way Americans called each other "sir." "There's something I have to ask you."

"What?"

"Were you really going to shoot him? The little boy."

"This is *jihad*." The Great Bear stared straight ahead into the oncoming traffic. "If it was God's will, I would have."

"But I was the one who pushed you out of there." Nasser let go of the key and looked once over his shoulder, to make sure they weren't being pursued.

Youssef shrugged. "Then that was God's will too."

2

A morning mist was burning off over the Atlantic and seagulls settled on the railings of the famous boardwalk along the southwestern rim of Brooklyn.

Nasser walked stiffly up the front steps of Coney Island High School, a salt-corroded, graffiti-insulted redbrick building on Surf Avenue. For the occasion he'd put on a black polyknit tie bought from an African street peddler in East Flatbush and a secondhand wool sports jacket that was much too warm for early October. He hadn't been back in the four years since he left school, and now, as he walked into the lobby with a battered briefcase in hand and was confronted with the metal detector, he was not sure how to proceed.

"Please," he said to the school security guard, "I have to see Mr. Fitzgerald."

Come on. Keep them focused. Ten minutes before the buzzer.

Up in a fourth-floor classroom, David Fitzgerald angled his glasses and smoothed his beard as he read aloud from *The Red Badge of Courage*.

" 'But here he was confronted with a thing of moment,' " he began, in a deep, chesty voice with a slight Long Island accent. " 'It had suddenly appeared to him that perhaps in a battle he might run. He was forced to admit that as far as war was concerned he knew nothing of himself.' "

He slammed the book shut with a dramatic pop, getting the attention of all thirty-six kids. They were jammed into the little dimly lit classroom with yellow walls, uneven wood-plank floors, and an old rotting hulk of a teacher's desk at the front smelling vaguely of formaldehyde.

"All right, let's throw this one out to our studio audience," he said, keeping his voice up so he could be heard above the constant drilling upstairs. "We're talking about this idea of being tested again. The whole notion of what a hero really is. So how many of you guys think you would run?"

The students turned on each other with incredulous snorts and fey high-pitched wisecracks. He was going at it too directly. These were Coney Island kids: you weren't going to get them to own up to fear and vulnerability that easily.

"Come on, guys, don't leave me hanging here." He picked up the gnarled old Rawlings baseball glove he had lying on his desk from the discussion of *The Catcher in the Rye* earlier. "The point isn't that I want you to memorize these books. The point is, I want you to find something of yourself in them. Or maybe to take something out of them that will become part of yourself." He looked around, thinking he saw a few glimmers of light.

He slipped his left hand into the glove and pounded his right fist into it, savoring the loud *wop* bouncing off the classroom walls, feeling the performing juices start to flow.

"A-right, let me give you an example," he said, wading in among them—all six feet two, two hundred and ten pounds of him—like a ship breaking through ice floes. "Back when I was a kid, I had a job being a lifeguard one summer at the Westbury Beach Club in Atlantic Beach. Can you imagine me in a bathing suit?"

He held up his arms and made a show of sucking in his ever-so-slack middle-aged gut, getting a round of giggles. "Yeah, right," he said. "I looked like the 'before' picture in one of those muscle-builder ads on the subway. Anyway, my father was this big war hero with all these medals and I used to dream of doing something great to impress him. And everyone else. You know, common adolescent fantasy, right? You save the girl and she swoons in your arms."

About three-quarters of the boys in the class smirked in recognition while the girls held back, waiting to be convinced.

"So one day, I'm up there on my lifeguard chair, waiting to be a hero, and I see this head bobbing up and down on the horizon. So I'm *on it*. Okay?" He moved toward the back of the class, hearing chair legs scraping on the linoleum floor as kids parted to get out of his way. "This is my dream girl, who I'm going to save. And I go running out there and I dive into the surf and I'm stroking against the current, man." He mimed thrashing in the water, pulling back great handfuls of the Atlantic. "And then I get there, like two hundred yards out, and *it's this big fat old lady in a bathing cap*."

"Oh, snap!" yelled a boy called Ray-Za in the third row, who up until this minute had been staring mindlessly into his tiny Game Boy screen.

A few of the others cracked up too. It's happening, David thought. After four weeks of school, they're finally beginning to wake up after the long summer's mental hibernation. Now was the time to grab them before they slipped back into indifference.

"So I'm trying to pull her out," said David, doing the gasping-for-air bit. "And they tell you when you're in lifeguard class, grab the hair—don't grab an arm or a shoulder, because the person you're trying to save may grab you and pull you down. So I grab for her bathing cap and it comes off and she's like *bald* underneath."

"Ho shit!" Merry Tyrone in the second row put a hand over her mouth.

"Oh yeah," said David, heading back toward the blackboard. "She's bald and she's losing it *big-time*. She grabs me around the neck and starts trying to pull me down with her. This big bald lady is trying to drown me in the middle of the Atlantic. It was like some Freudian nightmare. Anyway, make a long story short, the skinny girl lifeguard I had a crush on from the club next door had to jump in and fish us both out."

"*Whhooo-aaa, Mr. Fitzgerald!*"

The whole class went off, boys and girls equally. Well, that wasn't exactly what happened, but who cared? They liked it when he told stories on himself. You were trying to spark them, engage them, break up the frozen sea in each of them.

"All right, so somebody else give me an example of character being tested," he said, pounding his fist into the glove. "I'll take anything from life or one of the books we've read." He switched into his Coney Island sideshow barker's voice. "Step right up. Make your case or get outta my face. *Think fast!*"

Without warning, he whipped off the glove and threw it to Elizabeth Hamdy in the first row. That bright and radiant girl who usually came to class wearing a white Arab head scarf and Rollerblades. He wanted her to set the tone for the others. She caught the glove and looked around, half embarrassed and half proud. No head scarf today.

"Um, what about Holden Caulfield?" she said quietly.

"Yeah, okay. What about him? Speak. You have The Glove."

"Well, he has that dream near the end. About saving the kids falling off a cliff. That's why it's called *The Catcher in the Rye*."

"All right, but he only *thinks* about that." David bowed to her. "He's never really tested that directly. Can you give me a more concrete example?"

"Well, my father, when he crossed the river," she said quickly and then lowered her eyes, hiding behind a smile.

"Yeah?" he said, not sure whether to push her. "What river was that?"

"The Jordan."

"That's in the Middle East, you guys." David cocked an eyebrow at the rest of the class. You couldn't make any assumptions about people's knowledge of geography these days.

"Yeah, he's Palestinian." Elizabeth blushed a little.

"So why was crossing the Jordan such a big deal?"

"Because the Israelis shelled his family's village," she said shyly, not liking the attention but determined to answer the question diligently. "And his parents asked him to take his brother and sister across the river to Jordan. They thought everyone was going to get raped and killed by soldiers."

"And so did he do it?" asked David. He hadn't meant to delve so deeply, but the door was open now.

"Yes." She swallowed and lowered her eyes. "One time, he said that when he crossed the river, it was like his childhood disappeared over his shoulder. But, you know, not everyone in my family was happy about it." Her fingers curled up along the edge of the desk.

"Why not?"

"Some of them thought he should have stayed and resisted or something like that. But I thought it was more courageous, what he *did* do."

"Which was what?" asked David, who remembered Mr. Hamdy only as a squat and exceedingly polite sixtyish grocery store owner he'd met on Parents' Night last year.

"He survived," she said, tightening her mouth a little. "He moved around a lot and eventually he saved enough money to come to this country and try to start a new life for his family. So it was like crossing another river."

David sensed there was more to the story, but he decided not to push her on it. She'd said enough. In fact, if anyone else in the class had spoken that long, she would have been shouted down and called a loudmouth chickenhead. But with Elizabeth, the others hung back a little. They sensed she had a kind of glow about her, a special presence in the room. Look at her, thought David: she's a star and she doesn't even know it.

"Okay, thank you, Elizabeth." He gave her a thumbs-up and saw her slump down a little in her seat, relieved she didn't have to say any more.

"All right, somebody else!" he said, raising his voice so he could be heard above the construction racket upstairs. "Step right up. Make your case. All tales of guts and cowardice welcome."

There was a pause, but he didn't rush to fill it up. After fifteen years of teaching, he'd learned never to force the answers down their throats. Let them come to it, on their terms. That's the only way they'd ever learn anything.

Eventually, Kevin Hardison in the back row half-raised his hand. He was a runty wannabe-gangsta with monogrammed gold caps over his front teeth, a Dollar Bill cap, and two sets of baggy clothes which he alternated day after day because likely that was all he could afford. Having been in fairly serious trouble himself when he was young, David always had a soft spot for the roughnecks and knuckleheads. He signaled for Elizabeth to throw Kevin the glove.

"I was gonna say something about how I moved last year," the kid began with a soft lisp.

David started to stop him, saying he wanted to keep the discussion focused on heroism in literature. But then he remembered this was only the second time Kevin had spoken up in the first month of school. Better to let him go, to encourage him.

"All right, what's that got to do with this idea of being tested?"

He saw the boy hesitate and start to sink back down into his chair, sorry he'd raised his hand. It was going to be one of those make-or-break moments, David realized, where a kid either becomes part of the life of a class or starts the process of withdrawing and eventually dropping out.

"It's all right," he told Kevin. "Make your case. I got your back."

The kid licked his lips. " 'Kay." He began slowly, as if he were bouncing a ball at the foul line. "Like last year? My family moved outta the Coney Island Houses and got a apartment in O'Dwyer Gardens." He was talking about two massive housing projects a few blocks away from each other in Coney Island. "Anyways, these guys from my old crew at the Houses had a beef with my new boys in O'Dwyer. And then they both came to me and said what-all am I gonna do when they have a fight on Friday night. Whose side am I gonna be on?"

"So what did you do?" David said gently, trying to protect the moment and keep the space open for the kid.

"I stayed home, by my moms," said Kevin, trying to sound tough and unashamed of himself. "I was like just buggin' out with the WB, and jacking the sound up so I wouldn't hear them busting caps and the sirens outside and shit. And then in the morning, I found out my man Shawn De Shawn got shot in the head. They had him on life support for a month before they let him die. That was messed up, man. He was gonna play point guard for St. John's."

His voice trailed off and he looked down at his fingers, ill at ease over having exposed so much to the group. A couple of the other guys in the class started mumbling behind his back and pointing in contempt, but David cut them off with a cold stare.

"All right, *enough*," he said, before turning his attention back to Kevin. "Thank you, Kevin. I give you props for opening up like that. Shawn was in my class, and for the record, I think you did the right thing. And if anyone disagrees, they can take it up with me personally after class."

Okay, so it wasn't "Elegy Written in a Country Churchyard," but to have a kid like Kevin let his guard down so much was a small miracle. The kind—along with having Elizabeth in his class—that kept David going year after year in spite of budget cuts, school board politics, and plaster dust drizzling down on his desk.

He cruised by Kevin's desk, collecting the glove and quietly telling him, "Come talk to me later if you want." The morning was developing a kind of unusual gravity, with kids dropping their hearts on their desks. He made a U-turn back toward the front of the class and used his booming voice again, trying to lighten the discussion a little.

"Okay, I don't want to turn this into a therapy group or a talk show," he said, picking up a piece of chalk. "I want to bring it back to the books. Because that's what we're here to talk about. Right? So can somebody else give me an example of a character in one of the books who's either being tested or maybe even testing something?"

A Russian boy named Yuri Ehrlich slowly hoisted his arm in the fifth row, over by the radiators. He was a brilliant but unscrupulous kid, with long, straight brown hair and a disturbing habit of cheating when he didn't have to, as if the old Soviet habits of beating the system were too deeply ingrained in him. David wondered if he'd change this year.

"Raskolnikov." Yuri rolled out the name with a thick accent.

"Raskolnikov who chopped up the old widow and her sister?" David tossed him the mitt. "Should I have brought an ax instead of the glove to throw around today?"

Uneasy laughter. They were reading *Crime and Punishment* in Advanced Placement English, not in this class. But why make a deal out of it if the kid wanted to contribute?

"All right, I'll bite. Why Raskolnikov?"

Yuri sat there, silent and brooding, letting the glove tumble to the floor.

"Maybe he means that Raskolnikov is testing the definition of what it means to be an extraordinary man," Elizabeth Hamdy said earnestly, leaning forward on her elbows. She was taking A.P. for extra credit too.

"Okay, I can live with that," said David, thinking this really was the day for heavy topics. "So does he succeed or fail?"

"I think he fails, because his definition of 'extraordinary' is flawed," said Elizabeth in her perfect diction, obviously glad not to be talking about herself.

"Yuri, is that why you think he fails?"

A tensile moment of anticipation. Other kids looking at each other, checking their watches; David holding up his arms, wanting everyone to hush up and listen.

"No." Yuri stared down at his red Converse high-tops. "He fails because he turned himself in."

The period buzzer went off.

"Yuri, you're scaring me." David went to pick up the glove. "The rest of you give me three to five pages on this subject by next Friday."

With the change-over between classes, the hallways exploded in sound and visual chaos. Students stood around in exclusive circles and insolent clusters, as if daring people to pass.

Nasser moved by them gingerly, feeling just as invisible as he had felt when he was a junior here, repeating the grade, four years ago. Everything looked the same, except for some red-white-and-blue bunting on the walls. The green-tiled walls, the dull streaky floors, the chipped mahogany banisters, the names of war veterans and valedictorians of years past painted in gold letters on brown plaques, the sports trophies in glass display cases, the posters celebrating Italian American week with pictures of famous actors, pop singers, Christopher Columbus, Leonardo Da Vinci, and pasta dishes. But the feeling was a little bit different. He no longer wanted to fit in here, he told himself. He no longer wanted to be one of them. Let them swagger by, talking in code, flirting, fighting, making incomprehensible private jokes. With their bared midriffs, their pierced noses, dyed hair, black nail polish, foul language, their tight and baggy clothes, their frank appraising stares. Seeing him but not seeing him. Someday a Great Chastisement would befall all of them.

On the other side of the building, David Fitzgerald hiked a black Jansport book bag over his shoulder and walked past the gauntlet of kids on his way to the office. The inside of the school was like something dreamed up by a fun-house designer. Long, dark hallways that didn't go anywhere, stairwells that didn't connect from floor to floor, offices with tiny windows. Traffic patterns loosely based on Boston and Tijuana. Acoustics appropriate for a heavy-metal concert or a Manhattan restaurant. Buzzers going off for absolutely no reason.

A group of loiterers in front of the boys' room called out to him.

"Yo, what's up, Mr. Fitz?"

"Yeah, look out, don't step on me, Mr. Fitzgerald!"

"Yo, you're scaring me, Mr. Fitzgerald!"

Though he had a few inches on most of the kids, occasionally a hand would reach out to touch him on the head or the shoulder, either mockingly or affectionately. It was hard to tell at times. But there was something comforting about it anyway. A kind of assurance that he had a secure place in this intricate little municipal beehive.

"Yo, Mr. Fitz, you gonna call my parole officer for me?"

"Mr. Fitz, you gonna talk to my moms? Right?"

"Yo, Mr. Fitzgerald, how's the bike?"

Oh yes, the bike. An old-fashioned Schwinn with a banana seat he'd picked up for five dollars at a sidewalk sale. He'd first developed an image as an eccentric because of that bike. Some years back, he and his soon-to-be-ex-wife Renee had been living in Park Slope and he'd ridden it to school a couple of days a week, instead of taking the subway. So he became the bicycle man. Even after they moved back to Manhattan and he started taking the train again, he was still "the bicycle man" to the kids. He had a reputation to uphold. Funny Mr. Fitzgerald. Weird Mr. Fitzgerald. Not a bad thing. It was an identity. A way for people to think about him. One time he brought a baseball glove into class when they were talking about *The Catcher in the Rye*. So that became another part of his mythology. Mr. Fitzgerald brought in props. Now every year he had to bring in the glove for the imperfect hero discussions. The kids expected it.

"Yo!" he shouted out to a Dominican kid called Obstreperous Q from his seventh-period class, who was sweet-talking a girl by the fire stairs. "Come by my office later. I got that book of García Lorca poems I was telling you about."

When David arrived at the door of the English Department office Donna Vitale was standing in the doorway, waiting for him. Donna with her frizzy straw-colored hair, her wonderful warm shining smile, and her one wayward eye staring slightly out into space.

"You have a visitor," she said.

"Tell me it's not Larry coming to complain about my programs again."

Larry Simonetti, the school's principal, had been in a state of high fret for the past week, ever since Albany issued a report calling the school "one of the ten worst-managed" in the city. Test scores were fine, but the school had ricocheted from scandal to scandal in the last twelve months. There was the security guard running away with the ninth grader, the falling bricks that seriously injured an eleventh grader last spring, and of course the $75,000 from the annual budget that was mysteriously missing. The governor himself was scheduled to come next week and give a speech about "taking back our schools," possibly as a prelude to announcing his own candidacy for President.

"No, it's not Larry," said Donna. "It's a blast from the past. I told him he could wait at your desk."

"Thanks, Ms. Vitale."

He started to move past her, but she caught his elbow. "I also wondered if I could talk to you about coming over for dinner next week," she said softly.

He stopped short, flattered but awkward, suddenly feeling like a bashful ape. How did women handle this kind of attention? "Um, can I get back to you on that, Donna?"

"You got the number."

He wondered if he was missing a great opportunity here, waiting to see if he could still work things out with Renee. Ms. Vitale was smart, she had ballast, and something about her suggested a kind of rowdy availability. You could imagine sitting up in bed, drinking beer with her.

"But don't wait too long, David." She brushed by him on her way to the Xerox room. "I might not be around forever."

He continued on into the office. A narrow little blue room, off a main corridor, with a dozen desks for the twenty teachers in the English department. The junior staffers were expected to roam like nomads and put their papers and books down on any surface that happened to be clear, while the senior teachers hunkered down and defended their areas like mangy old primates. Three students loitered inexplicably by the water fountain and a work-crew guy stood on a ladder pulling down parts of the ceiling, looking for God knows what hazardous materials. A tattered print of Edvard Munch's *The Scream* adorned a wall above an overstuffed file cabinet, and a group of painters stood around with dripping rollers, trying to freshen the room up for the governor's visit.

The visitor was sitting in David's chair, studying the papers on top of his desk and the placard above it with the Melville quote *God keep me from ever completing anything.*

What did that mean? Nasser wondered. He'd never trusted this one, this Mr. Fitzgerald, with his patient smile and unruly brown hair. He'd sat in the back of his class for a whole term, too bored yet too intimidated to speak up. Feeling the work was both above him and beneath him. Not understanding most of what was said; not getting the jokes; not liking the fact that he'd been left back once already and was older than most of the other students. And especially not liking it when Mr. Fitzgerald would call on him in class, asking him to explain what he thought of *The Great Gatsby* or *The Deerslayer* or some other immoral American book. It was humiliating, like being stripped naked in front of the other students. He stammered and stuttered, wanting to crawl under his chair, while this man read him immoral poems and tried to force him to think and speak in an uncomfortable way.

He'd dropped out soon after that. But there was another part of Nasser that was confused, being back here. The weaker part that needed to talk to someone about the things he'd seen. He remembered how he'd watched other students talk to Mr. Fitzgerald, sharing jokes and intimate secrets after class, and how he'd wished he could unburden himself to someone that way.

"It's Nasser, right?" David set down his bag and offered his hand, grateful for the excuse to ignore the pink phone message from Visa lying amid the piles of uncorrected papers from his five classes on his desk.

The thought of the $2,500 he owed on his credit card made the back of his neck ache.

The visitor looked up, startled, with luminous brown eyes, just like his sister's. "I am surprised for you to remember me." His handshake was limp and cautious.

"Sure, I remember almost all my students."

Not that he'd done much worth remembering, this Nasser. Just sat in the back, looking pissed off all term. There was a certain number of kids like him every year, maybe twenty, thirty percent. The unreachables. Who either didn't speak the language or just didn't give a damn. After all these years, David accepted that triage went on in the classroom. You helped the ones who were going to make it and made the best deal you could with the ones who wouldn't. And once in a while, you found a gem in the gravel. There'd be a kid like Kevin Hardison, of no special promise, yet somehow you could find a way to buff him up and make him shine. You could signal him that there were life and ideas and mystery on the other side of the great divide of adulthood; it wasn't all just driving on the expressway, flipping burgers at Mickey D.'s, and selling drugs on the corner. High school was the last chance at true democracy, where everyone stood more or less equal. So you went to the wall for these kids. You bought extra books for them, went to their Friday-night basketball games, talked to the social workers when they had problems with their parents, took their phone calls from Rikers when they got in trouble with the law.

He'd offered to give this Nasser that kind of attention, thinking he'd seen something unusual in him. But the boy had stalked out before they could even make an appointment.

The real enigma here was how this Nasser's little sister, Elizabeth, could then turn out to be one of the best students he'd ever had.

David pulled over an empty chair and sat down. "So how have you been, anyway? What have you been up to?"

"I am good. I am very good. I am excellent, in fact." Nasser pulled on his tie nervously. "I am driving for the car service. I am doing very well. I'm making the money."

"I'm glad to hear it. Sounds like your English is better now too."

"Is still very difficult for me." He rolled the tie around his finger and stared out at the patriotic bunting draped in the halls, pride and embarrassment wrestling on his face.

"So the governor is coming next week—to share his sincere concern with the children and teachers of this state, no doubt." David brought his chair close so they were almost knee-to-knee, like passengers on a train. "What brings *you* back? You thinking about getting your GED?"

The boy looked over to meet David's eyes. "No," he said. "But I have something very serious to discuss." The tie unrolled, the Adam's apple bobbed behind the buttoned collar. "I must talk to you about my sister."

"Elizabeth?"

Nasser put his briefcase flat across his lap, almost defensively.

"What about her?" asked David. "She's terrific. She's a world-beater. She got fifteen hundred on her SATs. She can write her own ticket to any college she wants."

"This is not appropriate. For a girl like this to write her ticket."

"Why not?"

Nasser frowned, straightened his tie, and picked at his raggedy briefcase. So much tension. David thought about offering him a cup of coffee, but then decided he'd better not. The kid was wired enough already.

"A girl like this should stay home and make a good marriage," Nasser said firmly. "A girl like this should help raise a Muslim family."

A part of David rebelled, hearing that. Why did everyone want to control these kids and put them in a box? Sometimes it felt like half his job was breaking these boxes open.

But he tried to finesse the point here. "Well, what makes you think she can't get married if she goes to college?" he said, opening up his big palms.

"No." Nasser shook his head vigorously. "This will not work. There are things in the world."

"Things?"

"Bad things. Things she shouldn't be exposed to. The immorality and lasciviousness. I drive around this neighborhood, I see the drugs and prostitutes on the boardwalk. Every day, girls like this are raped in the newspaper. People are *shot* for being in the wrong place. *For no reason at all.* This is a terrible thing."

As Donna Vitale squeezed between them with a wink, a pile of secondhand *Jane Eyre*s in her arms, David found himself uncomfortable with all this brotherly interest. It wasn't unusual, traditional families not wanting their kids to go out into the world. Some of it was just cultural differences. But occasionally he wondered if the relatives secretly wanted to hold the kids back so they could feel better about their own lives.

"Can I ask why you're the one who's talking to me about this and not your parents?" David furrowed his brow and leaned in so close his shoulder almost touched Nasser's ear.

Nasser reared back from the contact. "Our mother is dead," he said, greatly agitated. "Someone has to look out for my little sister."

"So what about your father? I talked to him last year." David found himself wanting to defend the old man after hearing Elizabeth's story.

"*My father.*" Nasser pursed his lips and pulled hard on his tie. "My father is not the one to protect my sister. He is married to an American woman with no morals and he has daughters with her who are allowed to eat pork and watch filth on television! I'm sorry to say this to you, but it is the truth. My father is not a devout man. He tries, but it is not enough. Someone else has to be responsible."

Then all at once, Nasser fell quiet, turning and looking out into the hall.

His sister had just walked by with her best friend, Merry Tyrone, a stylish black girl who wore short skirts and chunky shoes and didn't like people knowing how smart she was.

"You see this?" Nasser clapped his hands in frustration. "She's not wearing her *hijab* today."

"Her what?" asked David.

"Her head scarf. This is what a proper Muslim girl should be wearing."

"Oh." David looked down at the top of Nasser's head, as if trying to see inside it. "Come on, Nasser. Your sister's a good kid. She's not going to get in any trouble."

"Oh no? Look at this." Nasser started to dig through his briefcase. "Look what I find in her room."

He began pulling things out. A copy of *Cosmopolitan*, a J. Crew catalogue, *The Catcher in the Rye*, and *The Color Purple* with various sections dog-eared and underlined in red ink. Her permission slip for Tuesday's field trip to the Metropolitan Museum of Art.

"You see?" he said. "*Haram. Haram. Haram!*" He pointed to each item. "None of this is permitted."

Haram. The word sounded like an engine revving. David sat back as if he'd just gotten a faceful of fumes.

"Nasser, I don't know what to tell you." He sighed, arching his chin at the ceiling and rubbing his throat with a knuckle. "This is the modern world. I don't like everything about it either, but you can't put on blinders and pretend it doesn't exist."

"But don't you see how this is harmful to a young girl?"

"Well, I don't know." David didn't want to say he'd assigned some of the reading himself. "Do you think it's possible you're overreacting a little?"

"No, this is not possible."

David watched Nasser's fingers slip between his shirt buttons, as if he were trying to control some terrible pressure building up inside of him. So tight, so held in. Did he want to say something else?

"Really, Nasser. I think it'll be okay." He tried to sound reassuring.

"So you don't help me keep her home from college?" Nasser asked with glistening, almost brimming eyes. "Is that it?"

David saw he was wrong about this guy. Before, he'd suspected Nasser was merely jealous of his sister's grades, her ease in assimilating. But something larger was at stake: here was a young man genuinely frightened by the late twentieth century. In fact, David remembered, that had been Nasser's problem as a student. He was too scared to step outside his familiar frame of mind and try out new ideas.

"I'm afraid I can't make anybody do anything they don't want to do," David told him. "Are you sure there's nothing else you wanted to discuss?"

He studied Nasser's face again. Amazing. Brother and sister hardly looked anything alike, except for the eyes. Most days, Elizabeth looked like a regular could-be-anything New York City girl, if you ignored the head scarf. But Nasser had an unmistakable Old World heaviness, as if he'd just come off the streets of Bethlehem. Even their first names sounded as though they came from opposing cultures.

"No, nothing else is important." Nasser loaded his sister's things back into his briefcase. "I am disappointed. I hoped you would help."

Every year, they come and go with the tides, David thought once more. The kids. Young, then not young. Some you save, some you don't. Like a lifeguard.

"I'm sorry, Nasser. It's a free country. I mean, I respect your beliefs and I'll look out for your sister the way I'd look out for any of my students. But people are entitled to make their own mistakes."

"No, I don't think this is so." He snapped his briefcase shut and stood.

David started to offer him his hand, but Nasser was distracted again, looking at the Melville quote over the desk.

"And this is not right either," he said, jabbing the placard with his finger. "A man should finish anything he starts."

3

"What's the matter?" Youssef was asking.

"Nothing." Nasser shrugged, not meeting his eye. "Why do you ask?"

"I see you looking very . . . dog-face."

They were leaning against the Plymouth, eating lunch outside the Temple Mount All-Halal Deli on Atlantic Avenue, across the street from a Pentecostal church and a bail bondsman's office. To people driving by, they looked like a couple of Brooklyn cab drivers brown-bagging it on a hot, sooty afternoon, not warriors planning the next stage of *jihad*.

"Are you still worrying about this thing we do at the check store?" Youssef bit into his falafel sandwich.

"No . . . well . . . of course not."

For the past few days, Nasser had been haunted by the memory of the robbery. He still kept seeing the woman falling away from life and the child with his tinfoil badge. But he was afraid to show any sign of weakness in front of his mentor.

"It's my sister, sheik," he said, trying to change the subject.

"What about her?" Youssef looked over. He'd always taken a strong interest in Elizabeth, staring at her in long, admiring silence the two times they'd met.

"I went to her school today." Nasser fidgeted. "I am very worried about what goes on there."

"Oh?"

"Yes, this is a very bad place," said Nasser. "No one is taught any respect for God. The girls dress like whores and the boys talk like hoodlums. *As if this is normal.* I tell you, sheik, I'm scared to death about how this will affect her."

He stopped and stared at the House of Detention down the street. Somehow, the killings the other night and his sister's well-being had become linked in his mind. A wild uncertainty hovered over him, as if something terrible were about to befall him or someone he loved as retribution.

"Yes, it's terrible." The Great Bear set down his sandwich on a bed of wax paper and took out a twenty-ounce bottle of Diet Coke. "A great judgment awaits them all."

The great judgment. The phrase made Nasser's stomach lurch as he took a wedge of pita bread out of his own bag. "And then they are having the governor come to see them," he went on. "As if it's okay with him too. The things that go on."

"The governor is coming to this school?" Youssef abruptly straightened up.

"Yes, next week, I think." Nasser tore at the bread absently, molding the dough into little balls.

He felt the Great Bear's weight shift against the car. A city bus moved by slowly and Nasser watched a damp, half-dressed model on all fours smile invitingly from an underwear ad on its side. She looked as if she'd been recently savaged and was ready for another go.

"Why does the governor come into the school?" Youssef had become alert and attentive, his eyes flicking up and down Nasser's face.

"I don't know, sheik." Nasser searched his bag for tahini to dip his bread in. "I was there to talk to my sister's teacher. I'm very worried about the things they're putting in her mind."

He was aware that something in the conversation had changed. For the past six months or so, he'd been Youssef's little acolyte. But now he had something of value to the Great Bear, though he had no idea what it could be.

"So did you look into the feasibility?" Youssef leaned in close and gripped Nasser's puny arm.

"The feasibility?"

"Of what we talked about," Youssef said harshly. "Of putting the *hadduta* there."

Nasser felt a slight tremor in his eyelids as the model on the passing bus seemed to wink at him.

"You remember this, right?" Youssef belched and covered his mouth. "We never say the word 'bomb' from now on. In case anyone is listening. We call it the *hadduta*. Like a fairy tale."

A Budweiser truck going by hit a pothole, and three thousand bottles rattled ominously.

"Well, I hadn't considered it." Nasser pushed back against the car with his buttocks, feeling defensive. "I was there to talk about my sister."

"You didn't consider it?" said Youssef. "In a week, the governor is coming to the school—this one who is running for President—and you didn't consider putting the *hadduta* there? All this time, we are talking, talking, talking, about *jihad*. About what we can do for *jihad*. We have almost three thousand dollars left over from the caravan raid and we still have the blasting caps I took from the demolition site last year. And you didn't consider putting the *hadduta* there? What's the matter with you? Have you lost heart?"

He burped again and looked around, annoyed, as if someone else was responsible.

Nasser stared after the departing bus, wondering if he had, in fact, lost heart. It had all started casually back in the spring, waiting around between calls at the American Way Car Service on Flatbush Avenue. Nasser was just a boy then, it seemed, still lost and confused in this new country, pumping quarter after quarter into the *Baywatch* pinball game. And then one night, Youssef spoke up, this big older man who'd been sitting in the corner reading the Koran and eating sandwiches night after night: "The Prophet says that when you see a wrong action, you should try to change it first with your hands, then with your words, and finally with your heart. *Stop putting money in that accursed machine.*"

And so they'd started talking instead, Youssef just throwing *haddiths* and sayings of the Prophet at him at first and then moving on to stories about the Holy War he'd fought against the Soviet oppressors in Afghanistan, where CIA advisers had given him special weapons training. Nasser couldn't help but be impressed; his own career as a warrior had begun and ended with throwing stones at Israeli soldiers in the streets of Bethlehem. But here was a brother who'd truly taken action and put his life on the line for *jihad*. Gradually, they started spending more and more time together: sharing meals, going to the mosque on Bond Street, occasionally even catching an American action movie (providing there was nothing overly *haram* in it). Until eventually, they were almost like father and son, and the Great Bear asked Nasser if he was ready to take a physical step for *jihad* too.

"No, I haven't lost heart," he said, watching a squirrel run along a telephone wire. "I am still for *jihad*. There's no element of doubt."

"Then why don't you find a place to put the *hadduta?*" The Great Bear picked up his sandwich again. "All this time we've been saying we should do something to one of their politicians, but then when the opportunity comes along you do nothing about it. How could you not have thought of that? It's as if God ordained it. Is there something wrong with your brain?"

"I don't know." Nasser lowered his eyes, feeling abashed. "I was caught up, worrying about things. Worrying about my sister."

The Great Bear stared at him a moment, rubbing his lips and curling up the corner of his mouth, as though he was about to spit. Yes, Youssef had spoken about setting off a bomb before, but that had just seemed like a vague and rough idea. Seeing the bald man's blood on the wall the other night had suddenly made it vivid and real to Nasser. Anything was possible.

Youssef seemed to let his annoyance ebb away a little. "You know," he said finally, looking around and making sure no one was passing too near them on the sidewalk. "I am thinking how we could get the *hadduta* into the school when there's so much security around for the governor."

"How?"

"Well." Youssef watched trucks making the turn off Tillary Street, heading toward the Brooklyn Bridge. "Maybe we could put the *hadduta* in your sister's book bag," he said finally. "Then when she goes to school on the day the governor visits, there's a big *boom* in the classroom. We make a very big statement for all the televisions."

"Oh." Nasser, who'd been listening carefully, suddenly felt his blood pressure drop. "I don't think I can do this, sheik."

"No?"

"No, no. Definitely *no*." Nasser put his bag down and pushed himself off the car. "This is my sister. I could never let anything happen to her. She is the last one I have left since our mother died."

Youssef sighed and looked away for a moment. Then he reached into his shirt pocket, took out the bottle of nitroglycerin pills, put one in his mouth, and washed it down with another swig of soda.

"My friend, have I ever told you how I got my scar?"

Nasser's eyes went to the ugly red line of flesh that could be glimpsed through Youssef's open collar.

"No, not this." Youssef touched his chest. "This is my bypass. They let the janitor do this at the hospital in Cairo. I mean *this*."

He pointed to a short white scar under his left eye.

"I've wondered," said Nasser.

"This is from the war against the Soviet infidels in Afghanistan. One of their soldiers, a devil really, shot me in the face when I stood up in a foxhole."

"Really?" Nasser had been staring at the scar for six months, afraid to ask about it.

"Yes, he thought he'd killed me, but it was only a graze wound. And then I rose up and shot this devil right through the heart."

Youssef smiled and stroked his graying beard. "Ah, that was a great victory for Muslims, little brother. I'm sorry you were born too late to be part of it."

"I'm sorry also," Nasser said, sticking out his lower lip.

"Muslims came from all over the world to take part." Youssef put an arm around Nasser's shoulder. "Egypt, Bosnia, Pakistan, Syria, even Gaza, where I am from. And this was perhaps the most glorious part of all. Most brothers my age never have a chance to prove themselves. Their lives are compromise and compromise and compromise. They don't understand how it's necessary sometimes to be drastic."

"Like my father," Nasser said glumly.

His father had never fought for anything. He was a coward. He'd spent his life giving away the things that mattered most: his land, his country, and now his daughter.

"I know," said Youssef. "We've spoken of this before, how most men of my generation only know how to live on their knees." He squeezed Nasser's shoulder. "But now you have the opportunity to take a stand, my friend. To prove yourself. To show you know what it is to be drastic."

"But my sister. I could never do anything to hurt her."

"Well, perhaps there's another way." Youssef hunched his shoulders and put the screw top back on his soda bottle. "Maybe you'd prefer not to be involved at all. This is okay. Not everyone is cut out to be a big hero. Perhaps there are other useful things you can do for the cause. Like handing out pamphlets at the Israeli embassy." He began to chuckle. "Or playing the pinball again."

Nasser watched him for a second, feeling dim and ashamed. Yes, he understood this was another test, to see if he was fit to be a warrior, to see if he would submit to something greater.

He looked out at the traffic again. He saw the bread-truck drivers, the bus drivers, the taxi drivers like himself and the Great Bear getting yelled at by passengers. Ordinary men caught up in a meaningless existence. He'd go out for coffee sometimes with other Arabic and Pakistani drivers at a diner near the mosque on East 96th

Street in Manhattan. Men who'd been doctors and lawyers and heads of bureaucracies back home, but were reduced to scrounging for tips and desperately trying to scrape together $240,000 to buy their own medallion for a cab. They'd sit there, listening to *News of the World* on public radio and discussing affairs of state, which they could never hope to affect themselves. It was not for him, this life. He wanted to be part of something better. To belong to the company of warriors.

He looked back at Youssef. "No, I am not afraid," he said. "I want to fight. I want to be part of this. I just don't want my sister to be hurt. This is not asking too much. Anything else I'm willing to do all by myself."

"Then eat something, thanks be to God," Youssef said, pointing to the bag still sitting crumpled on the hood of the car. "You're going to need your strength."

4

A man should finish anything he starts.

Nasser's words were still echoing in David's mind as he knocked on Renee's door at quarter past six that evening. He was jangling inside, standing there, wondering whether to kiss her or not. How forward were you supposed to be with your ex in the midst of a divorce?

Chains rattled, bolts shot back, and the door opened. Renee stood in the doorway, red hair spilling down over her shoulders, a green terrycloth bathrobe parted slightly at the waist showing off her long dancer's legs, Upper West Side twilight slanting into the room behind her.

"You're late," she said. "I was worried about you."

Kiss or no kiss. "I know. I'm sorry. The kids, the trains." He stepped past her into the living room. "I fucked up. I should have called."

"No, no, it's okay." She let the door close behind her and leaned against it. "It's just me acting crazy again. I mean, you're always at least twenty minutes late, so I try to allow for that. But tonight I started thinking something might have happened because it was *more like an hour*. I got scared you might've gotten mugged on the train and lost your wallet and then the muggers would have had your money, your keys, and your old address off your driver's license, *so they might come here first.*"

"It's all right." He moved to comfort her and cut off the speed rap. "There were no muggers."

"*I know, I know.*" She was wringing her hands. "I told myself that. I said, '*Renee, you're just acting paranoid again.* He probably just got delayed and he's going to be hungry by the time he gets here.' So I started to make you some pasta. But then I remembered you like to take Arthur out to dinner, so I threw half of it out and ate the rest. So I've been waiting for you, feeling bloated and guilty. Isn't that crazy?"

"It's good to see you, Renee." He touched the side of her face and kissed her cheek.

Even in her manic phases, she could break his heart. She was so anxious to please, yet she couldn't stop clawing at herself.

David took a moment to look around the place. Eight hundred ninety dollars a month for two little bedrooms looking out on 98th Street and Broadway. It was odd, what David missed about living here. Dust motes falling through the air. The poster of Dame Margot Fonteyn in *Swan Lake* over the couch. The garbagemen moving the Dumpster on the street at five in the morning, the car alarms, the radiators knocking, the way you could catch a glimpse of the Hudson if you stood right by the window and turned your head at a particular angle. The little moments of love that flickered like sunlight between the buildings.

"So anyway," he said. "How are you?"

"I'm good. I can tell I'm getting better," she replied, a little too brightly. "The new medication is really working for me."

"What's it called again?"

"Clozaril."

"And what does it do?"

"It really helps me settle down and focus my thoughts. The only downside is it can kill some people. But so far that hasn't happened. Knock wood."

Knock wood. Her brave, girlish smile pierced him again. It happened every time he'd come to visit these past four months. Those lingering shafts of love. He still felt guilty about his decision—their decision—that he should move out just before the end of the last school year, leaving her alone with her meds and their son. But he couldn't take it anymore: the unpredictable mood swings, the paranoid fits of jealousy, the vicious fights and weeklong silences. He needed a break, he'd told himself, just to recharge his batteries. He was sure he'd be back before the Fourth of July.

But instead, the separation had taken on a momentum of its own and Renee had started seeing someone else. So now everything seemed to be conditional. The state of their marriage, her mental stability, and most important, the question of what all this was doing to their mutually beloved son. It killed him not to be there when Arthur woke up in the morning.

"You look good," she said, brushing his wrist with her fingertips.

"You look better."

In fact, she looked stunning. She was always at her best just lounging around the apartment. She could take an ordinary Bloomingdale's bathrobe and set it on fire by wearing it just so. The problem was whenever she got herself dressed up to go anywhere, her nervousness would get the better of her and she'd put on too much mascara or put her lipstick on crooked.

"So what have you been up to?" he asked, following her into the middle of the living room. "Any more auditions?"

"Oh yeah, I'm trying out for Herbert Berghoff next week. The Stella Adler people said they didn't have any room for me, so I have to work up a monologue. Do you think I'm too old to do one of Laura's speeches from *The Glass Menagerie?* Maybe I should read for the mother, Amanda, instead."

"I'm sure you'll knock them on their asses either way."

Renee and her tryouts had always been a double-edged sword to David. On the one hand, it was good to see her getting out of the house and trying to build an identity for herself. On the other hand, he feared the cumulative effect of all her rejections.

She'd always been auditioning for things and trying to find herself, ever since he first met her in grad school. Always looking for some surrogate parental approval. First, she was a ballet dancer, then she applied to the School of Visual Arts, thinking she could be a painter. Later, she gave songwriting a try, and when that didn't work out, she decided to take up acting at the age of thirty. And the truth was, she was pretty good—if not particularly outstanding—at everything she'd tried to do. But what worried David was how hard she took each little failure to break into the big time. She'd lost her elasticity and stopped bouncing back from her disappointments. Instead, she'd started drinking and sinking deeper into her ineffable "moods," until David finally got her to a psychiatrist.

With the medication, she was certainly doing better these days, smiling, laughing, being more responsible, sometimes even joining David and Arthur for their boys'-night-out dinners. But David still quietly fretted about the black abyss that always seemed ready to open at her feet. A part of him wanted to say, *Fuck all the bad history, fuck all the old fights. Let me move back in and take care of you and Arthur*. But then he'd remember the complicating boyfriend and the image of a plate flying at his head.

"So you still seeing that guy?" he asked. "The musician, what's his name?"

"Anton."

"Right. The saxophone player."

Anton was a rich kid from her class at Columbia, someone she'd been seeing casually before she hooked up with David. Naturally, he'd started calling her as soon as word got around about the separation. How had Renee's friend Rachel described his music? *Adult contemporary*, that's right. *Sort of like Kenny G., but freer*. Musical wallpaper, David thought grimly, based on the one tape he'd heard.

"So how's it going with him?" he asked, with studied nonchalance. The last he'd heard they were about to break up.

"It's going okay," she said, digging a toe into the burgundy carpet. "We get along, most of the time. He's doing very well with his session work. He's gotten a bunch of commercials lately, and you know those corporate jobs pay really well."

"Is that right?"

"Yes, he's thinking of relocating out to L.A. to take advantage of how hot he is at the moment."

"Oh?" David felt his scalp contract. "So what does that mean?"

"Well . . ." She turned halfway away from him, as if she could soften the impact of her words by not speaking them directly. "He asked me if I'd consider going out there with him."

It took a few seconds to sink in.

"So what did you tell him?" David asked. He could hear the struggle for calm in his voice.

"I said I'd have to talk it over with you. I couldn't go without Arthur."

David cleared his throat and squared his shoulders, realizing he was rapidly approaching one of life's sad junctures, where pain becomes unavoidable. The only questions were how much and how long. At this moment, all his reasons for leaving disappeared and like a child he wanted only to be back here, with her, with *them*. He wanted that old feeling: lying on the bed with Arthur between them, listening to the ice cream truck chiming outside, the sun sinking between the buildings, the shafts of light fading as the child drifted off to sleep, his breathing heavier and heavier, as the sky turned arterial pink and then gray, and then finally black.

"I don't think that's a good idea, Renee . . ." David said.

But before he could say any more, Arthur came bounding into the room, a little redheaded love bomb in a Batman T-shirt and Gap jeans. He flung himself into David's arms and started roughhousing, pushing his father back onto the old brown couch which David and Renee had carted up from Ludlow Street one bright ambitious afternoon eight years ago.

"Daddy! Daddy! Daddy! I was playing Sir Gawain and the Green Knight in my room! I just cut off the Green Knight's head and stuck it on a pole!"

"You mean you started without me? How could you?!" David slipped his big sausage fingers into the boy's armpits to tickle him while Arthur giggled maniacally and tried to scissor his father's head with his skinny piano legs.

He didn't dare show the boy how upset he was at the moment. Ever since the separation, Arthur's little spirit had become almost as fragile as his mother's. His teachers told David the boy almost never talked in school, and sometimes he banged his head against walls when he was upset. His sleep was full of nightmares about scary clouds and threatening rocks. And he'd developed an absolutely terrifying case of asthma, which could come on without warning.

"Easy, you guys," Renee warned them. "I don't want to make another trip to the emergency room."

David, remembering the helpless feeling he had the first time his son started coughing uncontrollably, let go of the boy.

"It's all right, Mom," said Arthur, flushed and wheezing a little.

My boy, thought David, I can't let you go. In so many ways, Arthur reminded David of what he was like as a small child. Full of great tales of heroic medieval knights and glorious Nordic slaughter, but afraid to leave the sidelines to play in the Saturday morning soccer games in the park.

"So are you ready?" asked Renee.

No, David wanted to say. I'm not ready. I'm not ready to give you up, I'm not ready to give *this* up. She might as well have casually proposed taking his vital organs to Los Angeles without him.

"Here." Renee was hauling up Arthur's blue-and-red Power Rangers backpack and dropping it in David's lap. "I packed his inhaler, his pajamas, his good night book, soy milk in case you ran out . . ."

"I didn't run out," said David, rising.

How had his life come to this pass? These weren't supposed to be his themes, separation and dissolution. He thought his life was going to be about doing Great Things—turning students' lives around, saving the Western canon, maybe one day writing a great book of his own—not about watching his family fall apart. He couldn't allow this to happen.

"We'll talk," Renee said anxiously, watching Arthur get to his feet and put his sneakers on.

"We'll have to," said David.

"Nothing is etched in stone."

David looked over her shoulder and saw the sun had gone behind the neighboring buildings, bringing long shadows into the living room. "Oh, look," he said. "The light is going."

5

Nasser and Elizabeth Hamdy lived in what their father, George, called "the best-maintained home in Brooklyn"—a plain redbrick three-story house on Avenue Z with a postage stamp–sized lawn and a concrete driveway. Every weekend he spent hours on that lawn: mowing, weeding, trying to raise tomatoes in the tiny garden, and clearing away empty bottles crackheads had tossed on the grass. All in the name of convincing his old Italian neighbors that he was just like them, and not some dirty Arab. Completely unaware of how much he was actually irritating them.

Just before seven o'clock in the evening, Elizabeth sat cross-legged and barefoot on her bed in her second-floor bedroom, writing in her paisley-covered diary.

"I saw you."

Nasser stood in the doorway, wrapping his tie around his finger and then unwrapping it.

"You saw me what?"

"I saw you today at school, without your *hijab*."

"And I saw you too." She pushed the diary off her lap. "What were you doing there?"

"I was talking to someone."

"Yes, I know. You were talking to Mr. Fitzgerald, my teacher. Why were you bothering him?"

He leaned against the door frame, pulling on his lip. "I don't like these things they do there."

"Nasser, I thought we talked about this already!" She threw down her pen and stood up. "You are not my father and you are not my mother. We are not living on the West Bank. You can't control me like that!"

"I am only trying to protect you. People might not think you're a proper Muslim girl."

"I don't care what people think. This is America!"

"But what if you dishonor the family?" He turned away from her and looked down at the floor.

"Don't put all that weight on me! I'm just a regular girl!"

By now, Father had come upstairs, drawn by the sound of his children's voices. He was a thick-waisted man just starting the long march down into the valley of true old age. His eyes were tired and his hands were callused from unloading crates at his grocery store.

"So what is the big problem here?" he said. "Why are my children at war with each other?"

Nasser ducked his head and moved farther into the room. Elizabeth stared after him, with her hands on her hips.

"It's nothing. Just Nasser being stupid again."

Father tried to smile, but it looked as if he was in mild discomfort. Yes, he was getting old. He'd carried his brother and sister across the Jordan when he was sixteen and had carried the rest of the family ever since. Back across the river when he was twenty-one and the relatives in Jordan got tired of having them in the house, and then on to the terrible refugee camp where he met Mother and struggled for years to save enough money to bring the family to America. And then once he got everyone here, he'd spent seventeen years of eighteen-hour days running the little shop on Stillwell Avenue. Scraping and saving. The newest shoes he owned were three years old. He meant well, but every word out of his mouth made Nasser stiffen his spine.

"Be kind to your big brother. He's still trying to find his way."

He came over and kissed Elizabeth on the top of the head.

Then he tried to pat Nasser on the shoulder, but the boy moved away.

Father pretended not to notice. "We should be happy," he said, leaving the room. "Come downstairs soon. Dinner will be ready and I want to pray."

Elizabeth stared at the doorway, thinking: *yes, we should be happy*. But somehow they hadn't been these last few years. Not since her crazy brother had moved back from the Middle East.

She tried to tell herself it was not at all Nasser's fault. That some of the changes he'd brought with him were good. Religion, for instance. Before he'd come back, the five of them had been living like a regular little American family—her father, herself, her stepmother, Anne, and the two young girls, Leslie and Nadia. Beer in the fridge, hot dogs on Saturday night, and no one cared if she wore a miniskirt to school. But as soon as Nasser showed up, their home turned into a little outpost of Islam. Out went the beer, down came the miniskirts, and forget the Saturday-night hot dogs—this was not *halal*. Everyone except her stepmother was expected to start praying five times a day.

And the funny thing was, her father went along with it. Her father, who drove a Chevy and smoked Marlboro Lights, started going to the mosque all of a sudden. At first, Elizabeth thought it might have just been guilt over being separated from Nasser for so long. But lately, she was starting to think there was more to it than that. A certain wistfulness came over her father when he prayed, as though he was yearning for a connection with something he'd had before. And what was even stranger was that sometimes she felt herself yearning too.

"You know, you're starting to drive me crazy with all this tradition," she said. "What were you doing outside my room at four-thirty this morning?"

"I was calling the morning prayer. I thought you wouldn't want to miss it."

"I need my sleep." She picked up a pillow and thought of throwing it at him. "Did that ever occur to you? I'm still in school."

"I am sorry." Nasser started fumbling with that rusty key he kept on the chain around his neck. "I am thinking you are right. Maybe I'm being too strict with you. I should trust that you are being good and true."

"Well, yeah. Right." She stood before him, braiding her hair.

"It's just—how do you say it?—it's worrying me to see how the children grow up around here. With all the licentiousness and danger. I look at you and I think of our mother sometimes, God be merciful and rest her soul." He pressed the key to his lips. "I think how she is not around to help you know the right things and so this is my job instead."

"You think she would have been so worried about whether I was wearing a head scarf?" Her fingers kneaded strands of her hair together.

"This I cannot tell you." He smiled and then dropped the key again, letting it dangle in front of his tie.

A mystery. The whole family was a mystery to her. Especially Nasser. There were so many things he never talked about—his friends, his time in Ashkelon prison, their mother. Even after five years under the same roof, she sensed there was a side of him that she had never quite seen.

"You're too much, Nasser. Really you are."

"I know." He picked up one of her Rollerblades and ran a finger along its wheels. "But this is not what I want. For you to be so mad at me. How can I make it better?"

Elizabeth tried to keep scowling, but it was no good. He could be so sweet and bewildered at times. And there was too much she wanted to know from him.

"You promise me you won't show up at school like that again?"

"Yes, this is a promise."

"God, I don't know what I'm going to say to Mr. Fitzgerald." She decided to hold on to her irritation for just another second, to make him squirm a little.

"Don't say nothing. He's not in your family."

"Yes, but he's my teacher. He's helping me apply to colleges."

Nasser narrowed his eyes as if he were about to object to this too, but then he caught himself and put the Rollerblade down on the floor. She could tell he was thinking about something serious. She recognized the expression from looking in her own bathroom mirror, and seeing the resemblance again made her feel warm and protective toward her brother.

"Hey," he said, snapping his fingers. "Soon is your birthday. Is this right?"

"Yes, the week after next."

"So I am thinking I want to get you something. I like to take you shopping. Next Tuesday."

"I can't do it Tuesday." She sat down on her bed. "I have a field trip to the museum."

He looked down at her knees, with his face pinched in concern. "But this is the only day for me," he said. "The rest of the time I am working, working, working, like a crazy man. On Tuesday, I can buy you anything you want."

"Anything?"

He sucked in his cheeks and looked down at the Rollerblade on the floor. "How about the pads and helmet? I see you skating sometimes without a helmet. You need protection."

She crossed her arms. "Nasser, a good set of pads and a helmet from Canal Skates can cost you a hundred fifty dollars. You know that, right?"

He swallowed. "Whatever," he said.

One of those unconscious Americanisms he'd picked up without realizing it. He always ridiculed her for being too Western, but slowly it was happening to him too. He just didn't know it. Sometimes she'd catch him humming a song from the radio or strutting around in the pair of Timberland work boots their father had bought him for his last birthday. These little moments embarrassed him terribly, but secretly they made her feel closer to him.

"Well," she said. "I guess I could skip the class trip. It's not like it's for credit or anything. Everybody cuts sometimes."

"Exactly." He bowed his head and then looked up. "So this is a deal? I take you shopping Tuesday."

"Yes, it's a deal, Nasser."

"Very good, very good."

He smiled in relief and came over as if he was going to embrace her. But at the last second, he pulled back and just shook her hand instead. All this for a birthday present. My brother, the alien.

"I'm glad you don't go to the museum and see these immoral pictures and statues," he said. "These are the bad influences."

"You're so weird." She stood and screwed up one side of her face, ready to go downstairs. "I think you need to get a girlfriend."

"This is not appropriate," he told her.

6

The Wonder Wheel stood motionless against a crystalline blue sky and the Cyclone roller coaster was silent. Nasser and Youssef sat in the Plymouth, parked some three hundred yards down the street from Coney Island High School.

"How are you feeling?" said Youssef. "Are you good?"

"My stomach hurts," said Nasser, who had a McDonald's bag in his lap and wore the maroon windbreaker with dark slacks and a white shirt.

"It's only natural." Youssef was fussing with wires and two sticks of dynamite in the book bag at his feet. "I was nervous before every military operation I was ever involved in. This is completely all right. It keeps the mind sharp." He put the bag up on the seat next to Nasser and took out an alarm clock. "Here. Put your finger there for a second. In the middle of the dial."

Gingerly, Nasser put his index finger on the meeting point between the hour and minute hands while Youssef inserted a wire through the back of the clock. Inside his head, he was in a state of narrowly controlled hysteria.

"There," said the Great Bear, putting the cover back on the clock and placing it back in the bag, very carefully. "We're all set. Give me my hamburger."

Nasser took out the squarish yellow Styrofoam box and handed it to his friend. It was 1:25. In twenty minutes, the seventh-period buzzer would go off, and hundreds of students would spill out onto the sidewalk in front of the school, where carpenters were building a wooden stage for the governor's visit in two days.

"You know, I was asking the imam the other day if this kind of food is *halal*," said Youssef, opening the box and taking out his Quarter Pounder.

"What did he say?"

"He said it would be better if the beast was blessed before it was slaughtered. But we can make exceptions in the country of infidels. It's all right if we just say the blessing before we eat the food."

"It makes me uncomfortable sometimes, to ask for too many exceptions," Nasser said earnestly. "Did you ask the imam for his blessing on this operation?"

"Not too directly, but it will be okay," said Youssef, muttering a blessing before he took his first bite. "Don't worry too much. God will protect us. Everything is very strong, very simple. One more time: You go in with the *hadduta* and your old school pass. No one will stop you, because you used to be a student there and they've seen you outside with your sister. And don't worry about the metal detector either—the timer is made out of plastic. I took out all the screws myself."

"Really?"

"My God, don't ask. This was a pain." Youssef chewed with his mouth open. "So then you go downstairs and leave it in the boiler room next to the cafeteria. Put it *inside* the boiler if you can. You say you know where this is, right?"

"A thousand times I've been by it, sheik."

Nasser wrinkled his nose at the memory of the foul-smelling cafeteria food. "Flush hard, it's a long way to the lunchroom." The first piece of American bathroom graffiti he'd ever understood.

"You'll see. It will be okay." Youssef washed another nitroglycerin pill down with a sip of Diet Coke. "It would be one thing if we were trying to do this on the day this governor visits, with all the security around. This way we get the same message across without all the risk. You put this dynamite in a contained area like a boiler, it can maybe bring the whole school down into a pile of bricks and rubble. Then they know not even their children are safe. Very big story, on all the news tonight."

Nasser found himself starting to eat french fries out of the bag, methodically, compulsively. Hating the idea of them, but loving their salty taste. Trying to find a way to calm himself. The dashboard clock said it was nearly half past one.

"I am still noticing you look sad." The Great Bear was looking at him closely, as if probing for momentary weaknesses. "Are you thinking again if maybe you don't want to do this?"

"No, sheik, my heart is strong." Nasser tried to make himself very still, aware that any small movement could set off a disastrous tremor through the rest of his body.

"Then what's the problem?" Youssef said, his voice turning sharp. "Is it your sister you're worried about?"

"No." Nasser put down the french fries and wiped his hands with a napkin. "I've made arrangements so she won't be here."

"Then what is it?"

Nasser looked at himself in the rearview mirror, wondering. Trying to imagine how the next few minutes would unfold. He wanted to picture himself being cool, ruthless, and efficient, like a figure in an American action movie, leaving destruction in his wake. But instead he felt the sharp corner of his belt buckle digging into his navel.

"I have so many things in my mind," he said softly. "My mother. My father. Everything I want to do for the faith."

Dread. Why did he have such a feeling of dread? For three years, he'd wandered the hallways of this school, thinking he'd like to machine-gun everyone there. Now he had a chance to do it, and for a greater cause, something bigger than himself. And yet his nerve was leaving him again.

"You know, you can get up and walk away this very minute." Youssef put the burger down and stared at him. "No problem." He reached for the bag at his feet. "I can just stop the timer where it is. We still have almost seventeen minutes."

Nasser looked at the remaining french fries in his bag and felt the rusty key resting against his chest. He was afraid to say anything.

"Just let me ask you one thing, though," said Youssef. "How long were you in the Ashkelon prison?"

"Almost two hundred days."

"And how did you like it there? Didn't you tell me how they tortured you to get you to confess and name your friends? Didn't they give you the freezing water?"

"Yes."

"And didn't they put you in the banana position?"

"Of course." Nasser still could feel his spine threatening to break from the unrelenting pressure.

"And what about the bag?" Youssef asked. "Didn't they put the bag on you?"

Nasser nodded, experiencing that flush of nausea all over again. The bag. It was made of brown sack material and smelled strongly of feces. He was in an outdoor prison yard shackled and rear-cuffed in a backless chair when the Israeli guards stuck it over his head. For two or three hours, he sat there baking in the Jewish sun, breathing in the vile fumes, sweating and getting sicker and sicker. His joints aching. Wondering how he would survive this. At one point, he turned a little in his seat and one of the guards hit him so hard on top of the head that he saw a flash of light. That was when he thought he couldn't take it anymore, that he would throw up and die right there in the chair surrounded by concrete walls and barbed wire. But he didn't die. And after a while, all the pain and discomfort became relative and he willed himself into a state of numbness. That was how he got through it. By promising himself he would never feel anything ever again.

"Just remember, my friend," Youssef was saying. "The Book said it best: sometimes you must fight when it is the thing you least want to do."

Outside, ocean breezes stirred the banners of the closed-up amusement arcades, and the sounds of carpenters' hammers echoed down the boardwalk. Nasser slowly turned and looked at the Great Bear. The scars. Youssef was covered in scars. The one under his eye and the other one up and down his chest. And then the knuckles, which were like painfully swollen bulbs. His entire body was a record of the things he'd done. Nasser's own father had no scars like this, because he'd never fought for anything. He'd been too busy running away, crossing rivers.

"It's okay," he said. "I'm ready."

He decided he was going to have to stop feeling again, to stop thinking. This must be how all the brave men got from one side of an experience to the other. You had to turn yourself into a machine. Wasn't it all for a higher purpose anyway? You were but a tool in the hand of God, and if God wanted to stop you, He would.

"Fine." Youssef picked up the book bag and set it on Nasser's lap. "Then you know what to do. When the alarm clock completes its circuit, the *hadduta* will go off. Don't jostle it around too much and don't stop to talk to anyone you know. Trust in God and think like a gun."

He reached across Nasser and pushed the door open onto the clear blue afternoon.

Up on the fourth floor, David Fitzgerald emerged from the bathroom, still feeling hungover and sick to his stomach. He'd stayed up late the night before, drinking and worrying—as he'd been doing pretty steadily since last week when Renee told him she was considering following Anton to the West Coast. This morning his guts had finally given up on him. He came back into the classroom after a good twenty minutes away and found his students acting like subjects of some highly irresponsible hormone experiment. Kids were screaming at one another, climbing over desks, throwing wads of paper, doing strange things to one another's hair, and, most irritatingly, using some kind of orange-and-black Halloween clicker, which made a terrible racket to go with the constant hammering outside.

"Thanks for warming them up for me." David grimaced at his best friend, Henry Rosenthal, who was supposed to be watching the class and chumming him on today's after-school field trip to the Metropolitan Museum.

"It was nothing," said Henry. "Just remember: Hendrix once opened for the Monkees."

Henry, with his long gray hair and black radical-chic turtleneck, was not into crowd control. He'd been involved with the Free Speech movement and alternative education programs of the sixties, but not *too* involved, you understand. He preferred talking fine wine to politics.

"All right, everyone, settle down and put the clickers away." David stepped past him. "And the rest of you. If you're not going to let me talk, can you at least keep your voices down so I can sleep up here?"

The day had already been a blizzard of demands and responsibilities. Parents showing up unannounced, wanting to know why their kids were doing so badly; papers for his second period freshmen needing to be graded; Xerox machines breaking down; Shooteema Edwards, in tenth grade, finding out her mother had inoperable brain cancer. And of course, it didn't help that there was a TV news crew outside, doing a segment about the school's deplorable condition.

From out of the rabble, Seniqua Rollins raised her hand. A big, tough girl with cornrowed hair and tight jeans, who'd been suspended last year for smashing another girl's head into a locker, she was rumored to be the main squeeze of a jailed gang leader called King Shit, or something like that, and today she was sporting a tight pink T-shirt that said I'M UP AND DRESSED, WHAT ELSE DO YOU WANT FROM ME? and a navy Tommy Hilfiger jacket.

"Yo, yo, yo, Mr. Fitz, what da dilly?" she said in a voice louder than the subway. "I got a question for y'all."

"What is it?"

"Why you wasting our time taking us on a field trip anyhow? It's late, man. You supposed to let us out."

A little ripple of laughter went through the class, the kids titillated by the way she was challenging him. David slapped his attendance book against the side of his leg.

"I mean, you're always saying we shouldn't just accept things," Seniqua went on, getting high on the attention. "So what's up with that shit? I rather just like go home, chill, and read my girl Alice Walker."

Several rebel clickers seconded her dissent.

"Well," said David, taking a deep breath and trying to pull himself together for the occasion. "Number one, it's the only time we could fit it in. And number two, we're going to be studying the roots of our subject. Egyptians. Sumerians. Even our buddies, the Greeks. Check it out. Achilles, the first great hero of Western literature, refused to leave his tent to fight in the Trojan War because his general stole his mistress. Spitefulness, pride, jealousy. Can you relate?"

"No," said Seniqua, authoritative and boisterous.

"Really?"

David noticed she was sitting unusually close to Amal Lincoln, a backup forward on the basketball team and reputedly the worst amateur rapper in Brooklyn. What would King Shit make of that little alliance if he ever got out? He'd probably fly into an Achillean rage, tie Amal's skinny ass to the rear bumper of a LeBaron, and drag him around the walls of the school three times.

"I ain't with it," said Seniqua, wrestling with Amal for a clicker. "It all just seems so . . . *white*."

Ah, the old racial correctness bugaboo. David tried to swiftly parry her thrust. "Well, the Egyptians and the Sumerians, they're not exactly the Osmond Family, are they?" Immediately, he realized he'd slipped and fallen behind the popular culture curve again.

"Yeeeeeahhh, whatevah!" Seniqua dismissed him with a flat-handed homegirl swipe. "I'm just tired, that's all. I wanna go home!"

"Word!" Stray voices and clickers backed her up. What was wrong here? David wondered. It wasn't just him being hungover and worrying about Renee and Arthur. The whole rhythm of the day kept falling on the off beat. He looked around and noticed that more than a third of the class was absent—even Elizabeth Hamdy, who usually helped focus the group in her quiet way. *Et tu, Elizabeth?* Maybe that was the problem. Classes developed their own kind of chemistry over the course of a term. If you removed just one crucial element, the whole thing could collapse or combust.

"Anyway, we're running kind of late, so we ought to get going," he said, rubbing his temples and checking his watch. The hammering outside and the stray clicking in class seemed to italicize his headache. "Are there any other questions?"

"Yeah." Seniqua Rollins glared back at him. "What were y'all doing in the bathroom for so long?"

Trust in God and think like a gun.

Nasser kept repeating the words to himself as he drew closer to the school and the sound of the carpenters' hammering grew louder.

The sun was at his back and the book bag holding the *hadduta* was in his left hand. He wasn't sure if he could do this. He was sure he could do this. His attitude changed from second to second.

He was some one hundred yards from the school now, the weight of the bag and his own caution making him list to the left a little as he walked.

Up ahead, he saw students starting to come down the front steps of the school, ready to disperse to the various hot dog stands and clam houses along the boardwalk for a late lunch, rejecting the cafeteria food. He remembered this part of the routine from when he was a student here four years back. There'd been times when he'd wished they would ask him to join them. But then again, he was sure he would say no if they did.

Boom. He flashed on the image of them falling under the avalanche of bricks. The boys crushed and bloody. The girls crying inconsolably. Sirens screaming everywhere. Yes, this would be horrifying, but he wouldn't allow himself to feel anything about it. He'd seen many things just as horrifying back in Bethlehem. The rain of stones. The burning tires and the tear gas. The soldiers firing rubber bullets. The children lying in the streets and the mothers crying. They were inconsolable too.

He was within thirty yards. He could see the carpenters working on the stage raising their hammers and slamming them down, but the sound took a second to reach his ears. A flock of boys came flying past him, and one of them, an *abbed*, a black one in a yellow Polo Sport shirt and street-sweeper jeans, made a point of plowing into him, shoulder first.

Caught off guard, Nasser stumbled, twisted an ankle, and started to fall over onto his book bag. *The hadduta*. He reeled back and just barely managed to steady himself as the *abbed* kept walking, smirking over his shoulder. With no idea of how close he'd come to blowing both of them up. The black ones. They were supposed to be brothers, Nasser thought. But he'd always been a little afraid of them at school.

He straightened up and began walking faster, knowing he had little more than eight minutes to leave the *hadduta*. The rhythm of the hammering seemed to quicken. There were red-white-and-blue banners hanging from the scaffolding over the school entrance. More and more students surged past him on the front steps; it was like a dam breaking. So free and easy with the way they moved, swinging their arms and shoulders. As if they were born to rule the wide open spaces. He could never be like that. His steps were small and careful. He'd known confinement for too long. Even today, he felt his collar choking him. But the more he tried to relax, the more he found his legs locking.

Don't feel anything.

He tucked the bag under his arm as he walked by a band of laughing, singing girls in matching blue Nautica jackets and entered the lobby. He saw the blue plaster walls and the Celebrate Diversity Week posters. That familiar awful ammonia smell hit him. *Trust in God and think like a gun.* This would be the hardest part, getting through the metal detector. He turned, expecting to see the guard who'd let him in without a pass last week, a sluggish, sleepy-eyed Puerto Rican guy named Miguel who'd actually been in his class a few years back. But today, there was someone new; an alert-looking fiftyish black man wearing a blue blazer and gray slacks with sharp creases, carefully checking student ID cards. Nasser looked at those sharp creases and felt his heart jam.

Merciful God! This hadn't been anticipated, though it should have been. Unlike Miguel, this guard would surely check his ID and make him write his name down on the visitor's sheet, leaving a direct trail of evidence for the police. They'd find him right away and drag him off to jail with all the *abeeds* and the Spanish criminals.

All at once, the lobby didn't seem as vast as it once had. It felt as cramped and claustrophobic as a phone booth. His breath stopped in his throat and his intestines seized in torment. He had to get out. Without thinking, he turned toward the big square of sunlight pouring in through the front entrance and walked out. The steps down to the street seemed to go on for miles and miles, like the slope of a mountain.

He imagined he could hear the clock ticking in his bag, while down below the crowd on the sidewalk had thickened, with hundreds of kids leaving. For the first time, he noticed a burly man with a video camera and a slender, blue-suited lady with a microphone talking to a group of students over by a wrought-iron fence twenty feet away. Other kids were behind the woman, pushing one another out of the way trying to be photographed, grinning stupidly and waving. *A television program.* Somebody had actually come here to make a television program, perhaps because the governor was visiting. There was a chance they'd already taken his picture. Nasser looked at his watch again and saw he had a little over six minutes. His heart throbbed in time with the jerky quartz movement of the second hand. That was not scared, what he was before. This was scared.

He turned and started to walk around the side of the school, heading for the back entrance. He remembered there was a hatch for an old coal chute near the doors. But as he came around the side, he saw dozens of students lounging on the back steps, smoking, drinking from brown paper bags, kissing each other blatantly. No, this was no good either. Now that he finally *wanted* to be invisible among the kids, everyone was looking at him. Maybe he'd never been invisible after all.

He ran back around to the front of the school, knowing he probably had less than five minutes. Panicking. He was absolutely panicking. The *hadduta* would blow up in his hands. The camera man and the lady with the microphone were setting up on the front steps of the school, in order to interview students with the amusement park skyline in the background. The carpenters were still banging away at the wooden stage nearby, leaving no opportunity to slip the bag under the slats without anyone noticing. And just to complete the nightmare, here was Mr. Fitzgerald, his former teacher, coming out through the front entrance, trailed by that Jew, Mr. Rosenthal, and two dozen ill-behaved students from his sister's class.

This was the greatest mistake of all. They were supposed to be gone by now. If he stayed where he was, one of his sister's friends would certainly recognize him and ask Elizabeth what he was doing hanging around school on a day she was absent. What if Mr. Fitzgerald saw him? But returning to the car with the *hadduta* was out of the question. The shame of facing Youssef would have been killing enough. But he wasn't even sure if he would make it anyway. There might not be enough time to defuse the device. The throb of his heartbeat came up between his ears. He considered just dropping the bag on the sidewalk and running. But with the way this day was unfolding, someone would pick it up and run after him, shouting: "*Hey, asshole, you forgot something! Hey, sand nigger, this is yours!*"

The hammering was so loud now it was as if the carpenters were inside his head. He found he could not move. Indecision had frozen him. Was this his destiny? To blow himself up in front of his old high school? Was this what God wanted?

He saw himself, as if from far away. A lonely Arab boy in a crowd, holding a thunderbolt.

But then salvation came. It literally pulled up right in front of him. A yellow school bus stopping by the curb and opening its doors.

The path was clear. It was obvious what he had to do. Nasser waited for another wave of at least thirty students to come down the front steps, and then he joined them as they crossed the sidewalk and passed in front of the bus. Lowering the bag and carefully shoving it under the front wheels next to an empty Snapple bottle took less than a second. In the midst of the crowd, no one noticed. They were too busy shoving, giggling, touching each other within their little cloud.

Nasser moved past the bus, broke off from the group, and ran across the street without so much as a glance over his shoulder. Yes, he'd never gotten along with Mr. Fitzgerald. Perhaps this was God's will, after all.

"Come on, you guys! Let's keep it together."

As the school bus pulled up to the curb, David, sweating out vodka and lugging his Jansport bag, full of library books for Arthur, called to his class to line up on the sidewalk, but it was like yelling into the surf.

Three girls he thought of as the hip-hop sisters were on the front steps, doing a hip-swinging, booty-waggling dance for the TV news crew. Ray-Za, whose hair today was shaped like an English tea service, chanted the words to the latest rap hit, which seemed to be a kind of Sears catalog of bitch names: "Horny bitch, nasty bitch, crazy bitch, bitchy bitch, female bitch . . ." And the rest of them just dissed each other. Even the Chinese kids dissed the Korean kids about their mothers' hairy backs and loose ways. This was the style now: I dis, therefore I am.

"All right, party people," he said. "I'll wait."

This should have been one of those soaring anything-is-possible days. He loved getting the kids outside the school, opening new vistas to them. But something kept casting a shadow over his brain. *What was wrong?* It was something bigger than his divorce. A feeling that he was barely keeping a hold on things. There was too much pulling the kids away. Corrupt administrators, outdated textbooks, electronic billboards, HDTV, computerized banking, CD-ROMs, beepers and cell phones, eight-year-olds with handguns, teen pregnancy, indeterminate sentencing, Prozac, New Age philosophy, crumbling and overcrowded classrooms, incurable viruses, and broken homes. Most days it didn't bother him, the Great Divide. But today he felt rubbed raw. He just wanted to tell everyone to stop and listen for a second.

"Yo, yo, yo, Mr. Fitzgerald." Seniqua Rollins was tugging on his sleeve. "I wanna ask you something."

"What?"

She moved closer to his side, and he noticed she was wearing patchouli today. "I want to know if I can get on the bus first."

"Why do you want to do that?" He was a little sore and suspicious from the way she'd been acting up in class.

She lowered her voice. "I'm five months' pregnant. I like to sit at the front near a window so I don't get sick."

"For real?" David gave her the famous Fitzgerald hairy eyeball.

"Oh yeah, it's for real," she sighed, rolling her eyes and blowing out two big cheekfuls of air. "Didn't you notice I put on weight?"

Actually, she'd always been built like a water tank, but no matter. David regarded her with a mixture of tenderness and exasperation. He wondered if the father was Amal or King Shit in jail, and then decided he didn't want to know the answer. "You going to be all right?"

"Yeah, just gimme some space to breathe."

"We should talk later." David gestured for the bus driver, Sam

Hall, to open the yellow doors. "Hey, Sam," he called out. "You don't mind if this young lady sits by you, do you?"

"I appreciate all the company I can get." Sam, a courtly man in his early sixties with a face like old mahogany and beautiful long tapered fingers, waved for both of them to get on board.

David followed Seniqua up the stairs and set his heavy book bag down next to Sam. It was the *New Larousse Encyclopedia of Mythology* weighing him down, he realized. The thing had to weigh ten pounds all by itself.

"How you doing?" he asked Sam.

He hadn't seen the driver the last few field trips, and he remembered hearing that Sam had been operated on for prostate cancer last spring.

"Just keeping on keeping on," Sam said with an easy smile and only a slight tensing of the jaw. All the gangsta rappers in the world put together could never be so cool.

Most of the kids didn't know that Sam had been a singer in the late fifties. He'd even had a number three hit on the R 'n' B charts, a haunting echoey ballad called "The Loneliest Man in the World." But that was a long time ago and hence not worth much in the up-to-the-minute culture of Game Boy and Home Shopping Network.

"Hey, Sam, you mind if I leave my bag a second?" asked David. "I don't want to drag it around."

"Be my guest."

David started back down the stairs, still feeling as if he was coming at life from an odd angle. Everything he did and said seemed too slow and lugubrious for the world at large. The rest of the class, seeing Seniqua was already on board the bus, started to rush past him.

"Hey, not so fast, crew." He blocked them with his big leaden body and started pushing the group back toward the steps. "I want to do a final head count. Make sure we didn't lose anybody."

Yes, exactly. Everyone needed to slow down, stay in one place. Not move around so much, to sun-blasted cities three thousand miles away. He made them stand in single file and started to call the roll again. He wasn't sure why he felt such a need to impose order on them today. Maybe with the threat of losing Arthur and Renee, he was experiencing some existential need to prove that he, David Fitzgerald, could still have a minor effect on the world.

But then he heard it, or rather he felt it: a hammer blow to the ear.

He turned and saw the front of the bus suddenly rising up three or four feet off the ground and then coming down with a sickening crunch. The sound of the explosion seemed almost incidental.

For a second or two, his mind refused to accept the information. Of course, this wasn't happening. They were all going to get on the bus and make the long queasy ride into Manhattan with kids screaming, beating on each other, and probably committing various misdemeanors at the back.

But then the bus sprawled forward like a drunk with one elbow up on the bar, and the right front wheel went flying off. Broken glass came flying at David and he threw an arm in front of his face. He took a step back and saw that the whole bus was tilting forward. The engine was on fire and a column of charcoal-gray smoke was rising from under the hood. The front of the bus had crumpled with the force of the landing. Sam Hall had been thrown against the windshield, and his face was mashed and bloody against the cracked glass.

A wave of panic swept David up and put him down again. *What was this?* A second ago he was going on a school trip, now he was in a war zone. *All right, what am I supposed to do here?* He saw Seniqua trying to wriggle out a window near the front of the bus. A group of her friends ran over and stood under her, flapping their hands like bridesmaids throwing rice after a wedding. She'd managed to squeeze her head and shoulders through the frame, but that was as far as she could get. There was too much of the rest of her.

The wave of panic came in again. *Okay, you should try to save her. That's what you're supposed to do*. David coughed, feeling the heat pushing him away like a hand. Heavy black, acrid smoke was beginning to stream back from the engine, enveloping the rest of the bus. It dawned on David that soon the whole thing would be in flames.

"Seniqua, try the back door!" he shouted, approaching her.

But she was too busy screaming to hear him. The sidewalk around him was bedlam. Hundreds of kids had come running, from down the boardwalk and out of the school, to see the spectacle. But the hot reality of it kept them at a respectful distance of at least a hundred feet—the girls crying and shrieking, the boys staring and cursing in useless shock. The only calm one was the burly tattooed TV cameraman, who stood halfway up the school steps, anchored and efficient, keeping the burning bus in steady focus as if he were drawing strength and serenity from all the commotion.

"It's all right, David!" yelled Henry Rosenthal as he ran back toward the school building. "I'm going to call nine one one!"

For what? There wasn't time. David stood there, paralyzed with fear. He kept waiting for the disaster to subside, but it just went on and on. All his life, he'd waited for The Moment when he would discover whether he was a coward, as he'd always suspected, or whether there was a secret part of himself that was capable of great, thoughtless courage. But now that the moment had arrived and the beast had sprung, he wasn't ready.

The wave ebbed away. He had a son to take care of. If anything happened to him, who would look after Arthur? Surely that was justification. He began to back away from the scene. So now he had his answer. He was a coward, after all: the lifeguard who would never save anybody.

Seniqua was almost disappearing in the cloud of toxic smoke surrounding the bus.

"Oh Lord, somebody save her," he heard one of the other girls say. "She was gonna keep that baby."

David coughed into his hands and found he couldn't back up any farther. What would his father the war hero say about this retreat? No. It took nerve to be a true coward and David wasn't sure he had it.

The tide began to draw him in.

With a heart full of misgivings and a mouth mumbling curses, he made his way around to the back of the bus, where a sign said: IF THIS VEHICLE IS BEING OPERATED RECKLESSLY, PLEASE CALL 555-1000. He hesitated a second, then saw the hip-hop girls staring at him, expecting him to do *something*. "Oh, look!" one of them shouted. "He's gonna do it now! He gonna save her fat ass. I told you he was all right!"

With the bus tilting forward, its back was slightly elevated, and David had to stretch to reach the yellow door handle. Finding it surprisingly cool to the touch, he yanked on it, expecting nothing to happen, absolving him of all responsibility. But to his amazement, the door fell open easily and more black smoke billowed out, almost solid in mass. He choked and coughed, feeling as if he'd just had motor oil poured down his throat. The undertow had him.

I'm not really going to do this, am I?

"Here, I'll help you get up." Ray-Za was kneeling before him in the street, offering his back as a stepping stool.

David looked down at the black cloth of the T-shirt stretched across the boy's back. Here was a thing of moment; more than anything in the world he didn't want to get on the bus. Every muscle and nerve ending in his body was resisting. But he couldn't let them all down. He had to somehow force himself to act. Trying to ignore his wildly beating heart, he placed one foot on Ray-Za's shoulder and hoisted himself the rest of the way up onto the bus.

It was like stepping into a blast furnace. The heat wrapped itself around him, compressing his organs and curling his hair. He heard a sound like a giant breathing. More smoke came rushing at him, choking him, making him hack uncontrollably. He began to duck down, imagining a voice saying: *Go back, send someone more qualified.* Okay, fine, he thought. *Let me get out of here. I have a child of my own.* But the pull of circumstance was too strong and the slope of the floor sent him spilling toward the front of the bus where Seniqua was still screaming.

He was almost drowning in smoke and could hardly see anything. But every step he'd taken forward made it harder to take a step back. The bus's hard landing had jarred seats out of place and left cushions in the aisle. David tried to feel his way around their hot coverings as he crouched down, making his way toward the girl.

Why am I doing this? Why can't I just turn back? His head was getting light as his body started to shut down. But the undertow wouldn't release him. It kept dragging him farther and farther out. And then just as he began to grow dizzy and faint, he finally found her, still stuck halfway out the window near the front of the bus. He put his hands on her big churning thighs and tried to yank her free, to little effect. How was he going to do this? It was like trying to pull a pipe organ away from a church wall. He stepped between the seats to get a better grip on her from behind.

"Okay, honey. I'm just gonna give you a little tug."

He circled his arms around her waist, set his legs for traction, and pulled with all his might. As she fell back onto him, she shrieked in terror, thinking he was dragging her back into the fire and certain death.

"It's all right. It's all right." He squeezed her shoulder, trying to calm and reassure her. "We're gonna make it out of here."

But that was by no means a sure thing. The back emergency exit was at least thirty feet away, at an incline. It couldn't be seen. His heart was punching the walls of his chest. The smoke was stinging his eyes and quickly suffocating him. And he heard two sharp pops, telling him windows were breaking, letting more oxygen in, feeding the flames. At any second, the whole bus would flash over.

This was the middle of the cold dark sea, he thought paradoxically. *You're going to die*. The idea was overwhelming. You thought your life was about turning forty and getting a divorce. But it was about dying on a school bus. Everything else was just preamble.

The bus groaned and seemed to crush in around him. You're never going to see your wife again, never going to see your son again. He tried to remember the words to the Lord's prayer . . . *Our father . . . my father . . .* Oh, how did it go anyway? *Hail Mary, full of grace . . .*

No, he wouldn't accept death. Arthur and Renee still needed

him, didn't they? He had to get back to shore. With a sharp surge of strength, he balled up his fists and started pushing Seniqua back toward the emergency exit. *Live, baby, live.* What else was there? He looked once over his shoulder and, through the smoke, glimpsed little flames moving toward them along the floor runner. He began pushing Seniqua harder, threatening to steamroll her if he had to. His heart beating with fierce shuddering force.

And then it appeared before them, a silvery rectangle of light. The doorway, through the smoke.

Seniqua, however, had stopped moving, as if she'd been overcome by the fumes and gases less than ten feet away from safety. "Come on, you can do it!" David pleaded.

But she was hunched down and unbudgeable. This system was no longer responding. David heard the loud pop of yet another window blowing out. This was either the beginning or the end of something. What had his father said about facing the machine guns on Okinawa? *Just keep going.* He bent down, reared back on all fours and slammed ahead into her with his full weight. Seniqua pitched forward and went tumbling out into daylight.

A group of her classmates caught her and pulled her off the bus, and David quickly jumped down behind her, hacking mightily and hurting his knee with an awkward landing. His eyes were still stinging and black mucus streamed from his mouth and nostrils, but he'd made land.

Good man yourself, Fitzgerald! as his father used to say on the rare occasions when David pleased him. But then he looked over and saw Seniqua's friends laying her out on the sidewalk some twelve yards away.

"Hey, is she okay?" he called out.

His words were swallowed up in the mass of kids huddling around her while the cameraman maneuvered for position among them.

David came staggering over and the circle parted for him. He heard grim murmuring. Merry Tyrone, usually exuberant and chatty, looked at him, ashen-faced and silent. Seniqua was lying on her back, in the middle of the group, with her mouth slightly open and her Hilfiger jacket unzipped. David knelt beside her and put his hand over her mouth.

"She ain't breathing," said Merry, finally breaking the silence. "She must have got too much of that smoke in her lungs."

David looked at the other kids. They were staring at the sky, glancing back at the bus, retreating into themselves. He put his ear down to Seniqua's mouth, hoping somehow she'd start breathing on her own.

But all he heard was the sound of the fire burning nearby and glass breaking. Where was everybody? Where were the ambulances and fire trucks?

"Anybody here know CPR or mouth-to-mouth?" he asked the group.

The kids were slack-jawed and wordless. The burly cameraman was pushing several of them out of the way for a better angle.

"Hey, back off, will you?" David coughed. "This kid isn't breathing."

He looked down at Seniqua's dry useless mouth, a white crust forming in the corners. Couldn't someone else do this? Sure, he'd been a lifeguard, but even firemen didn't perform mouth-to-mouth anymore, because of AIDS. On the other hand, he couldn't bear having his student, this pregnant girl, die on him.

He bent over Seniqua and blew tentatively into her mouth. Come on, girlfriend. You can do it. You got the power. He felt the heat of the fire at his back and an ocean breeze in his hair. The presence of death nearby.

He pinched Seniqua's nose and exhaled hard. It was like kissing, it wasn't like kissing. He thought of Arthur's first blue moments in the world. Struggling in the nurse's arms, trying to catch his breath.

He turned his head, listening for a response, and then breathed in harder, desperately trying to blow open all the little hatches and constricted passageways. But it was like trying to blow up a Macy's Day balloon with a bicycle pump. The girl remained motionless, lifeless. David coughed and tried to clear his own throat. Remembering his father dead in the hospital, right after his heart attack. A bloated copy of what he'd been. He felt the cameraman shadowing him, kneeling to capture the real-time drama, the lens lapping up what life was left in the girl.

The roughnecks in the group began to withdraw, not able to face this. The girls, always more honest, fell into each others' arms. And David bent over Seniqua once more. Come on, baby, don't die on me. Don't die on me with everyone watching. He inhaled deeply and blew out with all his might, pushing the breath up from the very pit of himself, bringing along whatever horrible toxins and gases he'd taken in on the bus, and leaning into her, trying to will her back to life. Having exhaled everything that was inside him, he fell sideways, exhausted.

From far away, he finally heard the loopy whistle siren of approaching fire trucks and ambulances. The bus exploded again, much more powerfully this time. It was as if a fist had come down from the sky and smashed what was left of the vehicle. Everyone jumped back and a dense mushroom cloud rose from the front of the bus, filling the air with dark oily smoke. Only now did David allow himself to remember that Sam Hall was still on board.

"Oh shit, lookee, look at that." Ray-Za was dancing around, pointing.

David stared at him blankly and then looked back at Seniqua. Just in time to see an eyelid flutter. He leaned in close, heard a short cough and then another longer one. The cameraman stood up to get a wider angle as Seniqua suddenly sat up, retched violently, and took her first deep gasping breath.

"Oooooaaaaa!" Merry Tyrone cried out. "You go, girl!"

David steadied himself and saw Henry Rosenthal back at his side again. Where had he been these last few minutes? Somehow he looked smaller and older in the aftermath of the explosion.

"You did it, man," he said, patting David on the shoulder uneasily. "You saved her. You must be out of your fucking mind."

7

Judy Mandel, twenty-four years old, wearing a jean jacket and a skirt just a little too tight for her, already had a splitting headache and vicious menstrual cramps before she even got to the scene of the explosion.

She'd been out at the Red Hook housing projects, covering a granny-fell down-the-elevator-shaft story when her editor at the *New York Tribune* city desk beeped her and told her to get her hyperactive butt out to Coney Island.

It was, like, ridiculous, trying to get over there and cover it. Ten minutes before she could get a car to come to the projects, and then the driver instantly ran into mega-major gridlock traffic on the Gowanus Expressway. By the time she got to the school, John LeVecque, the pompous and deliberately unhelpful police spokesman, had finished briefing the rest of the daily reporters about what had happened, and the detective in charge—who truth be told looked a little like death warmed over himself—wasn't speaking to any of the press. All Judy could get out of anyone was that a teacher named David Fitzgerald had somehow saved one of the kids and stopped more of them from getting hurt. Which officially made him hero of the day, until someone else came along.

All the other reporters were already mobbing him in front of the school steps. A billowing mass of people. Just the sight of it made Judy's cramps worse as she came running over, orange laminated press I.D. bouncing against her chest. How was she going to get a piece of this story with all these other people around? They were already breaking her shoes at the city desk, threatening to send her back to celebrity stalking and covering Lotto mania. Within five minutes there wouldn't be so much as a nuance or a half-quote left to chew over. She recognized the short guy from the *Daily News*, the wild cowboy from the *Post*, the stylish political lady from the *Times*. And worst of all, that swanky bitch Sara Kidreaux from Channel Two with her beefy crew guys in tow and her broadcast truck parked by the curb, ready to go live.

All her life, Judy had been around long-legged, Chanel-wearing goddesses like that one; a merely decent-looking girl among the city's legions of beauty queens. She'd accepted that it was her lot in life to be the underdog, to have to work harder and fight dirtier just to stay on par. So she launched herself into the crowd like a heat-seeking missile. Fighting her way to the front, pushing bigger and more established reporters out of the way, making sure she wouldn't be ignored.

"Hey, what happened?"

"Hey, what happened?"

David Fitzgerald—still dazed and wobbling before the school's front steps—was slowly becoming conscious of a kind of frantic animal effort going on around him. Paramedics had just finished examining him and putting salve on his hands and face, when the rugby scrum of reporters and camera people suddenly closed in around him. There were at least twenty-five of them, pushing and shoving to get near him. Where had they all come from? At first, he was frightened and confused by the surge. *What did they want from him?* Were they going to trample him? He thought of the Who concert in Cincinnati and English soccer tragedies. But gradually things came into focus. He began to recognize individual faces and questions. People he'd seen fleetingly on the few occasions when he watched television news as well as names of famous newspapers on laminated press passes. They wanted to understand what had just happened. *They wanted him to help them.*

"Why did you keep the kids from getting on the bus in the first place?" asked a stocky young reporter from the *Daily News*, who was wearing a knit tie and jeans.

"I don't know." David rubbed his eyes. "I didn't want to lose anybody."

"I wonder if you can be a little more specific?" asked a girl with black bobbed hair and brown lipstick, whose name tag said she was Judy Mandel from the *Trib*.

For a moment, David stared at her. She wasn't beautiful, exactly, but she'd seized on a certain idea of attractiveness so forcefully, it was impossible to ignore her.

"Specific about what?" David inhaled deeply, realizing he was still having trouble catching his breath.

"About why you kept the kids off the bus."

"There was a bomb." He felt momentarily confused about the sequence of events, not sure what he was saying. Was it a bomb?

"Yes," Judy Mandel said gamely, looking up with big brown eyes and trying to hold her position as other reporters jostled her from behind, "but how did you know that beforehand?"

David's mouth opened, but no sound came out. Someone was shining a bright light in his eyes, from on top of a camera. He was aware of people paying inordinate attention to the surface of his face. Students were monkeying around behind him, throwing up gang signs and trying to get on camera.

"So how does it feel to be a hero?" Sara Kidreaux stepped in front of the girl from the *Trib*.

"Oh . . . I . . . huh." He stopped and looked back at the firefighters trying to hose down the remains of the school bus. "I don't think I was being a hero . . . I think it was just, you know . . . life."

"What subject do you teach at school?" a radio reporter called out from the rear of the pack.

"Um . . ." David choked and coughed more black phlegm into

a handkerchief. "Excuse me. Heroes, heroism. I mean, I'm an English teacher. That's what we were supposed to be doing on the field trip to the museum today. Studying heroism."

"But instead, you gave the kids a real-life lesson in heroism. Right?" Sara Kidreaux stood on tiptoe, rising out of her high heels, so she could stay in frame with David's face.

Even in his confused state, he could tell she was trawling for a sound bite.

"I'd still like to know how he knew it was a bomb," Judy Mandel said, peeking over the TV lady's shoulder. "Hey!" She called to David. "*How do you know there was a bomb?*"

The other reporters were still pushing and shoving behind her like passengers trying to get to the *Titanic*'s lifeboats.

"So you gave them a real-life lesson in heroism." Sara Kidreaux maintained her position, trying to get the quote she needed before she got stampeded away.

"I guess I did," David said absently, as an Emergency Service crew carried Sam's scorched and shattered body away in a black bag. Poor Sam. David shuddered and tried to focus again on the question. But it was hard. He felt as if he were trapped in a dream and trying to explain it to everyone at the same time.

"And what exactly did you teach them about heroism?" Sara asked, as if he'd already accepted the premise of her question.

"I don't know," David said once more. Breathing in, breathing out.

"Come on, give me something."

David held his breath, watching the paramedics checking out his students by the curb. Then he looked down and saw that a little black kid no more than eight years old had wandered over from one of the nearby housing projects and wedged his way in among the reporters, with a scrap of paper that said "reportr" in brown crayon taped to his polo shirt.

"I'm sorry, but I don't know anything about heroism," David said finally, exhaling. "The only hero I ever knew before was my father, and he never talked about it."

"Your father?"

"He was in the war." David looked across Surf Avenue at a torn and singed red-white-and-blue banner outside Astroland amusement park.

"Your father was a war hero?"

He sensed he'd said something that pleased the group.

"Ah, yeah. He was in the Second World War. He was in the Engineer Battalion. You know, one of the guys who handled explosives."

"And what did he do that was so heroic?"

"Well, um, I know one time he got wounded running up a hill on Okinawa, to throw a satchel charge at a sniper's nest when all the guys in his unit were getting picked off—I mean . . ."

"Oka-what?" one of the reporters further back in the scrum asked.

"And is he alive today?" Sara Kidreaux persisted. "Your father?"

David cast his eyes down, watching the little kid with the homemade press pass pretending to take notes. "Uh, no. Unfortunately he's not."

"But do you think he'd be proud of you?"

For a moment, David didn't know what to say. The reality of his father was too dense and complicated to explain here. On the other hand, he was aware of all these people looking at him anxiously, wanting him to be interesting.

So he said: "Uh, yeah, I guess he'd be proud . . . Sure. I hope so."

As he said the words, David felt part of himself shredding and then splitting off. An inauthentic self had suddenly risen out of him. Now it was flying through the air, jumping through the camera lenses and into the radio microphones. That was the self that would be broadcast around the city tonight.

The real David Fitzgerald was still crouched down inside himself, stunned and frightened by what he'd been through.

But the impostor was blustering on. "U.S. Marine Corps, Private First Class Patrick V. Fitzgerald, Sixth Division, Engineer Battalion," he said, answering a reporter's question about his father's name and rank. "He won a Silver Star, a Bronze Star, and a Purple Heart, and a bunch of other medals I can't think of at the moment . . . Yes, I think he would be pleased."

In truth, David knew his father had always been quietly disappointed that his only son had turned out to be a lowly public school teacher.

"Where did the sniper thing happen again?" asked a *New York Post* reporter.

"Okinawa," said David. "O-K-I-N-A-W-A."

He tried to swallow, but his throat felt tight and dry. His eyes were still stinging and his teeth were chattering. The little boy with the crayoned press pass was smiling at him. More than anything, David wanted to go home, hug Renee, and hold his son close enough to smell the playground in his hair.

"What do you want?" someone was saying, "he's a teacher."

David turned and saw Nydia Colone and three other girls from his class coughing and weeping on the school steps. The hip-hop girls were keening and in one case heaving into the gutter. Yuri Ehrlich stood by the curb, watching smoke dissipate above the remains of Dreamland with a kind of stoned-looking admiration.

The sky, however, was exquisite and indifferent. It was just going on with the business of being a beautiful day.

David looked out at the crowd and saw that black-haired girl from the *Trib*, Judy Mandel, staring at him with her brown eyes half-closed and her head tilted, as if seeing things just a little differently from the rest of them.

"Listen, I think that's about all I have to say right now," David said. "I have to go see about my kid." He caught himself. "I mean, I have to see about all my kids."

He turned and found himself facing a short, gaunt, balding man in a gray suit. The first image that came into David's mind was from F. W. Murnau's film *Nosferatu the Vampire*. The long hawk nose and the vulnerable bare scalp. The lonely and haunted eyes that looked as if they were rimmed with tight red rubber bands.

"I'm gonna need to talk to you," he said quietly, putting a

strong, sinewy hand on David's shoulder. "I'm Detective Noonan, from the six-oh precinct detective squad. We've got a few questions."

David felt jolted. Every time he thought he'd settled on the reality of the situation, there was another aftershock.

"Yeah, yeah, of course," he said, collecting himself as he started to push his way out of the crowd.

A small angry-looking young woman with a blunt hedge of auburn hair shoved a card at him that said she was a producer with one of the network morning shows.

"Call us," she said in a voice full of certainty. On the card, she'd written in sprightly red ink: "Top-rated in our slot! 30 million viewers."

A wiry young man in a white shirt and khaki pants cut in front of her. "We'll call you later," he said, pressing a card for CBS Morning News into David's palm. "We have your number."

"How?" David asked.

It was all too confusing. The explosion, the smoking remains of the bus, the attention to surfaces, the relentless friendly questions from reporters needing his help. He wasn't sure if he'd ever be able to put two coherent thoughts together again.

In the meantime, the detective began pushing him lightly but firmly through the crowd.

"Come on, come on," Detective Noonan grunted. "Let's get away from these parasites."

"Parasites" seemed a little strong, David thought, as he walked with the detective to an unmarked navy Ford parked across the street. These were just people doing their job. On the other hand, the detective needed him now. This was fine, the feeling of being needed. It gave him a momentary sense of groundedness. A chance to plant his feet and place himself amid all the confusion. Okay, here was what he needed to do next. He needed to be with the kids, who were no doubt upset and shaken up, and with the police, who needed a precise and accurate description of what had just happened.

So why did part of him still feel disappointed and resentful about having to leave the reporters and TV cameras so soon, as if he'd been hustled out of his own birthday party just as the fun was starting? The little boy with the press pass waved good-bye to him.

The detective's car smelled from the absence of women. Stale air, exhaust fumes, old upholstery, an overflowing ashtray, food wrappers on the floor, streaky windows. A speaker dangled from the passenger-side door like an eye out of its socket. Just the threat of a female sitting here should have shamed Noonan into cleaning it up a bit.

"Okay, you mind if I go through this one more time with you?" Noonan asked, taking notes with his pad resting against the steering wheel.

"No problem," said David, though he'd already gone over the narrative twice with the detective.

"You come out of the school with the kids. You let one of them get on first. You have a short conversation with the driver. You come off and line the kids up. And then the bus blows up. Is that it?"

"As far as I can remember." He stared at a large green vein in the detective's temple. "But like I said, I'm not thinking that clearly."

"And let me ask you again. Did you see anybody suspicious hanging around the bus before or after the explosion?"

"Not that I can recall."

David turned and saw more reporters interviewing his students outside the window. The who, how, and why of what happened were still flying around him like fragments. He hadn't had time to put it all together in his mind.

"You got off to a late start," said the detective.

"What?"

"You were running late. I wondered if there were mechanical problems with the bus."

"There might have been," David said, noticing there was a constant distant ringing in his ears. "I don't know. I was in the bathroom." He forced himself to pay attention. "Why, are you thinking that's what could have caused the bus to blow up?"

"Well, I don't know. It's something we're going to have to look at."

"Of course, of course."

The detective began to write faster in his notebook and the green vein in his temple started to throb.

"And so it was, what, just some kinda hinky feeling that you kept the kids off the bus for a few extra seconds," Noonan said. "Is that right?"

"Yeah. Hinky. I guess. I didn't want to lose anyone."

Noonan gave him a sidelong glance, and David wondered if by some instinct the detective knew that he'd been drinking heavily the night before.

Cops had always made him a little ill at ease. As a teenager, he'd halfheartedly taken a car from a beach club parking lot on Long Island and had almost gone to prison for it. The episode was enough to scare him straight and keep him away from the cretinous junior division thugs who'd talked him into the stunt in the first place. But to this day, he still often felt officers looking at him just a bit longer than they needed to, as if some aura of suspicion lingered.

"Detective, can I ask you something?" he said, trying to shift the focus.

"Yeah, all right." Noonan flipped a page in his notebook. "What?"

"Are you thinking it could have been a bomb?"

The detective put his pen down and stared at him for a long beat. "I don't know. You know anybody who'd want do something like that?"

Something in that look made David's joints ache. "No. Not that I can think of."

"You sure about that?" The detective held his gaze for a few more seconds. "You're a teacher. You must know plenty of angry kids."

"Not that angry, I don't think," David said quickly, the moldering stuffiness of the car starting to get to him. He needed some fresh air.

"How about anybody who was upset about the governor's visit?"

"Nobody who said anything to me." David coughed once more. It felt like weasels had been scratching the inside of his throat.

The detective took out his wallet and gave David a card with his number at the precinct. "You call me if you think of anybody or anything relevant. I'll be in touch."

"All right. Whatever you need."

Yes, Nosferatu. The throbbing vein and the heavy eyelids. The pale luminescence of the undead. David reached for the door handle, feeling some irrational need to be free of this man's presence.

"Oh, one more thing." Noonan grabbed his elbow.

"What?"

"How should I put this?" The detective let go of him and gestured rhapsodically with both hands. "A lot of people are going to be asking you about what just happened. Media people, I mean. Now I can't really tell you not to talk to any of them, though I'd like to. But just do me a favor. All right? Be careful about what you say. Because if this turns out to be a bomb or something, and this case goes criminal, you better make sure you have your story straight."

"Okay," said David, not quite absorbing the actual words.

The detective slapped him on the arm and reached over to open the door for him. "You done good today," he said. "There's guys been on the job twenty years wouldn't do what you did."

"You think so?" asked David, opening the door.

But the detective had already gone back to writing in his notepad, his jaw working and his green vein throbbing. Looking for a hundred different ways to dissect the moments just gone by.

8

Elizabeth Hamdy, managing a sort of elegance in baggy green fatigue pants and a black T-shirt, was sitting on the front steps of her father's house when Nasser and Youssef pulled up in the Plymouth.

"You're so late!" she said, standing up with her skates slung over her shoulder. "You were supposed to be here by one-thirty. I thought you were going to take me shopping. I skipped the whole museum trip for you."

"I'm sorry." Nasser got out of the car looking tense and distracted. "We went too far and got lost."

"Lost?"

"I mean, the traffic was very bad." He looked back at Youssef behind the wheel. "Ocean Parkway is blocked. I think something happened down the road."

"Yeah, I heard a big bang and saw some smoke from down by the beach. Was there a fire or something?"

"I don't know. These crazy things. I was in Manhattan with my friend."

She noticed Youssef was staring at her again, through the windshield, with his tinted glasses and his big bald head. He'd made her uncomfortable the two times they'd met, and now she had the unmistakable feeling he wanted something from her. She waved to him halfheartedly as two black crows landed on a slate roof across the street and gray smoke evaporated on the horizon.

"She is very beautiful, your sister," Youssef called out to Nasser, as he started the car and drove away.

"He gives me the creeps," she said, watching him turn left on Stillwell Avenue and disappear.

"He is a good religious man," Nasser replied stiffly. "Should we go?"

He started walking across the little tree-lined street to where his rented black Lincoln Town Car was parked.

"I wonder what the fire is." She looked again at the smoke on the horizon. "I hope it's nowhere near school."

"Probably it's the hot dog store. Maybe this is a chastisement for making the bad food."

He was even more tightly wound than usual today, she noticed, with his hair flat and his shoulders slumped. When he held the passenger-side door open for her, she saw little indentations in his lower lip where he'd been biting it.

"Please to put on your seat belt," he said as she climbed in. "I am very nervous to be driving with you."

She smiled to herself as he got in on the driver's side and started the car. The interior was ragged but comfortable. She liked it sometimes when he was sweet and protective. There was something very Old World about it. She could almost picture him holding their mother's hand as they crossed King David Street in Bethlehem or helping a Bedouin tribesman lead his flock to the Saturday-morning sheep market.

"You mind if I put on the radio? Maybe they'll have something about what happened down at the beach."

She reached for the dial as the car rolled down Avenue Z, passing the brick houses with Madonna statues on the front lawns.

"No!"

"Why, what's up with you?"

They made the turn onto the Belt Parkway entrance. A long

serpentine road lay ahead, with high weeds on either side and angry men hanging meaty tattooed arms out their car windows.

"I am just needing to be quiet for a few minutes, that's all." Nasser gripped the wheel tightly. "Hey, why aren't you wearing your *hijab?*"

"It's too hot today."

He looked over and saw her hair hanging free and loose around her shoulders. It looked so soft and rich that he had to restrain himself from trying to touch it. Other men would want to touch it too. He wished she would cover it immediately.

"I don't like for boys to see you like this. They get the wrong idea."

"Well, you say it's the wrong idea."

From the way he quickly switched lanes and cut off an approaching Lexus on the left, she could tell she'd picked a bad time to tease him. There was hardly a day that went by without his claiming to be disturbed or offended by some aspect of modern American life. But this afternoon it was more than that. He seemed profoundly shaken. She wondered if this Youssef had just said something.

God, God, God. What a terrible sound the *hadduta* made when it went off the second time. He couldn't get the noise out of his head. He was trying to talk to his sister, but all he could hear was that hollow boom. A sound you could feel all the way down in the bottom of your stomach. You knew such a sound would shake things loose and set them rolling wildly. The idea frightened him. What if a police car pulled up alongside him right now?

"All right, so you don't want to play the radio and you don't like my hair," said Elizabeth. "What else do you want to talk about?"

"I don't know," said her brother, as the road turned into Shore Parkway and swept past Dyker Beach. "Are you still thinking to go to college?"

"Now that's something *I* don't want to talk about. Not with you."

"Okay."

He shuddered a little behind the wheel and honked at an oil truck going by too close on the right. The yellow fragrance tree hanging from his rearview mirror swayed in the breeze.

"What about Mother?" she said.

"You want to ask me about Mother?" He took a deep breath and reached inside his shirt, fingering the key again.

"Yes, what was she like?"

Nasser let go of the key and put both hands on the wheel as his eyes followed the curving road ahead.

"She had soft hands, beautiful hands," he said. "But she was not soft. She was strong in her heart."

"And what was the name of the town she was from?"

"Dir Ghusun. It means the Monastery of Branches. It was an old Christian town, founded by the Romans. I have told you this three hundred times before."

"I know. But I like hearing it."

There was music in his voice when he described this place he'd never actually seen. Their mother's village on the coast of the Mediterranean. Where the soil was rich and black and the lemon trees and olive trees grew tall, and the sea carried the fine smell of the trees across the village. Every year at harvest time, children ran through the streets following the blind storyteller to a neighbor's house, where he'd tell stories of great Arab heroes and warriors like Saladin on his white horse battling Richard the Lion-Hearted during the Crusades, or the Prophet himself, who led three hundred brothers to victory over a thousand Meccans at the Battle of Badr. Even after the Israelis bombed the village in 1948 and forced her family to flee, arresting anyone who tried to come back, she'd carried the memory of this place, her connection to the land, in her heart. And, in turn, she'd passed that love of the land on to Nasser, even giving him the rusty key to the family's old house, so he could open the door on the day of return.

"So did she like me?" Elizabeth asked.

"Of course she liked you." Nasser forced himself to smile. "She loved you. You were her little baby girl. How could she not love you? I look at you and I see her sometimes."

He stepped on the gas again and maneuvered around a blue Honda onto the Gowanus Expressway. His head was full of hot tears but he didn't dare let them out.

Mother. She would have understood what he did today. She knew what it was to be drastic.

She was always at the front of marches in Bethlehem, lying down in front of the tanks at Rachel's Tomb. Screaming and rending her clothes at the funerals of martyrs. A little Arab lady in a white scarf with a voice that carried like the wind. She taught him that there was a special place of honor in heaven for the ones who fight, not for the ones who stay at home.

Not like Father. Getting his face slapped by Israeli border guards and trying to smile through the tears.

Nasser couldn't have been more than five years old when it happened but the memory tore at him in new ways all the time. It didn't even look like a slap. It looked more as if the young soldier was lightly patting his father on the cheek. They'd been making a special trip to Jerusalem—his mother, his father, and he—when their cab was stopped by the Israeli border patrol and the soldier on duty asked to see Father's identification card. Perhaps Father was slow to get out, so the soldier just reached out and put his hand to the old man's face, and that was that. Father bowed and got back in the cab.

It was only when Nasser looked up and saw his father trying to smile with tears running down his cheeks that he realized anything was wrong.

His mother just sat there, lips pursed and chin raised, refusing to look at her husband. Amina. She was pregnant, Nasser remembered, and Father had shamed her this day. So she stared into her son's eyes, not needing to say it out loud: *Don't be like him*. I would rather die than see you be like him.

Up until then, he'd thought they were a family like any other. Yes, he knew they had to move around a lot before he was born, leaving Jordan and eventually ending up in the Deheisha refugee camp outside Bethlehem, because Israeli forces had claimed the house Father grew up in and there was nowhere else to go. But all other families they knew had a story like that. After the slap, though, everything grated, everything hurt. Seeing the water carrying sewage down the middle of the dusty narrow street, so that flies followed you everywhere and the terrible smell infiltrated your clothes. Living eight to a room in a concrete-block house with a corrugated tin roof, where his mother would stack up mattresses during the day so they could have a living room and then spread them out at night for everyone to have a place to sleep. Wearing old UN food sacks for underwear, with Not for Sale stamped on the ass. Knowing his parents' first child, Maryam, had died of malnutrition before her first birthday. Watching his father stand on a street corner near the Damascus Gate every morning, with twenty or thirty other Arab men, jockeying for position, waiting for some sweaty, hairy-necked Jewish contractor to drive by in a Mercedes and say *you, you, and you* can come work for forty shekels a day, building houses on the land we stole from you.

"So what was it like when Mother came here?" said Elizabeth. "I can't really picture it. This little Arab lady in a head scarf riding the subway with us."

"She didn't." Nasser kept his eyes on the road. "She never crossed the water."

"What do you mean, she didn't cross the water?" Elizabeth cricked her neck, trying to get Nasser to look at her. "I thought she brought us to the States after Father had been working here a year, making money so he could get us out of the refugee camp. Didn't we all live together on Starr Street?"

"She came here but she never left there. Do you understand?" He blinked. "In her heart, she was still there, in the camp."

He flashed on the image of her in Deheisha, right after Elizabeth was born: A shrinking lady with two small children carrying rotting vegetables past barbed-wire fences, moving slower than the dirty water in the gutter. Her spirit wilting in the sun. A part of her was already dead. Things he could never put into words.

"Never mind," he said. "You're too young to remember."

"Explain it to me." Elizabeth touched his arm.

They were passing under the elevated tracks, near the Bush Terminal warehouses, a rough and dark industrial place where men did things that made no sense to their wives.

"She never accepted that she was here," said Nasser. "No place was home except for the Monastery of Branches. You see? She said she would go back there one day or die waiting for the Jews to leave Palestine. Okay? This is how it was."

America had done this to her, she'd say. *America has broken our hearts. America has taken your father from us. America makes it possible for the Jews to treat us this way*. There would be a *Great Chastisement* for those who'd been so cruel.

"Sometimes, she'd take us on this boat that goes around Manhattan Island," said Nasser. "This Circle Line. She'd stand by the railing and look out at the water, like she was thinking to be somewhere else. And I would never let go of her hand because I was so afraid she would jump over the side and leave us."

"Is that what happened?" Elizabeth turned on him. "Is that how she died?"

"No." Nasser pushed himself back against his seat, as if bracing for impact. "She just got sick and took too many pills. It was an accident."

"You mean she committed suicide?"

He took the question like a blow to the head. "Don't say this. It's against the Holy Book."

For a few seconds, he refused to speak or look at her. The road hummed under his wheels and he felt the pressure of tears building up behind his eyes again.

No, she wasn't a suicide. She was a martyr. That was the only way he could think of her death. He remembered seeing her lying on the bed, with hands folded over her chest. "This is not my mother!" he'd yelled at Father. "What have you done with my mother?" He had become a warrior to honor her memory. When he'd joined the *intifada* back home, every stone he'd thrown at the soldiers was for her, every rock was a piece of his broken heart. Today was for her too. She would have understood.

"Then what *did* happen?" said Elizabeth. "I have a right to know. She was my mother too."

"I tell you this was an accident—nobody says nothing against her." Nasser abruptly cut her off. "We don't talk bad about her." He took a deep breath and sniffed.

"I know, but sometimes I'll hear you and Father speaking in Arabic and I feel like you're keeping something from me."

"Maybe it's better that way." He blinked again and the tears began to recede, just a little trickle coming out on the side facing away from her.

"Why, what makes you say that?"

The Gowanus bent its elbow in Red Hook and splintered off into the Brooklyn-Queens Expressway, cutting through Carroll Gardens and Cobble Hill. Gray-rimmed clouds drifted in from the east.

"I think let's be quiet awhile." Nasser wiped away the stray tear and lifted his chin. "I don't want to talk no more. Let's just be together, like a family."

9

As the elevator doors shut, David closed his eyes and got that same visceral jolt of the bus exploding. But when he opened them again, he was back on the elevator, being carried up to see Renee and Arthur on the eighteenth floor. For a few seconds, he wasn't sure which was real and which was hallucination—the polished oak walls or Seniqua screaming, metal twisting, and the floor buckling under him. He had to see his family immediately. It was a physical craving. He needed the tactile sensation of being near them, touching them, to make him real again and assure him that he had indeed survived.

The elevator doors popped open and he stepped off quickly, coughing as if his lungs were still full of poison.

"Jesus, what happened to you?" Renee was waiting for him in the corridor, wearing gray sweats and propping open the apartment door with her foot.

"I was in a fire." He followed her into the apartment, realizing that he might still be a little raw and smelly in spite of the shower he'd just taken at home.

"For real?" The door closed behind her.

"Yeah, for real. Didn't you see it on television? Our bus blew up outside school."

"Shit." She came over to hug him. "Are you all right?"

"I guess so."

She reached up to put her arms around his neck and he closed his eyes, waiting to feel the bus explode once more. But instead there was only the sensation of stillness and her cool forehead resting against his chin. His metabolism was finally starting to slow down. He felt skin and hair and heard Joni Mitchell singing on the kitchen tape player. He opened his eyes and saw sunlight streaming between the buildings and Margot Fonteyn dancing above the couch.

"Hey, is that Daddy?" Arthur called from the other room.

They moved apart from each other a little, embarrassed by the Polaroid flash of intimacy.

"You better go talk to him." Renee touched his chest. "Show him you're okay before he hears anything and gets worried."

"Yeah, of course." He took her fingers and kissed them. "I'll be right back."

Hungry for more flesh-on-flesh contact, he went down the hall to the boy's bedroom.

"Hey, tiger. What's happening?"

"Odysseus is killing all the suitors."

Arthur was sprawled on the bedroom carpet, arranging toy soldiers around a plastic castle. The floor was covered with the detritus of a child's life: comic books, Disney action figures, Lego blocks, Playmobil fortresses, Transformers, and cap guns. An archeologist could come in and discover generations of pop culture buried in layers. David knelt and put his hand on his son's back.

"Why is he doing that?"

"He wants to take back his family," said Arthur, furrowing his brow in concentration.

David saw how enormous his hand looked on the boy's narrow back. From palm to fingertips, he could easily span Arthur's waist. This was good. This was real. This was life. He leaned down and nuzzled the boy's hair.

"Look, buddy, something kind of serious happened at school today. I'll tell you more about it later. But right now all you need to know is I'm all right."

"Okay," Arthur said casually, turning onto his side. "Dad, tell me about the Valkyries again."

For a second, David was disoriented. Was this relevant? "The Valkyries from the book we were reading the other night?" He blinked, trying to get on the boy's wavelength.

"Yeah. I really, really want to know."

David steepled his fingers and felt himself getting dizzy for a moment. He considered telling Arthur more about the explosion, but now the timing didn't seem right.

"Um, I guess you're talking about how the Valkyries look down from Valhalla and choose which warriors are going to die that day," he said slowly. "And then they swoop down and tap them on the shoulders."

"Yeah, yeah! Keep going."

David closed his eyes and breathed in, still trying to get himself oriented. You're okay. You're not going to die. You're with your son. The hard part is over. The fire is out.

"And so then," he said, opening his eyes, "the warrior who's been tapped knows this is the day he will die, and he rushes around killing as many of the enemy as he can until he falls. Because this is his last day."

"And what else?"

Breathe in, breathe out. You weren't the one who died today. "And then he's carried up to Valhalla, where he lives with all the Valkyries and great warriors in history, eating and fighting and fighting and eating until the end of time."

"Cool!" Arthur threw his arms around David's neck. "Thank you, Daddy."

"My privilege."

His exhilaration tempered by the knowledge of Sam's death, he kissed his son on the top of his head. Why me? he wondered briefly. Why am I the one who gets to live?

He looked down at the back of Arthur's red hair standing on end like a cock's comb and decided the answer was probably somewhere in there.

From the next room, David could hear Renee turning the television up, the traditional signal that it was time for him to leave. This was going to be a short visit after all.

"All right, buddy." He stood up. "So I'm going to see you Friday after school."

"Dad." Arthur rolled onto his side. "Mommy cut herself."

"What?"

Arthur turned back onto his stomach, playing with his soldiers again, blissfully unaware of the chill he'd put in his father's belly.

"What did you just say, buddy?"

"Nothing." Arthur made machine-gun sounds and banged his sneakers together, losing himself in his little world again. "I'm just playing."

Afraid to ask any more, David squeezed the boy's foot and started to walk out through the living room. Anton, the boyfriend, was sitting next to Renee on the couch. Wearing David's old red bathrobe with the belt double-knotted in the front.

Unbelievably, he was a couple of inches taller than David, so the sleeves were too short and the hem rose up above his knees. His hair was long and silky and much more poetic than his face, which had a mildly sluggish and complacent look. He wore a thin gold chain around his neck and an expensive-looking turquoise Navajo bracelet.

"David, you know Anton," Renee said cautiously.

So here was the final aftershock. Yes, he'd met Anton before, but never this casually. The coziness of the scene made him a little sick to his stomach. Another man in *his* house, wearing *his* bathrobe, sitting next to *his* wife, on *his* couch. How's that for cutting you down to size, big guy?

"How you doing?" David offered his hand.

"Yeah, what's up, man?" Anton gave him a kind of fey hep-cat hand slap and the bracelet slid down his arm.

David sucked at his teeth and sneaked a glance at Renee. What did she see in this guy? Was she impressed because he was a musician? Or was this evidence of some worrisome deterioration in judgment on her part? She used to have better taste.

As the six o'clock news began on television, David looked her over, trying to find the cut Arthur mentioned. But no bandage was apparent.

On the screen, a chiseled-looking young anchorman was introducing a segment about the bus exploding. And then there it was again, the nightmare starting, this time with a little graphic at the bottom of the screen that said: New York 1 News Exclusive. No longer just a vision in his head.

The camera turned just after the first explosion, so the bus was already tilting forward with its hood on fire and the kids running away, screaming. And then here was David Fitzgerald again, lumbering around to the back of the bus, opening the door, and getting a leg up from Ray-Za. Then David watched himself climb onboard and go charging into the smoke. The camera didn't record the fear in his head; it just caught glimpses of him through the smoke, making his way toward Seniqua, halfway out the window and bawling piteously.

Everything seemed so much faster and more offhanded than it did in real life. Watching it was beyond surrealistic; it made David feel slightly psychotic. Like he had no business still being in his body. The angle had finally shifted to the back of the bus; the cameraman had moved there just in time to catch Seniqua's friends carrying her off and David jumping down after her.

"Oh my God," Renee was saying. "Is this really you?"

The same question had occurred to David. He was aware of the fact that both she and Anton were looking at him strangely, as if they couldn't quite connect the man in the living room with the image on the screen. In the meantime, the angle had shifted once more and he saw himself trying to resuscitate Seniqua. The video footage here was much more frightening because it was so stark and ordinary. The cameraman had been leaning right over David's shoulder, and the feeling of death approaching jumped right through the camera lens. Without edits or dramatic music, the plainness of it was heart-stopping. And then David saw himself leaning over and breathing life back into the girl.

Watching it from this angle, he first felt scared again, and then oddly detached. He sat down.

"God!" Renee moved close to him and touched his arm. "Are you all right?"

"Yeah, I'm fine. Everything's fine."

"God!" She scrunched up her face, reabsorbing the shock of what she'd just seen. "What happened?"

"I don't know. The bus blew up. You know as much as I do."

He tried to tell her about the intensity of the flames and the detective who questioned him afterward, but she was staring at his forehead with a dreamy, faraway look.

"Oh, David. I always knew you'd do something like this."

"You did?"

She took his hand and squeezed it. For a second, the electricity of the contact bypassed his sense of time and reason, and he wished they could be alone for a few minutes to talk sense to each other. But then he noticed Anton staring over her shoulder with a mixture of dismay and disbelief.

"So you're the man of the hour," he said.

"Well, I don't know." David coughed.

"You saved those kids."

"Actually only one kid. Somebody else died. The driver."

Renee let go of his hand and drew away from him. "Shit, man, this is so weird," she said. "It's like, all these levels of reality. I'm sitting here, watching this, thinking *is this him or is this a movie?*"

She laughed a little wildly and he smiled to humor her. "Well, that was—"

"You know, I'm sitting here, trying, trying, trying to learn these lines . . ." She gestured at an open copy of *The Glass Menagerie* on the coffee table. "And then I turn on the television and *there you are*. It's like you were in a movie."

Her hands shook as she started to light a cigarette. He wondered if seeing the father of her child in danger had somehow unnerved her. Or did it mean she still cared for him?

"It didn't feel like a movie when it was happening, Renee," he said gently. "It felt real. The driver died."

That seemed to calm her a little. "But you're all right?"

"I'm all right."

She hugged him once more and then drew back. She was looking at him with that old glitter in her eyes. That crazy connection between them, he was feeling it again. That sense that it was just the two of them against the rest of the world. The way they used to believe in each other and egg each other on. On this very couch, they'd made love one morning after he'd called in sick to school on a whim. He remembered the green robe slipping off her bare white shoulders, as he reared up over her, covering her with his body but trying not to crush her. Maybe it wasn't too late to try to put things back together. They needed each other; a man needs his woman, a boy needs his mother and father. But then he recalled what Arthur had said a minute ago: *Mommy cut herself.*

"So you doing okay?" He looked her over once more, checking her wrists and ankles for scratches and abrasions.

"Of course." Her smile turned to bewilderment. "But you're the one who almost got killed today. So why are you asking me if I'm okay? Do I not seem okay?"

"No, you seem fine."

No visible cuts. It's all right, David thought. Kids make things up all the time.

Anton put a hand on her shoulder, as if staking a claim on her. "Shouldn't we be getting ready for dinner?" he mumbled.

Renee drew up suddenly, like a cat arching her back. "*I am speaking to David,*" she said.

"I know." Anton sulkily played with his Navajo bracelet. "But it's getting to be time."

"I know what time it is, Anton. But I am *speaking* to David."

So there was tension between them. Fine, thought David. Maybe their little West Coast swing wouldn't come off after all and he wouldn't have to fight to keep her and Arthur in the city.

"Maybe I should go," he said, starting to rise.

"Did I ask you to go? Is that what I was saying?"

"No, but it's late."

He recognized the mood she was getting into and knew enough to stay out of its way. A half-eaten green apple was turning brown on a plate next to the open script. Let nature take its course, he thought. If we can reconcile, we'll reconcile. No sense forcing the issue tonight.

"So I guess I'll see you Friday," he said slowly, moving toward the door. "I'll come by after school to pick up Arthur."

He decided not to remind her that they also had appointments with the psychiatrist and the judge in their divorce case next week. He didn't want to set off any more emotional depth charges here. His chest ached and his limbs felt heavy. This day had already taken too much out of him.

"God, David." Renee ran across the room and kissed him on the cheek as he put his hand on the doorknob. "I'm so proud of you."

He got a static shock from her. "Are you really?"

"Now I wish I could do something to make someone proud of me."

10

Down at the house on Avenue Z, Elizabeth Hamdy and the rest of her family were in the living room, sitting transfixed in front of the forty-inch-wide Pioneer home entertainment center, watching the *Headline News* at eight o'clock. Images of the bus burning in front of the school had already been repeated enough to become a kind of instant icon, a symbol of vulnerability. All over the country, parents were seeing it and thinking about how much it looked like buses they'd put their own children on.

"Jaysus," said her stepmother, Anne, holding Elizabeth from behind. "Thank God you stayed home with the headache this morning. I'd be worried sick about you."

"*Allahu akbar*. God is good, God is greatest." Her father stood there, hugging himself and murmuring, his neatly trimmed mustache rising and falling faster.

The two younger girls, Leslie and Nadia, were giggling and doing each other's hair as if they found the images silly and tedious.

Elizabeth sat with the helmet Nasser had just bought her on her lap and turned to say something to her brother.

But he'd already left the room.

This was *jihad*, Holy War, and in a war, there were casualties. Still, it bothered Nasser that he remembered Sam the bus driver from school. He told himself it didn't matter, that these were infidels, that there would have been far more casualties if he'd managed to get inside the school and put the *hadduta* in the boiler room as he'd originally intended. This would have been justified. The American people supported their government, and their government supported the Israelis, and the Israelis were the oppressors who stole land and broke his mother's heart. They only understood the language of violence.

Just the same, it was troubling to him, the way casualties that had so little to do with Palestine were mounting up. The three people in the check-cashing place, the bus driver.

He got into his car, stopped by to pick up his paycheck as he did every Tuesday night, and then drove into Manhattan, trying to work it around in his mind so he'd feel at peace. On the radio, there was more news about the *hadduta:* "Officials are saying what appeared to be a bomb exploded in front of Coney Island High School today . . ." The announcer's words made him too nervous, so he switched to an oldies music station—his secret vice—and found himself humming along with an insipid song about an achy-breaky heart.

He was exhausted, but he knew he wouldn't be able to sleep tonight. He was too upset. He needed to talk to someone older and more sensible to calm himself down. He'd heard his old cell mate, Professor Bin-Khaled, was in town, lecturing at City University, but he wasn't ready to face the older man yet. They had too many hard things to talk about.

Instead, he stopped by the Medina Mosque on East 11th Street, prayed for ten minutes with four full repetitions of the *raka* positions—standing, bending, putting his hands behind his ears, kneeling with his forehead on the floor—and then went to see Youssef at his residency hotel on West 23rd Street. He knew it would be a difficult talk too, but it was time to get it over with.

He found the Great Bear in the living room of his little two-bedroom apartment, freshly showered, wearing a blue bathrobe and drinking a white protein shake. Weight-lifting equipment surrounded him. Youssef's four children, whom Nasser had never met, were playing in another room, with their mother admonishing them to keep their voices down lest they make their father angry. On the television in the corner, a white-and-red fireball streaked across the city skyline. It took Nasser a few seconds to realize that he wasn't watching another film clip of today's bombing, but a bootleg video of the movie *Independence Day*. He remembered Youssef telling him he was doing a side business, making illegal duplicates of the tapes from the local video store to raise money for *jihad*.

"Okay," said Youssef, moving aside some American muscle magazines so Nasser could sit next to him on the sofa. "So let's talk about it."

Nasser tried to speak but couldn't for a few seconds. Fear still had his tongue locked up. His neck glands felt swollen and tired from having pumped so much adrenaline. The palm of his hand ached from having gripped the bag with the bomb so tightly.

"So tell me again, why do you put the *hadduta* under the school bus?" said Youssef, picking up the remote control and turning down the volume. "I'm ready to listen now."

Nasser was aware of the Great Bear staring at him, seething. On the TV screen, a huge alien spaceship was hovering over the White House and the President was rushing to escape with his daughter on an airplane. With the sound off, the images seemed even more frenetic and violent.

"I told you before, sheik, I had to put it there because they were all watching," Nasser said quickly, looking at Youssef once and then looking away. "There was more security than I thought. It would've been a mistake to go ahead with the plan."

On the TV, a green beam of light from space was incinerating a skyscraper in Los Angeles.

"Are you a fool? Is that what you are?" Youssef yelled.

"No, sheik . . ."

"Well then, why do you do this? Ha? The point was to put it in the boiler so it would have a greater impact. Instead, you put it under the bus where there isn't anything to push against! Don't you see?" He rubbed his forehead. "It's like a wet firecracker. I was watching the news before, and we don't get more than five minutes' coverage!"

"I saw it on the *Headline News*," Nasser offered meekly, not sure what Youssef had expected.

"Yes, but it should be on *all the time*, twenty-four hours. They should be in a total panic about this, talking about nothing else." Youssef sighed in disgust. "Now I'm not even sure if we should take credit for this. Do you want them to think we're clowns and incompetents? Is that what you want?"

"No, sheik." Nasser looked down and saw a long black-handled carving knife sitting on a stack of magazines on the coffee table. He pressed his back against the soft plush cushions. "I tell you, I'm sorry. I did what I could."

Youssef stared at him for a long time without speaking. He seemed to be swelling up with anger, right there on the couch. Nasser looked down at the knife again.

Fear went running like a rat through his brain, eating through all old notions of friendship and security. He'd seen the Great Bear kill a mother in front of her child.

Was it possible Youssef would stab him right here, with his own children in the next room? Nasser didn't think so, but he tensed up, ready to jump from the couch.

But instead of reaching for the knife, Youssef just picked up his protein shake.

"Well, it's okay," he grumbled, taking a sip. "But not really, if you know what I mean. We'll do better next time."

In the video, cars were flying through the air, women were screaming, and the White House was getting blown into matchsticks.

"Does anyone see you leave this bag under the bus?" Youssef asked, putting down the shake and wiping his beard and mustache with the back of his hand.

"I don't think so," said Nasser.

We'll do better next time. No, it was impossible for him to consider going through this again. Today had done too much violence to his insides.

"Sheik." Nasser looked up, folding his hands in humble beseechment. "I think I want out."

"What?"

"I'm scared to do this again. I'm not sure if it's right. The things we do."

The spaceship obliterated midtown Manhattan.

"You can't just walk away," Youssef said sternly, picking up the knife and pointing it at Nasser's face. "This is not possible."

"Why not?"

Nasser leaned back and saw light glint off the side of the blade.

"A man is already dead because of the bomb. *You are the jackpot, my friend*." Youssef said, switching to English for the phrase.

"I don't think this is how you say this expression," Nasser offered timidly.

"Of course it is." Youssef rebuffed him, switching back to Arabic. "Anyway, too much already is depending on you." He picked up a mango that had been lying next to the magazines on the coffee table and started to peel it. "Not two hours ago, I was on the phone with this brother I told you about from Egypt. This man who taught me everything I know about guns and explosives in Afghanistan. You remember when they stop the tourist bus in Cairo and shoot thirty-three of the Germans?"

"Of course," said Nasser, relieved he was not about to be stabbed to death, but aware he was still under a cloud.

"This was his operation. He personally shoots five of the passengers and two of the police before he gets away on a motorbike. And remember Flight 502 that blew up on the runway in Paris and killed seventy-five people?"

"Of course." Nasser remembered the film footage of ambulances and fire trucks screaming down the airport tarmac. The shrieking and crying relatives on the news.

"He was part of that too," said Youssef. "And he is coming here, next week. This good man. I told him all about you. How proud I was of you the other night. He'll be very disappointed if he hears you want to quit."

Hearing this, Nasser felt a crushing weight on his chest. One of the men who bombed Flight 502. He felt both terrified and exhilarated by the prospect of meeting such a man.

"But I'm just not sure I'm being effective," he said haltingly. "I know I made a bad mistake today . . ."

"Yes, it was a bad mistake!" Youssef slid the blade under the mango's skin, making juice spurt. "This is why you have to make up for it. To prove yourself again. I have already discussed this with my friend. What to do about you."

"What do you mean?" Nasser wiped his eye nervously.

"Well, he was very upset when I told him what happened at first. How you made a mistake. He's had men killed for doing less. But I explained your situation to him. How you are young and eager to help. So I think he's okay about it now. He's very compassionate, you know. He's made mistakes himself. A lab blew up. He was out of favor for a long time with some of our so-called leaders, who wouldn't work with him anymore. But now he's coming here, to make a big comeback and show them."

"So what did he say exactly? About me?"

Youssef leaned in and lowered his voice. "He says it sounds like you can still be useful and be a good soldier. If you can prove yourself. But I must tell you"—he cut off a thick slice of the mango—"you have a lot to make up for."

"I know, sheik. That's why I think maybe you should get someone else." Nasser stared at the pit sticking out through the pulp like a piece of bone.

The Great Bear offered the slice to Nasser. "No, it's too late to make a change," he said, as the image of the Statue of Liberty lying sideways in New York Harbor flashed on the screen. "When my friend comes next week, you'll see. Everything will be okay. He'll speak to you kindly. He's a very great man. He'll give you strength in your heart again."

11

The school was still in a collective state of shock the next day, with a quarter of the students absent and trauma counselors set up in the library for kids who wanted to talk. But David was determined to try to return to the landscape of reality.

The morning had been insanity. All last night, television producers from the rival dawn talk shows had been tying up his phone line cajoling, begging, pleading with him to come on—one of them actually saying, "I'll lose my job if I don't have you on before seven-fifteen!" But as soon as he agreed to appear on all three network programs in the order in which they'd called, it was as if a clandestine war had broken out. They canceled one another's limousine services, which were scheduled to pick him up in the morning, and then each tried to get him to stay overnight at a hotel near their studio. Finally, Stephanie Kwan, a booker from the third-rated *Morning Program*, showed up outside his apartment at quarter to six in the morning with a continental breakfast and a cappuccino. A petite young woman with a tight black leather skirt and stop-the-show-I-gotta-have-sex legs, she hustled him into a stretch limo, stroked his arm, and told the driver to take the West Side Highway while she made furtive triumphant calls on her cell phone and flattered David recklessly.

"Thank God, we have somebody real on the show this morning!" she'd said. "There are no heroes anymore. Just celebrities."

Once they reached their destination, she rushed him into a shiny building on Ninth Avenue as if she expected him to get snatched away, brought him up to the studio floor, and left him in the care of a brisk and efficient Southern makeup lady called Tammy who told him he had a good look for television and urged him to "lose the glasses." Then he was sat down in the greenroom with an Academy Award–winning British actor, a famous diet doctor having a panic attack, and a gimlet-eyed rock and roll girl singer who kept wandering around, asking production assistants, "Anybody got a Tuinal?"

A few minutes later, David was led out into the studio, outfitted with a microphone on his lapel, and seated next to the blond and genial host of the program, Brian something—a world's-smartest-tennis-pro type—who thanked him for coming and fawned over him effusively as soon as the red light on top of the camera went on. The video clip of Seniqua's rescue was played on an overhead monitor and David again had that peculiar out-of-body feeling, as he heard himself saying things about stoicism and responsibility. Only it wasn't really him. It was that inauthentic self that had been released before the cameras and microphones outside school yesterday.

Oh what utterly ridiculous bullshit, the real David thought. How can they stand me? How can they not see through me? But when he looked off-camera he saw Stephanie Kwan smiling giddily and sound technicians holding their chins thoughtfully, listening to him. After fifteen years teaching public school, it was gratifying to get such undivided attention. He wondered if Renee and Arthur were watching at home and seeing him in a different light.

Before the morning was over, he went through the whole routine two more times on the other two morning shows, barely managing to keep track of whom he was talking to. It all seemed to blend together in a weirdly giddy, intoxicating way. *People were listening to him.* The only thing that changed was the state of the rock and roll singer, who seemed to be disintegrating as she followed him from program to program. By the end of the morning, she was being escorted out of a greenroom on one high heel, muttering, "Beer and acid, beer and acid," as if it were a revolutionary political slogan.

But that was over now.

As fourth period began, Seniqua Rollins walked into the classroom, mumbled, "Thanks," to David, and sat down among the other kids, accepting high fives and chucks to the back of the head.

The rest of the class was buzzing. On the left, the hip-hop girls were doing their cheerleader/war chant thing. Ray-Za and Obstreperous Q were playing bumper cars with their chairs in the third row. And Kevin Hardison was standing up by the radiators in the back, giving his play-by-play version of yesterday's events at the top of his lungs.

"All right, all right, cool out, party people." David raised his hands. "Everybody take a chill pill. Since we didn't get to make our trip to the museum, I'd like to begin our *Odyssey* discussion now."

"*Get the fuck outta here,*" someone said.

"Yeah, get the fuck outta here," one of the hip-hop girls shouted out.

The Great Hormone Experiment was continuing. It was predictable, the kids being so agitated. Yes, a lot of them came from neighborhoods where there were shootings and murders every week and gutters strewn with used rubbers and drug paraphernalia, but still—they'd seen their school bus blow up, just seconds before they were going to board it. Their driver had been killed and one of their classmates had almost burned to death before their eyes. And by now, after being interviewed by detectives and counselors, as well as having their bags searched thoroughly, they had to be aware that someone within the school might have been responsible for the blast.

Homer had lasted for three thousand years; he could wait another day. The kids needed to talk. Besides, after making the morning talk show rounds, David hadn't done an adequate job of preparing for any of his five classes today.

"Okay, disregard what I said before—let's open things up a little this morning." He sat on the edge of his desk, more Cool Daddio–style than pedagogue. "Something pretty heavy went down yesterday, and I'd like to hear what you have to say about it."

He went to the blackboard and wrote the words: *To be afraid of oneself is the last horror. — C. S. Lewis.*

Then he looked over and saw Seniqua was wearing the same style Tommy Hilfiger jacket she'd had on yesterday. Unbelievable. Kids had stopped chucking her on the head and were now huddled around her, murmuring in awe and touching its hem and sleeves as if it were a war souvenir.

Okay, thought David, that's one way of dealing with it. Getting on top of the fear. Acting like you own it.

The real jacket was probably being tested for traces of explosives and accelerants by the investigators. The school was already crawling with cops. David had seen the bomb squad guys threading their way past repair crews outside school this morning. A sensory memory of the first explosion hit him again and he felt an uneasy stirring in his gut.

Who the hell did this? A side of him got angry thinking about it. Somebody had tried to kill them all. Not just him, but *his kids.*

But what if it was one of the kids? He found himself scanning various faces around the classroom, considering students as possible suspects. What about Yuri Ehrlich? He certainly had the technical ability to put together a bomb, and David remembered the odd look on his face after the explosion. Or how about jealous King Shit, the jailed gang leader? Maybe he'd gotten word of Seniqua straying and had dispatched an emissary to take her off the count.

It was too disturbing and distracting to consider, one of the kids being involved. The likelihood was that it was someone not connected with the school at all, he decided. Someone upset with the governor. A political statement.

"Anyway," he told the class. "You guys must have some response to what happened. Who wants to start off?"

Richie Wong's hand shot up. A motor-mouthed Cuban-Chinese kid who was always playing cards in the hallway.

"Yes?" David called on him.

"My mom said she saw you on TV last night. What show were you on?"

David laughed, caught off guard by the question. "I think it was just the regular news," he said. "There were a lot of reporters out there, in case you didn't notice."

Little eddies of conversation went around the room. Apparently some of the kids had caught his act. He wondered if they'd seen through him. Keep it real, they were always telling each other. Keep it real.

Kevin Hardison raised his hand. "I wanna know what that Sara Kidreaux is like."

"She was one of the people interviewing me yesterday?"

"She fly." Kevin nodded. "She slick."

"I don't know." David shrugged. "She seemed very . . . cordial. I guess. But listen, I don't want to get sidetracked here, talking about the media. There are important things we need to discuss. How did everybody feel about what happened? Were you scared? Shocked? Paralyzed?" One way or the other, he was trying to turn this into a lesson.

Seniqua Rollins raised her hand so suddenly it threatened to bring the rest of her body up out of her seat with it.

"I wanna know why they had you-all on the shows this morning, instead a one of the real victims. What's a matter? They don't wanna put niggahs on they program?"

"Um." David cleared his throat. "I don't know if it was a racial issue necessarily, Seniqua."

"Dawn."

"What?"

"Call me Seniqua Dawn. I saw God yesterday and he wanted me to change my name."

David stared at her again. Hadn't Seniqua just quietly thanked him for saving her life? On the other hand, what did you expect from a seventeen-year-old speaking out in front of her friends? It was practically a Board of Ed rule: every student must bring at least two personae to class.

He wondered if she'd been to a doctor to make sure the baby was okay after yesterday. "Anyway, Seniqua—I mean, Seniqua Dawn—I don't think they had me on because I'm white and you're black."

"Yeah, right!" An anonymous spitball of teenaged sarcasm hurtled from the back of the classroom.

David had no idea who said it, but he decided to press on. "Come on, you guys. You're being ridiculous. We've had discussions about thinking critically about what you hear in the media, and now you're letting yourselves be hypnotized."

Of course, he hadn't shown much critical perspective himself, getting sucked into the phony melodrama of today's interviews.

He noticed Elizabeth Hamdy staring at him intently from the third row, somehow both earthy and ethereal in her white head scarf. A Coney Island angel. She seemed to be looking right through him, like he wasn't there. Or maybe she wasn't there. She appeared to be staring at something far away, beyond the walls of the classroom. Probably she was just trying to picture the scale of the explosion, since she'd missed the whole scene.

Tisha Cornwall raised her hand, each nail painted a different color. Her hair was a history of hairstyles: some of it plaited, other parts dreadlocked, ponytailed, shaved, dyed, styled into bangs. "Are you-all gonna be on Howard Stern?" she asked.

David felt his jaw slacken and his shoulders sag.

"Yo, come on, y'all," Ray-Za called out. "Keep it real."

"Exactly," said David in frustration. "I think we're all losing sight of our priorities here. This isn't just some media package. This is real life. We've all been through a terrible trauma. A friend of ours died and a student here nearly burned to death. This isn't a television show. It's reality. Have we forgotten how to tell the difference?"

"Yes!" Seniqua Dawn Rollins called out enthusiastically.

12

"I'm not buying this," said Judy Mandel, perpetual-motion machine.

She was at her desk in the *New York Tribune* newsroom, tapping computer keys, chewing gum, and watching the President's morning press conference on a TV set suspended from the ceiling.

"Not buying what?" asked her friend, the columnist Bill Ryan, who was sitting across the partition from her.

The President was saying the era of big government was over. He said it was time for people to take charge of their own lives. He gave the example of parents in California who'd organized their own school, talked about a woman in Alabama getting off welfare after twenty years, and mentioned David Fitzgerald saving the children from the burning school bus in Coney Island.

There it was, a lightning strike from the heavens reanimating the story. Without the President, David Fitzgerald would be a trivia answer and a segment on *When Disaster Strikes 2* by next week. But now the story had new legs.

"He didn't happen to mention the California parents had median incomes of $70,000, did he?" Bill turned away from the set.

"There's something weird about this business with the teacher," said Judy, spitting out her gum and chewing on a pen cap. "I can't put my finger on it."

The press conference ended and the morning talk shows resumed.

"Can't go wrong distrusting authority." Bill cranked two sheets of paper into an old Remington typewriter, one to type on, the other to protect the roller. "Lord Acton said great men are almost always bad men."

"Why'd he keep the kids off the bus? And why did he say it was a bomb when the police haven't even announced that yet?"

Bill took an empty pipe out of his desk and stuck it in the corner of his mouth. "Are you going to ask Nazi to leave you on the story?"

She looked across the newsroom to the enclosed office where the paper's editor, a wiry, gray-faced Australian called Robert "Nazi" Cranbury, was pacing back and forth, berating his three deputy editors, known around the office as Prime Evil, Grudge Fuck, and the Death of Hope.

"No," said Judy, crossing and uncrossing her legs, unable to keep still. "Now that the President and the governor are getting into the act, it's going to be a major gang-bang political story too. He's going to let all the old hacks and police shack guys cover it."

"And what does he want you to do?"

She sighed and laced up her Doc Marten boots. "He wants me to stay on the Sex Change Singer."

"The who?"

"You haven't heard about this?" She framed her face with her hands, voguing in exasperation. "The guy who's had the number one record in the country the last four weeks is supposedly coming to New York for 'sex reassignment surgery.' "

"I'm an old man!"

"Nazi wants me to stake out the doctor's office."

"That's one of the advantages of being seventy-five." Bill chuckled and started to put on a Walkman so he could listen to Mahler while he wrote his column. "Our masters prefer to spare my gentle sensibilities and leave my column back by the used-car ads where it can't do any harm."

She watched him for a few seconds, a thin white-haired man tapping at his old machine and puffing away on a pipe deprived of tobacco by office rules. He was like some monument to mid-twentieth-century journalism plunked down in the middle of a modern corporate newsroom. Ideas and trends crashed around him, but he remained stolid and unchanging, anchored by his intellect and inner life, a rock in the middle of the ocean. She wished she could be like him, but she kept getting swept away.

She was still struggling desperately to make a name for herself at the paper. It had been easy in school, where she could command attention by sitting splay-legged and acting saucy in class. But New York newspaper people had seen that bad-girl act too many times. After a year and a half at the paper, she was still writing briefs for page 9 and actor-slugs-the-photographer captions. She felt herself slipping into a kind of lonely corporate anonymity. If she didn't watch it, she'd become one of those middle-aged "News Nuns," who worked all the time and came home to cottage cheese and white wine in the refrigerator.

"Hey, why don't they put Riordan on the sex change story?" Bill took off his headphones.

"What?"

"Your old boyfriend." Bill nodded in the direction of Terry Riordan, who was on the phone some twenty-five feet away, swiveling in his chair and applying Chap Stick to his lips. "Didn't he write a feature about the plastic surgeon to the stars last month?"

Judy looked over at Riordan, a vain young society reporter whom she'd dated briefly during the summer. "Yeah, he loves that crap."

"So tell Nazi to let him do it. Riordan's got all the show business connections anyway. You stay on the teacher."

"Think he'll let me do it?"

"Like you said, it's a major story because of the video and now the President. Nazi will do anything to stay out in front if he can. Make him think you have something."

"What do I have? The detectives on the scene wouldn't talk to me."

"But you're a hot number. Look at you, with your little skirt and your black stockings and your Lulu hair. Cardinal Spellman couldn't resist you."

He was an old man, but not that old, she realized. He'd dined with Bacall and danced with Monroe. If he wanted to pay her a compliment, she'd take it.

"Anyway," he said. "John LeVecque's the police spokesman now. That moron who used to be with the *Post.* Go down to Police Plaza and rattle his cage a little. Get him to tell you something he doesn't want to tell you about the investigation."

"And how am I supposed to do that?"

"Be provocative. Be ruthless. Ask the hardest question you can think of. Manipulate the manipulators. And for Chrissakes, be interesting about it."

"Is that it? Anything else?"

"Yes, always write in the active voice and try to hold on to a portion of your dignity."

"Easy for you to say. You're old."

He chuckled and started to put his headphones on again. She stood up, straightened her skirt, and flipped back her hair, getting ready for her talk with Nazi.

"By the way." She looked back at Bill, lowering his magnificent white mane toward the keyboard. "If great men are almost always bad men, what are bad men?"

"Worse than they seem." He pushed the typewriter's carriage all the way to the left. "Nose pickers and card cheats, the lot of them."

13

About ten minutes from the end of fourth period, there was a knock at the door of David's classroom and Michelle Richardson, one of the principal's secretaries, came in. She was usually aloof and contemptuous of mere teachers; for years, David had seen only the side of her face because she was always turned away, talking to somebody more important on the phone. But now she sidled up to him, as intimate as a kitty-cat.

"Larry King's people just called and there's a camera crew from NBC downstairs," she said softly, her lips near his ears. "They want to talk to you. The President just mentioned you in a speech."

"Well, it's really going to have to wait," David answered quietly, looking up at the clock.

Yes, it was nice, all this excitement, but he was still a teacher. Though a part of him was curious: *What did the President say about me?*

"The principal thinks it might be good if you spent some time with these newspeople this afternoon." Michelle breathed against his neck. "He thinks it can only help the image of the school."

"So I'll try to make time for them," David said.

"He wants you to do it *now*."

"Are you sure?" David glanced at the restless faces, the swinging legs.

"Oh yeah, I'm sure."

"Okay, guys." He faced the group. "You're getting early dismissal. Don't all start crying at once."

He could barely be heard above the racket of students laughing, giving each other high fives, and still using their clickers. He scanned the faces again. Still wondering: could one of them have done this? He'd only hurt their trust in him by asking too directly, but he decided to leave the door open a little. "And listen, guys. I know there are counselors in the library today, but if one of you wants to come by later and talk *to me* about what happened, I'll have office hours."

If any of them were interested, they weren't letting on. No one wanted to look weak or needy in front of the other kids. Instead, the students rose as one body and began their lemming-like trudge toward the door, ignoring David as he called out a reading assignment to finish the excerpt from the *Odyssey*.

From the corner of his eye, he saw Elizabeth Hamdy was lingering, still sitting in the third row, fidgeting with her books and staring at the blackboard.

"Hey, what's up?" he asked her.

She stood up and came to him with her head bowed. "I wonder if you have a minute so I could talk to you about something now," she murmured.

"Sure," said David. "I always have time for you."

"Oh no you don't." Michelle Richardson pulled on his sleeve. "The principal wants to see you with these media people *right away*." She lowered her voice. "*He got a call from the superintendent's office.*"

David looked back and forth between the two women, not sure what to do. The kids needed him. The camera crews were waiting. Things were changing and he realized he would have to reach an accommodation with this new multilayered reality.

"Can I catch up with you a little later?" he asked Elizabeth.

"I guess you'll have to." She drifted out of the room, like a sunstruck rain cloud.

14

The girl from the bus ad was staring at Nasser again. Only this time, she was atop a building in Times Square, with a hand thrust suggestively down the front of her unbuttoned jeans.

He tried to ignore her as he drove his Town Car down Broadway just before noon, through the valley of billboards and video screens. All these pictures and words trying to force themselves into his mind. Children in designer jeans behaving like adults; pulsating advertisements for camera equipment, computers, semiconductors, cable television, music stores. A huge American Express Card wearing a pair of black mouse ears. "Autumn in New York, presented by Diet Coke." The effect was to make him want everything, and then nothing at all. But what confused him most of all was the information circling the immense white building just ahead, One Times Square.

Police continue investigation into Coney Island High School explosion . . ., said the yellow lights speeding by on a rotating black beltway. *President praises schoolteacher David Fitzgerald . . .*

What was the sense in this? When he'd slipped the *hadduta* under the school bus, Nasser had thought it was God's will. But had it been God's will that this man he deplored, Mr. Fitzgerald, should become a hero instead?

He turned right on 42nd Street, where a giant Oreo cookie was revolving on top of a building, and stopped the cab for a young woman in a cream-colored pants suit standing in front of a tourist office with her arm raised.

He was still wondering what to do about Youssef's friend coming into town, whether he should continue with the bombings. Maybe it would take a while for God's will to fully manifest itself.

"How much to take me to Fifty-first Street and Fifth Avenue?" the girl in the pants suit asked, climbing in.

Nasser turned down his radio calls from the dispatcher and craned his neck to see her in the rearview mirror. "Four dollars."

What a stroke of luck, to pick up a fare in midtown. Perhaps Allah was smiling on him after all. He looked around cautiously, checking for police cars since only yellow cabs were supposed to pick up passengers off the street in this part of Manhattan.

"Why don't you take Eighth Avenue uptown?" the girl in the back said. "There's construction and traffic on Sixth."

"Okay, boss."

He wasn't about to argue. Most of his regular fares were radio calls from Brooklyn and Queens, which either landed him in slow-moving traffic or left him stranded in remote and dangerous neighborhoods.

The livery cab gave a little shudder as he started it west on 42nd Street. The girl in back checked her silver watch, a glint of moonlight on her wrist. Something about her reminded him of Elizabeth. Her poise, the length of her neck. But she was different too. A little older, a little darker.

Across the street, a backhoe and a pile driver were laboring in a vacant lot next to an old theater. Mickey and Minnie Mouse grinned down from the front of the Disney Store. Furious-looking men and women in dark business suits hurried by carrying navy Gap bags and attaché cases. Black clean-up men in red jumpsuits swept up trash for the Times Square Business Improvement District. A hell-fire preacher with a little microphone stood under an enormous cartoon Superman, braying about damnation. A double-deck tour bus nearly sideswiped Nasser on the left. Everything here was commotion for the soul. Nasser decided he had to shut it all out for a while and concentrate on the girl in the back.

"Is okay, without the air conditioner?" he asked her.

"Yes, I'm fine," she said, rearranging herself on the seat. "It's not that hot outside."

"You want I should leave on the radio?" He craned his neck, trying to catch her eye in the rearview mirror, eager to make her comfortable.

"Sure." She busied herself with her briefcase, really only half-listening. "Just turn it down a sec while I make a call."

He turned the volume knob the wrong way and a blast of trumpets jerked him back against his seat. He lowered the sound instantly and apologized as a mattress commercial came on. "What I am thinking?" he said, the words coming out in an awkward rush.

But she was preoccupied, trying to make a call on a little gray cell phone. He watched her in the backseat, turned sideways with one leg tucked up under her, brushing raven-black hair out of her eyes with long graceful fingers. Yes, she was like Elizabeth, a little. He sensed there were secret places inside her.

"Excuse me," he said, as she gave up on her call and closed the phone. "I do not want to be rude. But please may I ask you a question?"

"What is it?"

"You are Arab? Yes?"

In the mirror, she smiled in just a small way as traffic finally started to move and a breeze stirred her loose-fitting clothes. "Yes," she said. "I am Arab."

"Palestinian?"

"Yes, as a matter of fact."

"Ah, very good. This is the best. *Allahu akbar*."

He half-turned his head, waiting for her to return the blessing. But instead she lowered her eyes in embarrassment and began rotating a ring on her finger. "I'm sorry, I don't . . ."

"It's okay."

They swept past milk-fed tourists gawking at posters for *Les Mi-*

serables and *The Sound of Music*. Another Arab girl who didn't speak any Arabic, he thought. Just like his sister. He decided not to let his disapproval show, for the moment. She was young and pretty. She didn't know any better, he told himself.

"Please, if you don't mind for me to ask, where are you from?" It irked him having to speak English to her, the words feeling heavier than usual in his mouth today.

"Queens Village."

"No, I mean before that. Where is your family from?"

"East Jerusalem." She put away her cell phone and started looking for something else in her briefcase.

"Ah, Ras al-Amud? Upper Silwan?"

She pulled out some papers. "I don't know. I haven't been back there very often."

He looked at her in the mirror again, and felt that great loneliness once more. He'd had other Arab girls like this in the back of his car and still had not really found a way to talk to them.

"So," he said, "you are working?"

"Yes." She allowed herself just a little more of a smile but didn't look up from her papers. "I do have a job. In computers."

"My sister. She is wanting to work too. After she leaves school."

She picked up on the tension in his voice. "And that's not okay with you?"

He simply raised his hands from the wheel, as if to say, ah, what can I do?

Work and his sister. The subjects went around and around in his head. He'd never been able to get a good job in this country, and his sister was always saying it was his own fault. "You're too rigid," she'd tell him. Perhaps so. He wouldn't work for his father at the grocery store on principle. But then he wouldn't work at most restaurants either because he was trying to adhere strictly to Muslim dietary laws (except for the occasional McDonald's lapse). Working in the garment district was also out of the question since there were too many Jews involved. Finally, computer work was impossible because he hadn't graduated from high school. And of course, he didn't finish high school because of teachers like this Mr. Fitzgerald, who wouldn't leave him alone.

Around and around he went. It was easier, in some ways, being back home in the days of the *intifada*. At least he knew who he was then, throwing stones in the street. But this country had spun him around and made him dizzy.

"And now here's a song about a dwarf at a smorgasbord," said the announcer on his radio. " 'I Can't Help Myself' by the Four Tops!"

The girl in the backseat smiled again, but he didn't know why. Some of the phrases here still baffled him. A dwarf at a smorgasbord? What could this possibly mean?

He wanted to ask her to explain, but he felt shy.

"You like this song?" he said.

"Yes, I do. Why don't you turn it up?"

She'd put her papers away and he watched her applying lipstick in her makeup mirror. Somehow she'd solved the American dilemma. She'd figured out a way to live here without tearing herself apart.

"Sugar pie, honey bunch, I'm weaker than a man should be!" The song on the radio moved his knee with its solid thwocking beat. He hated this country, yet he found himself humming its song, feeling the heat in the singer's voice.

Maybe he should ask her out. The idea crept up on him unexpectedly. He would approach her gently about it, respectfully. He'd ask her out for coffee.

She was singing along softly with the song and he began to daydream at the wheel, letting himself get carried away in the river of his thoughts. Yes, they would sit and they would talk about things, and maybe he would ask her out again before evening prayers at the mosque. And eventually he would meet her parents and somehow come up with money for a dowry and they would be wed. They'd move to a house in the suburbs. She'd help him understand things, smooth his way, maybe help him get a proper American job.

If only she'd say yes. This would be the first step.

On the other hand, why should she agree to see him? Would she understand the life he'd come from? The throwing of stones. The freezing water. The stinking bag over his face. And worst of all, the horribleness they'd done to his friend Hamid in jail, which he could barely stand to think about. They'd tempted him with a woman too. How could anyone who hadn't been there understand it?

Nasser made a right on Eighth Avenue, passing a Sbarro pizza restaurant with a red-green-and-white canopy out front and gleaming gold surfaces and pink marble inside. He pursed his lips, still not sure if he had the courage to ask this girl in the backseat to have dinner with him. It was crazy; he had enough guts to plant a bomb, but not enough to ask an Arab girl out.

Things were so much simpler in Bethlehem, where parents would find mates from good families for their children. But here everything was a mad scramble. You had to prove yourself day by day. And he was so broke all the time. It was costing him $350 a week to rent the Lincoln Town Car and after giving 50 percent of his fares back to the car service—not to mention paying for tolls, gas, and insurance—he'd managed to save less than $250 in the last three months. Even though he was living rent free in his father's basement, he'd barely been able to buy a birthday present for his sister Elizabeth. Now he wasn't sure if he'd have enough to buy this pretty pants suit girl dinner at Sbarro. And would they have anything *halal* anyway?

"So," he said, trying to work up to the subject, "you are still living at home with your parents?"

"For the moment." She sighed and stared out the window as they passed more construction sites encroaching on the old boarded-up Eighth Avenue porn parlors and steak houses.

He realized his heart was pounding, almost as much as it had yesterday with the *hadduta* at the school. Would he ask her? Wouldn't he ask her? All of a sudden, everything was riding on it. If she said yes, maybe this new life would open up to him and he would forget all about the *hadduta* and Youssef and all the other rage and bitterness. He'd be able to live like Elizabeth.

If she said no, well, this was God's will, telling him to go ahead with *jihad*.

Finally he was ready. "I am wondering," he said, taking a deep breath, "if maybe some time, you would take coffee with me."

There was a long pause as they pulled up at a red light on 51st Street, facing a Howard Johnson's motel and Bagel Espresso cafe.

"No, I'm sorry. I don't think so," said the girl in the back.

"You don't think so?" Nasser cocked his head to the side as if he hadn't heard her properly.

Pedestrians passed silently before his silver fender. He looked down and saw his fingers twisting around the grooves in the steering wheel. Long, broken Arab fingers. Perhaps she only wanted American fingers touching her body. He tried to put the thought out of his mind before he became enraged.

"Okay!" He tried to pull himself up in his seat. "No problem!"

"I am sorry." In the rearview mirror, she'd gone back to looking through her papers.

The song on the radio changed to one called "The Loneliest Man in the World," and something about the singer's sad deep voice pulled at Nasser and made him uneasy.

She'd said no. He drove without speaking the next few minutes, trying to absorb the hurt. It was okay. He'd been rejected before in this country. In the streets, in the hallways at school, in Mr. Fitzgerald's class. *I can't pass you with the kind of work you're doing*. God be merciful, this was a maddening place.

"Okay, this is it," she said. "Thank you very much."

They'd arrived at her address. The building with the statue of a man holding up the world. Wasn't there a passport office around here? The girl handed him a five-dollar bill and jumped out of the cab before he could ask if she wanted change. A young black man was waiting for her on the sidewalk, with a shiny shaved head and a gold earring that winked in the sun. The girl in the pants suit ran up and threw her arms around him, kissing him passionately on the lips.

Watching this, Nasser felt his heart incinerate. How he hated America. The things that looked beautiful often turned out to be ruined inside. And things that seemed to be within easy reach were, in fact, a million miles away.

He stuffed the money into his front pants pocket, not caring if it got crumpled or torn. The stench from a nearby food vendor cooking sausages on a grill turned his stomach. Thanks be to God that Youssef was giving him a chance to make up for the mistake at the school. This was mercy and forgiveness. *Allahu akbar*. The life of this world was but a sport and a pastime, its riches transitory. In just a few days, Youssef's friend would come into town and there would be a much bigger *hadduta*, and everyone would forget about this schoolteacher. They'd be too busy with the Great Chastisement.

He looked once more at the girl kissing the black man on the sidewalk and then stepped on the gas and drove away downtown, past St. Patrick's Cathedral and Saks Fifth Avenue, with the Rolling Stones bursting from his speakers and the smell of burning flesh still in his nostrils.

15

"Of course, we're proud of David," Larry Simonetti, the school's waxy, cherubic principal was telling Sara Kidreaux, the television reporter. "But really, he's typical of the kind of teacher we've been able to bring into our school. And we're fortunate to have the kind of nurturing relationship that . . ."

The media, David Fitzgerald was discovering, was a physical universe unto itself, with its own laws of gravity, velocity, and entropy. Entering its atmosphere changed you and charged you with special properties, which attracted some bodies and repelled others.

He was standing in the school hallway with Larry and Sara Kidreaux, surrounded by a semicircle of cameramen, sound technicians, and light handlers. An outer ring of some three dozen students had formed around the media people to watch them watching Sara Kidreaux watching Larry watching David.

Apparently, he'd become a potent political symbol in the last few hours, with the President and the governor, who'd probably be running against each other next year, both invoking his name. And in the euphoria of the moment, the morning's tense state of alertness seemed to slip away, and David found himself beginning to let go of his own suspicions and apprehensions a little.

So now there was not just one but four camera crews working

the corridors and classrooms, trying to come up with footage to supplement the rescue video. It fascinated David to see how their presence altered his relationship to various people. Students he'd never seen before were speaking authoritatively to reporters about his presence in their lives. Gene Dorf, the department chair, who spent all his time avoiding students and playing the stock market, stood in a doorway, declaring that David was his best friend. David's actual best friend, Henry Rosenthal, was outside the cafeteria, riffing to interviewers in ever so slightly biting tones about "David's particular teaching philosophy." Since the explosion, David had noticed a mild undertone of tension between them, as if he'd violated some agreement they'd had to remain ineffectual white guys together.

And Donna Vitale, with her big frizzy hair and one errant eye, stood under the fire exit, simply saying she wasn't surprised. Somehow David sensed she was the one person who would have said the same thing whether or not there were cameras present. He gave her a long, admiring look, deciding that once all this excitement was over, he was definitely going to ask her out.

Meanwhile, Larry Simonetti was leaning closer and closer to David as Sara Kidreaux tried to interview them. After all the bad publicity of recent months, he was clinging to his famous teacher like a life raft.

"Because that's what it's all about, Sara," he was saying. "Education. And the kids. Making sure *they* get what they need."

"Absolutely." David took the occasion to move up right behind Larry and put a hand on his shoulder. "And that's why I was so glad to hear about the new books and special programs we're getting in next year's budget."

Larry's waxy complexion turned even paler and his eyebrows shot up toward his hairline.

"Riiight." A saliva bubble formed at the end of his tongue. "David, don't you have a class you have to teach now?"

Ninth period, David's last class of the day, was pandemonium. Not only were three camera crews set up at the back of the room to watch him teach, there were twice as many kids as usual. At least seventy of them sucking up the oxygen, sharing desks, turning around and hoping some part of their faces or bodies would wind up on the evening news. A few were even crouching at his feet to fit into the classroom, as if he were some aging rock star or spiritual leader of the moment giving a college lecture.

"He was a legitimate hero," David read aloud from *A Farewell to Arms*, "who bored everyone he met . . ."

"Hold it, hold it!"

Sara Kidreaux suddenly rose from the back of the class and made her way toward him between the tightly packed seats, a vision in red with sculpted blond hair.

"What's the matter?" David looked down at her.

"I'm sorry." She smiled, embarrassed, and looked back at one of her technical people, an enormously fat young man sniffling in overalls. "My sound man has a sinus infection and that last part you said isn't going to come out on the track. Could I ask you to do it over again?"

"Well, I, uh . . . hate to interrupt the flow of the class."

"Please." She stood on her tiptoes again, looking eager and adorably hapless. "It would *really* make our lives easier."

"Well . . ."

"Yeah, go ahead, chief!" The kids were into it, easily sliding into the roles of patient movie extras.

"Yeah, we don't mind!" a girl called out.

"Do what you gotta do, man." A macho go-along-get-along kid's voice that David didn't recognize.

He shrugged, wanting to please everyone. "All right, I guess I could do it again."

Sara Kidreaux gave a little shiver of delight. "Oh, one more thing."

She lightly licked her fingertips and smoothed back a lock of his hair.

"Aa-wooo-woo!" The kids loved it, supplying an overlay of sexual tension that David wouldn't have noticed otherwise. Sara Kidreaux blushed and wiggled just slightly as she returned to her seat.

"Anyway." David clapped his hands and moved back to the blackboard. "I think what Hemingway is saying is that a hero becomes a bore unless we can . . ."

"I'm sorry, again," Sara Kidreaux called out from behind her tremendous sound man. "That time you had your back to the camera. Can we try it just once more?"

David started to protest and say he felt like a performing bear, but something stopped him. On the one hand, television and the rest of the electronic media were everything he'd been fighting against. They shortened his students' attention spans, rotted their brains. His own son was affected. "Daddy, when can I get Playstation?" Arthur had asked the other day. "Who's stronger, Batman or Superman?"

On the other hand, it was irresistible. A part of him cried out for all this attention and acclaim. The same part that had sat longing to be noticed in the lifeguard chair, back in Atlantic Beach all those years ago. Or had stood in the outfield, waiting for someone to hit him the ball. Now here was the ball.

"Just one more, for me?" Sara Kidreaux begged with long lashes fluttering.

"Go 'head, chief!" the kids cheered him on.

"Yeah, well, I guess, all right." He took a deep breath and began again. "A hero is a bore . . ."

He stepped out into the hall afterward, feeling half elated and half abashed. How could he have given in so easily? But then again, how could he have held out? He might not have done much actual teaching today, but for once he had everyone listening, even the unreachables.

Michelle Richardson brushed past him, saying he had a message from Noonan, the police detective. The words barely sank in.

Three kids were waiting to talk to him by the library entrance across the hallway. He knew what two of them wanted. Scott Cunningham, a lanky science-obsessed senior whose mother and father had both died of AIDS, needed help filling out a college financial aid application. Next to him, Roberto Suarez, an aspiring artist from sixth period, wanted David to help him persuade his father to let him finish school, instead of making him go to work in the family fish store.

But Elizabeth Hamdy was standing a little bit behind the two boys, and David still didn't know what she was after. She looked as though she was lost in a private conversation with herself, as she stared down at the floor, contemplating her skates lying there.

"I'm sorry about before." He started to approach her first. "We really do have to talk. Your brother came by the other day."

"I know." She threw back her head and the sides of her scarf flapped like wings. "That's part of what I want to talk to you about."

They started to meet in the center of the corridor. But then Larry Simonetti suddenly came high-stepping down the hall, his wing tips making a busy slap-slap on the floor.

"Hey, David, you're not going to believe this," he said sotto voce as he moved between them. "We've got CNN *and* Dan Rather downstairs."

"Okay, but I've got to talk to Elizabeth and then Scottie and then Roberto." He threw the boys encouraging glances, letting them know he hadn't forgotten them.

Larry gripped his arm. "Maybe you didn't hear me the first time. We've got *CNN and Dan Rather*."

"Jesus, Larry." David shook him loose. "You sound like one of my kids."

But Elizabeth was already starting to withdraw, while Scott and Roberto peeled off in the other direction.

"Hey, where are you guys going?" David called after them.

"You're still busy," Elizabeth muttered as she faded down the hall, turned the corner, and disappeared.

A muted sense of having betrayed someone lingered with David for a few seconds. He'd always prided himself on being available to the kids, even giving out his home phone to the worst of the knuckleheads and telling them to call any time something was bothering them. But today he'd let them down. Despite all his intentions, he'd allowed himself to get glossed, glamorized, and artificially sweetened by the media.

"Okay, let's move." Larry was pulling him over to the stairwell. "We don't want to lose these guys."

Though he was a full five inches taller, David allowed himself to be dragged along. It was useless to resist. A part of him was already out there, being beamed up and carried aloft on the airwaves, rising above the boardwalk and Mermaid Avenue, over the skyscraper canyons and tenements of Manhattan, out past the farms of New Jersey and Pennsylvania and into the Great American heartland. Montana cattle looked up to see him passing and Pacific volcanoes yawned below. By nightfall, people in Budapest and Beijing would know his name.

"Hey, Larry, am I at least going to get some extra books for the kids out of this?"

"We'll talk about it later, smartass. Unless you want to go to your girlfriends in the media first."

David followed him down the stairs, glimpsing a patch of sky through a smudged window. It was happening.

Little bits of him were raining all over the world.

16

The next morning, Judy Mandel from the *Trib* burst into the public information office on the thirteenth floor of One Police Plaza with her skirt riding high and the top three buttons of her shirt undone.

"Goddamn it! Goddamn it! How come no one in this office has a tampon?"

John LeVecque, the former *Post* reporter who'd recently been named deputy commissioner for public information, looked up, startled and flustered.

"I'm afraid I can't help you on that count," he said, reddening slightly.

"Why don't they have tampon dispensers in the ladies' room in this building? Don't you think they should?"

She'd decided to throw him off balance by treating him the way cops had treated her for the last eighteen months. Like a rube. Except instead of talking about great blow jobs from strippers or bending a bit at the waist and farting for the amusement of everyone else present, she decided to stick her womanhood right in his face. It was no good being shy around these characters. You had to show you were tougher than them, that nothing they could do would shock you. In fact, you were better off trying to shock them first.

"So?" she said, helping herself to a seat before his desk. "When are you guys going to announce it was a bomb?"

LeVecque leaned back from the desk and made a big show of putting down the five-dollar cigar he'd been smoking, obviously recognizing there was a kind of territorial imperative at stake here.

"It's Murphy, right?"

"Mandel."

"Why am I talking to you, instead of Lippman?"

Ernie Lippman was the paper's regular police reporter, working out of the shack on the second floor. A burnout who was more interested in fly-fishing and dating dead cops' wives than in doing his job. It had been easier than she'd expected to get her editor to wire around him once she'd convinced Nazi she was the girl for the job.

"Lippman's chasing rainbows and bluefish." She crossed her legs and swung an ankle. "So should I repeat my question?"

"Yeah, why don't you?"

She flopped her notebook down into her lap as the fax machine in the corner beeped. "Everyone knows there was a bomb on the school bus. Why are you guys ass-dragging on announcing it?"

"You know, that's very naive. You don't know how naive that sounds. I never would have asked a question like that. We can't just pull results out of a hat. It takes days for the lab tests to come back."

She tensed her eyelids for just a second. Oh look at him, sitting there with his thinning blond hair, his little cigar, and his puffy I-gotta-start-playing-racquetball-again tummy protruding. An aging preppy thinking he's such a tough guy. She'd heard about this LeVecque already, that he'd been a complete buff and badge-sniffer when he was a reporter, ready to go into the tank for the police on any story. Word was, he rode around town with a police scanner and a cherry-top in his Volvo. The kind of middle-class guy who'd always wanted to be a cop, but his parents wouldn't let him.

She had to strategize here, to get around him. Think like a boxer, Bill Ryan once told her. Use what you have. Even if it's your body instead of gloves. Bob and weave. Feint and jab. Don't be afraid to get down and dirty. Manipulate the manipulators. God knows, the people you're writing about won't hesitate to do the same to you.

"So I heard a rumor that it was actually a fairly small explosive charge that happened to catch the fuel tank," she said, leaning forward and showing just a little cleavage.

"Could be." LeVecque lowered his eyes for a second and then raised them.

Brian Wallace, one of the sergeants who took calls in the outer office, walked in and dropped a file on LeVecque's desk. A big, tall guy with a walrus mustache and his tie askew, he didn't offer LeVecque so much as a nod, but he gave Judy a long once-over twice, which she tried to accept as her natural due.

For the briefest of seconds, she felt sorry for LeVecque. Quitting his newspaper job and going to work for the cops had left him a man without a country. Reporters certainly didn't trust him, but there was no way cops would ever fully accept him either. It didn't matter that the public information job had always been filled by civilians; he hadn't come up through the ranks.

"So do you have any suspects?" she asked after the sergeant left.

LeVecque put his brown loafers up on his desk, trying to reassert control. "How can there be suspects if we aren't saying it's a bomb?"

"Well, are you looking at anybody?"

"We're not prepared to say at this time."

Clearly he had no idea. She was going to have to try to embarrass him into finding out what was going on. When she'd approached that weird-looking Detective Noonan on the scene, he'd just given her that dead-eyed stare and the public information office phone number. She was stuck with LeVecque as her conduit, for the moment.

"So when will you know?" she asked.

"When will I know what?" He affected distraction, looking at the bank of televisions along the office wall.

"Whether it was a bomb or not? Whether this is going to be a criminal investigation."

"Oh."

She was going to have to keep sparring with him, and that was all there was to it. He had the weight of a huge institution behind him and she just had her imperfect little body and a notebook. She felt like she was facing a thirty-foot-high brick wall. She was either going to have to scale it or try to crash right through it. Otherwise, she was going to have to go back to the office and face Nazi and the Death of Hope empty-handed. And then it would be back to Lotto mania. Somehow she had to get this LeVecque to like her.

"I'll tell you what," he said, sitting up straight in his chair. "Why don't you check back with me in a couple of days?"

"You mean, over the weekend?"

"Whatever." He let his voice trail off. "I don't care."

To his right, the TV screens were showing that one image of the burnt bus in front of the high school over and over, as if it were on a tape loop.

"Just tell me this," she said. "Are you looking at terrorist groups?"

"We're looking at everyone," he sighed, turning back to her. "Give it enough time, we'll be looking at you. Reporters are behind everything."

She smiled, more at the concept of the joke than at the joke itself. "So you're not going to give this to the *Post* or the *News* before you give it to me, are you?"

"Everyone's going to find out at the same time. We don't play any favorites here."

Though even a small child could easily discern that was not true, and, in fact, had never been true of the office. There were always favorites, reporters who got the stories first, because they'd written positively about the department in the past. His own career was proof of that.

"Well, don't lose my number," she said, rising and smoothing her skirt.

"Oh, I won't. And by the way . . ." He mustered up his nerve. "What about your, uh, tampon?"

"I don't think I need it anymore." She paused in the doorway, the convulsive racket of the outer office going on behind her. "By the way, how is it that the teacher knew enough to keep the kids off the bus for the extra thirty seconds or whatever it was until the thing went off?"

"How should I know?" He lowered his eyes and tried to look busy moving pens and paper clips around his desk top. "Dumb luck. Isn't that always the answer?"

"Is it?"

17

"Can I offer you gentlemen some coffee?" Elizabeth Hamdy said.

"It's half-past four, but what the hell," said Detective Noonan. "We got a few more hours' work ahead of us. Might as well be awake for it."

"It's Turkish coffee, it's sweet," said Elizabeth, heading for the kitchen. "We put cardamom in it. I hope you don't mind. My father and I are always arguing about the best way to make it. Whether it's better to let it foam up once or twice."

Noonan shrugged at his newest partner, Tom Kelly. They'd just stepped into the living room of the house on Avenue Z. A regular working-family home, Noonan noted. A beige slip-covered Jennifer Convertible couch, an Oriental rug, an oak china cabinet, pictures of old relatives on the wall. In the corner, two little girls were playing a Nintendo video game on the big TV. The only unusual things were the plate-sized plaque with Arabic writing on it above the kitchen doorway and the picture of the mosque above the couch.

Even with twelve other detectives running around interviewing former and current students, teachers from the school, and witnesses from Surf Avenue, Noonan was still the primary on the case. It was just a matter of time, though, until the feds came barging in, trying to elbow him out of the way.

The girl came back with two espresso-sized cups and saucers and set them down for the detectives on the coffee table, next to a diary with a paisley cover. She was lovely, Noonan thought to himself. Not just her bright smile and her long, flowing hair. She had a lovely way about her. Reminded him of his daughter, sixteen, at home, and doing God knows what with boys up in her room. She didn't seem Arab at all to him, but what did he know? Anybody could be anything.

"Thanks for making the time for us," he began. "I know you weren't at school Tuesday, but like I said on the phone, we're talking to everybody from your class, gathering all the information we can get so we can figure out what happened out there. Okay?"

"Of course." She gave just a small smile, but somehow it changed the rest of the room, made it seem bigger. "Anything I can do to help. I really liked Sam."

"Terrific. I was wondering if you might have heard anybody say anything unusual at school in the days before this thing went off."

The smile retreated and her face turned somber, still lovely but taking the light a different way. "I'm not sure what you mean."

"I mean, was anybody acting strange, or angry. You know? Boys fighting over girls. Girls fighting over boys. Disputes about money. Did you hear anybody say they were going to get somebody else?"

She looked down at her diary and then at her feet, resting in thick white tube socks under the glass coffee table. "There are fights and arguments all the time, but nobody said they were going to do anything like this."

"How about the governor's visit? Anybody say anything about that? You know, he's a Republican, but he's got some views on abortion that aren't too popular with some of the Right-to-Life people."

"No, I didn't hear anything like that. But then I don't get involved talking about politics."

"Yeah, right," Kelly interrupted. "Just cut to the chase and ask her if she knows about any of the usual bomb-throwers. She's an Arab, isn't she?

Oh, there he goes. Noonan frowned. The man had been a burden since this case began, slipping off for drinks throughout the day and getting wobbly and dull-headed by the end of the shift. They'd be packing him off to go dry out with the God Squad upstate any day now. And then there'd be a new partner Noonan would have to fill in from scratch on the case.

"No," Elizabeth said, overlooking the insult with carefully measured patience. "I don't know anybody like that."

"I see." Noonan scratched his temple and noticed Kelly yawning. "You know, we're just looking for anything out of the ordinary. Like one of your classmates was telling us something your teacher said in class a couple of days ago about wanting to be a hero."

"Is that unusual?"

"Well . . ." He sipped the coffee and shifted around in his seat a little, trying to find the right angle to come at this. "Didn't he say something about how he'd always wanted to save somebody's life?"

"Well, he talked about being a lifeguard. But that's what he's teaching this term, 'Heroism in Literature.' " She sat up straight with perfect posture, but Noonan noticed the white socks moving under the coffee table a little, like bunnies in the grass. "Why do you ask about that?"

Noonan glanced at Kelly but got no reaction from him. Was he asleep, sitting there with his head thrown back and his mouth half open?

"It's just, you know, you wonder if a remark like that puts ideas in somebody's head."

She paused for a moment to ponder that, putting her hand over her mouth. "So you think somebody from our school put a bomb on the bus?"

"At this point, we don't know anything. We're just looking at every possibility."

"God."

"You sure you don't know anybody who'd do something like that? Somebody who's really been upset about something lately."

She lowered her hand to her chin and flecks of gold showed up in her brown eyes. "Um, no. I can't think of anyone like that." She smiled shyly.

Kelly yawned again and stretched his arms, looking at the watch on his hair-blackened wrist. "We gonna spend the night here or what?" he asked Noonan. "We got seven more interviews. The department says no more overtime for the rest of the year."

Noonan bared his teeth at him for just a second before he turned back to Elizabeth Hamdy. "We won't take up too much more of your time," he said. "I was just curious, though. Why was it that you were absent Tuesday, anyway?"

He noticed she was looking at a pair of Rollerblades by the video-game-playing little sisters in the corner. Under the glass coffee table, her toes were curling and uncurling like they couldn't wait to get inside the skates.

"I had a really bad headache," she said. "I stayed home."

"Probably too much Arab coffee," Kelly said, rising and stretching again. "You ask her about the bag?" He blinked at Noonan.

Noonan shook his bald head and looked up at the ceiling. It was the third time today Kelly had revealed too much with his questions. It was inevitable; he had to get another new partner.

"Right," he said, his hand forced and his rhythm thrown. "We just wanted to check. Does Mr. Fitzgerald have a Jansport book bag?"

"I think so. Almost everyone does." The feet stopped moving under the table. "Was there a bomb in a book bag?"

"We gotta go." Noonan stood and dropped his card on the coffee table. "Give us a call if you think of anything you want to tell us."

18

The publicity onslaught had continued all through Thursday afternoon and into the early evening.

First, the mayor's office called, asking David to come to City Hall on Wednesday morning to get a special award presented by the mayor and the governor. Then Diane Sawyer's people called, asking if he'd be available for an interview that same afternoon. Oprah Winfrey's people wanted him in Chicago the next Friday for a panel on "Profiles in Courage"; "*Grace Live!*" in L.A. wanted him for the next Thursday; an agent named Mark Feinberg called from International Creative Management, asking if David already had representation for book and movie deals. And finally, *Nightline* wanted him for Monday, not to talk about the explosion itself, but to talk about why the story was attracting so much attention. A *meta* story.

He stopped answering the calls just before eight so he could race off to Sam Hall's memorial service at Christ the Redeemer Baptist Church in Harlem. The governor, the mayor, and the police commissioner had already paid their respects and left by the time he arrived. He walked quickly past the two remaining camera crews on the sidewalk outside, not wishing to take part in the grief-as-public-spectacle phenomenon.

The church itself was modest, not much more than a storefront with wood-paneled walls, a water-stained ceiling, and a Casio keyboard instead of an organ up near the pulpit. But after a day in the spotlight, it felt like a sanctuary to David, a place where you could sit and contemplate the meaning of death in privacy and silence.

This day shouldn't have been about him, he decided. It should have been about Sam. David was sorry he hadn't gotten to know him better in life. He took a seat in the last pew, noticing how many of the five dozen people present bore some family resemblance to the dead man. Some were the spitting image, others just had one or two of his gestures; it was as if parts of his spirit were scattered around the room.

"None of us can know the hour or the day," the preacher was saying.

David felt pressure on his upper arm and turned to his right.

"How you doing tonight, partner?"

Detective Noonan gave a low, sandpapery chuckle and shook David's hand.

"Oh, I'm sorry I didn't see you when I sat down," David whispered as the pew creaked under him.

"That's all right." The detective laughed again, but it sounded just a little forced this time. "But I feel like you've been following me around all day. Every time I turn on the radio or pass a television, you're on it. I tell you, twenty years of police work, I never had press like that on all my cases combined. And let me tell you, I caught some big cases."

David banged his knees together, feeling as if he'd been admonished. "I know, really, it's out of all proportion. It's got nothing to do with me or even what happened. It's just the news cycle."

"Right. Of course."

David thought he could still hear a little crackle of resentment behind the words.

"Anyway," Noonan said quietly, "I was wondering if you had time to answer one or two more questions. Just things we needed to clear up."

David noticed people in the row ahead of them turning around and looking annoyed. "Sure," he said. "But maybe we ought to step outside and not interrupt."

"Yeah, yeah. Good idea."

David followed the detective out of the church and back out onto the sidewalk, where a familiar-looking black-haired girl was waiting.

"Hi, David." She approached. "Judy Mandel, from the *Trib.* I was wondering if I could . . ."

"Get outta here!" Noonan swung an arm at her. "I thought I told you to call LeVecque."

She lowered her chin like a fighter. "It's a public sidewalk, Detective . . ."

"Fuck it, come on." Noonan grabbed David's elbow. "We'll talk in my car again."

As he led David across the street and let him in on the passenger side, Judy Mandel remained on the sidewalk, taking notes and watching them.

"Pain-in-the-ass broad." Noonan slammed the driver's door and looked at David. "Should I cruise by the bodega and get you a soda or something?"

"No. Are we going to be long? I thought you only had a question or two. I have to go home and call my son before his bedtime."

Noonan's eyes looked at him with a blank intensity. "He doesn't live with you?"

"Uh, no. His mother and I are sort of getting a divorce." It was something he'd tried to avoid putting into words, as though saying it made it real.

"Is that so? I didn't know that." The detective took out his notebook and began writing notes against the wheel again. "That's interesting."

"Why's that interesting?" David felt a twinge in the back of his neck.

"It's just interesting, to know people's backgrounds. It's a nice part of the job. Getting to know people."

David leaned back against the door, touching the handle and making sure he knew where it was. He had a headache and a dry throat from having done so much talking today. "Anyway," he said. "What can I do for you tonight? I was surprised to see you here."

"Oh yeah, that's standard." Noonan turned on the car's dome light. "You always try to stop by the service. You never know who'll turn up. Sometimes it'll be the perpetrator."

"Really?"

"Yeah." Noonan turned to face him. His eyes were deep-set and the green vein in his temple was throbbing again. "People can't help themselves. They have to see how things turned out."

"And did anybody suspicious show up?"

"Not as far as I know."

There was a pause and David realized the car still stank from carbon fumes. He tried to roll down the window but discovered the button didn't work. The speaker was still hanging off the door.

"So how else can I help you, Detective? I'm sure you're under a lot of pressure."

"Oh yeah. Forget about it. Everybody's looking to take this case away from us. Noonan half-smiled and turned back a page. "So I just wanted to ask, did you by any chance have a black book bag with you at school Tuesday?"

David had to stop and think carefully. In telling the story so many times the last two days, he'd begun to emphasize certain details and subtly drop others. But now he was in danger of remembering the story he'd told better than he remembered the actual experience.

"Yeah," he said after a few seconds. "I think I did. In fact, I know I did. I remember, I was carrying all these library books for my son and I got sick of lugging them around." Again, he didn't mention how hungover he was on Tuesday.

"Okay! See, you didn't mention that before." Not even a rebuke, really. Just a point of friendly interest. "Do you think you left it on the bus before it blew up?"

Again, David tried to recall the exact sequence of events, but he was too tired and there were too many things cluttering up his brain. Television interviewers, Oprah's people, book deals—maybe he could finally get his novel, *The Firebug*, published, if only by a small press—and Arthur. What about Arthur? He needed to hear that sweet voice before he'd be able to sleep properly tonight.

"David?" the detective prompted him.

"What?"

"Do you think you left that bag on the bus?"

"Um, yeah. I'm sure that's right. I'm remembering it. I left it right next to Sam. He didn't mind."

He looked out the window and saw the girl from the *Tribune*, Mandel, still standing there, watching them and taking notes from across the street. As if the very fact that they were talking were newsworthy.

" 'Cause, you know, the bomb squad guys found what looks like part of a Jansport book bag in the wreckage," the detective was saying. "You think it could be yours?"

"Um, yeah, why not? If I left it on the bus." David looked at the dashboard clock and saw he had less than twenty minutes to call Arthur before his bedtime.

"Of course. We're just checking everything."

David looked back at Noonan and for some reason the image of a cell door slamming came into his mind.

"So do you think you might have left that bag anywhere before you got on the bus?" Noonan asked. "Like, would somebody have had a chance to put anything in the bag without you knowing it?"

"Well, I was in the bathroom, but . . . Wait. Are you saying somebody put a bomb in my bag?" Just the idea of it struck David as a gross violation. He felt himself getting angry all over again, remembering the vicious force of the destruction.

The detective started to laugh, a hoarse ragged wheeze. "No, no, no, no, no. Nothing like that. It's just these bomb squad guys, they want everything tagged and identified. You know? So there's no extraneous bits lying around. They want to be able to focus on the real cause. You understand that, right? We're waiting to get all the evidence back from forensics."

The answer left David feeling like the world was just slightly off-center and not at all what it appeared to be. "So who did this, anyway? Are you any closer to finding out?"

"We're narrowing it down in a hurry." Noonan smiled and the vein stopped pulsing. "Don't worry. We'll get the guy."

"Is there anything else I can do to help you?" David looked over at his door and was surprised to see Noonan had locked it while they were talking.

"Nah. I'll let you go for now." Noonan laughed and popped the lock. "But we'll talk again soon. You can tell me what it's like to be such a big shot."

19

Elizabeth's father was telling one of his stories again at the dinner table, but she was having trouble focusing on the words.

"Did you know I was sixteen the first time I saw a Jew?" He smoothed back his mustache. "It's true. Three of the soldiers walked into the shop where I was working. I'll never forget that one of them had clear blue eyes. I'd seen blue eyes before, but never quite that color. Like the blue of the sky or the bottom of the ocean, I tell you. They were beautiful, those eyes, but they scared me to death. Remember, we thought the Jews were going to kill us all. And so he stepped forward, this one with blue eyes, and pointed to a bag of beans. Then he gave me a fistful of Israeli money. And I didn't speak his language and I didn't have any idea how much his money was worth. But right then I wanted to give him *all the beans in the world*."

He chuckled and Elizabeth touched his hand. Normally, she loved hearing his stories of life back home. All the beans in the world, crossing the river, and childhood disappearing over his shoulder. Little touches of poetry from a deeply prosaic and practical man. But tonight, something was coming between her and her enjoyment.

Across the table, Nasser was boiling again. Grimacing at his food and shooting recriminating looks at both his father and stepmother.

Elizabeth's two half sisters were oblivious at the other end of the table, whispering to each other behind their hands. The sprites. Leslie, the older at twelve, was skinny and blue-eyed like her mother; Nadia, the ten-year-old, was round like her father and sallow like her older half brother.

"You're excused," said Anne, their mother. She was forty-four and as dour as a winter morning in Dublin. "But don't be turning up the TV too loud either," she told the girls. "The rest of us are still eating."

The two of them bounded out of the room and a certain heavy spirit came in to replace them.

"So why do you let them do this?" said Nasser, turning to stare at his father and deliberately striking the edge of his plate with a fork.

"What?" Father dug into his *coosa b'leban*, a zucchini stuffed with minced lamb and rice sitting in a yogurt and garlic sauce. Elizabeth could tell he was unhappy because his wife had made it without mint again, but didn't dare say anything to her about it.

"Why do you let them go watch this MTV in your bedroom?"

"It's all right," Father said, though he didn't sound entirely sure. He wasn't like other Arab men in that way, laying down his word as the absolute law.

"You know what this is about." Nasser wagged a finger. "You should have this removed from your cable TV box immediately. I have a friend who can do this for you."

Elizabeth rolled her eyes again and her stepmother put a sharp elbow down on the table. Nasser ignored both of them, holding down the citadel at his end of the table.

"This is how it starts," he said. "With the small things. The television." He waved at the bedroom. "The food prepared the wrong way." He pushed away his plate. "And the matters of dress." He glared at Elizabeth.

She glared right back, wondering what was causing him to turn on her so suddenly. There'd been a different feeling during their ride up the Belt Parkway the other day, a kind of closeness.

But now it was gone and he was full of cold fury. She thought of his friend Youssef behind the wheel of the red Plymouth, giving her that look. She imagined his breath would stink from old vegetables. Possibly Nasser had been spending too much time with this man.

Meanwhile, Anne was drumming her fingers on the tabletop.

She and Nasser had never gotten along. Their troubles had started back when he was seven and Elizabeth was just two. All the relatives talked about how Nasser screamed curses at her in Arabic on the day she married Father at the mosque on Bond Street. And from then on, he just became harder and harder for Anne to handle—defying her at every turn, hitting her when she tried to take him to school in the morning, refusing to look at her or take her hand when crossing the street. It was understandable, considering the boy's mother had just died, but nevertheless unbearable to be around. And then there was the time Nasser ran into the Bay Parkway traffic trying to get away from Anne and almost got hit by a car. Eventually, everyone agreed it was best that he go back home to live with relatives for a while. Somehow Bethlehem was easier on the boy's nerves than Brooklyn.

"If you don't like the way the food's done, the kitchen's wide open to you," Anne said. "You can take your best shot."

"May I be excused?" Elizabeth pushed her chair back from the table. "I want to work on my college essay."

She had no stomach for this tonight. The last twenty-four hours had pushed and pulled her in too many directions.

"And this is another thing." Nasser turned to his father. "We have been discussing this. You're going to allow her to go away to college, a young girl? You should be making a good marriage for her with someone back home."

"Well, it's not for you to decide, buster, is it?" said his stepmother, giving him a look as black as the end of a gun's barrel.

"You see? You see?" Nasser held out his hand to Father at the head of the table, waiting for him to adjudicate. "This too? Are you going to let her get away with this too?"

Elizabeth threw down her napkin in disgust. "Oh, why don't you just stop it?"

Father pressed his fingers against the creases of his brow. "*Insh'allah*, give me peace," he muttered.

His daughter looked at him pityingly. These fights were beginning to take a toll on him, now that he was older and diagnosed with diabetes. There were times when he got along with Nasser—after all, they had religion in common these days. But then there were other times when she could have sworn Nasser was trying to destroy the old man.

There was so much residual bitterness between them. Nasser had never stopped blaming the old man for coming to America and leaving the rest of them behind in the refugee camp for a year while he tried to make enough money in New York to send for them. Of course, Elizabeth had been too young to remember any of that, but Nasser had gone back to Bethlehem to live for ten years, so he'd had more than enough time to grow into his sacred outrage.

"You don't understand," Father said to Nasser. "Sometimes you have to be like the olive tree and bend a little."

"Mother never bent."

"Yes, exactly—Mother never bent." Father's features receded as if someone had put a hand over his face. "But this is because she wouldn't let go of things, even the ones she didn't remember that well. *Do you know she was four when she left her village? Insh'allah*. But still she acted like she remembered everything and her whole life was there! This is what killed her."

"No! *Askat!* That's not what killed her! You are what killed her! *Kha'in! Kha al-'ahad!*" He took the rusty key from around his neck and slammed it down on the table. "And this is what killed her!"

Silence fell over them again like a veil. Traffic breathed on the parkway nearby and the only sound in the house was Anne picking up her silverware to start eating again.

"Some policemen came by earlier," Elizabeth said. "They wanted to talk about the explosion."

The nature of the silence changed. Anne put down her fork and Nasser dabbed at his lips with a cloth napkin, keeping it there a beat or two longer than was necessary. Their father was still looking at the rusty key in the middle of the table.

"Whatever for?" said Anne. "You weren't there, were you? How would you know about it?"

Elizabeth made a show of nonchalantly rolling her tongue around her teeth as she went back to her food. "I don't know. I guess they're talking to everybody."

Father brought his fist down on the table. "I tell you. When they find whoever put this bomb there, they should kill him immediately. He is a bastard."

"*Akhra!*" Nasser hissed. "What do you know?"

"I know all about these men, the fanatics," said Father. "My father arrested some of them when he was a policeman under the British mandate in Hebron. They are shit, these people. All they want to do is make war with the Jews. They don't want the peace because then they know no one would pay attention to them."

Nasser looked at his sister quickly and then pretended to study the quotation from the Koran above the kitchen doorway. "So did they say this was a bomb?" he asked.

Elizabeth stared back at her brother, wondering. There was so much she didn't understand about him, so many more things she wanted him to explain.

But then again, there were things you were better off not knowing, things you didn't want to think about. She looked at her brother, with his brown eyes turned just a little bit away from her, but still not missing a move she made, and she thought about how late he'd been to take her shopping on Tuesday.

"No," she said. "They didn't really tell me anything."

"So okay." He picked the key up and put it back around his neck. "Nobody knows nothing. I'm going."

He stood and walked out of the room, without saying good-bye to any of them.

Elizabeth stared at the spot on the table where it had been lying, the key to the family home in the Monastery of Branches. She'd thought it would have been a skeleton key hammered by the village blacksmith. But the after-image in her mind was unmistakable: the word *Yale* had been etched on one side.

20

As he sat at the back of the Command Center, an enormous high-ceilinged room on the eighth floor of One Police Plaza, Detective Noonan watched the mayor metamorphose into a pair of gigantic lips attaching themselves to the governor's buttocks.

The transformation was subtle at first. Just a slight swelling around the mouth and a profusion of words.

". . . and of course, we all want to express our gratitude to our friends in Albany for making so many resources available to us on such short notice. And for the governor to come down and take time off from his busy schedule to talk is just . . . just unprecedented . . ."

Give me a break, thought Noonan. He was probably upstate, squeezing campaign funds out of a bunch of rich Republican farmers. Where else is the governor supposed to be when there's a major bombing two days before his appearance in the city? At a cheese festival in Iowa?

It was supposed to be a Friday-morning "strategy meeting" for the one hundred or so top law enforcement officials involved in the school bus investigation. "Coordination" was the buzzword everyone kept using now that the police were officially announcing it was a bomb. But Noonan took one look at the dais, saw Jim Lefferts, the big bohunk who ran the FBI office in New York, sitting up there and thought, *Katie, bar the door*. Everyone knew this Lefferts used to play football in Wisconsin, and he looked like he was about to jump up, tackle the bug-eyed ruddy-cheeked mayor, and wrestle the case right away from him.

Two seats down from Lefferts, Roy Miller from ATF rubbed his eyes and tugged on his ear. Next to him, Paul Schecter, the aging Manhattan DA, was scowling up at the mayor, who'd defeated him two elections back. This was a real gang bang, Noonan thought. The feds, the state, and the local cops all wanted a piece of this case. And with all these powerful agencies coming together and combining their resources, it would be a miracle if anyone could locate a bar of soap in the bathroom.

What they knew so far was this: The bomb was a fairly low-tech affair, made with ammonium nitrate, nitroglycerin, and a little bit of collodion cotton. Homemade dynamite hooked up to an ordinary Westclox alarm clock. Any idiot with a copy of *The Anarchist Cookbook* or a recipe off the Internet could have made it. The bomb had actually malfunctioned at the scene, because of some dampness on the materials. However, the small blast it did manage was enough to trigger the subsequent, more impressive explosions from the fuel line and gas tank, which effectively destroyed the front of the bus and made it impossible to determine the exact location the bomb had been in. That left exactly no real leads. Most of the elements of the bomb could have been found at any major shopping mall or high school chemistry class in America and the serial number had been filed off the alarm clock, which in one piece of bizarre sophistication had had all its metal screws replaced by plastic ones.

The mayor managed to reduce the level of suction long enough to introduce the governor, who rose from the dais and moved quickly toward the podium as if drawn by magnetic force. He was taller than he looked on television, Noonan noticed, with eyebrows so bushy you could see them when his back was turned. But he gave a good law-and-order speech, had a stand on abortion that liberals could live with, and his last poll had said he was trailing the President by only ten points, with more than a year to catch up.

"I just want to shift gears for a moment and remind everyone here how important it is to solve this case expeditiously," he began. "We need to send a loud and strong message that political terrorism will not be tolerated in this country."

Who'd said anything about political terrorists? Noonan wondered. Of course, that was in the back of everyone's mind. But they had yet to receive a believable call, fax, letter, or e-mail from anyone claiming credit. Yes, the kooks had come out of the woodwork. People who said they were with the Right-to-Lifers, the IRA, the IRS, the JDL, the Bosnian rebels, the Shiite Muslims, the Weathermen, the FALN, the tree-huggers, the bunny-huggers, the Kurds, the Friends of the Unabomber, the Colombian drug lords, the Chinese militants, the Black Liberation Front, the UFT, and the Shining Path. Who did that leave? The La Leche League?

The one thing Noonan kept coming back to, in his own mind, was the school. It had to have some connection with people inside the school. So far, there was nothing solid connecting Seniqua Rollins's boyfriend, the jailed gang leader, to the explosion, which left the other kids, and more immediately, the teacher, David Fitzgerald. And there was something that bothered him about Fitzgerald. How the hell did he know to keep those kids off the bus? And why did he keep harping on this hero thing with his students? And giving interviews? Did he want to be a hero himself? Even weirder: why didn't Fitzgerald mention the book bag he'd left on the bus until he'd been asked about it?

The thought fell into memories of the Herman Solloway case, that alleged kidnapping Noonan had caught in Holliswood twelve years ago. Solloway, who happened to be a schoolteacher too, said he'd left his wife waiting in the car while he'd run in to buy some Tylenol from an all-night Revco drugstore and that was the last he'd seen of her. Then he went on the local news shows, all teary and red-eyed as a basset hound, pleading for her safe return and saying he'd pay any ransom. Naturally, Noonan and the other detectives had found her buried under the kids' plastic wading pool in the backyard a week later, stabbed fifty-five times by her husband.

Up on the podium, the governor was finally beginning to round the corner. "In closing, I want to make two points," he said. "The first is that I think we would do well to crack down on any leaks to the press about this investigation. The wrong kind of information can only be detrimental in the long term . . ."

Right, so why blab to a roomful of a hundred potential leakers? Noonan asked himself. Over the last two days, he'd personally had a half-dozen conversations with various detectives about what kind of money they could possibly make from book and movie deals if they happened to be the one who solved this case. Ah, but then that was obvious. The point of this meeting wasn't really coordination. It was to show that the governor was doing *something*. That one image, repeated five hundred thousand times on television, of the burning bus in front of the school with the teacher's face imposed next to it was starting to make everyone crazy.

"And number two," said the governor, folding his speech with a flourish and putting it in his inside jacket pocket, "once this perpetrator is brought to justice, let us prosecute him to the full extent of the law, up to and including the death penalty. Let's be clear: you take a life, you pay with a life."

Right, off with his head and fuck the Constitution, Noonan thought. Oh well, what the hell. As the police commissioner liked to say, you're either on the bus or you're under it.

The governor finished his remarks to a round of not entirely satisfying applause and stepped down from the podium with a frown. The meeting broke up and Noonan headed past the steam tables and the door, anxious to get back to the squad, but then someone came running up behind him and grabbed his elbow. It was LeVecque, the chubby little blond guy who was running the press office these days.

"So am I going to see you this weekend? Weather's supposed to be nice."

Noonan stared at him blankly, as if LeVecque had just asked him for a date. But then he remembered the guy had left a couple of messages at the squad, inviting both him and his partner, Kelly, to his house on Long Island for a barbecue on Saturday.

"Yeah, we might stop by," Noonan replied in a surly voice.

Some matter of political expediency stopped him from saying no outright. He'd heard a rumor that this LeVecque had gotten close to the commissioner lately and therefore had to be handled with care. Besides, Kelly would want to be there for the free beer.

"Great," said LeVecque with a strained smile. "You can get me up to speed on the case."

"Yeah, right," mumbled Noonan, turning away from him, "you and every other square badge in the state."

21

At four-thirty on Friday afternoon, David and his son were surveying knights' armor at the Metropolitan Museum of Art. One way or another, he'd been determined to get here. The explosion wasn't going to alter the course of his life.

"Check this guy out, Arthur." David hoisted the boy up in his arms, giving him a better view of a mannequin with a stainless-steel sword and a red tunic with a white cross on it. "He's a Crusader. He's one of the guys who fought with Richard the Lion-Hearted to try to take Jerusalem back from the Moors."

"Cool!" Arthur jiggled, catching his father's enthusiasm. "And then they came back and helped Robin Hood. Right?"

"Wellll . . ." David did a U-turn with his voice. "Not exactly. Some people aren't sure Robin Hood actually existed. But the part about Richard the Lion-Hearted is true. He fought Saladin to a standstill after the Moors ripped the golden cross down off the Dome of the Rock . . ."

Oh listen to me, being a teacher with my own son. But David couldn't help it. He wanted to pass his love of these legends down to the boy. Arthur would get an almost spooky, enraptured look while listening.

"You know, I used to come here all the time when I was your age." David set the boy down and took his hand. "I'd make my mother take me practically every other week, all the way in from Atlantic Beach. I'd walk around for hours, pretending to be one of the Knights of the Round Table or St. George fighting the dragon."

"I wish you could take me that much." Arthur pulled on David's fingers, leading him to a German knight and his horse, both in etched armor.

"I know, buddy." David winced.

These little expeditions and adventures had been too few and far between since the separation. David worried the boy's childhood was being tainted and corrupted by all the tension around him. Three days a week wasn't enough time to spend together.

"So did Grandpa ever take you here?" Arthur asked.

David looked down, surprised. His father had died three and a half years ago and he wasn't sure how much of the old bastard Arthur remembered. "No, buddy. It was usually Grandma who took me."

"But he was a soldier!"

"Yes, he certainly was."

"Didn't he want to go with you and see the weapons?" Arthur peered up, eager for confirmation that David had some meaningful contact with his old man, the war hero.

"No." David half-smiled. "I think maybe he'd had enough of that."

The truth was, his father almost never talked about the war. To David growing up, Patrick Fitzgerald just seemed like an ordinary man living in the suburbs, working for the gas company, and drinking himself stuporous in front of the TV every night. Other than the old rifles and uniforms in the garage, there was no evidence of the eighteen-year-old boy who'd gone charging up a hill to kill half a dozen Japanese soldiers, some of whom were probably old enough to be his father. *Tell me how you did it*, David always wanted to ask him. *Tell me how you could be so brave when you were so fucking scared.*

But his father never told him much of anything, never really taught him anything. The closest he came to imparting any wisdom about life or war was one night when David was home from college and they went to see *Apocalypse Now* together. In the middle of the psychedelic bridge scene—with fireworks streaking the night, soldiers painting their faces, and no one knowing who was shooting at whom—his father had grabbed his arm, pointed at the screen, and gasped: "That's it! That's what it was like! Nothing happens and then everything happens! All you can do is *just keep going*."

David hoped he was offering his own son more sustenance than that, but he wasn't sure. The separation had drawn a curtain around parts of the boy's life.

"So how you getting along with Anton?" he said, following Arthur over to a display of samurai warriors.

"He's a dickhead."

David stopped in his tracks, an alarm clock ringing between his ears. "Who taught you that word?"

"Anton did." The boy pressed his nose against the glass, making a pig face to the samurais.

"Well, I don't like it. And take your face off the glass. They'll throw us out of here." David took the boy's shoulder and turned him a little. "So why don't you like Anton?"

"I just don't."

"Why?"

Arthur wriggled away from his father and went to sit on a bench. "He said you didn't save the bus driver."

"Hmm," said David, thinking: screw him. What did Anton ever do? "So did Mommy tell you what happened the other day?"

"Sort of. And we talked about it at school."

David sat down and watched Arthur swinging his leg, the toes of his sneakers barely brushing the stone floor. The boy was a bit scrawny for his age, which made David feel fiercely protective of him, especially in light of his own size. What made it almost unbearably poignant was that Arthur went to the playground every day chin up, shoulders back, imagining himself a tough little soldier, but inevitably came home wheezing and tearstained after some bully stole his tank.

"Well, I probably should have told you more when I came over the other night, but I didn't want to worry you," David said, looming over the boy. "I guess you heard the bus blew up and I had to help get one of the girls off it."

"You saved her?"

"Well . . . Yeah. I mean. Okay." David fumbled with the words, not wanting to exaggerate his bravery, but at the same time wanting the boy to be proud of him. "You could say I saved her."

Arthur's face lit up with that enraptured look again. "And did they catch the bad guys who did it?"

"No, but they will. I'm sure."

Arthur sat quietly for a few seconds, processing the information, his face a matrix of little-boy emotions. Back and forth went the leg, five more, ten more times, until his heel hit the bottom of the bench.

One of the museum guards came over, a stubby little man with pumped-up shoulders and a brutish-looking small mustache. David was sure he was about to tell Arthur to stop kicking the bench. But instead, he handed David a little pencil and a museum program.

"I wanted to know if I could get your autograph," he said with a low, hoarse Bronx accent. "I seen you on the *Today* show."

"No problem," said David, relieved and bemused, aware of Arthur's eyes on him as he took the program and started to sign.

What must my boy be thinking? The guard took back the signed program, smiled with gold-capped gratitude, shook his hand, and scurried away. Does he think I'm somebody important? David wondered.

"Daddy, I want to live with you," Arthur said suddenly.

"Why? Because someone asked for my autograph?"

"No, because Mommy keeps acting crazy." Arthur assumed that screwed-up little cartoon voice he always used when things were bothering him and he didn't want to show it.

"How crazy?"

"She thinks the neighbors are listening to us."

"Well, Mrs. Harris next door is kind of nosy." David remembered the old crone's stern disapproving looks on the elevator around the time he moved his things out.

"And Mommy burnt herself," said Arthur.

"Ayyyy . . ." The alarm clock went off in David's head again, a little louder this time. "Are you sure it wasn't an accident?"

"It wasn't an accident. She fights with Anton all the time and then she stays in her room and cries and she won't come out. And she keeps singing that dumb song, 'Kimono My House.' "

"Oh great." David hissed, like a tire running out of air.

Arthur looked disturbed. "Why did you say 'Oh great,' Daddy?"

"No reason." He shook his head. "It's just a stupid grown-up expression."

In the back of his mind, he'd always feared this day would come, but he'd put off thinking about it. She was beginning to unravel.

He looked down and saw that Arthur's frayed white Converse sneakers were now about a size too small for him. "Is she getting you to school in the morning and making you dinner?"

"Sometimes." Arthur wiggled his feet. "But she's sick a lot."

So here was the new issue. Up until this point, David had been going along thinking he could share custody with Renee amicably until they finally reconciled and got back together. A boy needs his mother the way a deep-sea diver needs oxygen, someone once told him. But now the line was getting tangled.

Reconciliation was looking unlikely, but a vicious custody fight with Renee was the last thing he wanted. She was sick; she needed help. He hoped she wasn't falling into a druggy thing with Anton.

And what would happen if he won anyway? Raising a child by yourself wasn't a one-shot deal like dragging somebody off a burning school bus. Arthur's life was all niggling little details—making sure he had his inhaler at all times, getting him ready for school, arranging play dates and doctor's appointments—you had to plan like Machiavelli and execute like Patton. But in his own life outside the classroom, David had never shown much aptitude for details like paying his bills on time or getting his apartment painted. He'd been too preoccupied waiting for Something Great to happen.

"You know, if I tell Mommy that you want to come live with me full-time, she's going to be very upset," said David.

Arthur just looked at him, as if to say: So are you going to betray me or not?

"And I'd have to get a bigger apartment."

At the moment, he had exact duplicates of most of Arthur's toys jammed into the corner of his little $798-a-month apartment on West 112th Street and two dresser drawers full of the boy's clothes in his bedroom closet. How would he swing it, anyway? He was making just a shade over $50,000 a year and spending most of that on support payments and lawyers. Ten thousand dollars each for his attorney and Renee's. And what were his prospects for doing better with an unpublished novel and an unfinished dissertation in the milk crate in his closet? At Coney Island High School, he was a great teacher. But on the social scale of the average Upper West Side playground, he was near the bottom.

It was going to be a tough sell to the court-appointed psychiatrist, whom he was seeing with Renee tomorrow. Fathers generally didn't get full custody of their kids. But then he saw Arthur was still giving him *the look*. The one that said, *if you saved that girl on the bus, you could save me*.

"You know, I'm still hoping Mommy and me can work things out," he said wistfully.

Arthur shook his head. "I don't think so," he said in his best approximation of a dubious big-boy voice.

"Well, we'll see."

David patted him on the shoulder and they went to look at more knights, stopping at a diorama of Italian noblemen in chain mail and sharp-looking visors. Can I really do this? David asked himself. Can I start a war with Renee and not get everybody hurt in the process?

It was useless to wonder, he realized. Momentum was already carrying him forward. He couldn't let the boy down by not trying. Arthur tugged on his wrist. "Hey, Daddy. Can I ask you something?"

"What?"

"Can I have your autograph too?"

22

The small man in the dark suit without a tie did not stand when Youssef brought Nasser into the living room on Friday night. He only sipped his coffee and looked to the side of Nasser a little, as if checking to see whether anything of greater interest was going on behind him.

"*Keef halik?* How you doing?" Nasser tried to introduce himself and offer his hand, but Youssef's friend ignored him and kept looking off to the side.

"So this is the idiot who puts bombs under school buses," he said in Arabic, putting down his little cup.

Nasser found he couldn't respond; his mouth was full of dust. Here was the great hero of the Afghanistan war, the Cairo bus shootings, and Flight 502. He was shorter and thinner than Nasser had expected, with hot black eyes, a narrow, long, horse-like face, and a sharp dagger of a beard. Youssef said they should call him Dr. Ahmed, though he didn't say what his degree was in.

He'd been everywhere and nowhere at all, according to Youssef. He had five different passports and five different names. He'd been Egyptian, Palestinian, Iranian, Syrian, even a citizen of Kuwait. He'd led student revolts against the Shah in the seventies, fought the Soviet oppressors, and before falling out of favor with his fellow terrorists he'd planted bombs that killed dozens of Jews in Israel. But there was something finicky, almost fussy about him. He did and said everything twice as fast as necessary as if to emphasize his impatience to get on with his great comeback.

"You say you are going to put the *hadduta* in the school and then you put it under a bus," said Dr. Ahmed, pulsating slightly in the easy chair Youssef never let anyone else sit in and viciously working a handkerchief around the bottom of his nose.

"There was a lot of security, sheik." Nasser sat down on the couch and started to defend himself. "There were too many witnesses and even cameras . . ."

"You are an idiot, my friend," the doctor said, quickly putting the handkerchief away and picking up the coffee again. "On this, we are all agreed."

Nasser looked around the room and realized Youssef had hidden all of his weight-lifting equipment and bootlegged videos, instead putting up a picture of the al-Aksa Mosque. There weren't any McDonald's containers either. *Sheik, how can you believe so fervently and live so comfortably in this godless country?* Nasser had asked Youssef before. *It's all just a ruse to fit in,* the Great Bear had told him with a shrug. *Always have two faces—one for your friends and one for your enemies—but never get them mixed up.* Clearly the visitor had little tolerance for such excuses.

"To target a school is not such a bad idea," said the doctor, blowing on his coffee and looking at a spot just below Nasser's chin. "But to do it so badly. To make it into a joke. What is the point? Can you tell me?"

"Tell him, sheik," said Nasser, turning to the Great Bear for support. "Tell him why we thought of it."

But instead of explaining how they meant to disrupt the governor's visit, Youssef just coughed and took another pill. "I think it was you who brought it up, my friend," he said softly.

Nasser stared at him. So this was how it would be. He was to take all the blame himself and Youssef the warrior, the father he never had, would not help him.

The corners of his eyes burned and his tongue thickened. But he swallowed hard and said no more.

"Now there is only confusion and no point has been made." Dr. Ahmed crossed and uncrossed his legs, seeming suddenly disgruntled by his own smallness. "I was watching the CNN *International News* in Egypt and this was hardly mentioned at all. There was nothing about it in *al-Hayat* newspaper. A *hadduta* like this should be in the news for weeks and weeks. Instead, the only thing you accomplish is maybe you have the police looking for you now."

"They don't know nothing," Nasser mumbled, again bewildered by what the others had expected to see on the news.

"And neither do you!" The doctor cut the air with an angry slash of his hand. "What do you do this for? To kill one bus driver? You son from a mother's asshole. We should not even take credit for this."

"I am very sorry," said Nasser.

For the briefest moment, he wondered if in fact Youssef had brought him here tonight not to help with the doctor's comeback, but to be killed for his mistake.

"Where did you find this imbecile, anyway?" Dr. Ahmed asked Youssef. "Look at him. Look how pale he is! Is he even an Arab?"

"Both my parents are from Palestine, sheik." Nasser rested a hand on his cheek, again feeling ashamed of his inability to grow a proper beard.

"Crusaders must have fucked your ancestors." The doctor glanced down, sneering at Nasser's Timberlands. "And what about these boots? Is this what the cowboys wear?"

"A gift from my father. I thought they were only work boots."

"It's like an infection, America. It works its way into you and makes you weaker. It destroys you if you're not careful." Dr. Ahmed stood up and began to walk in a circle around Nasser, limping slightly and taking him in from all angles. "Youssef tells me your father is married to an American woman. Are your sisters being raised as Americans?"

"No, sheik. They still have their honor."

"Well. That is something, at least." Dr. Ahmed sighed and blew on the coffee again. "There's nothing more important than a family's honor."

"*Allahu akbar,*" said Nasser.

It was amazing how quickly he'd fallen into the rhythm of wanting to impress this man. Part of it was knowing the visitor's history, but another part was simply the way the doctor was staring at him. As if he found the whole idea of human beings tiresome. You either crumbled before such a look or found a way to stand up before it. He reminded Nasser of the hard men back home. The ones who didn't let Israeli guards slap their faces.

"Sheik, I know I've done wrong," Nasser said. "But I'm ready to make up for it."

"I wonder if this is so." Dr. Ahmed kept limping around him him, faster and faster, as if he were trying to make Nasser dizzy. The black coffee swirled and smoldered in his cup. "I wonder if you know what it means to have *jihad*. To have a Holy War."

"Yes, I know."

He stopped and put his face right next to Nasser's. He smelled like stale crackers and airport lounges. "This means we don't stop. Okay? We kill all the bad ones and make them afraid every minute of their lives."

"It's what I tried to do."

"You failed. This is not *jihad*. It's humiliation." Dr. Ahmed's nostrils flared, as if he could actually smell failure. Nasser wondered if the little man was about to throw the hot coffee in his face.

"I know. It won't happen again."

"Well, it's okay," Dr. Ahmed said with an expression that suggested the opposite. "Some of our supposed leaders make mistakes too and don't acknowledge the warriors who've done and sacrificed the most for them." He paused and looked bitter. "But all of that is going to end now. So are you going to be part of this?"

"Yes, but . . ." Nasser began.

"No God but God," the doctor cut him off, starting to limp in a circle again, his fingers tensing on the cup. "This fight we have has been going on for fourteen hundred years. Okay? Maybe you know a guy, an American guy, and you get to be friends with him. All right? So you fight once and then you get along, and you're friends again. But it's not like that with us. Okay? We fight to the end. This next thing we do won't be just one school bus. Many, many more people will be involved. Bodies and bodies everywhere. We kill as many as we can. Do you understand? Even the women and children die. Okay? They'll be lying in the street with their arms and legs blown off. Just like at the Jerusalem mall."

"Of course," said Nasser, trying to ignore the shaking in his knees.

"Some people will say, 'This is not right, this is *haram*. The Koran forbids this. You should not kill the innocent.' But this is not a regular war with the soldiers. This is *jihad*, this is Holy War. And everyone is a soldier in the Holy War. We could kill their mothers and fuck their sisters nine hundred thousand times and it wouldn't make up for what they've done to us. Am I right?"

"No God but God," Nasser said.

"*Insh'allah.*" Dr. Ahmed nodded and sipped his coffee some more.

"*Allahu akbar,*" Youssef added.

Nasser hesitated, not sure if it was his turn to praise God or not.

He found himself imagining what it must have been like when the doctor shot the tourists on the bus in Cairo. He could picture this angry little man curling his lip at a wounded woman begging for her life, letting her crawl away a little, and then pulling the trigger. He was afraid to associate with such a man, but even more afraid not to associate with him. His fate had been decided the other day with the girl in the back of the cab. If God had a better path for him, He would have revealed it by now.

"So do you have the heart of steel?" Dr. Ahmed stopped and looked down into his cup, as if wondering whether the coffee was still hot enough to scald anyone.

"Yes, I do," said Nasser.

"God is greatest!" said Youssef.

But for some reason, Nasser found he could no longer look at the Great Bear. In a very small way, he felt his friend had betrayed him by not doing more to defend him. On the other hand, he had survived it on his own and was that much closer to being accepted by this man Dr. Ahmed.

"So you're going to be ready to do whatever I ask you, right?" said the doctor, finishing the coffee and circling one last time. "You're going to be a soldier in the Holy War, so no sacrifice is too much. You do whatever it takes. And you don't get scared about people dying. Understand?"

"I understand." Though as he said this, a part of Nasser was still struggling, still wanting to back away from all the destruction.

Somehow Dr. Ahmed seemed to pick up on his lingering reluctance. He paused to the right of Nasser and carefully put his cup down on a white saucer with a delicate blue border. "Of course, if this is not okay with you, you should just walk away," he said. "Nothing will happen."

Nasser noticed a stillness in the room, a quiet hissing awareness of death. The doctor was weaving in and out of his peripheral vision. "It's all right," he said. "If it's God will, I'll do it."

23

The weekend with Arthur had so far been full of joy and apprehension for David. Everywhere he went with the boy, people recognized him from the news. Two passengers on crowded subway cars offered him their seats, a waitress at a restaurant called Lucky's on 57th Street brought Arthur a special ice-cream dessert with luscious cherries and extra fudge on top, and guys in a Con Ed work crew on Columbus and 86th climbed out of a hole in the street to ask for David's autograph. As he signed their newspapers, Arthur hopped up and down next to him, declaring, "That's my daddy! One day I'm going to do what he does!"

Back at his apartment on 112th Street, his answering machine was bursting with manic energy. He sat on the rug, eating potato chips with Arthur, while Matt Lauer's people asked if he'd be available to play golf next week; Geraldo invited him to dinner; Barbara Walters's people wanted to put him up at the Waldorf for a few days. He knew it couldn't last, this orgy of attention. But still it was hard not to get caught up in it, as he sat in his cramped apartment surrounded by half-painted walls, books falling off shelves, and the few pieces of ratty furniture he'd managed to salvage from the old place.

On the other hand, there was Renee to deal with. When David

called her Friday night to talk about the conversation he'd had with Arthur at the museum that afternoon, she'd sounded tense and distracted. And when he repeated Arthur's comment about wanting to live with him full-time, she hung up the phone.

Now, at a special Saturday session, sitting next to her in the Upper East Side office of Dr. Allan Ferry, he was full of dread.

Dr. Ferry wore a white Paul Stuart shirt with red stripes that alarmingly matched the color of his office walls and carpet. His tie had pictures of small panda bears on it, and when he smiled his teeth looked slightly brown. He was a forensic psychiatrist, whose job was to interview both David and Renee before consulting with the judge about custody arrangements. Originally this was just supposed to be a formality. Husband and wife were going to work this out on their own.

"I thought I'd start off by asking the two of you what brought you here today," the doctor said.

David tensed up in his seat, anxious to impress this man, yet not wanting to show how desperate he was.

Renee was sitting a yard away in one of the doctor's other hardback leather chairs, her shoes off, her long legs drawn up in front of her, and an empty Diet Coke can balanced on the armrest for her cigarette ashes. She was in her hunkered-down, defensive mode, the one David found hardest to contend with. A light red welt appeared on the back of her left wrist, as if she had indeed burned herself there, as Arthur had said.

"I don't know," she said nervously, rubbing her leg. "I don't know what I'm doing here, anymore. I got this call last night from David, accusing me of not taking care of our son! It's crazy. Crazy." She took another drag on her cigarette, dribbling ashes on the doctor's red carpet. "He wants to take Arthur away from me."

The doctor studied her a moment, trying to put together the nattering bag-lady voice with Renee's high-fashion cheekbones and willowy figure. She definitely was deteriorating, David noticed. What happened to the pills she was taking? The thought of Arthur going home with her today made him deeply uneasy. The boy was playing peacefully with the doctor's wooden blocks in the other room.

"I'm just concerned about you, Renee," David said evenly. "That's all."

"Oh, you're so concerned, David. *You're so concerned.* Is that why you're divorcing me?"

"I didn't think *I* was divorcing *you*, Renee." He turned his chair toward her, trying to catch her eye. "I thought we'd made that decision together."

"Yeah, right!" Renee took another hard drag on her cigarette. "Tell me about it!"

Dr. Ferry smiled his brown smile. "Well, okay. Maybe that's a good place to start. Perhaps we can talk about what brought you and Renee to this point in your marriage in the first place?"

"But I don't know. See?" Renee flicked more ashes into her soda can, as her mood softened for a moment. "One minute I was married and I was happy and then I wasn't. I don't know what happened. It all blew away, like a dandelion. You ever think of that, Doctor? Love is like a dandelion. I just looked around one day and David wasn't there. You sure you don't have a real ashtray?"

What was driving her today? David couldn't get a feel for it. When they'd been living together, he could anticipate her wild moods sometimes and prepare for them, like pushing chairs out of the way for an epileptic. But with the separation, he'd lost that sense of continuity and he had no idea what she would do next. He teetered between feeling sorry for her and being a little afraid of her.

"Okay!" said Dr. Ferry, trying to get back on track. "Let's try to focus on some issues here . . ."

"The issues?" Renee exclaimed, her hands fluttering. "The issues? The issue is David thinks he can take care of Arthur all alone, but *he can't even take care of himself*. Have you seen his apartment? Have you seen his Visa bill? He can't finish his doctorate and get his Ph.D.! You ever see that sign over his desk? 'God keep me from ever completing anything.' That's him!"

"Okay, hold that thought!" The doctor cut her off with a referee gesture. "I'm thinking maybe it would be more constructive if I continued these conversations with each of you separately. Renee, would you—"

"Yeah, yeah, yeah." She was already gathering up her shoes and papers and going off to sit in the waiting room with Arthur. *"Take your pills, Renee. Take your pills."*

She left her cigarette burning on top of her soda can. Their marriage had always been a coiled and fragile thing. And Renee had always been her own worst enemy.

"Well!" Dr. Ferry took a deep breath and relaxed into his chair. "What were we talking about?"

"The divorce and why it's happening." David checked the doctor's degree on the wall. Forensic psychiatrist. Wasn't forensics about dead people? *We're waiting to get the evidence back from forensics, said the detective.*

"Sometimes I think the more key question is why a couple got married in the first place." The doctor drew a circle in the air with a yellow pencil.

"Interesting." David paused for a second and listened as Renee started talking to Arthur in the waiting room.

"So why did you get married in the first place?" the doctor prompted him.

"I don't know." David smiled in spite of himself, remembering more hopeful days. "She was in a section I was teaching at grad school at Columbia and I couldn't keep my eyes off her. She had this magnetism. She kind of moved like a dancer. It was like the air cut around her in a special way."

"So it was a physical thing." The doctor's tone was pleasant, soothing.

"No, there was more than that." David stroked his beard. "We fit together."

"How's that?"

"She had this burning need to be an artist of some sort because her mother was this failed big band singer and never gave her any attention. You know, 'Come-On-A-My-House.' And I, of course, wanted to be this big writer. So we kind of supported each other in our delusions. You know how it is when you first get together with somebody? It's like the two of you are in a conspiracy against the rest of the world."

"So what happened?" The doctor raised his eyebrows.

"I guess our conspiracy broke down." David stopped and stared at his hands for a moment. "The world found out about us and wasn't that impressed."

"And how did each of you deal with that disappointment?" The doctor rolled the pencil against his lips.

"In our own way." David shrugged. "It was probably easier for me, because I had teaching and my kids to fall back on. But with Renee, it was different. I remember she went to audition for this Madame Cecile or something, this famous ballet teacher who had a studio on Columbus Avenue, and she came back *devastated.* This was supposed to be her big break, like it was her mother who was finally going to accept her. And instead, this Madame Cecile videotaped her performance and then made fun of her afterwards, saying she was too old and heavy to be a real dancer. And from that point on, Renee just got worse and worse. She kept trying things and when they didn't work out, she wouldn't come back from them. She'd just get deeper and deeper into her hole. I don't want to oversimplify—there were all these other underlying problems you can't totally explain away by circumstance . . . But she just . . . kind of . . ."—he toyed with the words, trying to come up with the right expression—"got them old Kozmic Blues, mama."

A series of images flashed through his mind. Renee having a fit at her thirtieth birthday party and smashing a glass at an expensive midtown restaurant. Renee pregnant and weeping on the couch, under Margot Fonteyn's blazing eyes. Renee locked in the bathroom, with Arthur six months old, soiled and screaming in his crib. David grimaced, remembering how he accidentally gave her a black eye when he tried to break the door down.

"Bi-polar is the technical term," said the doctor, glancing down at a file.

"I didn't know that at the time." David frowned. "I just knew she was unhappy."

"So how did you try to help her?"

"Well, at first, I did everything I could." David turned halfway around in his chair, uncomfortable with this part. "I tried to get her to see a psychiatrist. I listened to her, I rehearsed with her, I told her I loved her . . . anything I could think of." He sighed. "But then after a while, I guess I just sort of got tired and started tuning her out. You know, I'd just sit in the kitchen, drinking bourbon and correcting papers when she was having her moods. Or I'd throw Arthur in the stroller and take him for a two-mile walk, just so I wouldn't have to deal with her." He looked down at his hands. "That wasn't very heroic of me, was it?"

"It's what life is like," the doctor said, waggling the pencil between his fingers. "A hundred thousand little decisions and then you add them up. You don't get a chance to save somebody's life every day."

David touched the armrests of his chair, aware he'd been subtly admonished. "That's like what my mother used to say to my father: 'It's no good being a hero one day a week and a bum the other six.' "

The doctor wrote that down. "That's a nice aphorism," he said.

" 'Tis," mumbled David. "Didn't make a damn bit of difference, though. He just stayed in that chair getting drunk all night anyway."

"But back to your marriage," the doctor prompted him again. "So you concluded that after a certain point there wasn't much more you could do to help Renee."

"Well." David cleared his throat. "I kind of have problems of my own. I felt she was . . . we were dragging each other down."

"In other words, you felt so overwhelmed by these problems of your own that you were unable to save your marriage?" the doctor was asking.

"Well, that's not putting too fine a point on it. I mean, I held on for as long as I could, for Arthur's sake."

Renee's cigarette butt fell into her soda can with a hiss.

"So what makes you think you're going to do any better in raising a son all by yourself?" the doctor asked.

"Oh boy." David worked his fingers together.

Busted! As the kids would say. He stared at a Francis Bacon print on the wall, a picture of a man trapped in a glass case.

"I don't know," he began slowly. "I guess you could say my life has this kind of loose improvisational quality . . . well, some people would call it immaturity. I mean, let's face it, I haven't accomplished a tremendous amount, except for being a teacher—*though, I'm a damn good teacher, mind you!* But I can change." He felt himself growing stronger as he spoke, turning to face the doctor straight on. "I love Arthur and I'd do anything to make him happy. What Renee said might be true—there may be some unfinished business in my life, but with Arthur, it's different. This is the one thing I want to complete."

He stopped speaking and stared at the doctor, trying to determine if he'd had any effect. He realized his pulse was racing. The urgency of the moment had sneaked up on him. Having lost his marriage, he was terrified of losing Arthur too, especially if Renee decided to move away with the boy.

"You know, it's a lot of responsibility taking care of a child on your own," Dr. Ferry said. "How are you guys getting along this weekend?"

"It's fantastic," said David, puffing out his chest. "We've had a blast. We went all over the city and he ate everything you put in front of him, instead of just nibbling on Pretzel Stix. It was the happiest I've seen him in months."

Dr. Ferry chewed on his pencil for a few seconds with a beaverish intensity, considering what he'd been told. It's adding up, David thought to himself. He's starting to take me seriously. Maybe I *will* get custody.

"You know, David," said the doctor. "I've seen Arthur a couple of times, and I must tell you he seems much better since your recent little run-in with fame."

"You think so?" David tried to sound nonchalant, but in his mind he was straining, waiting to see if this ball would go fair or foul.

He heard Arthur calling out, "BOOM!" exuberantly as a chair fell over in the waiting room. He could almost picture Renee frowning and lighting another cigarette under the doctor's no-smoking sign.

"I mean, he seems much more confident, all of a sudden," said Dr. Ferry. "Last week, I saw him and he was a wreck. But now he's beginning to come out of his shell. He sees your picture in the newspaper and hears your name on television. He knows the mayor is going to give you an award soon. His daddy's a hero. It has to do something for his self-confidence."

David resisted the urge to smile. "So what's the problem?" he asked.

"The problem," said Dr. Ferry, chewing his pencil again, "is what happens when it all ends."

24

Oh my God, that idiot's balls are hanging out of his shorts, Detective Noonan said to himself. It's disgusting.

He was at John LeVecque's backyard barbecue in Hempstead, watching his partner get progressively stewed as he lay on a white chaise, sucking down Budweiser after Budweiser with his angry-looking red scrotum dangling out of his loose-fitting jogging shorts.

If it was up to Noonan, he would have just skipped the whole thing. Work was piling up and he was never much for mixing. But there was no escaping the politics of this case. He'd gotten a call from his old friend Tommy Vaughn in the first dep's office telling him that this LeVecque had indeed developed a butt-link with the commissioner—and was even ghost-writing a column for the P.C. in the *Post*—and so attendance at this little shindig was strictly mandatory.

So now, here was Noonan standing around, trying to make conversation with two dozen cops without saying anything substantial about the school bus bombing. Anybody with real information didn't need to ask and the rest of them were better off outside the loop.

Kelly was starting to worry him, though. Standing by the hedges, Noonan watched him polish off his fifth Bud of the afternoon and then grab LeVecque's wife by the belt loops, begging her to bring him another. The man was a disaster. He was liable to say anything. The wife, however, didn't seem to mind. She was a slim, hard-faced number in designer jeans and a tight halter top who clearly enjoyed sticking it to her husband a little by flirting with the guests.

"You have enough to eat?" There was LeVecque trying to shove a hamburger on a paper plate at him.

Noonan stared at him until he backed off a little. "Ah, no, I'm all right." He patted his midsection. "I gotta watch what I eat these days anyway."

"I've got some no-nitrite hot dogs I could throw on the grill." LeVecque smiled, wanting to be liked. "It's no problem."

"Forget it, I'm a strict plain fish man these days." Noonan said preemptively. "My last partner had heart trouble."

He still remembered trying to give Frank Rowan CPR after he collapsed during a volleyball game on the beach last summer. Poor Frank never even made it to the ambulance. All his partners were doomed, it seemed.

"So the school bus investigation, how's it going?" LeVecque asked brightly.

Noonan turned and gave him the Dawn of the Dead look. "You keep the press off our back and we'll have it wrapped up sooner instead of later," he told LeVecque.

"It's a lot of pressure, I guess."

The detective twisted his mouth slightly, knowing the sympathy was just another pretense for him to see through. "I've had plenty of high-profile cases before. Doesn't mean a thing. They either get solved or they don't."

From the corner of his eye, he saw Tom Kelly almost falling off his chaise lounge as he tried to play grab-ass with LeVecque's wife.

Fortunately, LeVecque had his back turned and missed that little bit of byplay. "You've heard that the mayor and the police commissioner have been meeting every day, trying to make sure the FBI Joint Terrorist Task Force doesn't take this case away from us," he said quietly to Noonan.

"Like I said. Doesn't mean a fucking thing."

There was a blast of music and a puff of smoke from the screened window on the house's second floor. A touch of reggae and a pungent druggy odor joined the fumes from the barbecue. LeVecque's teenaged son was obviously smoking pot and blowing it out the window onto the party of cops. Christ, thought Noonan, the kid must hate his father's guts. He thought of his own son, Larry, doing the adolescent rebellion thing, piercing every inch of his body with studs and barely speaking to his parents. For a moment Noonan was filled with sadness, remembering a time when the boy was a sweet five-year-old, pounding a baseball glove and plaintively asking his father to play catch with him.

"So what should I tell the reporters in the meantime?" LeVecque asked.

Noonan turned his gaze to the press spokesman's jugular and raised an eyebrow. "Tell them whatever the hell you want," he said. "We've got thirty men working on this case full-time, not to mention the FBI, ATF, and God knows who else climbing up our backsides. We've interviewed everyone who was on the street that day, all the kids from the school, all the mechanics who've ever worked on the bus, and now we're going through all the recent graduates and former employees. Plus we've got the lab working on the wreckage day and night and the bomb squad guys going over the sidewalk with the dogs and the spectrograms."

"What about the teacher?"

"What about him?"

Noonan felt that vein throbbing in the side of his head again.

"How do you think it is that he knew enough to keep most of the kids off the bus for thirty seconds or whatever until the bus exploded?" LeVecque pressed on. "Doesn't that seem odd to you?"

"You asking this for your own information or should I frisk you for a tape recorder?"

Close with the commissioner or not, Noonan still knew this guy had once been a reporter. And reporters were never to be trusted. Bill Ryan, the old bird from the *Trib*, had once laid it out for him: in the pursuit of a story, everything must fall.

"Well, that girl Judy Mandel asked," LeVecque explained with a grimace of embarrassment. "But I figured it's worth following up on it, just in case the P.C. asks."

Noonan scowled. "If he does, tell him to call me direct," he said. "How the hell should I know, anyway? He kept them off 'cause he was doing a head count. Maybe it was just a lucky coincidence. Maybe he noticed something was just a little out of place and couldn't put his finger on what it was exactly. That's happened to you, hasn't it?"

No fucking way was he going to share any leads with some flack before he was ready. He'd told only four other people of his suspicions about Fitzgerald so far.

There was a shriek across the party, and Noonan turned to see Tom Kelly standing next to LeVecque's wife, both of them convulsed with imbecilic laughter. He saw Kelly put an arm around her and draw her close with little resistance. Oh fuck, she'd been drinking too.

This time, LeVecque was watching, and his ears visibly reddened. Almost in spite of himself, Noonan felt singed with pity for the man.

LeVecque turned back to him, trying to ignore the humiliation and get back to business. "You know, the mayor, the governor, and the police commissioner are supposed to give him an award on Wednesday. The teacher."

Noonan pinched the end of his nose for a second and then said something that he knew would probably haunt him for years to come. What he said was: "Ah."

There was no choice, he realized. He had to give the brass and City Hall some kind of heads-up. Especially now that he had gotten that little tip from Atlantic Beach. He only hoped LeVecque wouldn't press him on it too much.

"What's going on?" The flack's eyes opened wide and the hamburger plate almost fell out of his hands. "Is there a problem with that?"

"Ah-yyy . . ."

Noonan turned and watched his partner disappear into the house with Mrs. LeVecque. The party was edging closer to the line that separated extreme social awkwardness from outright catastrophe.

But LeVecque was so fixated on this conversation that he didn't notice. "Listen, is there something wrong with this guy that we ought to know about?"

"Ah, nah, he's all right." Noonan glanced at the house. Kelly had not come back out.

"Look." LeVecque said anxiously. "The last thing any of us need is to put the mayor and the commissioner into an embarrassing situation. So if there's a problem with this Fitzgerald, I need to know about it right away."

Noonan poked his tongue against the roof of his mouth, trying to figure out if there was another way to play this. On the one hand, LeVecque was the commissioner's guy. Telling him to fuck off was not an option. On the other hand, Noonan knew all about reporters like this Judy Mandel. They ran over you like road graders.

"Maybe you could find a way to put off the ceremony for a week or something," he said. "Just 'til we're done checking everything out."

"So you're looking at him?"

Noonan turned down the corners of his mouth and shook his head, finishing a silent debate within himself. "Yeah, we're looking at him," he mumbled, almost in disgust. "But no one else needs to know about that."

LeVecque's mouth fell open, and instantly Noonan knew he'd chosen wrong. He'd given the wand to the sorcerer's apprentice, and soon broomsticks would be marching.

"So he's *the guy*," said the flack.

"That's not what I told you," Noonan warned him.

"Jesus, that's amazing. I would never have thought of him."

Within less than a second, Noonan was in his face, pressing in so close that LeVecque tilted his plate and the burger slid back against his polo shirt. "Listen to me," he said with quiet intensity.

"I don't care how many columns you've written for the P.C., if I read one word of what I just told you in the newspapers, I will come over to your house in the middle of the night and I will shoot you. Okay?"

LeVecque checked the stain on his shirt and then looked up at Noonan, his face pinched as if it was caught between subway doors. "*I'm* not going to talk to anyone."

Noonan held LeVecque's gaze for almost a half minute, giving him some idea of what life would be like handcuffed to a chair in a Coney Island interrogation room.

Just then he heard the screen door slam and saw LeVecque's wife come running out of the house, pink-faced and sweaty.

"Detective Noonan, I think you'd better come quickly," she called out. "Your partner has gotten very sick in our bedroom and I believe he needs your assistance. I think he's had some sort of a stroke."

25

And then it was over.

David was in his office Monday afternoon, talking to Kevin Hardison and Elizabeth Hamdy about their upcoming papers, when the phone rang.

He picked it up and the ambient electronic hum of a speakerphone suddenly narrowed down to the closeness of a young woman's voice. "Hi, is this David?" Whoever she was, she sounded rushed, brisk, and eager to get rid of him—even though she was the one who called.

"This is David Fitzgerald." He held up one finger, asking the kids' indulgence.

"Hi, this is Amy Grossman from the mayor's office," she said. "God, they had me on hold forever—your phone system stinks. Anyway, I just wanted to let you know that the awards ceremony for Wednesday has been postponed."

"Oh?"

Something about her tone made him feel like he'd just had an ice cube dropped down his back.

"Yes, we have a conflict," she said. "The governor has to fly up to Buffalo and the mayor needs to be in Queens."

The mayor *needs* to be in Queens? She made it sound like some sort of irrational compulsion. "So when will our date be rescheduled for?" he asked, flipping open his appointment book.

"Our office will call you when that information becomes available," she said with a firmness beyond her years.

David looked over at Kevin in his black Dollar Bill baseball cap trying to nuzzle Elizabeth.

What the hell happened?

In the space of a few hours, he'd gone from being at the center of the media universe to nonentity status. He'd known he wouldn't lead the news today—the Speaker of the House had shot his mistress, her cat, and himself last night. But were his fifteen minutes really over? Half the shows he was scheduled to appear on had already phoned today to postpone his appearances and the other half, like *Nightline*, had simply stopped returning his calls. Everyone was busy chasing the Speaker's story. Geraldo and Barbara Walters didn't need him anymore. He'd dropped off the map.

"Okay, so we've spoken," said Amy Grossman of the mayor's office.

This came off like an ontological statement. Okay, so we've spoken. Okay, so we exist. Now what?

"Well, I'll be around when you need me," said David, not quite sure what else to say.

"Yes, we'll be in touch." Amy Grossman hung up, consigning him back to obscurity.

David sat there for a moment, staring at the pile of uncorrected papers and manila folders on his desk. All at once, disappointment fell over him like a stench. Suddenly everything seemed second-rate. The cold cup of coffee in the morning; the long lines for the ancient Xerox machine; the secondhand books and tedious meetings with the department chairman; the draftiness of the classrooms; Larry Simonetti and the school budget. Just a few days ago, the President had mentioned his name.

He was feeling the difference between real life and the hot thing. The hot thing was *swoosh;* real life was a grind. The hot thing was fabulous—it was orgasmic—it was insouciant—attractive—*sexy*—witty. Real life was hard work; it was frustration; it was pimples and cellulite; it was struggling along and then not having things work out. Much as he hated to admit it, it had been fun being a minor celebrity. Riding in limos and sitting in greenrooms with movie stars. Having strangers make a fuss over him in front of his son.

He leaned his head against his fist. It was time to get on with the rest of his life. He wasn't going to be like that fireman who'd rescued the little girl from the well down south and then committed suicide after people stopped paying attention to him. He had responsibilities. Classes to teach, students to talk to, a shy and troubled son to take care of. There were phone calls to be returned, evaluations to be written, Byzantine bureaucracies to be navigated, credit card bills to be paid, a dissertation to finish.

He turned back to the students standing in front of him. Kevin was still trying to make time with Elizabeth, but she wasn't giving him any. When he tried to snake an arm around her waist, she straight-armed him and raised her knee just slightly.

There was an analogy here, David decided: publicity and teenage sex rituals. The more you got, the more you were going to get. And the less you had, the less you were going to get.

"Okay, where were we?" He forced himself to focus again. Remember: you're a teacher, not a former talk show guest.

"Yo." Kevin snorted and started trotting in place like a stallion in a stall. "Like, about this paper?"

"What about it?" asked David, tugging on his ear.

"I was wondering if I could write about Shawn De Shawn," he said with his slight lisp. "Since you liked that in class the other day."

David half-smiled, tuning in on the little scam being pulled here. "Well, really, it would be better if you wrote a paper comparing Shawn to someone we've read about in one of the books."

"Aw, man . . ." Kevin's mouth fell open, flashing gold caps with dollar signs instead of monograms today. "You mean I gotta read one of them?"

"You seem incredulous, Kevin."

"Can't I just give you something from my journal?"

David shook his head. Yeah, okay, he thought. This is what I'm here for. To cut through the jive.

"I was touched by what you shared in class the other day," he said. "But I'm not going to let you keep using that. Okay? Because if you tell the same story the same way enough times, it starts to lose its meaning. And I speak from experience."

Kevin looked down at his Nikes, only slightly abashed at being caught. "So what do you want me to do?"

"I want you to stretch a little bit. Be a little bit better than the rest of the neighborhood. Reach into other people's spheres of experience. I mean, all the things we teach about improving your self-esteem are great, as far as they go. But then you have to make the leap beyond that. I mean, like, what, are you more brilliant than Shakespeare or Tolstoy?"

"No," said Kevin, amused by the thought.

"Then don't just keep writing about yourself. Read the books. You might even get something out of them."

All right, sliding back into the groove again. Kevin bobbing his head, getting it. Elizabeth listening intently, with that foxy little squint of hers. David felt his spirits lifting: yeah, okay, this is where I belong.

"Come back this time tomorrow." David made a mark on his desk calendar. "I'll have a novel picked out especially for you. I-ight?"

"I-ight." Kevin gave him a limp power salute, and then walked out.

"And now for you." David swiveled in his chair to face Elizabeth.

She smiled shyly and then cast her eyes down. He hoped he hadn't embarrassed her. No *hijab* today; her hair was loose and dark over her shoulders. In her denim overalls, she almost looked like an average American teenage girl. If you'd never seen her before, you probably wouldn't be able to put a finger on the difference. You'd just sense some fine long-boned *otherness* about her.

"I still need to talk to you," she said.

"I know. I'm sorry it's taken so long. There've been too many distractions lately."

Yes, exactly. Distractions. He felt like he'd allowed a part of himself to get reconfigured these last few days.

"Well, I, um . . ." She waved one hand in the air, smiled again, and looked down at his chair leg, wondering how to begin. "I . . ."

"Yes?"

She took two very small steps toward his desk and then stopped. Not ready to cross the breach. She seemed off-balance today. Something was on the agenda besides a paper.

"So I picked a topic," she said too quickly. "For the imperfect hero."

This sounded like a little detour but David went with it anyway. Kids were like that sometimes; you had to let them work their way around to the real point.

"Okay."

"Yes." She prompted herself, as if she was in danger of losing her place. "I was thinking of writing about *Tess of the D'Urbervilles*."

"Really?" David scratched his beard. "Whose class did you read it for?"

"Nobody's. I read it on my own. For fun."

He loved this girl, and in a weird way, he loved this school too. Where else would you have a class where a scruffy little aspiring thug like Kevin, who could barely make it through the sports section, would think he'd stand a chance of dating a swan-necked Arab girl who read *Tess of the D'Urbervilles* in her spare time?

"Well, Tess as the imperfect heroine," he said, tapping his fingers on his desk, mulling it over. "That sounds promising. I'll be interested to see what you do with it. You'll have to come up with some solid comparisons with more traditional heroes."

"Right, yes, of course." She frowned and moved her jaw around as if she was admonishing herself. "I should have thought of that before."

She fell silent and looked down at the floor. One black sneaker-clad foot was pointing toe-down, like a painter's brush poised on the canvas.

He peered up at her expectantly, not used to having the low angle. "Is there something else you wanted to talk about?"

There was a scuffle of activity behind him—most of the other teachers in the English department pulling themselves together in eager anticipation of the period buzzer.

"Yes, there is something," Elizabeth said, hugging her book bag to her chest and looking over her shoulder at students passing in the hall. "But, um, I don't know how to begin."

Was she pregnant or something? She didn't look pregnant. She looked somber, worried. But not pregnant-worried. There was a Spanish expression for anxiety: *eating your own head*. She looked like she'd been eating her own head.

He decided to take a guess and try to help her along. "Is this about your brother coming to see me the other day?"

She closed her eyes for a second; it was hard to tell whether she was relieved or mortified. "Well, yes. I mean. Sort of."

Donna Vitale brushed by, giving him a wink with her good eye.

"He's okay, your brother," said David. "I had him when he was a student here a few years back." He shifted his legs under a desk that was too low for his knees. "I think he means well."

Elizabeth went slightly pigeon-toed, standing before him. Looked twice over her shoulder, sucked in her cheeks, adjusted the straps on her bag. The windup, now the pitch.

"He has his . . . intentions," she said finally.

Hmm, a curve ball. "So what do you want me to do when he comes to me with his concerns about you?"

"I don't know." He had a feeling he'd fouled one off, rather than hitting it solidly. He'd have to wait for the next one.

The period buzzer went off, triggering stampedes in the halls and avalanches in the stairwells. David looked up at the clock and saw it was 2:30. In an hour he had to be in Manhattan to meet with his divorce lawyer, Beth Nussbaum.

"I'm sorry, Elizabeth. I'm running late. Can you walk with me to the subway a little?"

She threw her bag over her shoulder and followed him out of the office, through the hall, and down the caged-in stairwell. The first-floor corridors were clogged with thick knots of kids being noisy in the way kids always were: rude, exuberant, and absolutely certain that no one has ever thought to make such a racket before. Larry Simonetti roamed among them, waving his arms and bellowing, "Move on, people, move on!" to little effect.

Everything had almost gone back to the way it was. One or two kids even jumped up and touched David on the top of his head. But somehow he felt different and separate from all the activity.

He saw Noonan and another detective heading into a classroom down the hall and wondered when they were going to get around to picking up a suspect. Christ, the weekend had passed since they'd announced it was a bomb. In the back of his mind, he was still worried that someone within the school was responsible.

"Anyway, your brother," said David, holding the door to the parking lot open for her. "He doesn't want you to go away to college."

"He doesn't want me to do *anything*." Elizabeth came out and dropped her bag on the asphalt. "He's always watching me. Coming by school to check up on me. Insisting on picking me up, like today. He can't reconcile himself to the way things are here. I mean, he came back to this country so he could make money like my father, but then he can't accept the way other people live. Everything rubs him the wrong way. How people dress, how they talk. He doesn't like for me to have my head scarf off because boys will look at me on the subway."

"The imperfect brother."

"Yes." She laced her fingers between her dark curly ropes of hair, absently braiding the strands. "I remember once, just after he came back, my father took the whole family to the circus. And so one of the clowns got up and started doing this silly dance, I think it was the lambada or something. But then Nasser jumps up and starts pulling my father's arm, saying we have to leave immediately, because it's not proper for a girl to see this. It's *haram*. Can you believe that? The circus is *haram*. Movies are *haram!* Boys are *haram!*"

"So college is *haram* too?"

"Yes, but . . ." She touched the back of her neck and let her fingers trail along her collarbone. "But there's a lot more going on than that. There's something else I really need to tell you about. I've been trying not to think about it, but it keeps coming back to me."

"What is it?"

She looked toward the boardwalk, past Astroland, out to the old Parachute Drop, a giant rotting metal mushroom, near Steeplechase Pier. He had a sense something was ripening in her, about to burst out. He hoped she wasn't going to say she had a crush on him. Oh, to be eighteen again; he'd have her out on a date by nightfall. But you had to be vigilant about these student-teacher boundaries.

"God, why can't I just *say it?*" She looked back at him, stomping her foot in frustration. "You know how sometimes you talk in class about being willing to risk something? That's what I'm trying to do now."

"It's all right." He found himself putting a hand on her shoulder, and then quickly withdrew it. Rule number one, never touch the kids.

From across the parking lot, Nasser was watching them. He'd been there for twenty minutes in the Lincoln Town Car, waiting for his sister to come out the back entrance.

He'd been worried about her, ever since she'd mentioned the police stopping by the house the other night. He wanted to know more of what she'd told them, what kinds of questions they'd been asking. Would she tell them he'd been late to take her shopping? After his own cold interrogation by Dr. Ahmed, he wasn't sure how his little sister would stand up to such scrutiny.

But he didn't want her to think he was just spying on her, pressuring her, so he'd bought her a present today. A beautiful new purple *hijab* made from lighter cloth with studs and glitter on the fringes. The scarf cost him fifteen dollars from the Fertile Crescent clothing store, on Atlantic Avenue, but it would be worth it to see the look on her face. He wanted to show her that he understood her needs and concerns. Obviously, she didn't want to wear the old-style *hijab* because it made her look old and unattractive. This would be much more to her liking, he was sure, something stylish and modern, but not too modern.

He wondered if his mother would approve. In the wavering heat of the parking lot, he imagined he could see her again. Walking through the streets of the Deheisha camp. The sad, soul-eroding place. Old oil drums standing in the middle of the street, weeds growing over a crumbling concrete box of a house, women in *hijabs* lining up behind a truck full of rotted watermelons, old men in Bedouin headdress smoking filtered cigarettes, iron rods sticking out of bombed-out walls, cypress trees sagging, an empty cracked leather barber's chair baking in the sun, and Herod's Mountain with its Roman amphitheater baking above the hills of Judea in the distance. Children wandering the streets, rolling bike tires, playing war games with toy guns fashioned out of loose pieces of barbed wire.

Nasser remembered the Israeli soldiers coming to the house in the middle of the night, searching for a neighbor's boy. They were like shadow figures, monsters from a nightmare, waking the baby Elizabeth and pulling his mother out of bed half dressed. Laughing at him when he pissed in his underwear because he was so scared. This was a broken-pride place. This was not a place to hold your head up. This was a place to bring your head down.

And then all at once, he was back in Coney Island. Looking across the parking lot as his former teacher Mr. Fitzgerald stood by the school's back entrance, touching his sister.

Rage exploded in his head. An angry white sunspot glared on

the hood of his car. As he stepped on the gas and steered toward them, the white spot moved up onto his windshield, blinding him.

David nearly jumped as a horn blared and a Lincoln Town Car pulled up alongside them.

Nasser jumped out of the car, snarled something in Arabic at Elizabeth, and then walked up to David, stopping less than six inches away, about eye level to his chin. He cursed viciously under his breath, and with a look of childish bewilderment and fury he slapped his former teacher hard across the face.

David staggered back a step or two, more from the shock than from the force of the blow.

Nasser reeled back too, as if he'd been the one struck. "Before I said I was disappointed in you, now I am *very* disappointed!" he shouted, blinking over and over.

"Oh my God, Nasser! What are you doing?" Elizabeth grabbed her brother's arm before he could swing it again.

"I saw him touching you!" Nasser yelled hoarsely in her face. "This is totally *haram!* This is against God!"

He turned away from her and took a step toward David, standing on his toes, straining to go chest-to-chest with the teacher.

David, still seeing the flash of white from the slap, tried to resist the instinctual urge to fight back. "C'mon, c'mon, c'mon," he said, raising his arms in the international "hands-off" sign. "What's going on here? I'm just trying to help your sister."

"This is how you help?!" Nasser's voice squeaked. "By the touching? This is adulterating!" He poked David in the chest with his finger.

"Adulterating?" David didn't think Nasser knew any English words that long. He gently pushed the finger away, though a part of him was dying to take it and bend it back until it snapped.

A crowd of students had stopped to stare. They'd missed the slap, but they were picking up on its afterburn. Richie Wong and

Obstreperous Q were at the front of the pack, rotating their fists and barking, "FIGHT! FIGHT! FIGHT!"

"You guys get out of here." David turned on them. "You're not helping anybody."

"I'm sorry." Elizabeth was already dragging her brother back to his car. "This is all my fault. I shouldn't have said anything to you."

A few of the kids stayed, but most started to disperse into the warm afternoon.

"Look, Nasser," David said loudly, striving to keep a cool head. "You've got this all wrong. This is not the way we handle problems here."

"You don't tell me nothing!" The boy shook loose from his sister. "I know what you are! You are a bad man! A very bad man! If I see you touch my sister again, I will kill you."

Before the force of the words could set in, Elizabeth grabbed her brother around the waist and pulled him back into the car. "I'm sorry. I'm sorry. I'm sorry," she called out to David. "I shouldn't have let this happen."

He wanted to tell her not to worry, that he understood what she was up against now, but there was no time. Brother and sister got back into the car. The doors slammed and the Lincoln started with a sudden jerk. David watched it fishtail out of the parking lot and turn left past the Fascination arcade. A beat-up livery cab carrying off two thousand years of tradition.

David touched the side of his face, still feeling the sting of Nasser's slap and the place where fingernails had scratched his cheek a little. It was, he realized, the first real connection he'd ever made with the kid.

26

"You are sick," said Elizabeth as the car raced down Surf Avenue, narrowly missing a school bus turning on West 8th Street.

Nasser was clutching the purple *hijab* to the wheel and fighting back tears of outrage. "In another country, they would take this man and they would cut off his hands."

"He's my teacher."

"He doesn't look at you like a teacher should!" Nasser shouted, shaking the scarf at her. "You should be home anyway."

"You're out of your mind," she said.

He dabbed at his eyes with the scarf and stepped on the gas. "You should be praying and starting to make dinner."

"That's it. Stop the car."

She had the door open before he'd even moved his foot to the brake.

"What are you doing?" The car slowed in front of the New York Aquarium.

She jumped out by the boardwalk entrance and began walking back toward the subway. "I'm not talking to you anymore. I've had it. I have to get away from you."

He began to panic, watching her go. For some reason, he flashed on the image of his mother standing with him by the Circle Line railing. How he feared there'd come a day she'd fall over and he'd lose her to the river.

"Elizabeth, you are making craziness!" He put the car in park and jumped out after her, still holding the new *hijab*. "How will you get home?" he yelled out. "I have to drive you!"

"Leave me alone," she called over her shoulder. "I don't want to be with you!"

With his car stopped in the middle of the street, traffic was starting to pile up behind him. Drivers honked their horns and leaned out their windows to curse him: "Hey, get back in the car, you moron!"

Tears running down his cheeks, Nasser shook a fist at them and cried out for his sister again. "Eeeeeeleezabetttt!!!"

"C'mon, she don't want your sorry limp dick no more!" An *abbed* in an orange Datsun right behind him called out, taunting him. "Yo, get back in your car and find yourself another shorty, man. There's plenty of fish in the sea."

Wounded and freshly enraged, Nasser ran up and kicked the man's bumper. But Elizabeth was already disappearing on the horizon, probably going to join the throng of kids leaving school.

He threw the *hijab* into the street in disgust and then realized he still wanted it. Before he could reach it, though, a stiff ocean breeze took it and blew it down the gutter—thin, glimmering, and purple—just out of his reach among the white plastic bags and discarded Burger King napkins.

27

John LeVecque and Judy Mandel stood on the corner of Mott and Canal in Chinatown, watching a funeral procession pass with nine Cadillac hearses, three horn players, and a car carrying the deceased's picture garlanded in flowers.

"Probably the head of one of the tongs," said LeVecque.

"He ran one of the local trade organizations," Judy corrected him. "Totally legit. We had a story about him this morning." She touched his sleeve and watched him get a little stirred. "But hey, you never know."

Gotcha. She'd done it again, played him perfectly. Slammed him and lubed him simultaneously. It was the strategy she'd mapped out to keep him off balance. Beat him with her brain, make him ogle her breasts, never let him forget he's dealing with a real woman. Make him feel he has something to prove.

They'd just had an early lunch at a restaurant called Wong Kee and were wending their way back to their respective offices at One Police Plaza, past disoriented men in vinyl jackets and women dressed in layers of clothes, looking like they'd been suddenly transported here from the distant Chinese provinces.

"Ow, my thighs are killing me," said Judy as they got pushed together maneuvering past a crowded fruit stand.

"Oh yeah?"

"You know how it feels when you've been up all night having sex and . . . oh, never mind."

He blushed and looked away. She was beginning to get to him. She could tell. He was letting things slip. Over lunch, he'd mentioned that the chief of detectives and the first dep were at each other's throats, and talked about how his wife didn't like his new hours. Obviously, there were problems at home, but she didn't push him on it.

They stopped for a streetlight on the corner and she turned and straightened his tie.

"Now you're perfect," she said.

Would she get away with this? *Yes.* He stiffened and beamed a little at her touch. Her flirty little bad-girl act had never really flown at the office, but clearly it was spinning LeVecque's propeller. The thing was to not go too far too fast. Like any other kind of electricity, you could short it out.

"So what's going on with the bomb investigation?" she asked, brushing his arm with her fingertips. "Are you going to make an arrest?"

"I thought we weren't going to talk about that."

She realized she'd been a little too blatant here. He was pulling back from her, sensing how she was trying to play him. She was going to have to change tack quickly.

"Hey, I know your legs are hurting but can we pick up the pace?" He checked his watch. "We need to get back to the office. The commissioner has a press conference at two."

"My thighs," she said.

"Pardon me?"

"It's my *thighs* that are hurting."

"Right."

She looked up to see six headless chicken bodies perched on a third floor tenement windowsill, like men getting ready to jump to their deaths.

"Hey," she said, seizing the inspiration. "Have you ever played the chicken?"

"The what? What the hell are you talking about?"

"The chicken at the arcade," she said. "You know, the one that plays tic-tac-toe?"

"Come on. We're late."

"You mean in all the years you've worked down here, you've never played tic-tac-toe with the chicken?"

Before he could argue, she'd grabbed his hand and led him past an open fish stall and into a small storefront at the end of Mott Street. A sign out front advertised CHINESE MUSEUM—VIDEO GAMES—LIVE CHICKEN. Inside, wire-thin boys pumped quarters into noisy games called Sink and Aggressor and Virtual Fight II.

"Listen, I don't know if I'm supposed to be in here . . . ," he began. "What if this place is mobbed-up . . ."

She took him by the shoulder and quickly turned him, so that he was face-to-face with Bird Brain. A fat white rooster sitting behind a pane of glass in a yellow booth, like an old derelict in a flophouse. To the right, there was an electronic tic-tac-toe board, and a sign above him challenging all comers: HE'S NOT CHICKEN, ARE YOU? BEAT BIRD BRAIN AND WIN A LARGE BAG OF FORTUNE COOKIES! Small letters below the window advised "Bird Brain Has Appeared on *The Joel Siegel Show* and *That's Incredible*." This chicken had good press.

"You're not serious," said John LeVecque.

She had already inserted a quarter into the machine. The wire mesh turned into an electrified grid and the chicken stood up and looked at LeVecque as if in great consternation. Then it took a quick, deliberate step to the left and a large *O* appeared in the center block of the tic-tac-toe board.

"Your turn," she said.

"Christ." The back of LeVecque's neck turned red and he loosened his tie. "I can't believe I'm doing this."

He pushed a button and an *X* appeared in the upper left-hand corner.

"So," she said. "When is there going to be an arrest?"

He didn't dare take his eyes off the bird. "We're not going to talk about that."

The chicken took a step backward and another *O* appeared, this time in the lower right-hand corner. LeVecque scratched the back of his head, looking irritated and preoccupied.

"Are you telling me that after all this time you guys still don't have any leads?" Judy asked.

"I didn't say anything of the kind."

He was beginning to sweat. Impulsively, he placed an *X* in the middle top square and stepped back from the booth. The chicken quickly moved to the upper-right-hand square, blocking him and setting up two possible wins. LeVecque could only block one.

"Oh my God." His voice cracked. "I'm going to lose to a chicken. What have you done to me?" He placed his *X* in the middle right square.

Bob and weave. Stick and move. Sometimes she wished she could be more like Bill Ryan and just ask a straight-up question. But then again, she told herself, she didn't make the world full of horny, confused bureaucrats.

LeVecque stared at the floor in abject humiliation as Bird Brain completed the diagonal line of Os, winning the game.

Judy hummed to herself.

"My mother was a hummer," LeVecque said, without looking at her.

"Oh yeah?"

"She always used to hum when she was about to do something bad, like drop a pot of boiling water or drive the wrong way down a one-way street." He turned to face her, the two beers from lunch suddenly hitting him and turning his eyes slightly pink and watery. "Can we go now?"

"Certainly."

She took his arm as they left the arcade and led him down a trim alley called Mosco Street, taking him back to One Police Plaza the long way.

"So you're not in the loop," she said. "Is that it?"

"What?" His voice cracked again.

"I'm just figuring the people actually investigating this case are keeping you out of the loop and not telling you what's going on."

"I know what's going on."

They were walking through the small public park behind the criminal court building. LeVecque stared at a basketball lying on the asphalt nearby, obviously wanting to pick it up and throw it through the hoop just to show her what he was capable of.

"Out of the loop, my ass," he sputtered.

"Is that so?"

"We have a couple of suspects we've been looking at all along," he said.

There, that was supposed to show her. She wondered if she should act impressed by his manly certainty, but decided it was too soon.

"So why haven't you picked them up?" she asked, leaning against him just a little.

"You can't just go barging in there, lousing things up. We have to gather evidence. We don't want to alert anyone before there's a grand jury."

She turned on him. "So is that why they postponed the awards ceremony with the teacher?"

He froze, realizing he'd said too much. "I don't know."

Her eyes bored in on him. "Is he one of the people you're looking at?"

"I'm not confirming anything." He shoved his hands deep into his pockets and slowed his stride.

"Off-the-record."

"No, not off-the-record."

"Just for background. Not for attribution."

"No fucking way."

"Oh, you don't know anything." She strode on ahead of him, twitching her butt in her tight little skirt.

All of a sudden, he was a boy chasing after her, bursting with a secret.

"Where'd you get it was the teacher?" he said, catching up.

"Everybody knows."

In fact, it was only an educated guess. Bill had taught her the value of counterintuitive thinking. If the kids are dead, look at the mother. If the wife is dead, look at the husband. If a school bus blows up, look at the driver. And if the driver's dead, look at the teacher. Besides, why the hell else would they postpone the awards ceremony indefinitely?

"All right." LeVecque drew a deep breath. "But you didn't get it from me."

"You're only confirming it."

"Right." He looked around anxiously, thrusting his hands deeper into his pockets so his pants got tight. "You could've got it from a hundred other places."

"Of course."

"It's typical, you know. A typical situation. He wants everyone to think he's a big man."

"He *is* a big man."

"I mean, he creates a situation where he looks like a hero. Haven't you seen the way he's been running around giving interviews to everybody?"

Now it was okay to act impressed, she decided. She parted her lips and smiled.

"So that's it. Right? This David Fitzgerald is the main suspect."

The joy she felt at that moment was not like sexual abandon. It was something steadier, more dependable. *She had done her fucking job*. This would be a major story in tomorrow's paper. She could almost feel Bill Ryan slapping her on the shoulder, instead of patting her on the butt like Nazi would.

LeVecque shrank back a little, realizing the mistake he'd just made. *Oh, the tragedy of male vanity*. She'd rolled him.

"You didn't get any of it from me," he said once more.

" 'Police officials say . . .' "

"Maybe 'law-enforcement officials' . . ." He scrambled for cover. "You could put it like that, if you wanted."

He glanced at the back of the gray criminal court building, as if he'd suddenly sensed he was in a rifleman's sights. Pigeons gathered on benches and old Chinese women went through garbage barrels, looking for redeemable soda cans.

"You know, you could get me killed out here," he said with a nervous laugh. "Maybe we should go back to the office separate ways."

She felt a momentary twinge of guilt, hoping she wouldn't get him fired for this. On the other hand, screw him. He was a spokesman for one of the most powerful institutions in the city, maybe even the country. He lied to reporters and covered up horrendous scandals constantly. All she'd done was to get him to tell her the facts for once, which was *only* supposed to be his job.

"So I'll be seeing you," he said, bowing and backpedaling, not sure what to do with his hands. "Nice lunch. And, uh, it was interesting, you know, with the chicken."

"Don't worry." She reached after him and grabbed his hand. "I won't tell if you won't."

28

David was sitting at his desk the day after Nasser slapped him, talking to Kevin Hardison and wondering what to do about the incident in the parking lot.

He'd had problems with students before. In his first couple of years at Coney Island, he'd been spit on, pushed down a flight of stairs, even had a chair thrown at him. But this was a little different. Nasser wasn't a student anymore and Elizabeth was his prize pupil. If he filed a report about what happened, it might raise a few uncomfortable questions about what he was doing talking to her so intensely in the first place. "*What do you mean, you touched her?*" Maybe he was better off just mentioning it casually to Larry and a couple of the school security officers, in case Nasser showed up again.

"Okay," he said to Kevin. "I got a book for your paper."

He took a war-torn secondhand hardback of *The Great Gatsby* out of his new book bag and placed it on the desk in front of the boy.

Kevin leaned over and wrinkled his nose, as if David had just presented him with a dead mackerel. "That? You want me to read that again?"

"Why not?"

"Get the fuck outta here with that shit. It's about a bunch of fuckin' rich white people. How'm I supposed to relate to that?" He made a ticking sound and waved disgustedly at the book.

"Did you read it?" David gave him the hairy eyeball.

"Yeah, *I read it*." Kevin thrust his chin out. "It's got nothing to do with me. What am I supposed to say about it? Why don't y'all give me a book by someone I can relate to?"

"Well, I don't believe everything has to be spoon-fed to you. Sometimes you fight a little bit to bring a book close to you. But I'll tell you what." David put his hand over the book cover, blocking out the title and the author's name. "Suppose I were to give you a different kind of book. About someone you could identify with."

Kevin rocked in his seat, not wanting to get drawn into David's game but knowing it was inevitable. "Yeah, all right. What is it?"

David kept his hand over the cover. "Suppose I were to give you a book about a poor kid starting out with nothing in life. A guy who just wants to make some money—okay, a fortune—and get a little rep for himself."

Kevin, again wearing the Dollar Bill hat and the dollar gold caps, sniffed, mildly interested. "Yeah?"

"So this guy starts to fight his way up out of the gutter and he gets involved in all kinds of rough business. Machine guns, gambling, women, the whole deal. Okay? He becomes like an eighteen-karat original gangster. Right?"

Kevin was hooked. "For real? This is a book you want me to read?"

"Definitely." David still hadn't moved his hand. "But then when he finally makes it in society, this guy finds out the people at the top of the heap are just as corrupt and immoral as the people at the bottom." He snapped his fingers. "So you think you could get into a story like that?"

"Sure." Kevin nodded. Gassed, stoked, ready to go.

"Then read the book." David took his hand off the cover and slid *Gatsby* to him. "It's all in there."

The phone rang and Kevin smirked down at the novel, acknowledging he'd been tricked into opening his mind.

"David? David Fitzgerald?" Another young woman's voice on the line, but this one was familiar.

"That's the name. Don't wear it out."

"Hi. It's Judy Mandel from the *Trib*."

And here he'd been thinking everyone in the media had forgotten about him. Kevin picked up the book and started to leave the office. "I bet you only assign this 'cause your uncle wrote it or something," he said, pausing in the doorway and running his finger under F. Scott Fitzgerald's name on the cover.

"Get outta here." David laughed and waved him off. "I'm sorry, Julie," he said into the phone. "I wasn't talking to you."

"Um, it's Judy."

"Then I'm sorry again."

There was a long pause on the line and he heard her humming to herself. Through an open doorway on his right, he saw Gene Dorf, the department chairman, sitting in his office reading the *Wall Street Journal* while teachers in the main room worked frantically correcting papers and holding conferences with students.

"So what can I do for you, Judy?"

Phones rang and voices called out on her end. "David, I'm wondering if you could help me with a comment on a story I'm working on for tomorrow."

"Sure. Shoot." He picked up a Styrofoam cup and saw it was half full of cold coffee.

"I wish you wouldn't put it like that."

She made the humming sound again and for some reason it made him feel as if a fly was crawling over his skin.

"Okay, then just ask."

"David." She took a deep breath and shoved the rest of the words out. "I have it from a law enforcement source that you're a suspect in the school bus bombing."

"Excuse me?"

"I was wondering if you had any specific response to the allegations that you planted the bomb on the bus . . ."

He dropped the cup, and soggy black grounds spilled across Nydia Colone's paper. He felt like he'd been stabbed.

"What are you talking about?"

He realized he'd spoken too loudly. Henry Rosenthal and Donna were staring at him from across the office. Gene Dorf even looked up from studying the stocks he couldn't afford to buy.

"Who told you this?" David crouched in his seat, lowering his voice and feeling the center of his chest seizing up.

She kept humming what sounded like "Smoke Gets in Your Eyes." "Well, you know I can't really tell you that, since it was off-the-record," she said. "But I promise, if you give me a comment, I'll . . ."

"I'm sorry. I have to go."

He put the phone down and just looked at it. Praying it wouldn't ring again. Then he turned and surveyed the rest of the office. Everyone was pretending to go back to work. They all knew he was in the middle of a divorce. Donna Vitale went back to going over a paper with a Chinese girl named Li. The work crew was still taking down parts of the ceiling. Henry got up to leave and Shirley Farber was talking on the phone. But David couldn't hear any of them. His ears had shut off, and he was only aware of the sound of his own heartbeat.

He found some napkins to clean up the mess on his desk and saw he had two minutes to hit the bathroom before his next class. *You're a suspect in the school bus bombing*. Had she really said that?

The school hallways, usually so crowded and noisy, were silent and empty as he stepped out, like the streets of a western ghost town. David heard his own footsteps echoing faintly as if from far away. Where did everyone go?

He found his keys and went into the faculty men's room to try to collect his thoughts. Henry was already standing at one of the urinals, face turned up in serene meditation as if he were at the foot of a great mountain.

"Henry," he said.

And then there were no other words. What was he supposed to say? Do you know what's happened? Is this real? Am I still actually in bed, dreaming under the covers?

But Henry barely acknowledged him as he stood there, taking what seemed to be the longest piss in the history of mankind. David focused on the sound of the sprinkling on porcelain and the sight of condensation on the old chrome fixtures, eerie and conspiratorial.

"David." Henry zipped up quickly and walked out past him with a curt nod.

Did he know something was up?

David watched the door close as he stood at the sink. Then he stared at his own reflection in the mirror. A tall man with a beard and glasses. Is this really you?

He taught the next period in a daze, and when he stepped out into the hall afterward, Larry Simonetti was waiting. "Excuse me, David. These gentlemen would like a word with you."

Detective Noonan and a Hispanic man he didn't know were standing by some lockers a yard away.

"Good morning, Mr. Fitzgerald," said the vampire detective.

Just the sound of his voice turned David's stomach into a waiting room full of anxious commuters. He turned to the principal.

"Larry, what's going on?" he said. "I don't have time to talk to these guys right now."

Larry gave him back a waxy, awful smile. "It's all right, David. Don't worry about your next period. Gene Dorf is going to cover for you."

Amal Lincoln and Ray-Za walked by in clothes as baggy as flotation devices. From a glance, they knew what time it was. They'd seen friends and relatives pulled off the streets of their neighborhoods and beaten senseless by cops for no good reason.

"Come on." Noonan stepped up to him. "We're old friends here. We just have a couple more questions for you to help us out with."

Larry Simonetti turned and headed back to his office without saying good-bye.

"I'd like you to meet my new partner," said Noonan, turning to the Hispanic man, who wore a V-neck sweater, a scraggly beard, and a gold hoop earring. "This is Detective Bobby Gomez. Best undercover in Brooklyn before he came to our squad."

Gomez smiled disarmingly, but David wasn't fooled. "I know what's going on here," he said, struggling to keep his voice steady. "The girl from the newspaper just called."

"Oh?" Noonan looked at Gomez, obviously not ready for this.

"Am I under arrest?"

"Whooa-ho-ho-ho." Gomez made himself laugh. "Where'd you get that idea? Nobody said nothin' like that."

"No, nobody said that." Noonan looked perplexed.

The game was getting away from them. Clearly they'd had another rhythm in mind for this afternoon.

"I don't think I want to talk to you guys."

David saw both detectives register surprise and then suspicion. He was feeling a little surprised himself. Where did he get the nerve to say no to them?

"Come on," said Noonan. "You're not a suspect. Let's just get this cleared up as quickly as we can. Maybe if you could just answer a few more questions."

"Yeah." Gomez wagged his scraggly chin. "You don't want us to think you have anything to hide, do you?"

"Well, I . . ." David saw Seniqua Rollins and Elizabeth Hamdy walk by slowly, almost as if they were under water, staring at him. Figures in a nightmare.

"Yeah, come on, really," Noonan prompted. "Let's just step into one of these little offices a minute. You don't want to embarrass all the kids standing out here, do you? There must be someplace to talk."

David felt his scrotum tightening. If he just tried to walk away now, they might throw him facedown in the hall in front of all his students. If he insisted on calling a lawyer, though, they'd surely find it suspicious and leak the information to the media, perhaps damaging his chances of getting custody of Arthur. Everything was happening too fast; he needed a chance to figure out all the ramifications.

Trying not to panic, he led them down the hall, through the fire doors, and past the work crews on the stairway to the second floor. *Think critically*, he told himself. That's how he'd tell a student to handle this. Don't just accept the scenario. Consider alternative interpretations.

Kids he passed along the way avoided meeting his eyes, somehow sensing he was in trouble and not wanting to embarrass him. He could hear his heart beating in his head, a bass thump rattling his skull. He wondered, would Arthur see this story on the front page of tomorrow morning's paper or hear about it on TV?

They found an empty office next to the science lab and went in. Noonan pulled over a steel-and-ripped-vinyl chair and turned it around so he could straddle it. David felt the ache in the middle of his chest radiating back to his shoulder blades.

"So," said the detective. "I don't know what's going on either. You gotta understand none of us ever talk to the media. I hate the fuckin' press. And I'm still the primary on this case. So if they write anything without talking to me, it's bullshit."

David noticed the way the detective's pant cuffs rode up on his legs, revealing droopy mismatched black socks and pale hairless shins. Irish Catholic shins. The veins on the backs of Noonan's hands stood out like worms among faded grass and it occurred to David that these men might be at least as nervous as he was today. And for some reason, that knowledge allowed him to step back a little and consider his situation in a different light.

He remembered being arrested when he was seventeen. Being thrown in a pissy gray cell after a Nassau County cop named McNally got done barking at him and trying to scare the wits out of him. *Keep your nerve. Remember who you are.* That's what David had learned from that little encounter. *Don't lose your nerve.*

"So why is this happening?" he asked. "All I've done is try to help." He glanced at the clock above the door.

"I know," said Noonan. "You've been very cooperative."

"So why am I a suspect? I didn't have anything to do with the bombing." David sat with his hands folded in his lap, measuring his words carefully. Think critically. Why do they have you here?

"We know you're all right." Gomez stood up straight with his arms hugging his chest.

"Yeah, yeah, we know you're the good guy." Noonan smiled his Nosferatu smile, which just made him look old and mournful. "We just wanted you to answer three or four more questions so we could narrow down the list of suspects."

"You must think I'm a moron," David said, remembering Detective McNally's gray crew cut and the way he switched moods, playing good cop–bad cop all by himself.

"What?" Noonan's smile disappeared.

"Nothing. I think I'd like to talk to a lawyer." Something else he'd learned when he was seventeen.

"Well, just bear with us a second." Noonan quickly took out his slim notebook and began flipping through its tattered pages. "So what time was it that you said you started getting the kids ready for the field trip?"

"I believe I said it was just after lunchtime."

"And what time was that?"

"I think around one-thirty. Let me ask you again. Am I going to need a lawyer here?"

"Why do you need a lawyer?" Gomez leaned against a radiator. "We haven't charged you with anything."

David looked toward the door, considering the alternatives, recalculating the actual obstacles that would keep him from walking out right now. He was bigger than both of them. But then again, they could slap some cuffs on him and charge him with resisting arrest.

"So why didn't you tell me you left something with the driver on the bus the first time I talked to you?" Noonan asked.

"I don't know. It just slipped my mind. It was pretty confusing out there."

"Right." Noonan scratched his hairless shin.

"Look, I think I'd like to go now." David felt a little damp spot growing on the back of his collar.

"Just a . . . just a minute." Noonan turned to another page in his notebook. "Tell me again, how it is you knew enough to keep those kids off the bus?"

"I don't know," David said tersely, deciding he needed to parcel out his words carefully. "I just had a feeling."

Noonan gave Gomez a meaningful look. "A feeling," he said.

"Yeah, I told you before. I just had a feeling everything wasn't right." Two separate rivulets of sweat raced each other down his back.

"So what time did you go on your break?"

"My what?"

"Your break, your break. Everybody says you disappeared for about twenty minutes just before the class went downstairs for the bus."

"Yeah, I was in the bathroom."

The divorce anxiety and hangover giving him an upset stomach and diarrhea. He felt his intestines going end over end again here. He was falling into their rhythm, dancing to their tune. But he wasn't sure how to get up and walk out without seeming totally guilty.

"Twenty minutes," said Noonan. "It takes you that long?"

"It takes whatever it takes."

The door opened and a wan, parchment-skinned little man in dark clothes walked in with a power drill. He was like a character out of a Buñuel movie. Without a word, he plugged in the drill and began boring holes in the wall.

"Excuse me," said Noonan. "What do you think you're doing?"

"I got a work order." The little man took a yellow slip out of his back pocket, looked at it, and then put it back without bothering to show it to the detectives.

"We're using this room," said Gomez, displaying his shield. "Beat it."

The little man shrugged, unplugged his drill, and left. A few seconds later, the drilling sound started up again from the room next door and the drill bit began poking through the wall in front of David.

"So why didn't you tell us about that before?" said Noonan. "The twenty minutes."

"It didn't seem relevant."

David was struggling to get back into that cool place within himself, but they kept dragging him away from it. Forcing him out into the light. Panic closed in on him. Objects on the other side of the room—a globe and glass beakers—suddenly loomed much larger and he began to feel dizzy.

"Anybody see what you were doing in there?"

"I wouldn't think so."

"You sure?"

"I was in a stall." David tried to remember which stall he'd used and what the graffiti was on the walls, in case the detective tried to trip him up by asking about it.

"See, that's a problem."

Noonan moved his chair, and the scrape of its legs on the floor made David's heart jump.

"Yeah, it's a problem." Gomez tugged on his earring.

" 'Cause you disappeared for twenty minutes, and people are going to say that was enough time for you to set the timer on a bomb and put it in your book bag." Noonan dipped his head and looked up at David from an angle. "See what I'm saying?"

"There wasn't any bomb." His heart began to pound harder. His collar was getting completely soaked and he became aware that he was about to start getting facial tics.

"Hey, David." Noonan moved closer to him, ready to share an intimacy. "How come you never told us you been in trouble before?"

"What are you talking about?" David looked away, focusing on a chemical table chart on the wall.

"The little problem you had on the island before. I got a call from a retired detective name of McNally. He saw you on the news and remembered you."

"What does that have to do with anything?" David snapped back at him. "It was nothing. I was a juvenile. I took a car from a beach club where I was working. I'm not even supposed to have a record for that anymore."

Though he dreaded the idea of this part of his past becoming public. Somewhere in a file cabinet, there might still be a mug shot of him as a long-haired, dopey-looking teenager.

Having scored a point, Noonan put a hand on David's shoulder, keeping him in his place. "And let me ask you something else," he said. "How come you didn't say your old man was an explosives expert in the war? And he probably taught you all about dynamite."

"I thought I did, but . . ." David was scrambling to remember everything he'd said these last few days. "He . . . what?"

"Because you did it, right?" Noonan was smiling, a crooked half-moon hey-we're-a-couple-of-Irish-guys-in-a-pub kind of smile.

"I did what? What did I do?"

"You put it in your bag. It was your bag that blew up with dynamite in it."

"No, it wasn't." David felt like he'd just caught a flat hand in the middle of his face.

"Yes it was." Noonan gave a sidelong glance to Gomez. "We have witnesses who saw you playing with the timer."

For a brief moment, the unreality of the situation overtook David and he realized he was no longer in control. He was back in the Atlantic Beach police station, a terrified kid listening to the detective tell him that this night would determine the course of the rest of his life.

These men were trying to scare him just as badly now. They wanted to hurt him, to take his freedom away, to keep him from his son. More than twenty years had passed, but nothing had changed. He still had to find a way to hold on to himself.

"If anybody says they saw me with a timer, they're lying," he said slowly and deliberately, looking from cop to cop.

"No, *you're* the one who's lying. Because *you* did it. Right?" Noonan's voice had changed. He sounded flip and disgusted, as if he'd just noticed vermin in the room. He got out of his chair and walked across the room. "You didn't mean for anybody to get hurt. You just wanted to save the day."

"You're making a mistake." David found one scuffed-up piece of black-and-white floor tile and just stared at it, telling himself this was the anchor that would keep him in his place in the world.

"Come on." Noonan stopped at a desk covered with books and test tubes. "It's gonna be a lot easier on you if you open up about this now. If you just admit it, the judge will understand you didn't want for anybody to get hurt. You were just trying to be the hero. Like you talked about in class."

"That's not right."

"You did it!" Noonan pounded the desk and the test tubes rattled. "Goddamn it! I wanna hear you say you did it!"

"I'm not comfortable with where this interview is going," said David, still hanging tough, staring at the floor tile.

"Hey asshole, this isn't one of your kiss-ass celebrity interviews!" Noonan shouted. "You don't get to say where this is going."

David stood up abruptly. "Then I'm not answering any more questions."

He couldn't go back any further. It was the same point he'd reached in the police station all those years ago. The point where he said to himself: "Fuck you. I'm Pat Fitzgerald's son. My father is a *fucking hero* and you cannot treat me this way."

"Sit down, Mr. Fitzgerald." Noonan's vein throbbed in the side of his head.

"Yeah, sit the fuck down," Gomez chimed in.

"I'm going," David said, surprised by the strength in his own voice. "And if you have anything else to say to me, you can say it in front of a lawyer."

It was okay. He'd been here, done this before. He was not going to be intimidated. Somehow his father must have transmitted some notion of stolidity and stoicism after all. *Just keep going.* David found himself pulsing with anger and the conviction that one way or another he would get through this.

"Now you're the one making a mistake," said Gomez, moving to physically block the door.

"Yeah, this isn't over." Noonan stood next to him and rolled up his sleeves.

"Excuse me, gentlemen." David threw back his shoulders and stepped around them. "I believe I have some work to do."

On returning to his squad some thirty-five minutes later, Detective Noonan was duly informed that this was now a federal investigation and he would be expected to turn over all his notes to FBI agents. He calmly walked to his phone and called John LeVecque.

"Hey asshole," he said. "You may have fucked me, but my ex-partner fucked your wife."

29

So this was what it felt like to be a success.

Judy Mandel filed her story at six o'clock and then stuck around for three hours to answer editors' queries and make phone calls to double-check facts. By the time she was finished, Bill Ryan had gone home to be with his invalid wife and the only ones left for her to go out and have a celebratory drink with were the Death of Hope and the paper's editor-in-chief, Robert "Nazi" Cranbury, who everyone knew was a notorious whoremonger and grossly sentimental when inebriated.

Instead, she went home alone to her tiny $1,200-a-month East 50th Street studio to eat two-day-old salad, drink cheap chardonnay, and watch *Seinfeld* reruns until she started to fall asleep on her couch. But just before consciousness slipped away, the phone rang and her beeper went off. She picked up the receiver and Nazi's sloshed, frantic voice yowled into her eardrum.

"They're after us, love! It's your bloody bomber story!"

"Why, what's the matter?" She sat up and looked at the clock. It was after 11:30, and the early edition was already hitting the streets. She panicked, knowing that if she had gotten anything wrong it was too late to take it back.

"Nothing's the matter!" Nazi shouted. "You've got them all chasing you. *Now what have you got to follow it?*"

All of a sudden, word of her story had scattered around town like broken glass. The *Times* was trying to match her piece about David Fitzgerald. So were the *Post* and the *News* and all the major television stations. She'd managed to beat them all, for the moment. She was running hard, leading the pack. This was the place she'd always wanted to be in her career. But already the moment was passing. Dozens of reporters and producers were working the phones and combing the streets, trying to overtake her. Now she had to start worrying about staying ahead. And she hadn't even gotten to sleep yet.

30

The knock on the door came just before midnight.

Leaving the chain on, David opened it and saw an unassuming-looking bald man with an egg-shaped head and light-colored eyebrows standing in the hallway. Six young Visigoths in blue vinyl jackets were behind him.

"David Fitzgerald?" The unassuming man held out an FBI badge and a thick document with a federal seal on it. "I'm Special Agent Donald Sippes. We have a warrant to search your apartment."

David took the chain off the door and looked at the papers. "But this isn't right," he said. "I haven't had a chance to call my lawyer."

In fact, he didn't even have a criminal lawyer yet. His divorce lawyer, Beth Nussbaum, was supposed to be helping him find one as quickly as possible.

"Sir, *we have a warrant*," Sippes said carefully, like he was addressing a mildly retarded child.

Then he stepped into the apartment and held the door open for his six colleagues.

Within seconds, they were tearing the place apart, bagging and cataloging the most private and intimate parts of David's life. They took personal letters from his students, shirts Renee bought him when they were first in love, old Marvel comic books he'd been saving for Arthur, pages of his great unpublished novel, *The Firebug*. They grabbed photographs, divorce papers, floppy disks, old newspapers, Tupperware, old Delaney books, lesson plans, a papier-mâché solar system that Arthur had made as a school project. The sheer scope of the violation was nauseating, and the agents were utterly indifferent to David's response. It was like having a high school football team hold a scrimmage in his house.

They threw the mattress off his bed and confiscated the sheets. They dusted Arthur's Lego castle in the corner for fingerprints and took away his Playmobil pirate ship. They rifled his file cabinets, chipped paint off his unfinished walls, collected fibers from the carpet in his living room, carted away his old Schwinn bicycle. David felt as though his very identity was being deconstructed piece by piece and he was powerless to prevent it.

"Listen, I don't think you guys should be doing this," he protested. "Isn't there some matter of due process you're skipping?"

"Sir, you're not under arrest," Donald Sippes politely countered. "We have probable cause to search your apartment. I'm sorry, but we've already had one bombing. We're not going to wait around for another."

In the meantime, the phone kept ringing and David's answering machine kept taking messages from reporters. Apparently, Judy Mandel's story had just come out in the newspaper's early edition, setting off a Monster Rally Demolition Derby of new frenzied media interest.

David found himself getting enraged. How could this be happening? He was an innocent man in America. A teacher. He'd heard stories from his students about the police destroying their homes because they'd hit the wrong house in a drug raid, but he'd never imagined it could possibly happen to him.

He went to the phone and tried to call his divorce lawyer again, but her machine was on now, leaving him terrifyingly abandoned.

He turned and saw an agent with a mustache and a head shaped like a pumpkin go into his closet and pick up the Cal Ripkin Spalding baseball mitt he'd been saving for Arthur's next birthday in November.

"You don't have to take that," David said angrily. "It's for my kid."

"It's evidence." The pumpkin-head shrugged, dropping the glove into a large Ziploc bag and sliding his finger along the seal. "The judge says what's yours is ours. From here on in, you might as well get used to that."

31

Mr. Fitzgerald's fourth-period class was canceled the next morning and with three consecutive free periods ahead of her, Elizabeth decided to go home early to have lunch and put her thoughts in order. News about the FBI raiding her teacher's house had left her confused and edgy. She went into the kitchen to make herself a tuna fish sandwich but lost her appetite after one bite. Should she feel relieved or disturbed about Mr. Fitzgerald being named as a suspect? She didn't know. After all, now she could be sure her brother had nothing to do with the bombing. But the idea that Mr. Fitzgerald could have done it had no immediate resonance in her mind; had he done or said something she'd missed? She was going to have to consider this carefully.

From upstairs, she heard a footfall in her room. Someone was in there. She raced up the stairs and found Nasser sitting on her bed, with her books and papers strewn all over the floor.

"What are you doing?" she said.

Her closet door was open and her chest of drawers had been ransacked. Nasser looked up from reading her diary.

"What does this mean, what you've written here?" he demanded, holding it up by its paisley cover: " 'Things are building up inside of me. I have to tell Mr. Fitzgerald.' Are you talking about the sex?"

"Give it to me!" She lunged at him and grabbed the book away.

"He is putting these things in your mind, this bad man!" He jumped up and came after her. "He wants to seduce you. You have to control yourself!"

"Control myself? I have to control myself?! You slapped my teacher. You're in my room!" She hugged the diary to her chest.

"I am trying to help you. You have an obligation."

"I don't have any obligation to you."

"Yes, you do! Yes, you do! You have an obligation to the family honor."

"Family honor? You have no right to come in here and talk to me about family honor." She turned on him with her hair flying wildly in her face.

"Yes, I do! Yes, I do! Because I am the only one who cares! I'm the only one who remembers how it was back home!" He took the rusty key on the chain from around his neck and brandished it at her like a weapon. "You see? You see?!"

"What?" Her body sagged in weary disgust. "You think you can run my life just because you have some stupid key?"

"Stupid key? You call this a stupid key?" Nasser looked mortally wounded. "This is the key to Mother's home. How can you talk this way?"

"Nasser, have you ever looked at it closely?" Elizabeth shouted. "Have you? Have you even noticed it says 'Yale' on the key?"

"What are you saying?" Cautiously, Nasser took the key from his chest and studied it in his palm.

"I'm asking you how many old locks there are in Palestine made by an American company. Didn't you ever wonder about that? *It's not the real key!* Okay? It probably opens a door on Fourth Avenue somewhere."

He slowly raised his eyes from the key and looked at her, fearful and stunned, as if he'd just realized the floor was about to give way. "This is not true," he said defensively. "It's this teacher who's making you question things."

"Nasser, look at the key yourself if you don't believe me," she said, shaking her diary at him in exasperation.

But instead of looking, he put the chain back around his neck and dropped the key down the front of his shirt again. "No, it's not right," he said tightly. "It's the teacher making you blind to what you should believe. He's not a teacher, he's a poisoner. He's trying to break up our family."

"He's not." Elizabeth hugged the diary tighter, trying to maintain some control.

"Yes, of course, he is." Nasser came toward her. "He wants to make you into his whore. I can see this! It's in the book you wrote yourself! Why don't *you* look at the truth?"

He reached for the diary again, but she punched him in the shoulder. "Get away from me! Get out of my room!"

He drew back, startled and furious, looking at the place where she'd hit him.

"What's happening to you?" he said, staring as if she'd just spoken in a strange language. "I love you. Don't you see what he's doing to us?"

"Just get out of here. I'm starting to hate you."

"What did you say to me?" He reared back a step.

"I said, get out. I hate you."

Then all at once, he came at her and pushed her down on the bed, still trying to wrestle the diary away. She kicked and scratched at his face, screaming, "Get out of here, you're sick!" They'd rough-housed for fun a few years back, but the feeling between their bodies was different now. The sinews and muscles stretched and pulled in other directions. The two of them were bigger and the house was smaller. He was trying to subdue something within her. She reached for the helmet he'd bought her and started banging him over the head with it.

"For the love of God!"

They both looked up at the same time and saw their stepmother, Anne, in the doorway, holding a basket of laundry.

"What the hell d'you think you're doing?" she asked Nasser.

Everything stopped. Elizabeth struggled out from under her brother, and Nasser got up slowly, breathing hard and tucking his shirt into his pants. The static charge between them was still in the air.

"You can't understand." He looked around the room, like someone else was to blame for the shambles. "I'm trying to save my sister. This wouldn't make sense to you. You are not a good Muslim woman. You're not part of this family."

"I understand. I'll not have you living in my home anymore."

"Elizabeth, tell her how I was trying to help you."

But his sister was already busying herself, picking up her room and putting her diary away. "It's time for you to go, Nasser."

32

The little bits of David Fitzgerald that had been raining all over the world had finally landed and now he had no idea how to put them back together again.

Larry Simonetti had called the first thing in the morning and told him not to report to school. "I've already talked it over with the union," he said. "You can still get your salary, but it might be better if you stayed home for a while."

Meanwhile, federal agents had raided his mother's house on Long Island, seizing his father's old rifles and souvenir grenades from the garage, as if they were evidence of a connection with some sort of right-wing terrorist militia. David had to call his mother in Florida to calm her down and reassure her before returning to the business of talking to the steady stream of criminal lawyers interested in representing him. It was hard getting used to the idea that from here on in his life was going to be in a constant state of emergency.

"Looks like these guys did a full Rudy on you," said his latest visitor, an attorney named Ralph Marcovicci, who was surveying the heap of shredded bedclothes, silverware, and dismantled fixtures in the middle of the living room. "Imagine if they didn't like you. How's your landlord feeling these days, anyway?"

"Testy," said David, bringing in a cup of coffee he'd poured through a strainer, since the agents had broken his coffeemaker. "It's Columbia University. I worked a fiddle with somebody in their real estate department, so I could be near my kid. I'm only supposed to hold on to the apartment until I finish my doctorate."

"Well, now you got a good excuse," said Marcovicci, a bell-shaped, pink-cheeked man who wore his hair like a '70s classic rock guitarist and weighed at least three hundred pounds.

He was accompanied by another lawyer, named Judah Rosenbloom, who wore a graying ponytail and horn-rimmed glasses and was so skinny he looked as if he let Ralph eat off his plate at every meal.

"So I know Beth recommended you," said David, jittery and trying to get his bearings. "But you guys look very familiar to me. Where do I know you from?"

"I've handled a lotta high-profile cases the last few years." Ralph took the coffee from David and sat down, almost breaking the one good chair left in the living room. "Remember the Larchmont Lolita? That was one of mine."

"Oh."

"And the Boom Boom Killer? The stripper who shot two customers at the club where she worked? That was another one of mine. Also, the Centerfold Cop. I've been on Howard Stern a lot."

"Really," said David.

"Yeah, Howard's a good friend of mine. I'm supposed to go over to his house for a barbecue."

David was already shaking his head no. He knew he was in desperate trouble, but he wasn't that desperate. "Well, I . . ."

But now Judah Rosenbloom, tugging furiously at his glasses, spoke up. "David, I want you to know I've been a passionate advocate for the poor and the dispossessed for many years now and I've never hesitated to take on unpopular clients. In fact, I believe that's my mission as a lawyer." He spoke swiftly and insistently, as if he expected to get thrown out of the room. "I believe that people of good conscience should not only challenge the apparatus of government but dismantle its institutions when the cause of justice is not being served . . ."

David suddenly remembered he'd seen Rosenbloom on television, representing various terrorists and local drug dealers.

"Uh, listen, I don't know if I want you guys to represent me."

"Can I ask if you've spoken to other lawyers?" asked Judah.

"Well, I've seen a few already and I think the union's talking to some others for me." He felt his heart sinking as he remembered last night's conversation with his chapter leader.

"Come on, get real." Marcovicci looked over at the smudged, empty spot in the corner where Arthur's toys had been. "Some UFT lawyer's going to help you with a homicide charge?"

"I haven't been charged with anything yet." David stiffened. "As far as I know."

"Don't kid yourself, pal. You're already on trial. Have you taken a look outside lately?"

Marcovicci got out of his chair and walked over to the window. He pulled up the blinds and pointed to the sixty or seventy media people lining West 112th Street with their cars and broadcast trucks.

"You get it, don't you? You're on trial in the court of public opinion. You're getting the thermonuclear screw."

"The what?"

"The thermonuclear screw." Marcovicci mimed turning a big tool, grinding it in. "Don't you know what that is?"

"No."

"It's when the media starts bearing down on you and keeps boring in till there's nothing left. They don't have to put the cuffs on you. Your reputation is already on the block. Have you heard your mother's neighbors and your students on the news? They can't wait to bury you. 'He seemed like a nice, quiet young man, I never would have suspected.' "

With most of his furniture disassembled or confiscated, David found himself sitting on the bare carpet. "But that doesn't matter in a court of law. Does it?"

"Oh yeah, right." Marcovicci chuckled as he sat down again. "Like a jury isn't going to see any of that."

"But I'm innocent!" David said, balling up his fists in anger.

"Sure you are." Marcovicci smiled indulgently, facetiously. "Everyone I've ever represented was innocent."

"But I'm really innocent. I'm the one who kept the kids off the bus."

He found himself struggling to keep his composure. The wrongness, the sheer perversity of his situation, had literally knocked the breath out of him for the last twenty-four hours. And his lack of sleep was adding a blurry edge to the proceedings.

"David, we feel it's imperative we begin to fight back and start a counteroffensive immediately." Judah Rosenbloom, who'd remained standing, took off his glasses and wiped them with a Kleenex. His eyes seemed younger than the rest of his face. "We have to define the terms of the dialogue."

"But when can I expect to get my name cleared? I can't have this hanging over me. I've got a conference scheduled with the judge in my divorce case tomorrow."

"Well, the problem is, you haven't been arrested."

"What? Why is that a problem?"

"Because if you'd been arrested, then we could go to court and get you acquitted—or better yet, force them to drop the charges." Rosenbloom nodded at Marcovicci. "But as things stand, there's only innuendo and suspicion. It's like shooting arrows at ghosts."

Again, David felt that momentary spasm of claustrophobia-tinged panic, that feeling that things would never be the same. All this time, he'd been thinking Hemingway and acting Henry James, but now his life was going Kafka on him.

"So I'm just supposed to sit here while the roof caves in? What about my job? What about my custody case? You mean to tell me I'm going to lose my job and my son because there's not enough evidence to charge me, so I can eventually be cleared? That could go on forever."

"Exactly." Marcovicci tipped back his coffee cup. "That's why you've got to fight this case on every front. With Judah, you got all the legal angles covered if it comes to that. And with me, you've got the most media-savvy lawyer in the tri-state region. I know every radio- and talk-show booker in the city. I could have you on *Dateline* by tomorrow night, proclaiming your innocence . . ."

"Oh no." David smacked the floor. "I'm not going through that again. The media's probably what got me in trouble in the first place." He stood up. "Listen, thanks for your time, guys. But I think I have to talk to some other lawyers."

"Are you sure about this, David?" Judah Rosenbloom raised his eyebrows in sincere concern. "With Ralph and me working together, you get the best of both worlds. Go to the library and look at the clips. I had sixteen years in solo practice before I hooked up with Ralphie, and I'll put my record up against any high-priced defense lawyer in town."

So this was a marriage of convenience. David took a business card from Judah.

"I'm sure you guys are great," he said. "I just don't want to get caught up in the whole circus."

"Hey, guess what, pal." Marcovicci stood up too; it was like a mountain rising. "The circus already hit town."

"I still think I'd like to take a more low-key approach."

"Suit yourself." Marcovicci fixed his collar and threw back his hair. "You know, sometimes people say, 'Ralphie, you're a clown. You don't know the law.' And sometimes, I even say to myself I should have studied more at school, read more of the great books. Oliver Wendell Holmes, Aristotle. Truth and beauty. Perhaps I should have tried to be more of a scholar, a man like yourself or Judah here. But you know what? *It's not a scholarly age we live in.*" He stuck out his hands to indicate jiggling breasts and wiggled his enormous butt. "It's a *BOOM-BOOM KILLER AGE!* It's a *LARCHMONT LOLITA* age! And every-fucking-body knows it.

So if you just let it roll over you and crush you, you got no one to blame but yourself, pal."

The phone rang and David waited a beat before picking it up. He couldn't deal with another reporter right now. "Yes. Who is it?"

"David, it's Renee." She sounded skittish and far away, like she'd crawled out on a tree limb with the phone.

"What's up?"

"You need to get over here. Right away. *They've been here.* And I cannot handle it."

"Oh shit."

"That's what I say." She hung up.

David rubbed his knuckles on his beard. He couldn't wait any longer. He had to make a decision and pick a lawyer. Judah and Ralph had started for the door, and he pictured a rescue barge pulling away, leaving him stranded on a tiny shrinking iceberg.

"How much are you guys going to charge me?" he blurted out.

The lawyers looked at each other and shrugged. "I guess we're willing to take you on pro bono," said Judah.

"But of course, we get the usual percentage on the civil suit later," Ralph cut him off. "You got a helluva case, provided you're innocent."

Oh yes, provided you're innocent. That little detail. David hesitated just a second or two before he told the lawyers they were hired. It wasn't just the need to make a quick decision. There were larger forces at work. Ralph was right. It was a Boom-Boom Killer age, a Larchmont Lolita age. He couldn't just get his good name back on legal technicalities and precedents; he had to change people's perceptions out in the world.

"So I guess I'd like you guys to represent me," David said, almost swallowing his words.

"Good man," said Ralph, pumping his hand. "We're going to have a lot of fun. Just remember, 'Life is an adventure or nothing at all.' "

"Who said that?" asked David.

"Helen Keller."

33

Immediately after the fight with his sister, Nasser packed his bags and moved out, with no particular destination in mind.

First he stopped by the school, hoping to see Mr. Fitzgerald again. The one who'd started all his misery. He sat in the parking lot, listening to the radio and watching the school's back entrance, not sure what he'd do when he saw the teacher. But then he heard the news stories saying Mr. Fitzgerald had become a suspect in the bombing, and he drove on.

Confusion was clouding his mind. Everything was backward. First, the teacher tried to seduce his sister. Then Nasser had been thrown out of his own family's home. Now the teacher was being blamed for the bomb Nasser had planted. It was hard to understand how this was all part of a Divine plan.

He tried calling Youssef, but the Great Bear wasn't in. So instead he took the Brooklyn Bridge into Manhattan, thinking maybe he'd try to talk to Professor Bin-Khaled. He was at loose ends, directionless, like a marble falling through the universe. He needed a place to stop. He tried to call Youssef and Dr. Ahmed from a pay phone, but they were out. It was just as well he couldn't get in touch with them; he wasn't ready to get sucked into their plans for another *hadduta* just yet. He was too unsettled. The key was still dangling against his chest; he hadn't dared to look at it closely since arguing with Elizabeth.

From having checked the schedule before, he knew the professor was due to be giving a lecture today in one of the City University buildings on West 42nd Street. The halls inside were gray and careworn and reeked of ammonia. They reminded him of Bethlehem University back home, where he'd visited friends occasionally, but the feeling here was different. There was more of a hopeful, industrious bustle in these corridors. People here thought they had a future.

He found Room 106 and went in. The room was packed; some three hundred seats were arranged in ascending rows, amphitheater-style. He took an empty chair at the back and sat down, feeling a wave of discomfiting nostalgia. *Back in school again.* But most of the students here looked at least a decade older than the ones at Coney Island High School. They were more like people you saw on their way to work on the subway. They were focused and purposeful in taking their notes, determined to avoid distractions. The curly-haired Hispanic guy on Nasser's right was using a tape recorder so he wouldn't miss anything. He wore a sports jacket and a tie as if he'd come to class straight from a job in a bank. The black woman on Nasser's left wore starchy beige office clothes with a baby-picture button clipped on her denim book bag. She'd covered both sides of a notebook page with painstaking felt-tip writing. These weren't spoiled America children caught up in television and frivolity. These were adults sacrificing something to be here, *to learn.* And Nasser felt itchy and out of place among them.

Down by the blackboard at the bottom of the room, his old friend and cellmate, Ibrahim, Professor Bin-Khaled, was lecturing. At first, Nasser almost didn't recognize him—the intervening years had dropped a heavy snowfall into Ibrahim's hair and turned his mustache white as well.

He couldn't have been more than forty-five, Nasser calculated, but he looked like he was in his sixties. His movements were slow and gingerly, like something was still broken inside him after all this time. *Insh'allah* the man had suffered so much, getting tortured in prison and then losing a son in the struggle. Nasser felt a current of shame go through him, wishing he'd tried to make contact sooner.

"In *A Passage to India*, we see the colonizing force confronting the Other and collapsing utterly in the face of it," Ibrahim was saying as he drew a picture of a cave on the blackboard. "But what we have is not a polemic. Forster also gives us these impossible friendships, this sense of people straining to reach beyond boundaries . . ."

It wasn't what Nasser wanted to hear, right now. Impossible friendships. He wanted white-hot cleansing anger, words to direct him. He knew Ibrahim could give them to him, if only these other people weren't around. The Hispanic man on his right flipped through his copy of *A Passage to India*, looking for references. The woman on his left gracefully folded one leg over the other and brought her face down close to her page. She reminded Nasser of that perfect-posture girl he used to see in the high school cafeteria, Aisha Watkins, another one he never got up the nerve to talk to. Except this girl next to him had grown up and moved on in her life, while Nasser felt exactly the same: tongue-tied, mystified, and locked into himself.

Insh'allah. He couldn't stand to wait for Ibrahim. Too much was burning him up inside. He walked out of the lecture room and drove downtown to pray at the Medina Mosque on 11th Street. He washed his eyes, ears, nose, and privates, then took off his shoes and offered up an *ishkatar*, a prayer for guidance. The storm was still raging in his head as he knelt and prostrated himself in the bare white-tiled room alongside a half-dozen other men. A side of him wished something magnificent and violent would happen to him, while another side kept thinking about women: his sister, the girl at the cafeteria, the woman in the classroom. What did God want him to do next? Why didn't He make His will manifest? Nasser began to blame himself; perhaps he wasn't doing enough for the faith. The Prophet said when you saw a wrong action, you should try to change it first with your hands, then with your words, and finally with your heart. Maybe he needed to do more of each.

He drove around for an hour or so, picking up fares and earning about $24, and then at five o'clock, he found himself outside a neon-lit club on Lower Broadway called the Pussycat Lounge. He'd never been inside, but he knew immoral things went on there. No, he wasn't just going in because he'd never seen a woman in a state of undress before. To do it for that reason would be strictly *haram*. His reasons were righteous; he wanted to stop the wrongful actions without a bomb and spread the teachings of God. Perhaps he'd even find a convert in there.

But as soon as he walked in carrying his tattered copy of the Koran, he felt himself diverted from his mission. The warm throb of the music went right down into the pit of his stomach, reminding him of the songs Elizabeth would play late at night in her room while he was trying to sleep in the basement. It would come through the ceiling, soothing him to sleep at night. A secret thing that he shared with her.

But here he looked around in terror at the smoked-mirror walls and the chrome-topped bar. He saw bottles of liquor lined up behind the counter and had to fight the urge to smash them with his bare hands. Nearby there was a pool table and display cases full of dusty "I Luv NY" trinkets and souvenirs, but even Nasser understood their only purpose was to get around city regulations banning a club from devoting all of its floor space to "adult entertainment."

"Excuse me, sir, can I help you?" A bouncer, a bulky white refrigerator of a man in a black bow tie, was talking to him.

"Yes . . . I . . ." What to say here, what to do? "I would like to talk to someone."

"Right this way, sir."

The bouncer guided him past the bar and into a grotto-like darkened room full of mostly empty tables and chairs. It took Nasser's eyes a second to adjust to the purplish ultraviolet light before he saw a woman dancing on the stage, her movements undulating, serpentine. On the wall behind her, there was an electronic zipper sign, showing stock prices swimming by in red lights. To his right, he saw a man in a suit slumped back in a seat, as if drugged. A blond woman in a skimpy white bathing suit was presenting her rear end to him.

Nasser stood there, transfixed and horrified. The Great Chastisement would surely start here, but he found he couldn't move. A powerful force was holding him. The dancing girl's swaying hips and the swimming red numbers had him hypnotized.

"Care for a dance?" A brown-haired girl in a red sequined gown approached him with a dazed, glassy smile. "Only ten dollars until six o'clock."

He felt himself trembling inside. By God, this was the Devil himself tempting him. Tearing him apart from the inside. Yes, no, yes. He wanted to be touched, but he didn't want anyone to touch him.

He thought again of his friend Hamid in Ashkelon prison. Hamid, who was born a week before him and grew up twenty-five kilometers down the road from Deheisha. The Jews had put Hamid in a room alone with a beautiful Nablus girl, who told him he'd be given an early release and a big house in Jerusalem where they could make hot passionate love forever if he'd just cooperate a little and become a jailhouse informant. And then Hamid, who'd promised his friends he'd never break, had gone back to his cell and at the first opportunity cut his own throat with a razor he'd been given, so he wouldn't be tempted.

The same thing was happening again here.

"Can I show you to a seat?" the girl reached for his hand.

Nasser jumped back, as if she were about to engulf him in flames. "No! No thank you. I must go. I can't stay in this place."

He turned and ran out while he still could.

The street outside was full of people hurrying for the subways, hustling to their homes, to their families, to someone waiting for them. While Nasser stood by his car, feeling lost and crushed by the pressure of his loneliness.

At last, he knew he couldn't resist anymore. It was getting late and he needed a place to stay the night. He got in the car and started the drive up to the residency hotel on 23rd Street. It was his destiny and God's will that he fall in with Youssef and Dr. Ahmed again, he realized, so he could help them with their mission. There was nowhere else for him to go.

34

David finished his meeting with the lawyers and rushed over to the old apartment on 98th Street as fast as he could. As soon as Arthur opened the door, though, he knew he was too late.

"Mommy's in the bathroom and she won't come out," the boy said in his cartoony, sing-song, I'm-so-upset-I-can't-let-it-show voice.

"I'm sorry, buddy. Are you all right?" David knelt to give his son a hug.

Arthur felt stiff and cold in his arms. "Some big men came."

"I know. They were at my house too."

Arthur looked at him carefully, trying to take his cue whether to fall apart or not. "Did they touch my toys over there?"

"Not much," David lied. He'd have to get the place cleaned up before letting Arthur back in. "Did they mess with any of your things here?"

"Just a little." The boy sucked on his shirt collar. "But they went through Mommy's stuff and she got mad at them and started yelling and wouldn't stop."

David put a hand on the back of his neck and sighed deeply. The living room was disturbed in more subtle ways here than at his apartment. Everything had been picked up and put down just a little bit wrong. The couch was pulled away from the wall a few inches. The edge of the carpet was curled up. The TV and stereo were unplugged and the computer equipment was rearranged, as if someone had been checking the hard drive. That same half-eaten green apple was still sitting on a plate on the coffee table, though, and turning black.

David felt his rage giving way to weary frustration. What were these people trying to do to his family? Why were they trying to destroy everything he loved?

"Daddy, what were they looking for?"

Okay, Fitzgerald. Keep it together. The boy's whole world depends on your maintaining a brave face.

"They were looking for a bad man," David said finally. "But they made a mistake coming here. Somebody must have given them the wrong directions."

The boy's eyes went from side to side, searching his father's face for reasons to trust him. "When are they going to find him?"

"Soon, buddy. I'm sure it'll be soon."

"And when is Mommy going to come out of the bathroom?"

"I don't know. I'll go talk to her." He ruffled the boy's hair and listened to the sound of his breathing. "You gonna be all right, buddy?"

"Yeah." The boy wandered back toward the Lego castles in his room, trying to slough it all off. "They should arrest Anton. He's an asshole."

David followed him halfway down the hall and then made the detour to knock on the bathroom door.

"Renee, honey. It's all right. They're gone."

"C'mon-a-my-house, a-my-house . . ." She was singing softly and out of tune to herself.

He rested the top of his head against the door, the effects of a sleepless night catching up with him. Why was this happening?

"Look, babe. You gotta come out. Arthur needs you."

The pipes squeaked and water began running into the sink inside the bathroom.

"Renee, what are you doing? You're not going to hurt yourself, are you?"

"Why were those men here, David?" Her voice was barely audible over the rush of water. "What did they want from me?"

"Renee, open the door so I can talk to you. I'm losing my voice."

He hoped it wouldn't be necessary to knock down the door again. He'd accidentally given her a black eye the last time he tried that stunt. The water cut off and the pipes grunted. Renee opened the door less than half an inch. A sliver of pale light slanted into the darkened hallway and one bloodshot green eye appeared at the crack in the door.

Immediately, David understood that whatever thread she'd been hanging by was now broken.

"They scared me," she said, cautiously opening the door the rest of the way.

An awful smell hit David. His first thought was that she'd been washing the walls with her own vomit.

"Come on out a minute." He reached for her hand. "It's all right. They were *trying* to scare you. But they're not here anymore."

She grasped his fingers and slid one bare bruised foot into the hall. She'd been crying and drinking. Cigarette ash spilled down her fingers as she brought the filter up to her lips.

"What happened?" he asked.

"These men, they just come in here. I mean, they say they have a warrant, but what do I know about warrants? I'm a dancer." She began to babble, wiping her nose with the back of her hand. "Why would they show a dancer a warrant? Why would they show an actress a warrant? Do I look like I know about warrants?"

"There, there." David led her back into the living room and sat her down on the couch, noticing the Margot Fonteyn poster was slightly crooked.

"And then they started going through my things. They looked in my closet. They opened Anton's saxophone case. They asked me all these intimate questions."

"What kinds of questions?"

"Ba-ha!" She threw open her arms, leaving a trail of smoke in the air. "They wanted to know what you were like, who your friends were, what you talked about at home. Whether you were capable of hurting anyone. If you knew anything about explosives. Crazy things."

"So what did you tell them?" David asked cautiously.

"I told them they were wrong. That you weren't like that. That you were a good person. Basically." She stopped and touched her lip. "I mean, when you added it all up in the end. I think."

He sensed her mood was changing. The hollows of her neck were deepening. "What's the matter?" he asked.

"Well, it's just that they kept after me." She moved down the couch, away from him. "Telling me about guns and uniforms in your mother's garage. And how one of your students was on television this morning saying you brought an ax to class. They kept asking me these things and after a while I started to get paranoid. I thought, what if they're right? What if everything I thought was wrong? You think you know someone, but you don't. I mean, really you don't. I thought we'd be married forever and now we're not, so how can you ever really know anybody? There are things in my head I've never told anyone. Nobody knows anything."

"Renee, listen to me." David sat down next to her and put his arm around her. "I did not do this. Okay? They're doing a number on you. Something else is going on here that has nothing to do with you or me or Arthur or the divorce."

He felt her body quivering. He felt irritated with her and then sorry for her and then angry with himself for not being able to do more to comfort her. This is tremendous, he thought. She's having some kind of major breakdown, I'm under investigation, and we have a conference with the judge tomorrow.

"Oh God." She stubbed out her cigarette and hugged herself. "They showed me pictures of the bus driver. They told me how he died, with his skull fractured and his neck broken. It was awful. I feel like climbing into bed and never getting out."

"You can't do that, Renee," David said steadily, as if he was trying to talk her down from a bad acid trip. "Arthur needs you."

"I know, I know." She turned away from him and started to pick at her lip some more. "But I keep seeing the picture of the bus driver in my mind and I can't get rid of it. I keep thinking how lonely he must have been when he died. Nobody was there who loved him. I told them, how can you really know anything about anybody? It's the loneliness of existence. The fragility. Oh, god-damn it. Look what they did to my rug!"

She bent down and started scratching at a perfectly clean spot on the carpet.

"It's okay, babe, it's okay." He got off the couch and patted her on the shoulder until she stood up.

"They fucked it up." Her cheeks bunched up like little fists on either side of her face. "They just fucked everything up."

"Look, Renee." He exhaled. "I think the best thing to do from now on is not to talk to them. Not to the press and not to the FBI. If they call or come by again, just tell them to talk to my new lawyers. I'll get you the numbers." He wiped his brow. "This is all just an insane mistake. I'm sure it'll be over in a few days."

Though probably not in time for the custody hearing tomorrow. He wondered if there was any way to put it off.

"I'm trying to be strong, David." Renee put the top of her head against his chest. "Really I am."

"I know, Renee. I know."

He wrapped his arms around her, as if he were literally trying to hold her together. My fault, my fault, my fault. Somehow, it's all my fault. He felt like she was wounded and bleeding and he was a medic with no instruments to help her. "Do you want me to stay?" he asked.

"No, Anton will be back soon. He'll . . . do . . ."—she gestured lamely—"something."

He kissed her lightly on the forehead and then went to say good-bye to his son. He found Arthur lying on the bedroom floor with his legs in the air, reading a Batman comic and pushing his cheeks up with his fingers.

"It's going to be okay, buddy." David sat down beside him. "Someday, you won't even remember this."

A lie. A blatant lie. A pathetic lie. And even worse, a lie he was telling himself instead of the boy. Arthur didn't look at him.

"Okay," he said blandly.

David nuzzled him and stood up. "By the way, Arthur, did they ask you anything, the men who came here?"

"Just what I wanted to be when I grew up."

David looked down, and felt that tightness in his chest again. Just a few days ago, the boy had been running around telling people he wanted to be just like his dad. "So what did you tell them?"

"I told them I wanted to be a cop."

35

Sheik Abdel Aziz Ayad was a thin-boned, fiftyish imam with broken teeth and smiling impish eyes. Dressed in a white robe and a red prayer cap, he sat in the living room of his Atlantic Avenue apartment, talking to Nasser, Youssef, and Dr. Ahmed.

"There are some calling themselves holy men, who say there are other interpretations of the Holy Book—but this is ridiculous!" the imam said with a crooked, slightly mischievous grin. "There is only one way, one interpretation, one God. Is there more than one way to get an egg out of its shell? No. You have to break the egg. So that is what we talk about here."

Youssef started to rise. "Can I get you something from the kitchen, sheik?"

"No, thank you, brother. I had a *halal* candy bar before." The imam, who was sitting cross-legged on a brown rug, reached up to get his cup of tea from the table and then turned to Nasser. "This nation we are in is an abomination before God. Of this, there can be no doubt. God himself has put a blanket over the hearts of the nonbelievers and stuffed wax in their ears. This is the way it is! They cannot know the truth. They can only inflict suffering on others. God has no mercy for those who have no mercy. And this is why there must be *jihad*."

Dr. Ahmed was rocking back and forth on the floor with his

knees drawn up to his chest. "Ah, now, see, this is what I want to talk about. The Great Chastisement. About what form it will take."

The imam smiled without quite seeming to hear him. "We must afflict them in their homes. We must not allow them to feel comfortable in their Godlessness. Why do they support Israel? It's because they worship money and the Jews give money for bribes to the White House. They say they care about human rights and then they allow the Jews to oppress us and torture our peoples. They are hypocrites and cowards. So we must fight them everywhere and make sacrifices when we have to. There is nothing holier before God than a martyr. No greater hero than one who fights for the cause of Allah."

"*Allahu akbar!*" cried the doctor.

"No God but God." Youssef tapped Nasser on the knee.

"A man who stays at home to pray is nothing in comparison." The imam turned his smiling imp eyes to Nasser. "He will not enter Paradise as quickly as the warrior. One hour on the battlefield is worth a hundred years of prayer."

"*Insh'allah!*" Dr. Ahmed said loudly.

It felt good to Nasser, hearing this after being thrown out by his family. It felt right. To be here with these men, in this room, talking about things that were real, belonging in the company of warriors. It brought him back to the feeling he'd had in the early days of the *intifada:* the weight of the stone in his hand, his brothers alongside him in the crooked little streets of Bethlehem, that sense he once had of standing in the exact right place at the exact right time. Before he came to this country and lost his way.

"But of course, we must be cautious." The imam poked him with a long, gnarled finger. "Trust in Allah, but tether your camel. You know this saying?"

"No," said Nasser.

"One of the Prophet's followers asked him whether he should tie up his camel or trust in God when they were traveling. So the Prophet said, 'Trust in Allah *and* tether your camel.' "

Nasser bit his lip, considering this. Perhaps he'd been wrong, depending on God to arrange so much in his life.

"I want to talk about the place we should target next," the doctor interrupted, tapping the floor with his fingers. "Where we can do the most damage with the *hadduta*."

The imam leaned away from him. "Well, this must be studied," he said vaguely.

Dr. Ahmed's brow became a hardened ridge, and he began to rock more quickly. "I was thinking one of the great institutions they are so arrogant about. It's true the brothers missed their chance at the World Trade Center a few years ago. But that doesn't mean it's wrong to try something of this scale. The loss of many lives is important to make our point, to cause the disruption. . . . I was thinking about the United Nations again. It is possible to put the *hadduta* perhaps in the parking lot."

The imam's smile grew faint and he started to fidget. "Well, of course, this could be studied too," he said. "I don't know if it is necessary to go into such detail right now."

Dr. Ahmed missed the hesitance in the imam's voice and went on with his rocking and his planning. "I was also thinking to consider one of their great bridges and tunnels. The Lincoln Tunnel or the Holland Tunnel. My God, can you imagine? We could drown them all and stop traffic for days."

The imam folded his lips and said only, "Sometimes, it's best to keep things simple."

Nasser watched him closely, wondering why he'd suddenly fallen silent. Was he afraid someone was listening in on their conversation? *Were they not alone?*

Youssef had told him: The imam was not just a holy man, but a man of the world. He'd studied at the University of Cairo and for a time even went to classes at the University of Wisconsin. Naturally, he'd fought alongside his brothers against the Jews in Israel, but he was also a pragmatist. After all, he'd negotiated with the CIA to get military support for brothers repelling the Soviet invaders in Afghanistan, where he'd met both Youssef and the doctor. So perhaps he was aware of certain things in the air, attuned to potentials for calamity.

Trust in Allah, he'd said. *But tether your camel.*

"So what do you think, sheik?" Dr. Ahmed was asking. "Which should be the target?"

"I think," said the imam, standing slowly, "I am late to prepare for the evening prayer downstairs and there will be another time to discuss this. Remember, it is more blessed to worship among enemies than it is to worship among friends."

His smile came back as he made his way to the door. Youssef jumped up to open it. "Peace upon you, brother! God is greatest!"

"*Asalam allakem.*" The imam nodded his acknowledgment as he looked back at Nasser and Dr. Ahmed. "Stay as long as you like, brothers. My home is your home. Or join me for the prayer downstairs in a few minutes."

"*Allahu akbar.*" Dr. Ahmed waved. "We'll be along."

"*Insh'allah*," Nasser called after him.

The door closed and Nasser noticed there was a brown Snickers bar wrapper sticking out of the garbage can next to it. Dr. Ahmed clapped his hands gleefully and turned to Youssef.

"So now it's all set," he said.

Nasser looked at him quizzically. "What's all set?"

"He has given us his blessing. Didn't you hear that?"

"Not at all."

Nasser was still trying to decode the words the imam had said. Was some deeper meaning eluding him?

Dr. Ahmed stared to the left of him and worked the side of his mouth into a sneer.

"What's the matter with you?" he said. "He could not have been any clearer. Does he have to spell it out when people could be listening? He wants us to do away with many of them."

Before Nasser could protest that the imam had said nothing of the kind, Youssef came over, sat back down beside him, and put an arm around him.

"It's okay, my friend," he said. "You are young. But you must learn to listen with your heart and not just your ears."

36

The next morning, David sat with Renee and their respective divorce lawyers in Judge Katherine Nemerson's chambers at 110 Centre Street. He had tried to get this conference delayed for at least another week until the investigation blew over, but both the judge and Renee's lawyer, a blustery former prosecutor named J. Randy Barrett, insisted on going ahead, since David's new notoriety presented a slate of complicating issues that needed to be addressed immediately.

So he slumped down in his chair, looking at one of the claw feet of the judge's Louis Quatorze desk. Its nails were digging into a ball and he imagined that it was his heart being punctured.

"Okay, so what's the problem?" asked the judge, a hard and leathery New York lady in her mid-fifties.

"Your Honor, let's cut to the chase," said Randy Barrett, who had wavy black hair and jowls as big as a woman's purse. "Mr. Fitzgerald over here is the target of a federal probe. He's accused of planting a bomb meant to kill at least twenty-four school-age children. He's under constant surveillance and intense media scrutiny. So for the sake of the child, I want to terminate all visitation rights immediately and seek a waiver for my client to take Arthur out of state."

"Hardball, eh?" The judge made a note to herself and pushed her bifocals up on her nose, liking his style.

David winced, feeling like he'd been struck in the chest with a sledgehammer. He waited for his lawyer, Beth Nussbaum, to respond. But Beth was anything but a hard-charger. An old school friend from Atlantic Beach, she was a gentle, kind, loving person, with a soft heart-shaped face and billowy yellow hair. More than once, David had worried she wasn't vicious enough to make it in the matrimonial business.

"Your Honor, with all due respect, what counsel is saying is ridiculous," she said, shuffling papers on her lap. "My client hasn't been convicted of any crime. He hasn't even been arrested or charged."

Though at the moment, it was hard to tell that. Stories about him were appearing in every newspaper and on every television station, twisting his image and taking everything he'd said on the air and in class out of context.

"Judge, I'm not stupid," Barrett fired back. "I know the difference between arrest, arraignment, and conviction. What I'm saying is just look at the practicalities. Forget all of Mr. Fitzgerald's shortcomings for a moment—we'll get to those later. How is he going to care for his son and simultaneously mount a vigorous defense for himself? He could be going to prison for the rest of his life."

Prison. David had been struggling hard to keep that image out of his mind the last two days. He'd visited students on Rikers Island, heard about the strip searches, the fingers up the butt, the shanks driven into chests, the systematic loss of identity and manhood.

"I'm not going to prison," he spoke up. "I'm innocent."

He felt Renee looking at him. Dark circles under her eyes, a little scab in the middle of her lip. Christ, why couldn't they work this out between themselves? She wasn't that far gone, was she?

"So what's the story, Mr. Fitzgerald?" asked the judge. "Are you working in the meantime?"

"I'm still getting my salary," said David, pulling himself up in his chair.

"That's not what I asked." The judge scrubbed away the excuse in her steel-wool voice. "I asked if you were *working*. So I take it the answer is no, they want you away from the kids."

Before David could respond, Beth put a hand on his wrist, reminding him she was the mouthpiece here. "Judge, we're confident that Mr. Fitzgerald will be cleared in due time and get his job back. He's engaged the services of the criminal attorneys Ralph Marcovicci and Judah Rosenbloom."

"Oh great, the Laurel and Hardy Show!" Randy Barrett snickered. "See, this is what I'm talking about, Judge! Ralph Marcovicci is the all-time clown master of the media circus. There's going to be cameras around this case for months to come. This poor fragile little boy, Arthur, won't have a moment's peace. We've gotta protect him and get him out of town."

David bared his teeth and looked sideways at Renee. "Don't let him do this to us," he murmured. "You know it isn't right."

"Judge, please tell him not to address my client." Barrett cut him off, jabbing a finger at David. "He's trying to play games with her head."

"All right, all right, enough already." The judge waved her hands. "I've never heard so much acrimony over so little money." She touched the center piece of her bifocals and picked up a file. "Ms. Nussbaum, what say you about Mr. Barrett's request to let his client take the boy out of town?"

David and Beth looked at each other sorrowfully. They'd discussed bringing up Renee's deteriorating mental condition and had decided only to raise the issue in the most delicate way possible. But here Randy Barrett had gone nuclear on them.

"Your Honor," Beth began slowly. "My client still loves his wife, but he's beginning to grow concerned about her. Based on what he's seen and what the boy has told him, he's afraid she may be experiencing some kind of a breakdown and won't be able to take care of the child. So we would strongly oppose any effort to take Arthur out of town."

David saw Renee shudder in her seat. Her lawyer grabbed her elbow, meaning to reassure her but just startling her more.

"Your Honor, this is outrageous!" he bellowed. "Even I didn't think Mr. Fitzgerald would sink to this level of character assassination. He has no right to cast aspersions on my client's mental state."

"Well, actually he does." The judge was still studying the file, her mouth strained and dubious. "I'm reading Dr. Ferry's report and he had some serious concerns about Mrs. Fitzgerald's mental condition." She dropped the file on her desk with a *thwap*. "So here we have a problem. On the one hand, Mr. Fitzgerald is being followed around by the press and the feds, which could have traumatic effect on both the wife and the child. But on the other hand, Mrs. Fitzgerald doesn't seem entirely capable of caring for him all by herself. So what are we going to do about this?"

She threw her hands open to the room, as if asking for suggestions, but everyone was looking down. David gripped his armrests and saw Renee digging her heel into the carpet.

"Does anyone want to see this child in foster care or sent to live with a grandparent?" Judge Nemerson asked.

"No," said David, clearing his throat and raising his eyes.

"No." Renee's voice slid under his.

David looked at her gratefully, but she'd already turned away and started picking at her lip again. He reminded himself how much it must have cost her to keep it together as long as she had.

"All right, so let's figure out what we're going to do." The judge took off her bifocals and rubbed the bridge of her nose. "Mr. Barrett may have a point about all this pressure having a traumatic effect on the child." She turned her eyes to David. "Mr. Fitzgerald, have your criminal lawyers told you how long they expect this investigation to last?"

"Oh, it shouldn't be too long, Your Honor," he lied. "The government has no case."

Judge Nemerson cocked her head to one side, unconvinced.

"Well, until this gets cleared up, I'm afraid I see things from Mr. Barrett's point of view. I'm not going to cut off all visitation rights, but I am going to curtail them a little. The potential for damage is too great."

David felt the talons digging deeper into his heart. Stay focused on Arthur and the kids, he told himself. That's how you're going to get through this.

"All right, here's what we're going to do," said the judge, flipping open a desk calendar. "I'm going to schedule a custody hearing for four weeks from today, the sixteenth of next month, so we can settle this matter once and for all. Mrs. Fitzgerald"—she nodded to Renee—"I want you to continue seeing your psychiatrist and taking the medication he prescribes. If the drugs don't work anymore, get new drugs. I want full and regular reports from your doctor about how you're doing. If you try to leave the city with your son, the consequences will be *serious*. And Mr. Fitzgerald—" She drew a bead on David. "I suggest you get your situation with the investigation and your employment straightened out before the hearing. Those are going to be very important factors in my decision about who gets permanent custody of the child."

"But Your Honor, that's completely unfair!" Beth Nussbaum looked like she was about to start crying. "These matters are out of my client's hands. You're penalizing him just because he's been falsely accused of something."

"And what about the damage to my client and the boy from being in the middle of this media zoo all the time?" Barrett protested.

"Hey." The judge shrugged. "Who do I look like, Solomon?"

37

The day after meeting with the imam, Youssef, Dr. Ahmed, and Nasser got down to the serious business of preparing for the next *hadduta*.

They drove out to Sunset Park, Brooklyn, and rented a garage for $1,200 a month on a quiet block, where they could mix the chemicals for their explosives in peace. Then they walked around the corner and rented a dirty little hovel of an apartment behind a taxi stand for $686 a month, so the doctor and Nasser could stop sleeping on the floor of the Great Bear's living room and have a place of their own for a while.

Just before lunch, Dr. Ahmed gave Nasser a list of some of the ingredients they'd need, including two hundred pounds of the chemical fertilizer ammonium nitrate and five hundred gallons of diesel fuel, plus a half dozen fifty-five-gallon drums to mix them in. What he didn't give him was enough money to pay for everything; after renting the apartment and the garage, there was little left over from the check store robbery.

"Buy what you can," Dr. Ahmed said, pressing four crumpled twenties into Nasser's hand. "We'll raise the rest. And remember: don't buy too much at any one store. Spread it around. You don't want these bigots to wonder what an Arab boy is doing with all this material."

Nasser took the money and drove out to a garden supply store in Borough Park. He frowned, seeing the Orthodox Jews on the street in their black silk robes, fur hats, and nineteenth-century-style stockings. He parked his car in front of a vegetable stand selling "Israeli tomatoes" for 79 cents each. Israeli tomatoes? He felt like picking one up and smashing it on the sidewalk. These were *Palestinian tomatoes*, grown on land drenched in Arab blood. By God, these infidels deserved their punishment. It was getting easier to convince himself.

He went into the little store crammed with rakes and lawn mowers, wondering what they would finally select as a target. A synagogue? A great landmark like the United Nations? Some small part of him wished he could try again at the school. Every time he saw Ahmed, the doctor would remind him of his previous failure.

Nasser found two fifty-pound bags of the fertilizer back by the leaf blowers and checked to make sure the nitrogen content was at least 34 percent, as Dr. Ahmed had specified. Yes, it would be even better if he could go back to the school and find Mr. Fitzgerald there. This one who was trying to seduce Elizabeth. The idea of it filled Nasser with sickening rage. How could he stop this from happening? He felt ashamed and powerless. What would their mother have said about the loss of family honor?

He heaved the two sacks up onto the counter and the muscular kid in a Viva Puerto Rico shirt at the cash register did a double-take.

"Whooa, son," he said. "How much a that shit you need?"

"I need a lot." Nasser busied himself, digging into his pockets for the money.

The Puerto Rican kid looked at the instructions on the side of one bag. "Says here each of these bad boys covers fifteen thousand square feet. You sure you need that much?"

"I have a farm," said Nasser.

Yes, he thought. Somewhere I have a farm. But the Jews stole it and I've never seen it.

"Twenty-seven dollah niney-nine cent each, plus tax." The cashier patted the bag nonchalantly and started ringing it up on the register. "I hear this is good shit. People say it give your lawn a nice thick green color. Like the Emerald City. Right?"

"What?" Nasser carefully placed three twenties on the counter and looked around, sure he was missing something.

"You know, man. The Emerald City. *The Wizard of Oz.*"

"Oh, yes." Nasser pursed his lips and drummed his fingers on the counter, waiting for his change.

He hated these little references Americans made to their own culture, as if they expected everyone else to be just as enthralled. They made him feel small, resentful, and stupid. Didn't these people know there was an older world with more sacred traditions? Some things couldn't be mocked, packaged, and turned into television shows.

"Hey, man, where's your farm?" the cashier asked.

"Bethlehem," Nasser blurted out, and instantly regretted it.

I am an idiot. A complete idiot. He was aware of other customers looking at him. Jews with hats, beards, and curls. Swarthy men with heavy arms and broad faces. And sallow beardless boys like himself, whose ethnicity he couldn't trace. Wouldn't one of them remember him if they were questioned later? Especially after he made such a foolish slip.

But God was looking out for him. "Bethlehem, Pennsylvania. Right?" The cashier counted out his change for him.

"Exactly," said Nasser, hesitating for a moment and then grinning in relief. "You have it exactly."

"I thought that was steel country."

"It is." Nasser stuffed the change into his pockets and pulled down his bags, grateful to be getting out of there. "But there's farmland too. Chickens, cows, everything just as God made it."

Yes, this was surely a sign from God that he was going in the right direction with his life and this plan. Otherwise, he would have been stopped and caught immediately.

"Hey, you need your receipt?" The cashier pulled the white tape out of the register.

Nasser started to say no, and then caught himself. *Trust in Allah, but tether your camel.* That's what the imam had instructed. The less evidence around, the better. "Yes, thank you very much," he said, taking the sales slip and then starting to lug the bags out to his car.

"All right, my brotha." The cashier waved after him. "Follow the yellow brick road."

38

"I didn't do it," said David.

"What?"

The cute little Dominican girl at the corner bodega, who usually had a sweet smile and a kind word, wouldn't look him in the eye.

"I didn't do what you think I did." The need to declare his innocence had come upon him like a fever.

But the girl put his change down on the counter, instead of in his hand. "I didn't say anything."

He left carrying two six-packs of Rolling Rock in a brown paper bag and started up Broadway. In these last thirty-six hours or so, a sense of paranoia and isolation had begun to creep over him. Old friends like Henry and his occasional jogging partner, Tony Marr, acted strange and distant when he called, as if the David Fitzgerald they'd known before was just a sham. People moved down the counter when he visited Tom's Diner for a late breakfast. At the college bookstore, he picked up Conrad's *Secret Agent* and then put it down quickly because its plot involved a bombing and he was worried the store's clerk would tell someone he'd looked at it.

Outside his building, the camera crews, reporters, and various federal agents were maintaining an intimidating presence. There were at least thirty of them at all times, and various detachments would follow him on his jaunts to the grocery store and the dry cleaners, where the Korean men behind the counter would eye him with newfound suspicion.

"Hey, David, turn around!"

"David, just one picture please!"

"How are you holding up, David?"

He was turning into one of those horrible anti-celebrities, people famous for making a spectacular hash of their lives. He wished he could just turn it all off and ignore the racket, but his lawyers, Ralph Marcovicci and Judah Rosenbloom, had given him responsibility for clipping every newspaper article he could find about himself and recording as many radio and television stories as possible with rented equipment in preparation for a civil suit.

And God, the stories were relentless, humiliating beyond belief. He turned on the television when he got home with the beer and there was his old Little League coach, Murray Samuels, who'd always stood too close giving him tips in the batter's box.

"He always was a funny kid, that David," said Murray, who'd gone completely gray and had conspicuous hair growing out of his ears. "I remember whenever a simple fly ball would come to him in the outfield, he'd have to dive for it and make a big dramatic show of catching it and holding it up, so everyone could see what a big deal he was."

David turned off the set in disgust, leaving the VCR to record the program. He switched on the radio and there was that awful woman again, the pop psychologist Patty Samson, referring to him as David Brian Fitzgerald (in all his life, he'd only heard his mother call him by all three names, and that was just when she was upset). She started off saying David fit the classic profile of the murderous "loner" and then began harping on his "obsession" with *The Catcher in the Rye*. "The same book Mark David Chapman was carrying when he shot John Lennon," she noted cheerfully.

"We're clearly talking about the kind of person who experiences an almost orgiastic excitement at creating a disaster and then watching everyone rush around to deal with it. It doesn't take a great leap of imagination to guess what kind of sexual dysfunction might be behind that . . ."

He turned on the tape recorder and walked out of the room to call his lawyers.

"Jesus Christ," he said, once he finally got Ralph on the line. "I can't take this anymore. What if my kid hears what they're saying about me?"

"Hey," said Ralph. "I can have you on six syndicated shows tomorrow to deny the whole shebang if that's what you want. My friend Lindsay Paul is dying to get you up in front of a live studio audience."

"That's not what I want, Ralph. Can't we just sue them or something?"

"Heh, heh, David." Ralph made a burbling sound. "It's a free country, remember? Freedom of speech, our forefathers, all that crap. By the way, did you see me on *Live at Five* last night, defending your good name?"

"I'm afraid not." David twisted off the top of a Rolling Rock bottle. "I just recorded it."

"Well, short of you going on the air to deny everything yourself, that's best we can do for the moment. Judah's working the law angle."

David's eyes fell on the pile of newspapers he'd been collecting. Most of the morning's stories were meaningless rewrites of the previous day's news, plus or minus the sinister detail about the twenty-minute gap in the bathroom and quotes from unnamed students and teachers intimating there'd always been something creepy about him (*so why didn't they say so before?*). The only new development was that Sam Hall's sister was blaming him for the bombing and threatening the school with a civil action. That was bad enough. But the photos were even more excruciating. They made him look stupid, sinister, angry, shameful, haunted, loaded, and most of all, *guilty*.

Enough already. He felt like his throat was closing. "Ralph, I'll be talking to you. I gotta get out of here."

He hung up and just sat there for a minute, finishing his beer. What to do now? He realized how much of his day-to-day life was tied up with the routines of teaching. Getting up early, preparing lesson plans, correcting papers, filling out forms, keeping class discussions on track, talking to parents, meeting with kids after school, writing college recommendations, talking to admissions officers. Without these little patterns, he literally didn't know what to do with himself. How did other people get through the day?

He decided he needed to get out of town for a while, even though he had no money to travel anywhere. He wasn't due to see Arthur for four days anyway. He remembered a camping trip he'd taken with his father to a state park in Westchester called Fahnestock. It was one of the few fond memories he had of spending time alone with the old man. He recalled the smell of firewood and the blue glow around the marshmallows on a stick.

It was too bad that later in the evening his father had frightened him with stories about bears and snakes in the woods and then refused to comfort him by keeping his sleeping bag close.

"It's a man's journey," he'd said. "Get on with it."

Judy Mandel was still way out in front on the story, but worried about falling back. The last thing she needed was to hang out with every other reporter and camera crew in the city outside David Fitzgerald's apartment. She needed something fresh. Find the gravedigger, Bill Ryan used to say, quoting Jimmy Breslin. When they bury the President, talk to the gravedigger. That's your fresh angle.

Instead of the gravedigger, she went looking for the wife. Other reporters had been trying. Channel 2 had a crew in front of the building on West 98th Street for half the night, but all they got was a lousy comment out of her lawyer, pig-face Randy Barrett. The rest of the time, the doorman was keeping the press away and helping Renee sneak in and out of the building. But high on adrenaline overdrive, Judy took the next step and got the address of the son's school off the Internet.

That morning, she showed up outside the schoolyard, in her best soccer-mom get-up: sweatpants, old sneakers, oversized man's shirt, and unwashed hair. Sure, she was a little young to pull it off completely, but at least she didn't draw undue attention from the other parents dropping their kids off.

She spotted a nervous-looking redhead coming out of the school just after classes started at 8:30 and recognized Renee from the driver's license photo she'd also pulled off the computer the night before. Definitely a caffeine addict: looking over her shoulder, picking at her lip, lighting up a cigarette before she was even down the limestone steps. Judy was glad she'd stopped by Starbucks and bought her subject an espresso before even attempting this interview. The woman needed something.

Like maybe a talk with an old friend. Judy pushed herself off the chain-link fence, affected a nonthreatening neighborhood slouch, and started waving in a reassuring familiar way before David Fitzgerald's wife even got to the sidewalk.

"Renee! How are you?"

The representatives behind the counter at the Hertz car rental office on West 76th Street became giddy and excited when David showed them his driver's license and then they disappeared into the back to whisper and peek out furtively at him. Even the guys from the garage kept coming into the office to gawk.

What do I care? he told himself. I've got my dad's old army surplus tent, a cooler full of beer and cold cuts, and a beautiful autumn day ahead of me. At noon, he set off in a white Ford Tempo, trailed by a convoy of agents in three unmarked cars, plus the regular ragtag band of reporters in secondhand import cars. They followed him up the Henry Hudson and onto the Saw Mill. At the exit for the Taconic Parkway, two television broadcast vans fell in line behind them.

As he reached the edge of the campground and parked, he noticed roughly a dozen agents and a dozen reporters keeping a respectful distance but definitely still trailing him. The beautiful autumn day was fading, the air was getting unusually chilly for mid-October, and he realized he should have brought a jacket. Nearby, the reporters looked comfortable in stylish barn jackets from Orvis and Land's End, while the agents had more pragmatic department-store coats.

Apparently, they were all under the impression that he was heading for some arsenal in the woods where he might have buried additional evidence. Though why he would lead them to it so blatantly was not clear to him.

He followed the line of pine trees out past a scummy frog pond and up over a steep hill until he settled on a tall gray rock overlooking a gulch full of brown leaves. The ground nearby was hard and cold with wide, vein-shaped cracks in the black soil. A hawk flew by overhead. With the agents and reporters watching him from behind the trees some 150 yards away he felt like an animal being stalked by hunters and *National Geographic* photographers, but to hell with them. He decided to tough it out and ignore them. He started trying to figure out how to set up his tent poles without the long-lost instruction book.

As the temperature fell into the low forties and the bleak white sky turned gray and then navy, the news people finally departed, realizing nothing much was going to happen here. He cooked his hot dogs over the little hibachi and retreated into his tent just before eight, to drink Rolling Rocks and read Emerson by flashlight. He felt himself settling in, becoming part of the natural order of things, a man in his element. Why hadn't he done this before?

Then the rains came. There was no light drizzle beforehand, no heavy moisture in the air. A curtain in the sky just seemed to part and the water came straight down, through the trees, through the loosely rigged olive canvas of David's tent, through his clothes and into his skin. Within two minutes he was soaked to the bone and shivering. The wonders of the natural world. He moved around the tent frantically, trying to reset the poles, but everything he did just let in more water.

Eventually, he stumbled out of the tent with his flashlight, dripping and sneezing, and found himself surrounded by the wild darkness of the woods, with no idea where his car might be. The rain was coming down in walls, not sheets, and the only light he could see was from a tent a football field and a half away on the right. He staggered toward it like Frankenstein's monster pursued by mad villagers, trying to avoid the precipice of the leafy gulch.

It was a good five minutes before he finally reached the edge of the light-filled tent and took hold of one of its flaps.

"Excuse me," he called out. "Can I come in and get dry a minute?"

"Sure thing."

He lifted the flap and stepped inside, feeling a breath of hot air move through his clothes. The tent had been assembled with a kind of manly assurance, imposing a comfortable living space—a kind of instant apartment—on the rough landscape. Six perfectly dry people were sitting around a portable heater and a radio, listening to a Rangers hockey game. Donald Sippes, the FBI agent who'd led the raid on his apartment, half-stood and offered David a steaming mug with I SUPPORT OUR TROOPS written on the side.

"Glad you could make it," said Sippes. "You want some hot chocolate?"

David took it gratefully, as well as a plaid blanket offered by a blond female agent.

Sippes knelt down next to him, looking doleful. "I don't suppose you want to make some kind of a statement, do you?"

David hoisted the blanket over his shoulders as he sniffed and shook his head no.

"Then we should just turn him out in the rain again," said a man sitting in the corner, whom David now recognized as the pumpkin-headed agent who'd taken his son's baseball mitt.

"Chris?" Sippes furrowed his brow.

"What did I say wrong?" The pumpkin-head flexed his thick neck. "We're not in the business of coddling suspects, are we?"

"Come on, Chris," Sippes said, the reproach in his voice unmistakable. "He's just going to stay until the rain lets up. Right?"

"Right." David crouched near the opening of the tent, facing away from Pumpkin-Head Chris.

"Besides, he's not a suspect yet. Officially."

The crowd roared on the radio and the announcer began babbling excitedly. Sippes picked up a mug with a picture of Snoopy on it and gestured at David. "You like hockey?"

"No, not much." He almost felt like apologizing.

"Suit yourself." Sippes went back to his sleeping bag in front of the radio.

David remained crouched by the opening, watching the hard rain make a mist rise from the earth. His thoughts fell into the relentless rhythm: I can take this, I can take this, I can take this. If this is as bad as it gets, I can take this.

39

"Pull the trigger, love."

A few minutes before eleven o'clock that night, Judy Mandel sat at her computer terminal with her finger poised on the send button, listening to Nazi bark orders over the phone. He was actually standing less than twenty yards away, behind his office glass, but somehow it made him feel more powerful, more omnipotent, more like the image of an American tabloid editor, to growl into the phone instead of coming over to speak to her directly.

"What's the holdup, doll?" he said with the exaggerated New York accent he put on when he'd been drinking too much. "We've got the story, we've got the edge. We've been holding the front page for five hours for you."

"I just want to try him one more time. This is a very big deal, Robert. It's much more damaging than all the other stories we've had put together."

"How many messages have you left already?"

"Three. But he's been out in the woods all day and all night. We can't just run this without any comment from him, can we?"

Amazing. The further ahead she got on the story, the more she worried. It was like a rabid animal chasing her.

From across the newsroom, she saw Robert do a little skip-hop and pirouette with a Scotch glass, as if he was remembering being a lithe young boy from Perth trying to pick up girls at a posh London party. It was a bizarrely private scene; he must have forgotten people could see him through the glass.

"Come on, lover," he crooned into the receiver. "You've given him every goddamn chance to answer back and he hasn't done it. You've got the comment from his lawyers. This is going to be your biggest story yet. If we don't do it, one of these other fucking bastards will and then we'll have to kill ourselves. Pull the trigger."

"Give me a minute, Robert."

She was having *a moment*. She'd thought she wouldn't have them anymore, now that she was sure of her role in life. But here it was again. The confusion boiling up in her. The whole world was chasing her story and she wasn't sure how she could stay ahead.

How had she gotten this far? Were they about to find out she was a fraud? Who was she supposed to be anyway? When she was fourteen, she'd looked through her mother's *Vogue* and thought she should starve herself and become a super-model. But then she'd gone off to Vassar and the lesbian separatists had convinced her she should stop shaving her legs and be one of them for a while. And just lately she was trying to walk the walk and talk the talk to impress Robert and all these Neanderthal cops. What she still didn't have was a full sense of who she should be in these little in-between moments when no one was watching her.

She looked around for Bill Ryan, but he wasn't there. So she put Nazi on hold and tried David Fitzgerald's number one last time. After the fourth ring, the answering machine kicked on again and that was that. David Fitzgerald's life would never be quite the same. She switched back to Nazi.

"Happy now?" he said, tipping back his glass.

She watched the drink go down and heard the ice clack against his teeth at the same time. "I gave him every chance."

"That you did, love. That you did. Now pull the fucking trigger."

She hit the send button and the green letters on her screen jumped. Words flew out on fired electrodes and fiberoptic wires, making their way to Robert and the copy editors, who'd eventually send them on to the plant in New Jersey, where a half million papers would be printed up and sent out on trucks in time for the morning edition. Within hours, the story would be picked up by radio, television, and Internet providers around the world.

Thrilling and frightening to consider, what was beginning at the end of her finger. It could be the start of a new role for her. They'd have her on television news shows to talk about the story. And if she made a good impression, maybe they'd make her appearances a regular thing. Eventually, she'd have her own program, her own web page, she'd become the kind of personality other people wrote about and chased after. They'd write wonderful things and then awful things about her. Building her up and tearing her down. She felt exhilarated and ashamed at the same time. Is this what she wanted?

She looked across the newsroom and saw that Robert had settled down in front of a terminal and was reading her story. It was too late to take it back, and she felt a tiny spark of apprehension.

She wondered if somewhere out in the dark, wet woods David Fitzgerald was feeling that spark too.

40

David dropped the car back at Hertz just before two o'clock the next afternoon and took the subway uptown, feeling sore and still slightly chilled. Yes, the camping trip would be a fair addition to his ever-expanding collection of personal disasters, but at least he hadn't had to read or listen to any stories about himself for the last twenty-four hours

When he came around the corner of 112th Street and Broadway, though, they were waiting for him. Except instead of the motley band of thirty, there were at least a hundred and fifty press people gathered outside his building. Where did they all come from and why were they so angry all of a sudden? Up to this point, there'd been a certain collegiality among them. Now they'd turned vicious. They were baiting him like an animal. The photographers stood on car hoods, braying at him. The attractive female reporters, who'd once looked on him with open-mouthed interest, were plainly sneering. And the TV camera crews at the back were cursing him out loud.

"Fuckin' degenerate lowlife!" an enormous bull moose of a sound man called out, hocking phlegm into David's path.

"They ought to lock you up forever, you piece of shit!" shouted a cameraman.

"What did I do?" David struggled through the group, looking for a friendly face. "What's going on?"

Sara Kidreaux thrust a microphone at him. She'd always seemed kind and attentive when she'd interviewed him before. But as she drew closer, he saw her face was a mask of indignation.

"David," she said. "What do you have to say in response to these newest allegations?"

"What are they? I've been in the woods since yesterday afternoon."

The crowd pressed in around him and everyone began talking at once. Jeering, shouting questions, repeating accusations, asking him what he was going to do next. It was all furious and indistinct. A boom mike smacked him on the ear and a camera lens caught the end of his nose. Someone pulled the back of his shirt. It was like a gang initiation. None of these people would be so wanton and cruel on their own, but together they'd conjured a toxic atmosphere. David couldn't breathe. He had to get away before they accidentally strangled him with their cables and wires.

He bolted from the group and started to run for the building's entrance, almost colliding with Judy Mandel.

"Where have you been?" She stared at him strangely, as if he'd caused her great concern. "I called you four times yesterday."

He was about to ask why when the rest of the mob came storming across the sidewalk after him, knocking aside an old woman with a cart full of secondhand vegetables from upscale Dumpsters. He pushed through the front door and into the building's narrow alcove with the rain of voices at his back.

He could still hear them when he reached the second floor and brought the morning papers into his apartment. They were calling up from the street.

"Hey, David, why'd you do it?!"

"Hey, creep, show your face!"

And then he saw it. The "exclusive" on the front page of the *Trib* by Judy Mandel.

TERROR TEACHER WAS ABUSIVE, SEZ EX.

He staggered into the living room, tearing off the plastic and reading:

> In an exclusive interview with the *Trib* yesterday, the former wife of alleged school bus bomber David Brian Fitzgerald described her ex-husband as an erratic, unpredictable personality who once gave her a black eye and may have touched their seven-year-old son "inappropriately."

He fell back on the couch and read the sentence twice, realizing that he had reached the final destination on the road to sorrow.

He forced himself to go on to the end of the piece, where the denial from his lawyers sat like an irrelevant footnote. The rest of the story was just too devastating. It described someone familiar, yet completely strange. Renee described his father's war record, his own interest in the literature and mythology of heroism, his dark moods, his occasional intemperate drinking, his youthful arrest in Atlantic Beach, and his inability to communicate with her. She even mentioned his unpublished novel, *The Firebug*, neglecting to explain that the title was a metaphor for the unreliability of memory and not a reference to pyromania. Pulled together in print, the plainest and most mundane of details seemed sinister and incriminating. Especially "the inappropriate touching," which clearly referred to his tickling of Arthur, and the mysterious black eye, which occurred when he tried to break down the bathroom door.

> "He wasn't always the person he seemed to be," said Renee Fitzgerald, a leggy redheaded actress and former ballet dancer. "Was he capable of doing what he's accused of? I don't know. How can you know anyone? What if everything you thought was wrong?"

It was all true in small ways and absolutely false at the same time. But the distinction was absolutely meaningless. The story had destroyed him.

The room revolved as he tried to stand. He steadied himself on the couch arm, but it was too late. He was already falling, falling inside and falling though space and nothing would stop him.

What if everything you thought was wrong?

This was it. This was the abyss. This was the worst that could happen. There were few things pure in modern life, but this was pure despair.

He tried to grab hold of something, anything, to stop the falling. This wasn't the way it was, was it? He'd never hit Renee, had he? Never laid a finger on her. Except for that time she locked herself in the bathroom and he whacked her with the door—the old trying-to-get-in, trying-to-get-out—but that was an accident. Or was it? Perhaps, maybe, possibly there'd been a quarter second when he'd realized she was standing there and kept pushing anyway. It was possible, wasn't it? Anything was possible.

He was falling faster now, trying to grasp on to certainties, but the ground was dropping away.

Had he ever touched Arthur in an inappropriate way? No. Had he ever hit the boy? Certainly not. Was it possible he'd raised his voice? Of course, all parents yell sometimes; childhood is never as pristine and idyllic as we'd like it to be. Had he struggled to get Arthur into the bathtub? Hundreds of times. Had they fought over getting dressed? Hundreds more times. So was it possible there'd ever been a slip and a hand had struck flesh and the boy had wound up sitting on the floor crying as his mother walked into the room?

He tried calling his lawyers but they were out. So instead, he went into the kitchen to pour himself a drink. What could he be sure of anyway? The ball in his baseball glove. The one Coach Samuels described on television. He tried to project himself back into the moment of being ten years old again, lying facedown in the outfield. The grass stains on his face and his pants. Had he held the ball up to show what a great catch it was? Probably he had. He'd never caught a ball in a real game before, and perhaps a surge of boy-pride had overtaken him. So who the hell was he, anyway? How could he be so sure everyone else was wrong about him? These little moments added up and after a while you had an identity in other people's eyes. That's what his mother always told him. Who cared how you saw yourself? Perception was an amusement park with fun-house mirrors. And Hitler thought of himself as kind to animals.

David finished the quart bottle of Smirnoff he'd been keeping in the refrigerator and started on the Gilbey's gin, neat with no ice. But still the falling wouldn't stop. Black space surrounded him, roared around him. If a body catch a body. He was plummeting through time. He'd been turned into a monster. What was there to say? Should he go out there and try to talk to the reporters again? Shielding his eyes from the lights and murmuring, "I didn't do it," as they chased him down the block? Who would believe him? He wouldn't believe somebody else in the same position.

He put the bottle down for a second, thinking he should stand and fight. The judge said he had less than a month to get his job and reputation back if he wanted custody of Arthur. Come on, you can do it. You have the heart.

Or maybe he didn't. He thought he'd glimpsed something better about himself—some character, even—amid the oil smoke and the tumbling fireballs from the school bus. But that was just a fluke, he realized, an almost involuntary muscular reaction. He was low, base, and vile, even if he wasn't a child abuser. And once the accusation was repeated often enough, the truth wouldn't matter either. Arthur would lose ownership of his memories, just as his father was losing them. He'd forget that wonderful weekend of the workmen coming out of the hole and the subway riders jumping up to shake his father's hand. Instead, he'd grow up brainwashed, thinking his father had hurt him, with no chance of ever learning the truth. Even if he didn't believe his mother (who was going through her own confusion), he'd go to the library and look up the stories on microfilm or CD-ROM or hologram or whatever it would be in ten years, and he'd see those ugly words and they would wound him all over again.

What could David do to erase them? At the moment, he wished

he could erase himself, his whole life. No, that wasn't true, was it? He'd done some good in the classroom, hadn't he? Just the other day, Elizabeth Hamdy had come up to him in the parking lot, desperately wanting to talk. There were a few of them every year. Wasn't that right? Kids who'd connected with him. He got a letter or two every month from a former student, thanking him for something he'd said or done in helping them get into college. What about that Jean La Roche? The Haitian kid from a family of eleven, another one whose mother worked two jobs and had only two sets of clothes to send him to school in. David had helped him get into SUNY at Purchase, called the admissions officer over and over until he'd memorized the number, and now the kid was going on to Cornell Medical School. Didn't that count for something? And there was Arthur himself, a beautiful child, and David at least contributed half his genetic material. But maybe that was as far as he should go. Maybe the heroic thing to do would be to disappear before he gave the boy any more sad memories. Maybe a real man would end it all, he thought drunkenly.

No, he couldn't consider suicide, that was the coward's way out. On the other hand, why not? There were some pills in the house and enough booze left to wash them down. He could end it all and leave a note saying he didn't do any of the things they said he had and he couldn't live with the lies. Who would argue with a dead man? It would be clean and final and it would be over all at once. Yes. Papa himself did it. Hemingway in Idaho. Holed up in Ketchum with a shotgun to his head, sure the FBI had him surrounded.

And Hemingway was merely delusional. The FBI really *did* have David surrounded. He thought of Robert Jordan at the end of *For Whom the Bell Tolls*. His body broken, his heart beating against the pine needle floor of the forest, trying to hold on to himself and his submachine gun as he waited for the fascist troops to descend, trying to decide whether to finish himself off before they arrived. Oh, let them come. Let them come. Stop that, David told himself. You're acting badly. You're drunk. You should be good at this. You should. You should be good at something. You should be good at least at ending things. That way you can keep it under your own control. A man should be able to complete something.

He went into the bedroom and found one of the duffel bags of his mother's things that Ralph and Judah had forced the FBI to give back. She had a three-year-old Valium prescription and several dresses wrapped in plastic from the dry cleaner. It would be easy. Taking the pills, finishing the gin, and wrapping plastic around his head. Lying there with his heart beating against the bare parquet floor. Let them come, let them come. He opened the pill bottle, finished the gin, and sat on the end of his bed facing the window. Waiting for night to fall and the television reporters' klieg lights to rise.

He woke up perhaps six hours later with the phone ringing. He stumbled, fell, and hit his head on the end of the night table, trying to pick it up.

"David, I think you better come to the hospital right away," Renee said in a preternaturally calm, anesthetized voice. "Arthur needs you."

41

"Put the tape in! Put the tape in!" Dr. Ahmed was shouting when Nasser arrived at the 23rd Street apartment with another bag of fertilizer after Friday midday congregational prayers. "Show him what he missed!"

Youssef went over to the VCR and slid in a cassette. The screen went black for a second and then the CNN emblem appeared. The image wavered, blurred, and then coalesced into something familiar: scenes from a bombing. A device had exploded in a Jerusalem shopping mall earlier in the day and an announcer was saying 147 people were dead. There were overturned fruit stands, young girls in Spice Girls T-shirts with shredded bloody faces crying out in confusion, a pregnant woman with both her legs blown off, a man on a stretcher with half his face gone, smashed watermelons on the ground. Bearded ambulance workers in yarmulkes and rubber gloves scurried by, collecting limbs and pieces of skin for burial.

"This is Mehdi!" The doctor cried out, limping over and pointing at the screen. "This is totally and completely Mehdi!"

"Who's Mehdi?" Nasser looked at Youssef.

"Mehdi is the doctor's friend from back home," the Great Bear muttered, as he sat on the couch drinking orange juice straight from the carton. "They did many operations together. Then a lab blew up and Mehdi's brother got killed. And after that, Mehdi gets stronger and no one wants to work with the doctor anymore."

"This is what we should be doing!" The doctor slapped the top of the TV. "This is exactly what we should be doing! We should have bodies lying in the streets right this very second. Mehdi is probably laughing at me back home."

Nasser stepped back a little, changing his perspective. Ahmed seemed anxious all of a sudden. And for the first time, Nasser saw they had something human in common. The doctor was a man with something to prove too.

"It's the second time they bomb this mall in two weeks!" The doctor thrust his hands into his pockets and began limping around the room. "And what are we doing? Talking and talking and talking. This is not *jihad*, this is a talk show. A week I've been here and what have we accomplished? Nothing! We sit around watching television and talking. I am working with a bunch of women!"

Though he was far bigger, Youssef seemed to cower a little from the doctor's fury. Nasser was beginning to notice a sharpening of differences between them. Youssef was becoming lax and logy, as if he'd eaten too many American cheeseburgers, while Dr. Ahmed was wired and slithery, looking for a place to throw more sparks. Instead of inspiring the Great Bear with his righteous fury, though, he just seemed to be relieving him of the pressure to create all the violence by himself.

Nasser set down the fifty-pound bag of fertilizer which he'd just bought in Forest Hills. "What else do you want us to do, sheik?" he said defensively. "Every day, we are out, buying material and preparing. Praying. Getting ready to fight."

"We have to act. We have to act. I am going crazy with the sitting around." Again, the doctor was doing everything twice as fast as he needed to: scratching his beard, gritting his teeth, blinking his eyes as though he was transmitting in furious Morse code.

In the meantime, the picture had changed on the TV screen; it showed an old man lying on the ground with his guts sliding out while his wife screamed in horror.

"So how much material do we have for the *hadduta?*" asked Dr. Ahmed, snapping his fingers in Youssef's face.

Youssef flinched and read what was written on the side of the fertilizer bag. "Well, this has a nitro hydrogen content of thirty-seven percent, so with what we have already it's enough for one big bomb or three smaller ones." He took a sniff inside and then closed the bag. "But we still need to buy diesel fuel and I need to start making the detonators. Also, I'm trying to get hydrogen compressors from Jersey City to use as boosters, and we're very low on money . . ."

"Enough—we should decide what to do immediately." Dr. Ahmed pulled on his beard, one hand after the other, as if he were trying to lengthen it. "The imam said keep it simple, so we keep it simple. I've been thinking. We hit three targets simultaneously, all before Ramadan. I'm thinking maybe to do it in two weeks, before Mehdi acts again."

Nasser froze for a second, wondering if he had anything else he needed to do in that time. Any place he had to be. But then the sourness rose in his throat and he remembered that he'd wound up here because everything else in his life had collapsed. "So what do we do?"

"While you were out, we discussed two possibilities." The doctor stopped pulling his beard and walked toward the TV screen, as if drawn by magnetic force. "Since soon will be the holidays, we're thinking one of the targets should be a department store." He rested his hand on top of the set. "One of the kind they're so proud of. The Macy's or the Bloomingdale's. Jews dead everywhere."

Youssef nodded and started playing with one of the kitchen timers he'd bought earlier that day in Connecticut. "It's a simple idea," he said, setting it ticking. "Lots of people around, not much security. We go in on the first floor and boom! Out go the store windows. People stampeding each other for the exits. Blood and body parts all over the clothes and jewelry."

"Or even better, we put it in a van on the street outside the store and kill all the tourists and passersby," Dr. Ahmed suggested.

Nasser sat down and tried to conjure the picture in his mind. But of course, the only image he had of the *hadduta* he'd planted was what he'd seen on the TV news. He'd missed the actual explosion.

"The second one is easy too," Dr. Ahmed continued. "We just put a *hadduta* in the middle of Grand Central or Penn Station at rush hour. A nail bomb, maybe. Like the one we made in Peshawar." He took the timer from Youssef. "It kills everyone within a hundred and fifty feet. They'll be dead before they can run."

Nasser had nothing to compare this scene with either. "So what's the last one?" he asked.

He realized he was getting tense and prickly, listening to persistent ticking, like an insect in his ear. Yes, he wanted to be part of this, to play his role in *jihad*. But a small part of him was still terrified.

"What about inside one of the subway trains?" Youssef was asking. "The containment would make the blast much bigger and disrupt service for hours."

"No, it's too much like Grand Central." The doctor waved his hand, dismissively. "We need something distinctive, to send a message."

"What about one of the bridges or the tunnels, like we said before?"

"Too impractical." Dr. Ahmed shook his head in regret. "I've explored the possibilities and they won't work with what we have."

"The floor of the Stock Exchange?"

"Too much security, I think." Ahmed said, giving it a moment's consideration. "And it might be popular around some parts of this country."

"What about the school again?" Nasser said suddenly as the timer went off and its ringing made his eardrums shiver.

The two older men turned to face him, their stares like harsh spotlights. He immediately wanted to take back what he'd said, but knew it was too late.

"Again with the school!" Youssef laughed contemptuously. "You're making this too personal! This is not about Nasser. This is about *jihad*."

But the doctor was examining him with a more refined kind of interest. "Why do you bring it up again?"

"I don't know," Nasser mumbled, staring down at his feet.

But the truth was that it had been in the back of his mind since the day at the garden store in Borough Park. He'd never stopped brooding about the mistake at the school bus and Mr. Fitzgerald. Perhaps trying again was the only way he could both redeem himself and stop the teacher from dishonoring his sister.

"How would you get back in the school?" Dr. Ahmed, clearly intrigued, limped over to sit next to him. "This was disaster last time."

"I know." Nasser retreated back into himself for a moment, chewing a cuticle and remembering the failure, the sense of worthlessness. If he wasn't a warrior, what was he? He'd gone too far to go back to the way he was, a lost boy playing pinball. He had to will himself into a state of confidence. "This time I'll say I'm reapplying to come back and graduate, so I have to talk to the principal."

Youssef wasn't convinced. "What if you run into this teacher again, the one who knows you?" he asked, grimacing and belching. "What will you do then?"

"Mr. Fitzgerald?" The corners of Nasser's mouth turned down. "I put the bomb right in his hands and run away. This would be perfectly all right."

The others started chuckling and he felt his ears burn. "No, you are getting laughing and I am getting serious," he said indignantly. "If he gets hurt by the *hadduta*, it's completely okay. Then they'll know they were wrong about him and it's another thing for them to feel insecure about. They'll realize they have no idea what's really going on in the world."

Ahmed and Youssef stopped laughing and regarded each other

thoughtfully, each raising a thumb and then lowering it, weighing the decision. For a few seconds, Nasser felt like he had probably said too much.

"You know, it's not a bad idea," Dr. Ahmed said finally. "To go back to the same place again, like Mehdi does back home? This could be tremendous, to do it in the United States. It shows them we can hit them anytime, anywhere we want. They can never feel safe."

"I still don't know if I like it." Youssef huffed and picked up his orange juice carton, not wanting to look at Nasser. "Too many things could go wrong again."

"Nothing will go wrong this time." Dr. Ahmed leaned close to Nasser, suddenly wolf-like and intense. "You get inside the school building. You bring the *hadduta* to where it belongs, maybe the lunchroom or a classroom, and then that's it."

"Still, I don't know if it's okay." Youssef sulked. "If the plan didn't work the first time, maybe it's God's will. Shouldn't we ask the imam if this is permissible, to go back to the same target?"

But this part of the conversation barely registered with Nasser. He was distracted by the television again. The camera showed a young bearded man lying dead near a jewelry store, half-covered in orange tarp with the top part of his body mysteriously intact. The announcer identified him as the suicide bomber. Two young Israeli soldiers stood guard over him with their Uzis raised, as if they expected him to spring back to life and attack them at any moment.

Nasser held his breath, taking in the image. The young bomber seemed strangely calm in death. What kind of courage must it have taken to stand there, with the bomb ticking, knowing everything was about to end? What must his family be thinking? Would they understand what he'd done? Would they be proud at his martyr's funeral?

"Don't worry about the imam," said the doctor. "I'm sure he'll give us permission. Now let's go pray."

42

Poisonously hungover, eyes bloodshot, pupils dilated, guts on fire, and balance seriously questionable, David somehow got himself into a cab and made it to the hospital in twenty minutes.

He found the waiting room for the ER full of stupefied, devastated people watching the Psychic Friends Network on the TV. The nurse at the registration desk was a round, olive-skinned woman with bright-red blemishes and a tight, surly mouth.

"I'm here to see Arthur Fitzgerald." David leaned on the glass partition, feeling the heavy thump of his heart against his sternum.

She shuffled some papers and tapped some computer keys. "What are you, a relative?"

"Yeah, I'm his father."

"His father's already here." She reached for a ringing phone. "Ain't nobody else allowed back."

His father's already here? David stared at the smudged glass for several seconds, but there was no reflection. Was this it? Was this the final stage of dissociation? That not only was there a free-floating media image of himself that he didn't recognize, but there was an actual person running around with his name? He waited until the nurse got off the phone.

"What do you mean, 'his father's already here'?" he said angrily. "I'm the only father he has."

"Well, whose name is on the insurance?"

"Mine, goddamn it." He was perhaps two or three muscle movements away from breaking the glass and grabbing her by the throat. "It's my insurance plan. I have it through the school system."

She turned and shouted something to a woman sitting behind her. Then she buzzed him in.

"Is he all right?" David realized his hands were shaking as he came through the metal door and the quality of the air changed. "Is my son all right?"

The nurse barely looked up from her keyboard. "You're going to have to speak to the doctor on that," she said, gesturing toward a corridor on the left. "He's in Room A-121."

David headed down the scuffed hall, past bodies on gurneys, old men hanging on to IV poles, grotesque and desperate scenes of cutting and transfusing glimpsed through open doorways. A harsh antiseptic smell made his insides squeeze together. Okay, God, let's make a deal.

He found Room A-121 on the left side of the hall and went in. Arthur was sitting calmly on an examination table with his legs dangling over the side and a white nebulizer mask over his nose and mouth.

"Hey, Daddy." His voice was muffled. "It was the cloud again."

Renee and Anton were standing there talking to a nurse, a long-faced woman in papery green clothes.

"What the hell happened?" David asked.

"I had a fight." The boy smiled with his eyes.

David stared at him blankly. Arthur fighting? It was one of those images that was hard to visualize, like a Greenwich crack den or a riotous Jesuit.

"Oh, David, I'm so sorry." Renee came to him, her eyes smeared with mascara and her cheeks sunken.

"Will somebody tell me what's going on?" he said, looking over her head, not bothering to see if she was apologizing for the newspaper story or Arthur being in the hospital.

His eyes fell on Anton, who just hunched his coat-hanger shoulders and tossed his long black hair. "Hey, don't look at me, man," he said. "He's here because of *you*."

"What?" Instinct made David raise his fist.

Anton held up his hands, as if he was staying out of it. "You're the one in the newspaper."

Arthur, picking up on the conflict, began coughing and wheezing into his mask.

"All right, all of you, out of here." The nurse stepped between the three of them, her face etched in bitter sleeplessness. "Give us two minutes and then you can knock yourselves out."

"Just tell me if my son's okay," David said, his eyes returning to Arthur.

"He's fine." The nurse was pushing all three of them out the door. "And he'll be even finer if you get out of here."

They moved out into the corridor and took up positions near an emaciated gray-toned man with an IV pole, who looked like a wire sculpture in an open-backed hospital gown.

"What happened?" said David.

"It was nothing." Renee wiped her eyes and studied her sandaled feet. "He had a little fight at school."

Through the doorway, Arthur smiled and waved to his father. David tried to smile back but his face felt heavy and numb.

"A fight put him in the hospital?"

"Well, he had a little asthma attack in the middle of it." She stood on her toes and tensed up, as if he were about to start screaming at her.

"Oh God." David put a hand to his forehead, struggling for civility and sobriety. "What did he have a fight about?"

"You."

"Me?"

"Another boy was picking on him in the yard." She bum-rushed the words, trying to get through them. "Something to do with the story in today's paper. The other kid said you were a bad guy and Arthur hit him. Okay?"

"Okay. Okay." David closed his eyes. "I got it."

All at once, the falling that had been going on all day stopped. He felt something turning over inside him. His son was having to fight to defend him in the schoolyard. Finally, he knew he'd hit bottom and it was time to start climbing up.

"So what does the doctor say?" he asked, slowly beginning to rearrange himself, hitching up his pants and tucking in his shirt. "Does Arthur have to stay overnight?"

"They gave him a shot of Ventolin and they think I can take him home." She started to reach for David's hand, but then caught herself and left her fingers hanging in the air.

"Well, nobody asked me, but . . ." Anton interrupted with a lazy drawl. "Maybe it'd be better if everybody just cooled it and tried to change the atmosphere a little."

"What's that supposed to mean?" David turned on him, seeing at last a place to put all his anger.

"I mean, you should go home." Anton fussed with a black beret in his hands. "Renee is stressed out, Arthur's stressed out, and I'm stressed out. It creates an atmosphere. So maybe you should make yourself scarce awhile. Chill. Give us some space. Let the pot simmer. Take two aspirin, and call back in the morning."

"What are you, the king of clichés?"

Anton puckered his purplish, slightly oversized lips. "You know, I can see where he gets it from now," he said.

"You can see where who gets what from?"

"Arthur. That little way he has."

David turned on him. "You got a problem with my son?"

"No, man." Anton stepped back. "I'm just saying he needs a lot of attention. That's all."

"He's seven years old."

"Okay." Anton said in a mopey voice. "I understand. I'm just saying sometimes you can spoil a kid by giving him too much attention."

"You think he fakes having asthma?"

"No, man . . . I don't know." Anton toyed with his Navajo bracelet again. "I just . . . never mind . . ."

The man was a child himself, David realized. He wasn't going to help Renee out with Arthur.

"Anton, I'd like to have a few words with my wife," he said, resisting the urge to slap the taller man.

Anton looked back and forth between Renee and the man with the IV pole, not so much protective as worried about a scene. "Is that cool?"

"Yeah, let us be. I'll give a shout."

Anton walked down the hall, miming a saxophone and singing cocktail scat to himself: "*Bwada-dee-dum-dum-bwada-dum-dum-dum . . .*"

David glared after him, shaking his head. "What do you see in him, anyway?" he murmured.

"I don't know." Renee dabbed her eyes with a tissue. "Maybe I thought he could help me get over myself."

"And has he?" David asked.

"Not exactly." She touched the dent she'd made in the middle of her lip. "I don't seem any better to you, do I?"

"Is that why you said all those things about me to the newspaper girl?"

She shut her eyes tight. "David, I don't know why I did that. I'm so sorry. She just came up to me and started talking and I needed someone to talk to, because of all the pressure I've been under with the judge, and Arthur, and the FBI, and Anton and—" She stopped mid-rant and cringed. "I don't know. The words just came out angrier than I meant them to. I mean, I knew what I was doing, but I didn't know. Do you understand? The words kept coming and she kept listening. She seemed so nice and I . . ." She touched the side of her face. "I guess I got out of hand again, didn't I?"

"I guess you did." David stared down at the frayed cuffs of her jeans, trying to sort through fury, sympathy, and anxiety.

A gurney came rattling down the hall carrying a hairless old man on a ventilator, with a Jamaican nurse and a Filipino doctor arguing on either side of him.

"Look, Renee, we can't—I mean, *I* can't allow this to happen," David said, fighting down the vodka sickness and the waves of exhaustion. He could still feel the dampness in his bones from last night's rain.

"What?" She looked over her shoulder, as if someone had just tapped her on it.

"I'm going to have to . . . *going to have to*." He stopped, forcing the words to take on shape and muscle in his mind. "*Just get through this*. Okay? I have to do it for Arthur's sake and for my sake. Understand? If you're there when I come out the other side: great. If you're not, then I guess that will have to be okay too."

"What do you mean, if I'm not there?" She looked scared.

But he was already moving past her, into Room A-121. He was reaching back down into himself, trying to find that core of solidness again. The one he'd first felt when he was a boy, trying to grow into his oversized body. He'd always been too big to hit anybody back at school, so he'd just learned to *take it*. To remain in that secure place within himself. Now it was time to go back there.

Arthur was still sitting on the examining table, but the nebulizer mask was off. On seeing him, David felt himself becoming more vivid. The little pulse next to his heart. He knew there was a reason he hadn't gotten around to killing himself today.

"Daddy, the cloud almost got me."

"The cloud?" David sat down beside him on the table, still a little green and churned up inside.

"The bad cloud. The one from my dreams."

Oh yes, the nightmare cloud that always appeared after he'd seen his parents fighting.

"I was fighting with Maxwell and then the bad cloud came in my chest and I couldn't breathe."

"Okay. Okay." David put his arm around the boy and pulled him close, like he was pulling him to shore. "The cloud almost got me too."

"What?"

"It's all right. I've got you now. I've got you."

43

After last night's cold snap and rain, the weather had warmed up again, a final gasp of Indian summer. And from the way the sun was roaming on top of the water and the wind was carrying the carousel music up the Coney Island boardwalk, Elizabeth could tell this was going to be an American day.

There were days she felt more Arab. But this Saturday—as she put on a pair of denim cut-offs, a black tank top, and her Rollerblades and went skating down the boardwalk with her friend Merry Tyrone—she felt more American.

"Come on, girlfriend, shake that thang," said Merry, keeping pace with her in a blue Spandex tank top and tight navy shorts with the Adidas stripes down the sides. "Put some rhythm into it."

Elizabeth wobbled a little, hoping none of her family would see her like this. She'd had it with Nasser and the insanity of him going through her room. It made her just want to shuck off all the tradition, all the relatives, all the history, all the pressure of being part of an oppressed people without a real homeland. *Enough already*. She just wanted to skate.

She pushed off with her right leg and then her left, feeling the tendons and muscles stretch as she sailed past the hot dog stands and the old burned-down Dreamland amusement park, its disused Thunderbolt roller coaster shrouded in moss and ivy. The sun played lightly on her skin, making her shoulders shine and her arms look golden. She was wearing the new pads that Nasser had bought her but not the helmet. It was too small and it made her feel like she was suffocating. Besides, she liked having her hair in the salty breeze. She wanted the sensation of things rolling off her today.

"Yo, what about Mr. Fitz?" Merry said.

"I know. Did they arrest him yet?"

"No, but everybody's buggin' out about it. None of us knew he was, like, the *mad bomber* an' shit. So now, I'm like, thinking like a detective, you know. Going back over things he said in class. Re-*examining*. I always thought there was something a little *out* about him. What was that shit he wrote on the blackboard the other day? To know yourself is the final horror. Now we know *why*."

"It was, 'To be afraid of oneself is the last horror,' " Elizabeth corrected her. "That's not at all the same thing. He was being a teacher."

"If you say so."

Elizabeth pushed off hard on her right leg, hearing the roar of the herringbone boards under her skates as seagulls scattered from her path. "I don't believe what they said about him in the paper anyway."

"You liked him. Right?" Merry was grinning at her.

"What you talkin' about, girl?" Elizabeth was trying out that homegirl speak; it never sounded right coming out of her mouth.

"You were sweet on him, Mr. Fitz. I seen the way you looked at him sometimes."

"He's my teacher. What's up with that? Why's everybody think I've got something going on with him? It's just because he takes me seriously."

She passed through scents of perfume and cigarette smoke, thinking about him. Mr. Fitzgerald. It still made no sense to her, the accusation. He never seemed that strange in class, not like they said in the papers and on television. He just liked to push things a little. In fact, she'd enjoyed that about him. The way he could pull ideas out of you that you didn't know you had. Not like her other teachers, declaiming the same boring lessons from the same books in the same can't-be-bothered voices. When Mr. Fitzgerald talked, the words moved around in your head. Of course, he'd touched her, lightly, that day in the parking lot. But somehow she hadn't minded.

"Yeah, I know what that's about," Merry was saying. "You got that *older man thang* going on with him."

"I do not."

"Yeah, that's what you say. But you thinking about that mad bomber love."

The carousel music grew louder. Elizabeth pushed off on her left leg as they approached the entrance to the Aquarium. Four boys from school were standing there, some thirty yards away, smoking blunts and hoisting forties. One of them was that cute Dominican guy, Obstreperous Q, with the shaved head and the earring, and another was Ray-Za with the funky hair and the gangsta-style, whom Merry dated sometimes.

"Speaking of bad boys," said Merry, skating on ahead. "Excuse me a minute. I have to *communicate* with this *fine* young Nubian."

Elizabeth hung back a little, watching Merry's hips do the side-to-side swivel and wondering what it would like to be so free and easy with your body. To be so relaxed. To be a hot American babe, instead of a demure Arab girl. To have men stare at you, enthralled. She thought she'd seen Mr. Fitzgerald look at her that way once or twice. And why not? Why should she be different from anyone else? She had more in common with kids here than she did with her crazy brother from Bethlehem. She was raised in America, she had an American stepmother, she read American books, had American thoughts. But something wouldn't let her go all the way over to that side. The one night she'd tried hanging out on a street corner, drinking beer with Merry and a couple of other girls from school, she'd found herself getting restless and uncomfortable, liking the idea of what she was doing, but hating the actual taste of it. With boys, it was the same. She'd look at a guy for weeks, fantasizing about the absolute coolness of being on a date with him. But if he dared to approach her, she'd shrink away in terror.

What was the matter with her? She was seventeen years old, a healthy American girl, with a good mind and a good body. A rockin' bod, as the other girls in the class would say. A slammin' bod. So what was holding her back? Why couldn't she play? In fact, why couldn't she do anything she wanted? She wasn't wrapped up in a veil in a Middle Eastern village somewhere, about to be bartered away in an arranged marriage. She had the run of the country—the open sea on her right, the arcades, merry-go-rounds, and everything beyond on her left. She didn't have to stay home until she got married, though that was what Nasser and her father would have liked. She could go away to college, maybe even to Boston, where Merry was probably headed next year. She could have her own life, her own career, she could marry who she wanted. She could even make her own mistakes.

She started picking up speed as she drew closer to Merry, who was already sweet-talking with the *boyz* by the Aquarium entrance. There was nothing for her to be afraid of, she told herself. She wanted them to see her, to see she was just like them, and maybe even to chase her if they had the nerve.

But as she zoomed past the crew, and heard Obstreperous Q call out, "Ooow mama, I like it like that," she saw something that scared her. An old woman in a black head scarf feeding seagulls by the benches on her right. She couldn't see the woman's face, couldn't even tell if she was Arab, but for some reason, the thought came into her head that this was what her mother would have looked like. She turned, glancing back over her shoulder as she kept skating forward, twisting herself into a kinetic sculpture of confused emotions. She wanted this, she didn't want it. And so she tripped and fell.

44

Okay, this is who you are.

You are not a man who beats his wife. You are not a man who would ever hurt his child. You are a father and a teacher. That much you know for sure. It's a start. And you are not going to kill yourself. At least not yet.

Thus David Fitzgerald began trying to reassemble himself.

You are going to go on with your life. You are going to walk out of the apartment this morning. You are going to ignore the photographers on the sidewalk, yelling, "Hey, fuckface, look over here!" and "Hey, shithead, have you beaten your kid today?" to try to get a rise out of you. You will ignore the vicious animal gnawing at your insides and you will get on the subway, bury your face in *Darkness at Noon*, and start the long ride out to Coney Island. You are going to survive this somehow. You are not a victim. You are going to get back to being yourself, whoever that is.

You will show up at school for the first time in almost a week and you will not be embarrassed when Charisse, the sullen, spherical security guard, insists you go through the metal detector like a student when all the other teachers routinely step around it. You will go to the principal's office and you will ask to see Larry and you will not get upset when Michelle, his bitchy secretary, tells you that you'll have to wait most of the morning and gets on the phone with her crazy boyfriend. You will do this because you cannot continue to sit around the apartment waiting for further disaster to strike.

When Larry finally makes time to see you a few minutes before lunch, you will smile and grasp his hand warmly and try to summon up memories of when you were an eager young teacher. When Larry gives you a look of glacial seriousness, you won't be discouraged. You will ask for your job back.

"David, you have got to be kidding me," he will say. "Do you know what the people in the district superintendent's office and the Parents' Association will do if they even find out you've set foot in the school after what you've been accused of?"

You will remind him that no one has any legal standing to keep you from doing your job. You are yet to be charged with any crime, and though Ralph says that could change at any time, you still have your rights. You also have lawyers who are more than willing to sue the school if it comes to that. You will be making Larry very, very unhappy. When he tries to argue that you should be fired for not mentioning on your original application that you'd been arrested for stealing a car, you will point out that it happened when you were a juvenile and the record was sealed, so it can't be counted against you. You will cause his already waxy skin to turn slightly gray. You will make his hairline recede. You will make him reach for the Maalox. But this isn't your problem. You have been punished for a crime you didn't commit and you need to be made whole again. You have to re-apply to the world. The fact that you're still getting paid is irrelevant. A man is his work, and you need to work again.

A fighter fights, a writer writes, a teacher teaches. You need to get back in the classroom again, because it's the only place you've ever truly felt at home. But just as important, one of the kids may know who did the actual bombing. And in your heart, you know they're far more likely to tell you than a cop.

So you have to get back to work. It's impossible, Larry will tell you. The parents will go ballistic. Be reasonable. Take a reassignment back to the district office, he'll say. But that's not what you had in mind.

After going back and forth with him for ten minutes, you'll work out a compromise. College applications are due in a few weeks and someone has to review the students' essays with them. You will have some contact with the kids but it will be limited enough to keep everyone else satisfied. This seems like a fair alternative until the case is resolved. Until forces beyond your control determine whether you spend the rest of your life as a free man or a convict in a faraway prison, who gets to see his son maybe two or three times a year. But you will not think about that for now. You will try to get on with things. You are not a victim.

You will leave it to Larry to work out the details with the other administrators. It's not your concern who has to be stroked and who has to be bludgeoned. You just want to come back and find out who did this bombing. Hands will be shaken and eyes will be averted. You will walk out of there with a sense of purpose. You will still be scared and dreading every minute, for fear that you will suffocate, but you will put one foot in front of the other. You are going to live until you die. You are going to be a father to your son and a teacher to your students. You will have lunch at Nathan's down the street. Two dogs with relish, a large Coke, and those sublimely greasy fries. And for the first time in weeks, your food will taste decent.

45

With the bombing targets selected, Nasser, Youssef, and Dr. Ahmed arranged to have breakfast with the imam, Sheik Abdel Aziz Ayad, at the Skyview Diner in Bay Ridge.

The purpose, Nasser assumed, was to try to get some money and obtain blessings for each of their choices, especially since Youssef had expressed reservations about the school as a target. Getting permission was no easy matter, Nasser knew, for out of the literally thousands of imams in the tri-state area, almost none would sanction acts of violence against innocent people.

"I would like plain pancakes with no butter on the side," the imam told the waitress in English with his crooked smile. "And please have them wipe the grill for me, so my food doesn't touch any of the pork."

"Yes, keep my eggs away from the bacon too," chimed in the Great Bear, who was wedged into the booth next to the imam and across from the doctor and Nasser. "I only eat what's *halal*."

Nasser noticed the bigger man trying to puff himself up in front of the imam. Things had changed in their little constellation lately. Nasser sensed that he'd elevated himself to a new level of respect in Dr. Ahmed's eyes by suggesting they bomb the school again, while Youssef had forfeited some status with his hesitation.

It was strange about the Great Bear. Once he'd appeared so

masculine and dominating to Nasser. But now he was just another follower. Nasser realized the weakness must have been there all along—with the hamburgers and the American videos and the muscle magazines. Despite his size, Youssef was ready to go wherever a strong wind pushed him.

Nasser and the doctor both ordered plain toast, and the waitress, a tired busty blond, took their menus and headed back to the kitchen.

"So!" The imam smiled, switching back to Arabic and flashing the mischievous grin that had captivated Nasser at their last meeting. "What are my brothers up to?"

Dr. Ahmed leaned across the Sweet'n Low packets conspiratorially, being a little too obvious, Nasser thought. "We have three questions we've been discussing among ourselves, sheik."

"Good!"

Nasser looked around, trying to make sure no one was eavesdropping. From sharing an apartment with the doctor, he'd begun to notice the little man was swinging back and forth between fits of unfounded paranoia and moments of troubling heedlessness.

"I want to ask about the schools they have in this country." The doctor coughed and cleared his throat. "What do you think of the way the children are taught here?"

"This is surely an affront to God." The imam folded his hands and looked thoughtful.

"Good. Then it would not be *haram* for someone to attack such a place again, right?

The doctor coughed again and Nasser was reminded he'd smelled burning tobacco through the bathroom door last night. Did Ahmed have a secret vice?

The imam looked ill at ease. "Well, I would rather not say exactly—"

"It's all right, I understand." Dr. Ahmed cut him off and looked around. "There may be other ears here."

"Exactly," said the imam, receiving a cup of coffee from the passing waitress.

Nasser felt the vinyl seat cushion move under him as Dr. Ahmed fidgeted to his right. Was this all they needed? Had the imam really sanctioned bombing the school again, or had he just evaded the subject entirely?

Dr. Ahmed was undeterred. "There's something else I have to ask you," he said, lowering his voice so the imam had to lean across the table to hear him. "Even more serious."

"Go ahead." The imam's eyes twinkled.

Okay, so now he's going to ask about the other targets. Nasser picked up a glass of water and then put it down quickly, worried his shaking hands would betray his mood.

But the doctor suddenly veered in another direction. "The other day, there was a *shaheen*—a martyr—in Jerusalem," he said quietly. "One who blows himself up and kills these so-called innocents. We need to know if such a thing is against *sharia*, the laws of Islam."

The question stunned Nasser. Nothing had been said about a suicide bombing.

The imam's smile fell away. "Well, this is very serious indeed," he said, with raised eyebrows and a turned-down mouth. "The Holy Book is very specific that such things are strictly *haram*. Suicides are condemned, and so are ones who would kill innocent women and children."

"Oh?" Dr. Ahmed shot Youssef a questioning glance to the side of the imam.

"However." The imam paused and sipped his coffee. "There *is* a long, honorable tradition of martyrs. And remember: we are living through a time of Holy War. And in a war, it is not always possible to live exactly by the Book."

Oh my God. Nasser pitched his head forward into his hands. "Why are we even talking this way?" he asked the others. "No one has talked of doing such a thing here."

Silence fell over the table as the waitress brought the imam's pancakes, Youssef's scrambled eggs, and plain toast for Nasser and

Dr. Ahmed. "There you go, guys," she said, heading back to the kitchen. "Give a whistle if you need anything else."

"Of course we're not talking about such things," Youssef hissed across the table at Nasser. "*Inte mej noon.* Are you crazy? We're just trying to find the limits we have to work within."

The limits? Nasser was completely confused now, but afraid to say anything, lest he appear weak-willed in front of the imam and lose his newfound status. He had thought they were supposed to be getting the blessing to bomb the school and the other locations. What was the point of going into all these abstractions if they weren't going to put them into action?

"We have one last question," said Dr. Ahmed. "It also has to do with limitations. We are limited by money. We have three operations we want to do and we're running low on funds. This is a terrible thing about living in this society. One always needs more. So we were hoping you could help us. For the sake of *jihad*."

"How much do you need?" The imam spread a small lake of syrup across his plate, dipped a chunk of pancake, and stuck it in the corner of his mouth.

The doctor checked with Youssef, eyeball-conferencing and leaving Nasser out of it. "Maybe five, six hundred dollars?"

The imam raised his chin and rested his hands on the table, chewing thoroughly. "*That* is a considerable commitment," he said after a minute. "Are you sure the time is right?"

The question seemed to shrink Dr. Ahmed a little. "I know it in my heart, sheik," he said quickly, as if he sensed his request was about to refused.

The imam turned to Nasser and smiled. "You hear this?" he said. "He knows it in his heart. This is splendid, isn't it?"

"Yes, it is."

Nasser realized this entire meeting had been a waste. They were going to leave this diner without getting any money or even a sanction to bomb the school. The idea of going forward without a blessing left him feeling profoundly unsettled, as did the question about the suicide bombing. He kept seeing the image of the martyr lying there on television, half-destroyed in front of the jewelry store. Why did the others ask about this?

"So if it is meant to be, and you work righteously and pray, God will make it easy for you," the imam told the three of them. "Now let's have breakfast."

46

The night before he returned to school and began the arduous task of reinventing himself and getting back his good name, David had reread *The Great Gatsby*.

Again, he was struck by the scene at the end where Gatsby's father pulls out a faded old book with his son's boyhood schedule and "General Resolves" for making himself into a better person printed on the inside.

Exactly, thought David. He needed his own list of resolves:

1. Most important. Reestablish contact with your students. One of them may have seen something or heard something about the bombing.

2. Get people around the neighborhood to talk to you and find out what they might have seen.

3. Fight back. Have the lawyers issue more vigorous denials of the stories that have appeared so far in the press. And think about making an appearance yourself. People may need to see you to believe you're not a monster.

4. Publicly demand the FBI put up or shut up about arresting you.

5. Assume if the first four steps don't work, you were probably destined to be screwed anyway.

But as soon as he arrived at school the next morning, he realized he hadn't done enough to prepare himself. Just as Larry had predicted, some of the parents went nuts, showing up with with placards and bullhorns, protesting that an alleged wife-beating, child-abusing terrorist was being allowed back in the building. WHAT ABOUT OUR CHILDREN'S RIGHTS! said one sign in electric-purple letters. Naturally, the press corps was out in force to record the debacle with their dense packs of microphones and cameras. David bulled past them as best he could, pausing to notice that same little black kid with the homemade press pass hanging around on the fringes.

Inside the building, the reception wasn't any warmer. Larry had assigned him to a dank, smallish basement office next to the cafeteria—actually a converted storage closet—jammed with video equipment, shelves of books, workmen's tools, and rolls of toilet paper. Squeezing himself in among the clutter, David felt like a character in a nineteenth-century novel, forced to dwell beneath the surface of respectable society.

For most of the morning, he sat idle, quietly burning, waiting for students to come see him, wishing he could do more to seek them out. But he knew if he was too aggressive and obvious about pushing his cause and asking questions, he'd give Larry an excuse to have him removed. Better to play it cool, at least initially.

Slowly they began to trickle in. Kevin Hardison came first. Instead of one of his alternating outfits with the Dollar Bill cap, he had on a brand-new, pressed, green-and-white-striped Oxford-style shirt with a silver stickpin in the collar and stylish khaki slacks.

"Hey, how you like my Gatsby look?" he said, slapping the novel down on David's desk defiantly.

"You read it?"

"I read it."

"And where'd you get the threads?" David took his feet out of the drawer, where they'd been resting.

"Don't ask," Kevin said darkly. "I got a new job for after school."

Probably grilling hot dogs at Nathan's, thought David. But still, how about that? The kid might not get into an Ivy League college, but he'd gotten something out of the book. It might have even inspired him to get a job. More than you could say for most readers.

"Here, I wanna give you something." Kevin dropped a wrinkled, coffee-stained business card into David's lap.

"What's this?"

David picked up the card and saw it had the name and phone number of a Court Street lawyer in the Heights.

"Myron Newman, attorney-at-law." Kevin touched his stickpin, which on closer inspection looked like something you'd win at an amusement park by throwing a ball at a clown's head. "He helped my cousin out last year, off a drug arrest. Got him probation when he was carrying like a gram of coke. I figure you could use a hand."

David fingered the ragged edge of the card, secretly touched not just by the boy's concern, but by his efforts to spiff himself up.

"Thank you, Kevin." He shook the boy's hand and decided not to mention that he already had lawyers.

"Now do I still have to write that paper for you?" Kevin leaned against the edge of the desk, flashing his monogrammed gold smile, looking to take advantage of the moment.

"Hell yeah," said David. "You're still in school, aren't you? Besides, you're gonna have to show them you can write if you want to get into CUNY."

He took a sample application out of a folder and gave it to Kevin, knowing he had to make at least a token effort to do the job he'd agreed to do.

"Yeah, i-ight." Kevin took the paper and pushed himself off the desk, accepting that he wasn't going to get over this time.

"Hey, Kevin, let me ask you something." David gave Myron Newman's card another look and then put it in his pocket. "You hear anything?"

" 'Bout what?"

"You know." David glanced out the door, checking for eavesdroppers. "About my case. About who really might have done the bombing."

"You didn't do it?" Kevin seemed genuinely surprised, his voice cracking a little and his gangly arms swinging.

"You thought I did?"

"Well, I didn't know. You were arrested before. I seen it in the paper."

"And you were going to help me anyway?" David wasn't sure whether to be pleased or alarmed.

"Hey, man. Half my family been locked up. It's rough out there." He studied the back of his hand, as if figuring out the moral algebra of growing up in a bad neighborhood. "Besides, you did that shit stealing cars when you were young and you grew up and got to be a teacher anyway. That's all right, man."

David shook his head. If he'd known students would take it so well, he would've owned up to being arrested years ago.

"Do me a favor, Kevin. Let me know if you hear anything."

The rest of the day didn't go as well.

"I will not serve this man."

Rosalyn, the cafeteria lady with the suave Clark Gable mustache, was glaring at him over a pot of soup and a vat of meatloaf that looked like a little buffalo squatting in a muddy swamp.

"What's the problem?" he asked.

"I have a seven-year-old grandchild," she said. "And I won't serve you. I don't give a damn what they do to me neither. They can fire my ass, far as I'm concerned. But they can't make me serve a man who'd do something *like that* to a child."

David reached across the counter and took the ladle to pour his own soup. The other teachers in line in front of him moved along, murmuring to one another, not acknowledging the awkwardness. Before—when he'd just been "the mad bomber"—people had a lurid interest in him, peeking out when they thought he wasn't looking. Now there was only outright revulsion.

He picked up his tray and took his ocean-sediment coffee and experimental-looking soup to an empty table in the green faculty lunchroom. Why would anyone join him? He'd been branded the worst man in the world. Given the choice, I'd stay away from me, he thought.

"Hey, how's the Underground Man?" Donna Vitale suddenly appeared across the table, sitting down and focusing her good eye on the left side of his face. She had an extra plate of meatloaf on her tray.

"Brooding and plotting. Larry send you over to make sure I'm not making another bomb or something?"

"No, I just wanted to make sure you were getting enough to eat." She slid the extra meatloaf across the table to him. "How's it going anyway?"

"Great. I've had two kids come to see me since eight-fifteen. And I caught one of them plagiarizing *The Gulag Archipelago* in his essay."

She laughed and her wild eye glimmered. "Well, that's original, at least."

"Not really. It was Yuri Ehrlich. He's from Moscow. They may do it all the time over there. The sad thing is, he's a bright kid. He just has this weird compulsion to get over on people."

"So what'd he say when you called him on it?"

David tried his coffee, but it was gritty and cold. "He said, 'Oh, who cares what you say? You are terrorist and child molester. No one will believe you.' "

"Well, what did you expect?"

"I don't know." He put down his cup, surprised but not really displeased by her sharpness. "I guess I just wanted to make contact again."

He didn't dare tell her his ulterior motive for talking to them.

"Perhaps it's a little too soon to expect them to come flooding in to see me," he said.

"Yeah. *Perhaps*. Give me a break. They think you're a wife-beater who tried to blast them to Far Rockaway. Maybe they have a little problem with that."

She was like a faceful of cold rain and he laughed, refreshed by her directness.

"So what am I supposed to do?" he said. "How can I win them back?"

"A little bit at a time." She looked in her handbag and took out a lipstick. "Just be around. Be yourself. You lost them when you let the cameras into your classroom, if you don't mind my saying so. That's when they started not to trust you. You've got to come back down to earth. Hang out a little. Eventually they'll get the idea you're not the Terror Teacher and start talking to you again."

"Think so?"

"Well, either that or we could put bars on your office and make you part of the Sideshow by the Seashore."

She tied her straw-colored hair back into a ponytail. She wasn't conventionally beautiful, but there was a strong character to her face that made her more attractive every time he saw her.

He looked down at the slice of meatloaf, not sure if he wanted to try it or not. "I didn't do it, you know."

"What?"

"The things they're talking about. I don't know anything about bombs and I would never, ever hit my wife or my child. I'd cut my own hand off first."

He glanced around the lunchroom, aware the other teachers were watching them and then looking away.

"Yeah, I know."

She said it casually, as she closed her handbag. As if it was obvious. As if his world didn't depend on it.

"You know?"

"Yeah, sure. I know."

She smiled and the sides of her face creased up nicely. She was used to smiling. Not like Renee. In fact, she might be the anti-Renee. Whatever life had done to try to knock her down, she'd gotten back up again. He tried the meatloaf and found it only semi-indigestible.

"So." She stood up. "You want to have dinner?"

"You putting me on?"

"I figured you could use the company. Yes? No? Am I pushing too hard?"

"No, you're pushing about right."

"How's tomorrow night, my place?" she said.

"Fine. You're sure you don't mind having an accused terrorist over?"

"You bring the wine, I'll bring the rocket launcher."

He wanted to reach over and kiss one of her hands. Thank you, you wonderful woman. I was drowning, I was fucking drowning. She started to go back to the table where she'd been sitting.

"Hey, Donna."

She paused, hands on hips. "Sounds like a fifties song," she said. "What is it?"

"You haven't heard anything, have you? About what happened to the bus?"

She screwed up her mouth and half-closed her good eye. "Don't you think I might have gotten around to mentioning that before?"

"Yeah, of course." He pawed the air uselessly. "You're right."

"Hang in there, David." She looked back, making sure he was still in one piece. "And try not to get arrested before tomorrow night. I'd hate to buy a lot of food and have it all go to waste."

47

With the imam turning down their request for funds, Nasser worked a double shift the next day to try to make up the difference. As he finished up at eight o'clock and walked back into the American Way Car Service on Flatbush Avenue, he saw Bilal, the plump Pakistani dispatcher, talking to a big-shouldered blond man with a large, round head and a mustache.

"Ah, here he is." Bilal pointed at Nasser with his cigar. "I told you he'd be back soon."

The blond man turned and fixed Nasser with a direct, appraising stare.

"What's going on?" Nasser backed up a step toward the door.

"This man wishes to speak to you." Bilal put the cigar in his mouth and went behind the counter to take radio calls.

"How you doin', Nasser?" The blond man stepped forward and took a billfold out of his front jeans pocket. "I'm Chris Calloway, with the Joint Task Force."

All the saliva in Nasser's mouth spontaneously evaporated.

Calloway showed him his detective's shield. "I'm just asking some questions about the bus bombing a couple of weeks ago."

"I don't know anything about that."

Nasser was suddenly aware of everyone in the dingy little storefront looking at him. The black lady on the couch reading *The*

Crying of Lot 49. The ragamuffins in bomber jackets playing pinball in the corner. Bilal behind the counter.

"It'll only take a couple of minutes," said Calloway, who had a nose that looked like it had been broken and reset several times. "Mind if we go somewhere?"

"I am in a hurry," said Nasser, pursing and unpursing his lips. He looked over at Bilal and realized he'd spoken too quickly. "But I'll answer anything you want to say. This was terrible, what happened."

"Okay, we don't need to make a soap opera out of it." Calloway smiled and put away the billfold. "We're just going through the whole list of former and current students from your school, making sure we don't miss anyone."

"Yes, I understand." Nasser heard his voice go high and wondered if the others noticed.

"First of all, have you been around the school lately?"

"No, I, ah, didn't make the graduation." He laughed and looked down at the floor. "I was not very good at the school. I am thinking maybe to go back sometime."

"So you haven't been there for how long?"

"About four years ago. That's when I stop going."

"So were you there the other day? For any reason?"

"Oh no." Had someone seen him? Perhaps he should have mentioned his meeting with Mr. Fitzgerald.

A beeper went off, and almost everyone in the place looked down at their waistbands.

"It's mine," said Calloway, gritting his teeth as he pressed a button and checked the number. "Fuck 'em, I'll have to call him back. Anyway. Where was I?"

"You ask about school," Nasser reminded him, trying to appear relaxed and eager to help. "But I haven't been there."

"So what have you been up to instead?"

"Oh, you know. Not very much. I drive my cab. I see my family. Pay my rent." He decided not to mention going to the mosque, lest that raise any suspicion.

"You involved in politics at all?"

"No. I don't know what you mean."

Was this detective playing with him? Nasser couldn't tell. One minute, Calloway seemed blunt and obvious, the next he was sharp and unreadable.

"I mean, do you belong to any political groups? There's nothing wrong with that."

"No, I'm not involved."

"You sure about that? You have any friends who are involved?"

"No, I don't get involved with the politics. I am happy where I am. I love America." Just saying the words made Nasser's gums hurt.

"Where you from anyway?"

"Ah. I am Jordanian." His eyes started to slide over to Bilal, hoping he wouldn't protest. "My family is from Amman."

"You're not Palestinian?"

"No. Absolutely not."

Calloway was looking at him more carefully. His mustache tight against his teeth and his eyes gliding over Nasser's face, suggesting the physical distance between the two of them could be closed very quickly. No, he wasn't playing. *He knew something.*

He touched various parts of his windbreaker, as if making sure he still had his gun and handcuffs with him. "Anyway, about the bombing," he said. "You have a sister, don't you?"

"Um, yes." Nasser tensed up, not expecting this angle. "My sister is very nice."

"Yeah, I know. One of the other detectives on the case interviewed her already."

"I thought it was the teacher who did this," Nasser spoke up, trying to divert him. "Mr. Fitzgerald."

"Yeah, well, that's what they say on the news. But we're still checking it out."

He's torturing me. He knows something. Mr. Fitzgerald must have told the agents about me, so they wouldn't suspect him anymore. Nasser licked his lips, trying not to panic. What if he knocked this man down and tried to grab his gun? Would he make it out the door alive?

"So do you or your sister know anyone who could have done this? Are there any friends of hers you don't like?"

"No, her friends are all right. I think."

The beeper went off again. "Oh, for crying out loud, will you let me do my fucking job?" Calloway rolled his eyes in aggravation. He didn't even bother checking the number this time. "I'm going to have to get back to you and follow up," he said to Nasser. "Understand?"

"Okay." Nasser clenched and unclenched his fists.

Perhaps he would get out of this after all.

"But just one more thing," said Calloway. "Where were *you* when the bomb went off anyway?"

"I wasn't at the school. I told you. I don't go there anymore."

"I know. But I asked, *where were you?*"

Had someone remembered seeing him? Nasser felt a gag reflex seize the top of his throat. He was trapped. If he said he'd been working, Calloway could simply turn around and ask Bilal, who kept a careful log book.

"I was with my sister," he said.

Oh merciful God, what have I done? The words had simply jumped out of him without permission, and he realized he'd made his worst mistake yet. He was through, for sure. The other detective had interviewed Elizabeth, but Nasser had never had a chance to find out everything that she'd said to him. They'd had the fight in the school parking lot before he could get the whole story. Now he was flailing around in the dark, with no idea if she'd given him an alibi or not.

"You were with your sister," Calloway repeated skeptically, reaching around to his back.

He was about to pull something out. A gun? Handcuffs? Nasser glanced toward the door and calculated that in three long strides he could make it to the street, but he'd probably have a bullet in his back. *Allahu akbar*. If he got through this conversation a free man, it would truly mean God had a special plan for him.

"Well, I'm going to have to check that out," said Calloway.

To Nasser's astonishment, the detective straightened up a little and brought his hand back empty, as if he'd just been touching the small of his back. God be praised! He wasn't going to be arrested.

"So if I go back to the detective's notes and talk to your sister, your story is going to hold up?" Calloway asked.

"Absolutely," said Nasser, knowing somehow he'd have to get Elizabeth to talk to him again. "I'm as sure of it as God's eternal grace and forgiveness."

"Whatever," said the detective, handing him a card with his phone number.

48

With no money to hire a private investigator, David moved on to Step Two of his general resolves, trying to question people around the neighborhood about anything suspicious they might have seen on the day of the bombing.

During his free periods in the middle of the next day, he went out onto Surf Avenue and talked to the Russian owner of a mattress store, a Yemenese guy selling Lotto tickets out of a bodega, kids from the O'Dwyer Gardens housing project, and the fierce, ambitious little men with their stalls full of bric-a-brac, broken radios, and secondhand polyester clothes by the subway entrance.

Naturally, none of them had seen anything.

At one o'clock, he took a break and bought lunch at the hot dog stand across the street, by the Boardwalk ramp. The guy behind the counter had a shaved head about the size of a shopping bag, big, hairy shoulders bulging out of a muscle shirt, and florid red-and-green tattoos flowing over almost every inch of his visible body, even spilling across his neck, face, and scalp.

"How's it going?" said David, ordering two dogs and a Coke.

He thought of how good a beer would taste right now. With panic and depression threatening to engulf him every minute, he needed something to keep the black dogs at bay.

"Can't complain." The tattooed man drew a soda from the tap

and handed it over. "Well, I could, but who would care? Nobody wants a two-hundred-and-fifty-pound whiner."

"I know what you mean." David took a sip and wiped his brow. He found himself sweating all the time these days.

The man turned his back to get the hot dogs; eagle's wings stretched down the backs of his arms.

"Hey, can I ask you something?" David said.

"Sure thing. My regular advice will cost you nothing. Advice requiring some thought will run you a buck and a half."

"Fair enough." David took the dogs in their little paper gondolas and squeezed mustard on them. "Were you working the day the bomb went off?"

"Yeah." The guy leaned forward on his meaty arms, and David saw he had a dragon's face tattooed on the top of his head. "Are you the guy?"

"Well, they say I'm the guy."

"Hey." The tattooed man offered his hand, with a blue snake on the palm. "One freak to another. We gotta stick together."

"I'm innocent," said David, shaking the hand. "Really. I am."

"I am too. But somebody keeps drawing these damn scary pictures on me."

David laughed, for the first time in months it felt like. "Where'd you get those anyway?"

"Ah." The tattooed man squinted at the sun, as if he were mad at it. "I used to work at Bobby Reynolds's sideshow down the street. But then it closed up. There's only room for the one Dick Zigun runs down here now. People don't want to pay to see freaks anymore. They get them for free on television."

"You got me." David high-fived him and drained his soda, the caffeine buzz lightening him up for a minute. "Sorry I put you out of business."

"Hey, the difference between you and me is I chose to be a freak." The man looked at David's empty cup. "You want a beer?"

"No, I'll only hate myself later. I gotta go back and talk to the kids some more."

The collapse into alcoholic defeatism had a definite appeal. A part of him wished he could just hang out on this sunny day, drinking and talking to his fellow outcast. It was a relief being out of the spotlight for a few minutes. But the dire business of his life kept coming back at him like a wrecking ball.

"By the way," he said, "you didn't see anybody or anything unusual the day of the bombing, did you?"

"Just crackheads, hookers, bearded ladies, and sword swallowers." The tattooed man shrugged and took David's money. "This is Coney Island, you know."

Back at the school, a few more students came to see him. Some just to gawk at the Amazing Terror Teacher of Coney Island, but others—perhaps prompted by Ralph Marcovicci's more heated denials of all the accusations on the news last night—wanted to help.

"I think it was the bitches," Seniqua Rollins said immediately after sitting down.

Almost six months pregnant, she could barely fit into the little office space with all the video equipment, books, and school supplies.

"What are you talking about?" asked David, leaning back to try to give her some room. With the two of them, it was like a couple of hippos in a phone booth.

"The bitches, man. The Right-to-Life bitches. They blew up the bus."

"What makes you say that?"

"I don't know. *Somebody* did it."

He looked at her belly, swelling under a blue-and-white shirt, and decided it showed a certain broad-mindedness to see beyond the politics of her own pregnancy, even if it was to venture into totally unsubstantiated conspiracy theory. More important, she took it for granted that he was innocent.

"Seniqua, what did the police ask you about the explosion?"

"Same-o-same-o. They wanted to know like what did you say

to us before. And how you didn't come into the class for twenty minutes. And why you would've done it."

"So what did you tell them?"

"I told 'em you saved my fuckin' life, and if they didn't like it they could kiss my ass *two times*."

"I appreciate that."

Something was rolling around just beyond his fingertips. An idea. An image that could save him. What was it? He heard the tramp of feet overhead and distant raised voices rehearsing for the School Sing in the auditorium upstairs.

"What about the book bag? Did they ask you about my book bag?"

"Uh-huh." She nodded. "They wanted to know if I saw you bring it on the bus."

"And you told them you did. Right?"

She nodded again. So much for having any wiggle room on that issue.

"Sorry," she said. "I'd a lied for you, but I can't afford to get myself jammed up with the police right now. I'm already on probation for a fight I had on the subway. Some bitch got slashed."

"I understand." He cracked his knuckles. "I wouldn't have wanted you to lie for me, anyway. But is there anything you didn't tell the police about the bombing that you want to tell me?"

"Nope. I'd a given it up by now. For real. I don't want nothing bad on my conscience when I'm about to have my baby."

She patted her stomach tenderly. He noticed her face suddenly looked much older, as if she were getting bum-rushed into adulthood by having a child so young.

"By the way," he said, still not wanting to intrude too much on the question of paternity. "What are you going to do about that baby? Are you going to get any help from the father?"

"No, I'll raise 'im up myself." She smirked defiantly. "None of those tiny-dick bitches I was with are worth a damn anyway."

During a lull in the next period, David walked upstairs and asked Michelle, the principal's secretary, if he could borrow the key to the bathroom across the hall. Instead of going there, though, he used one of the other keys on the ring to open the door to the records room down the corridor. He slid his maxed-out Visa card into the lock space to keep it from closing, returned the keys to Michelle, and then crept back into the file room when no one was looking.

He wanted to see for himself if there were students who had anything suspect in their disciplinary records. But as soon as he flipped on the light, he knew the search was doomed. The room was an ancient archive, with a permanent haze of brown dust particles and a smell like old horses. Even worse, he quickly discovered, as he pulled open cabinet drawers with his pulse racing, the student files were arranged not by year, but by alphabet, so the records went back to the turn of the century, when Coney Island was the honky-tonk jewel by the sea and Luna Park lit up the boardwalk. Joseph Adler, class of 1905, was suspended for a week for swearing in the hallways, said one file. Miriam Avery, class of 1952, was caught smoking in the ladies' room. The whole room was a shrine to more innocent days and not of much use to him.

He was about to reach for another file anyway when the door suddenly opened and Michelle came in.

"What do you think you're doing here?" she asked in a voice that would shrivel the erection on a chimp.

He slammed the drawer shut, nearly crushing his finger. "One of the kids needed a transcript to go with his application," he said lamely. "I didn't want to bother you."

"The next time you want something from this room, you ask me *in writing*. All right?" She fixed him with the death-ray glare of a bureaucrat violated. "Now outta here before I call security on you."

He went back downstairs, appropriately chastened and rattled. He didn't like what he'd just done. He was supposed to be protecting his kids, not trying to dig up dirt on them. But desperation was pushing him into strange, ugly corners.

Elizabeth Hamdy appeared in the doorway just toward the end of ninth period. She stood there for a few seconds, studying him as he corrected essays, not wanting to make her presence known. When he looked up, she backed away a step, like a fawn encountering a hunter in the forest.

"Come on in," he said. "I promise I won't bite."

She came in slowly and cautiously, all watchful eyes and books clutched to her chest.

"Have a seat. It's all right."

He looked over and saw Donna Vitale had stopped in the doorway behind her. They were supposed to have dinner tonight, but her presence at this moment seemed intrusive. He wondered if she had, in fact, been sent down to spy on him. She mouthed "Talk to you later," and moved on.

"So do you have something for me to read?" He turned back to Elizabeth, aware she'd been staring at him while he was distracted.

"Oh yes." She dropped her eyes quickly and deposited an immaculate five-page typescript onto his desk. "This is my paper."

He picked it up and read the heading "Crossing the River." The rest of the piece drew him in immediately. It was about her father crossing the Jordan. All the details she'd omitted in telling the story in class were there. How his family had been in the same village for four hundred years until the Israelis shelled it. How his old, enfeebled father begged him, a boy of sixteen, to take his brother and sister across the river to safety. How he could see the brown-and-white stones under the swift, shallow water as he carried his little sister on his back and held his brother's hand, with his childhood disappearing over his shoulder. How the prospect of the alien world ahead terrified him.

"This is beautiful," said David. "It's exquisitely written and brilliantly organized. There's only one problem with it."

"What?"

"You're not in it. I thought I was going to be reading your college essay."

Her knees turned inward slightly. "Well, I guess I haven't made up my mind about that yet."

"What do you mean?"

"I haven't decided if I'm applying or not."

"You've gotta be kidding me." He frowned and put her paper down. "You could go to any Ivy League school in the country. Why wouldn't you apply?"

"It's hard to explain." She wouldn't look at him. "I'm not sure if it's the right thing to go."

"This wouldn't be your brother influencing you, would it?"

He'd noticed she'd been high-strung and a little withdrawn ever since Nasser came by to talk to him a couple of weeks back. And after the fight in the parking lot, he could imagine the kind of pressure she was under at home.

"It's my whole family," she said. "We've been apart so much. I don't know if I should go away too."

"Well, it would be a shame if you missed this opportunity."

Again, she was staring down at the floor and sucking in her beautiful sculpted cheeks. He didn't blame her for being nervous and uncomfortable. It must have taken a certain kind of courage to come and talk to him. Or some type of desperation he didn't understand.

"I'm not sure if it's an opportunity I want. It's hard for me to explain. Sometimes I don't know if I want to be part of the modern world and forget all the traditions. I mean, I want to, but I *can't*. The traditions in my family, they're still part of me. Girls in Arab families aren't supposed to move away. They're supposed to make good marriages for their families."

"I didn't know you were so committed to that."

"I'm not." She played with the ends of her hair. "I mean, I don't know what I am. It's like I'm stuck in the middle of the river. Maybe you're right. Maybe it's Nasser who has me all mixed up."

"Look, would you just do me a favor?" he said. "Just try it out. You know how I'm always pushing you guys to experiment with new ideas in class? Just write the college essay and then decide. Lay it all out for yourself, so you can see the scenario and imagine what it would be like. Define who you are and what you want out of life. There's no future until you make it with your own hands."

Right. He could have been talking to himself. Define who you are in the world. Don't let them plow you under. Take a stand. Be a man. Save your own life, you stupid son of a bitch. No one else is going to do it for you.

"But how should I do it? What should I write about?"

"Try writing the rest of the family's story. Tell us what happened on the other side of the river."

She said nothing. She was watching him again, with that otherworldly look. A conversation going on behind the eyes. He remembered Nasser looking at him the same way. He had the same feeling of something urgent being left unsaid.

"Well, I'll think about it." She gathered her things and stood. He noticed she was leaving the paper on his desk.

"Elizabeth, can I ask you a question?"

She stopped in the doorway, twisting her hair again. "What?"

It was lovely hair, he noticed once more. A shame she'd kept it under a scarf for so long. Had she added a red streak to it?

"You didn't by any chance notice anything strange happening before the bus blew up?"

"Strange?" She was looking at him directly for the first time in the conversation.

"Yeah, there are all the stories and rumors about what really might have happened." He tried to smile.

A small line bisected her forehead and her mouth closed. Her knees were even more expressive; turning out and then in and then out again.

"I wasn't there."

He kept his eyes on her, listening to some kind of soft thrum in the distance. He wondered if it was the school's boiler or the sound of the ocean somehow carrying through the walls of the school.

"I know you weren't there," he said. "But I wondered if you'd heard anything."

"What makes you say that?" She dropped her hair and then picked it up again.

"I just remembered that you kept trying to talk to me the week after the bombing and I wondered if it was because you had something to tell me. I wasn't being very receptive at the time, was I?"

"No." Her mouth formed a small tense circle. "I mean, yes. It was nothing. Nothing I need to talk to you about anymore."

The thrum grew louder, but she was edging toward the door. "Are you sure?" he asked. "I'm ready to listen now."

"It's okay." She stepped out into the hall and started to disappear into a crowd of passing students. "I think I'm working it out on my own."

49

Elizabeth was coming up the path to the Avenue Z house a half hour later when she saw a husky, blond man with a light, almost translucent mustache waiting by the front door.

"Elizabeth Hamdy?" He took out a badge and showed it to her. "I'm Chris Calloway, from the Joint Terrorist Task Force. You mind if I come in, talk to you a minute?"

She was just getting over the queasiness of her conversation with Mr. Fitzgerald, and *now this*. She'd been looking forward to having a little time alone in the house with her thoughts and her diary.

"What's the matter?" she said, fumbling for her keys. "I already talked to a detective. Mr. Noonan, I think."

"Oh yeah, sure, I know." He smiled, waiting for her to unlock the door. "I just wanted to follow up."

"Follow up?"

He moved up behind her in the doorway, and she was aware of the neighbors peering at them from behind their window curtains. Those bitter, clannish people with their baggy eyes and soap opera afternoons, always looking for a reason to dislike the one Arab family on the street.

"Yeah, I'm just following up," Calloway said, a little steel glinting in his smile. "You understand. This is a huge case. Everybody's looking over everybody's shoulder. I just want to make sure we have all our details straight, for the files. In case my boss gets called on the carpet. You don't mind helping me out, do you?"

She felt her clothes tighten on her, like someone was pulling them from behind. "No, of course not."

She let him in and was immediately sorry she had. He strolled through the alcove and into the living room, taking in everything, revealing nothing. He looked like he might buy the house or just as easily trash it.

"The Dome of the Rock, right?" He stopped in front of the picture over the couch.

"You recognize it?" His presence in the room was like a bad smell, turning her stomach a little.

"I was in the reserves in the Middle East," he explained. "I spent some time in Israel, learned some of the history. It's the third holiest site for Muslims. Right?"

"Right." She composed a demure smile. "I guess the other detective who was here didn't know much about that."

"There's a lot Detective Noonan didn't know." He sat down on the couch, spreading his legs wide and putting his arms on the tops of the cushions, taking up as much room as possible.

"Can I get you a cup of tea?" she asked.

"No, I don't want to take up a lot of your time." He reclined like a sultan. "I just have a couple of questions."

"Okay. I want to help."

He looked at her for a long time without saying anything. Perhaps half a minute, as he continued to spread out. She became aware of different parts of her own body, squirming, itching, needing attention.

"So I talked to your brother," he said, crossing thick legs in stone-washed blue jeans. "Nasser."

"Oh yes?"

Her brother's name was like a little firecracker in her ear. This was going to be bad, she knew. Something upsetting. She paused and listened a moment, making sure her stepmother and half sisters hadn't stopped by the house for money on their way to go shopping at the Kings Highway mall. She didn't want them to be scared and confused by this strange man being here.

"Yes, we had a very interesting conversation." The detective flopped a thick beige notebook onto his lap and made a show of turning the pages. "He told me he was with you on the day the bomb went off at school."

"Oh." Elizabeth began to fuss with her hair, pulling two tendrils down in front of her eye and then letting them go, lest it appear she was trying to hide something. "Yeah, I guess that's true."

So that was why he was here. To find out about Nasser. No wonder her brother had been calling and leaving messages for her since last night. She tried to make herself relax, putting her hands in her front pockets and rising slightly on the balls of her feet.

"He took me shopping for a helmet and pads for my Rollerblading," she said. "It was close to my birthday."

She paused, remembering that day again. Nasser showing up late. The smoke from down at the beach. Traffic on the Belt Parkway. And then she couldn't make herself think about it anymore.

"Is that right?" Calloway casually flipped back two pages in his notebook and raised his eyebrows.

"Yes, I'm sure of it."

"Then why'd you tell Detective Noonan you stayed home with a headache that day?" he said suddenly.

She dropped back on her heels, caught off guard. "I . . ." Her eyes darted around, waiting for her mouth to come up with an explanation. "I guess I didn't want my teachers to know I was playing hooky."

Calloway sat up and focused, like a dog hearing the word *bone.*

"Is that right?" he said. "You were worried about your teachers?"

The room began to feel pressurized. She felt blood leaving

her head and half-turned away from him, fearing she would crumble. "I have good grades," she said. "I didn't want to get in trouble."

Sensing her weakness, he got off the couch and stood in front of her, no more than a foot away, intimidating her with his size. She realized how few men had ever stood this close to her before.

"Let me tell you something, hon." He breathed ham and eggs in her face. "A man died in this bombing. Do you know what that means?"

"Yes, of course." She nodded vigorously. "It was Sam. He never hurt anybody . . ."

He cut her off, not interested in the sentiment. "It means this is a homicide. It means whoever did this is going to get the death penalty. And believe me, *we are going to find out who did this*."

"Yes, I understand." Her fingertips pressed into the seams of her pockets.

"So if I find out that you and your brother had anything to do with this, you are going to get the death penalty. *Capisce?*" He pinched his fingers together and wagged them in her face. "The fact that you are a young girl will cut no ice at all. You are an Arab in America. It's going to be an eye for an eye. So if you got something to tell me, *say it now*," he barked. "Otherwise, I am not going to be able do a damn thing for you."

She looked down, trying to process all the information that had been thrust at her. Nasser. The smoke from the beach. The Monastery of Branches. The key on the table. The slap in the parking lot. Her father. Her mother. It was too much and not enough. She needed time to sort through it all.

"I had nothing to do with it," she said, looking up at the detective and struggling to keep her voice steady. "I went shopping that day with my brother. He bought me pads and a helmet for when I go Rollerblading. It was close to my birthday."

"Prove it," said Calloway, his pale mustache twitching.

"Well, we were stuck in traffic for a while on the Belt," she said, exaggerating the delay for both herself and him at the same time.

"But I kept the sales receipt from later that day. I wasn't sure the helmet fit right."

Calloway seemed to inflate and then deflate, hearing the news. Clearly, he'd been hoping to catch the break here that would solve his case.

"All right, go get the slip," he said. "I haven't got all day."

50

"I think she has a crush on you," said Donna Vitale.

"Who?" David finished the spaghetti on his plate and took another helping. Comfort food.

"That little Arab girl I saw you talking to in the office today."

They were having dinner at Donna's apartment on Carroll Street in Park Slope. A modest one-bedroom floor-through, with period details and garden access. A self-sufficient kind of place, with a tiny kitchen, a futon in the back, and a writing desk at the front bay windows, which no doubt let in drenching sunlight during the day.

"You don't like her, do you?" said David.

"I don't *know* her." Donna helped herself to some salad and refilled her glass of white wine. "I had her brother in my class a few years back, though. A world-class jerk. The one time he spoke up in class was to tell me he didn't think it was right for there to be women teachers at the school. Also, I think he somehow got the impression I was Jewish, which didn't sit too well with him either."

"Yes, he had some adjustment problems."

David found himself taking greedy gulps of food. Left to his own devices, he was a determined but awful cook—always putting in he-man amounts of spices and herbs to disastrous effect—so it had been ages since he'd had a good homemade meal.

"Kids like that, I don't know." Candlelight played off Donna's plain here-it-is hair and shone in the one eye staring off dreamily into the distance. "They can sap you, if you don't watch it. Troublemakers. Did I tell you I had a couple of Russian girls in my class last year who were giving boys blow jobs for rides in their cars?"

"Are you serious?"

"On my mother's." Donna raised her hand, taking an oath. "Then you got your druggies, your gangster wannabes—white and black—and your kids whose parents are just too stupid to let them concentrate on school."

"Actually, those are sometimes my favorites." David twirled a strand around his fork. "The ones who need a little extra."

"Well yeah!" Donna picked up her glass. "Me too. That's not what I was talking about before. I was talking about the knuckleheads who don't want to work. But the others, the ones who have to overcome something, who maybe have some little imperfection but keep trying anyway? They've got my heart."

Is that why you invited me over tonight? David wondered. Because I'm so fucking imperfect? Who cared? He was grateful to be anywhere people would have him.

She smiled and went to the kitchen to get him a second beer.

"So what are you going to do?" she asked when she came back.

"About what?"

"About your life. About the mess you're in." She twisted off the bottle cap and poured it into his glass mug for him.

"Well." He thanked her with a nod. "I could make up T-shirts. 'I Bombed Coney Island High.' "

"You could."

"Other than that, I'm just going full-tilt, three hundred miles an hour in no particular direction." He stared at the fizzing head of his beer, trying to fight the abysmal feeling inside. "I'm talking to the kids, talking to the neighborhood people, talking to my lawyers. But nobody knows nothin'. The bomb got there and went off by itself."

She smiled sympathetically. "So do you throw up your hands now?"

"No way. I can't." He gulped down half the beer and then remembered he needed to be more cautious with his drinking. "Did I tell you my lawyers want me to take a polygraph and do a live TV interview with this guy Lindsay Paul later this week?"

"Think that's smart?"

"Well, I wasn't going to do it," he said firmly. "But then I was at the playground with my son the other day and I noticed that none of the other kids would play with him because their parents recognized me." He winced, remembering Arthur's bewildered expression. "And then I realized there was a team of three or four FBI agents watching us from outside the fence. While I'm *at the playground. With my son.* So I just lost it with them." He closed his fist around the mug. "I went over and started screaming at the guy in charge, Donald Sippes. 'Get the fuck away from me, you motherfucker. Are you trying to give my son an asthma attack?' And then I turn around and Arthur's behind me, and he's screaming at the agents too. All red-faced and wheezing, going, 'My daddy's not a bad guy! He's not! He's not! He's not!' "

"And that killed you," Donna said.

"Yeah, it kind of tore me up a little," he said quietly, trying to hold in his emotions. "So then I called back my lawyers and said, 'Okay, let's pull out all the stops. I'm not letting my son walk around with this anymore.' "

He fell silent, listening to voices passing on the street and leaves rustling on the trees. He hadn't see the surveillance agents when he came up the street tonight, but he knew they were out there.

"So can I ask you something?" Donna wiped her lips with her napkin.

"Sure, go ahead."

She hesitated, seeming to take his measure for a moment. "Have you thought about what would happen if you got locked up?" she asked.

"We're still a long way from that," he said, finishing his beer.

She saw through his bravado right away. "Big man," she said. "Think you could handle Rikers Island?"

"Well, it wouldn't exactly be my first time around."

"Oh?"

He put his mug down hard, rattling their plates. "You knew I got arrested before, didn't you? It was in the papers."

"I think I read something about it." Her wandering eye wandered farther away from him.

"I was a kid." He turned the glass around, studying the way the light changed color in its contours. "I had this job being lifeguard at the Westbury Beach Club, and, you know, I was just a local kid working for the rich summer people. So anyway, I hooked up with a couple of idiots. Pete Spano and Dickie Bergman. Pete really, really wanted to be in the Mafia and Dickie was just insane—he had white hair, like an albino, but not quite. It was like coming that close without achieving albino-ness drove him crazy." He laughed, and then felt a tug of shame. "So what happened was, they got me into stealing cars from the club's parking lot at night."

"Oh yeah?" She rested her chin on her palm.

"Yeah." He retreated into himself for a moment, the second beer hitting him as he wondered if he should continue. "I wasn't so much into stealing as I was into just driving them around and bringing them back. Pete and Dickie went straight to the larceny. They actually took some of the cars out to Patchogue and sold them to wise guys." He shook his head, knowing he'd gone too far in the story to stop. "I don't know why I got involved. I was just this doofy kid, who was always reading war books and trying to get good grades and taking my grandmother to the market in her wheelchair every week. So I don't know. I thought it would be cool and I'd get girls to pay attention to me if I showed up driving a bitchin' Corvette."

"No wonder you get along with all the misfits." She turned a little, focusing her good eye on him. "So what happened?"

"I got caught." He studied the dregs at the bottom of his mug. "I guess maybe that's what I wanted all along, taking cars from the club where I was working. I took this beautiful red MG-BGT for a spin down Ocean Boulevard and I lost control of it and rode it up onto this guy's lawn, smashed it right into his porch jockey. He comes out in his bathrobe, says, 'Are you all right, son?' I said, *'Fuck you!'* and hauled out of there. But the police caught up to me by the time I made it back to the beach club. It turned out they'd sort of been looking at us for a while."

"So did you give your friends up?" Donna asked, cutting to the heart of the story as only a public schoolteacher could.

"Nope." He watched the candle guttering. "This cop took me into the stationhouse, told me he was going to tell my father what I did, and wasn't I a terrible kid, and my whole future would be ruined if I didn't make a clean slate of it and rat on my friends."

"And you said?"

"And I said, take me to the judge. I'll take what I've got coming."

"Bullshit," she said.

He shrugged. "It's the truth. I spent the night in jail with the drunks, and then the next morning I went before the judge and said, 'Your Honor, I'll own up to anything I did and that's as far as it goes. All I ask is you take into account everything that I'm about. Don't just judge me for this one mistake. Add everything else into it before you make your decision.' "

"You must've been a pretty ballsy kid," she said, as she finished her wine.

"Yeah, maybe. I don't know." He suddenly felt abashed, remembering how scared he was standing up in the rickety little Nassau County courtroom that day. "I just knew it was what my father would've wanted me to say. Not that he gave me instructions of any kind. I just had this feeling about it. That if I laid it all out and didn't forget who I was, everything would basically be all right. And it was. The judge gave me probation and sealed the record, so I wouldn't have a problem getting a job later on."

He watched little droplets of wax fall and harden on the table's surface. He started to scratch them away, but then thought better of it. Let them be.

"And what happened to your friends?" asked Donna.

"Ah, they both thought they were tough guys and never owned up to doing anything. So the judge gave both of them a little jail time. Hard-core, right? I think it kind of messed both of them up for life, you know. Petey never really hooked up with the Mafia. He just became a junkie and eventually killed himself. And Dickie went all the way over to the dark side. He became a telemarketer." He rapped his knuckles on the tabletop. "I guess, it was just this big parting for us. They went their way and I went mine. So maybe that cop was right, in a sense. What happened that night probably *did* determine the rest of my life. Only not the way he thought."

He sat back, tired and dry-mouthed, feeling like he'd been talking for eight periods in a row. "So I suppose the point of this whole thing," he said, "is if I can just hang in there and keep my head straight, basically everything will be okay again. I hope."

"I hope so too." She reached across the table and squeezed his hand.

He looked down at her fingers. "Now can I ask you something?"

"Go for it, dude."

"What makes you so sure I'm not the bad guy anyway?"

"I don't know." Her good eye scanned his face, as if trying to see the edges of a mask. "You seem too . . . I don't know, *invested.* Is that the right word?"

"I'm not sure. Is that what you're trying to say?"

"I mean, you seem too present with the kids. I hear you on the phone sometimes, in the office, when you're talking to your son. And I know I shouldn't be listening but"—she leaned forward and looked up at him, the glow from inside her stronger than the candlelight—"I just get a good feeling about you. About the kind of man you are when no one else is watching. Besides, I've seen how you are at the coffee machine. You couldn't make a bomb if your life depended on it."

He waited a beat and then lifted his empty glass to her. "Why did it take me the better part of a year to have dinner with you?"

"Ha!"

She clinked empty glasses with him. In its subtle way, tonight was a sort of turning point for him. It was the first time since he got married that he'd been potentially serious about another woman, and the idea that he was ending one part of his life and starting another made him feel both melancholy and elated.

"Look, I really ought to get out of here." He checked his watch. "I don't know if I mentioned this, but they've probably been watching your place all night."

"I figured as much. It seemed kind of exciting."

She got up and started to clear the dishes. He liked talking to her, he realized. She didn't make him feel light-headed and full of false promise. She made him feel real. This was a woman who took no shit and gave none without warrant. He wondered how Arthur would like her.

"Next time, I buy you dinner and we talk about *you*," he said, going to get his jacket. "Instead of me blathering on. Maybe by then, they won't be following me."

"That would be nice." She came over and fussed with his collar.

He put his fingers under her chin and kissed her softly on the lips. She let his arms encircle her and then gently pulled back after a few seconds. "Hey, you're doing eighty in a fifty-five. Slow down a little."

"Sorry."

"It's okay," she said. "I know what I want and I know when I want it. And I just don't happen to want that right now. We'll talk about later, *later*, big guy."

"Good deal."

He touched her shoulder lightly and started for the door.

"Something else I wanted to ask you," she said.

"Go ahead." He paused with his hand on the doorknob. "I owe you."

" 'God keep me from completing anything'?" She put her arms out as if to say, What gives?

"Oh yeah, everybody's asking me about that lately."

"So why don't you want to complete anything?"

His hand dropped off the knob. This was slightly different from what Dr. Ferry, the psychiatrist, had been asking. "I don't know. I guess I used to think that if I didn't complete something, I'd always have a chance to start over and do it better. And then there'd never be a finished *thing* for people to judge."

"I hate to tell you, but it didn't work." She helped him button his jacket. "The not-getting-judged part."

"Yeah, I noticed."

51

At half past nine that night, Elizabeth Hamdy came out of West Side Storage on Tenth Avenue, looked around at the meat trucks and off-duty post office workers passing by, and ran across the street to join Nasser, who sat waiting in his Lincoln Town Car.

"You know, I'm still furious at you," she said, after she got in.

"I know. I'm sorry for the bad things I did."

She stared out the windshield at the slow-moving Lincoln Tunnel traffic up ahead, lightning bugs inching their way under the dark river.

"A week and a half we haven't spoken and you only call because you need a favor." She folded her arms and looked somber. "You missed my birthday dinner at the Moroccan Star. Nice."

"I am sorry. I have been so busy. And I felt shy because we fought."

"I shouldn't even talk to you anymore," she said. "I should have just torn up all your messages and forgotten about them."

"I know. I don't know why I act this way. I lost control." He nodded sadly and then waited a beat. "So did you do it?" he asked.

"Yes, I did it," she sighed. "I rented your storage locker for you. Two hundred dollars a month for a twelve-by-twelve room. Are you happy now?"

Headlights flickered across his eyes. "Yes, I am very happy. I appreciate you doing this for me. This favor."

She untied her hair and let it fall around her shoulders. "I don't even know why I bother. You're not even that nice to me. It's not like I need your approval or anything."

"I understand. You are too nice." He glanced up at his rearview mirror, making sure no police were in the area. "So okay. I'll take you home."

He turned the key in the ignition and felt his guts rev. It was a bad thing to get Elizabeth involved in this operation, he'd told Youssef and Dr. Ahmed, even in such a small way. But they'd insisted. The Americans they were dealing with were getting too wary of all these Arab men buying the material for the *haddutas*. It would be better to have a girl—especially a non-Arab-looking girl—rent a storage locker where they could keep the materials overnight and have the compressors delivered without raising suspicions. Leaving everything in the unsecured garage when they weren't there was out of the question; the neighbors were nosy enough as it was and Dr. Ahmed was getting worried that the junkies on the block would try stealing the chemicals.

"So what's it for, anyway?" she asked, as they rounded the block on their way back toward the West Side Highway.

"What?"

"The locker. What do you need it for?"

"Equipment. Business equipment. Compressors. I want to go into the refrigeration business. I'm trying to be—how do you say it?—*independent*."

He fell silent as they turned south onto the West Side Highway. Lower Manhattan glowed as if it were radioactive, and the blue Caprice directly in front of them had a bumper sticker that said: "My Karma Ran Over My Dogma." Elizabeth was eerily still in the seat next to him. Something was swelling between the two of them, but he didn't have the language to name it.

"So why'd you need *me* to rent it for you?" she asked finally. "Why couldn't you do it yourself?"

"They need the driver's license for the I.D." He lowered his eyes from the harsh glare of oncoming headlights from the other side of the road. "And I have a little problem with my license."

"Then why are you still driving?"

It was only a small lie, but she'd seen through it instantly. He'd never been good at fooling her. She understood him too well; the same tuning fork vibrated in both of them. He wondered how he would bring up the subject of getting her story straight in case this Detective Calloway came to interrogate her.

"You ask too many questions," he said, turning his head toward her as high beams flashed over the car's interior.

There was more of a family resemblance than he used to see, but it was subtle. A certain curve to her cheekbones, a softness of skin, the color of her eyes. He wondered how he would keep her safe when he brought the *hadduta* into the school this time.

"Hey, what do you do to your hair?" he asked. "What's the matter with it?"

The passing light had picked out a few purple-red streaks from her mass of dark strands.

"I dyed it. What's the big deal?"

"This is totally *haram*," he said, stepping on the brake quickly to avoid plowing into the back of the Caprice. "It's against the tradition."

"I doubt the Koran says anything about the use of hair color."

"It makes you look like an American. It's adulteration."

"I *am* American." She put a sneakered foot up against the dashboard. "I'm from Brooklyn."

"You are still listening to this teacher too much," he said, rocking slightly in his seat. "Your mother was an Arab and your father is still an Arab."

"Yeah, but now I'm thinking. I've never been back there, so I don't know what it has to do with me."

"One day, you will come," he said. "You will see. You will go to the sheep market in Bethlehem on a Saturday morning and you'll see the Bedouins come in from the desert with the white Oriental sheep and the goats and you'll see the farmers from Moab bring in the wheat and the barley and the corn. And the wheat, it's so fine and thin and crisp, it's like nothing they have in this country. Everything is just as it was one thousand, five hundred years ago."

"So will you take me there?"

He said nothing and kept driving.

This was when she felt closest to him. When he talked about things back home. The things she'd always felt but never actually seen. They were like scenes from a half-remembered dream. Reminders that there was a void in her, a sense that she'd never felt truly at home. Yes, she was an American, but sometimes she felt herself reaching out for something else, something less corporeal, another world, another time. Sometimes her father would read the Koran out loud to her and the words would sound like music, even when she didn't understand them. But throwing on a veil and a head scarf wasn't the answer either; she rebelled against the very thought of binding herself up in all that black cloth. No, the truth for her was somewhere in between these two places, the New World and the Old World. She wondered if Nasser felt the same pull of opposing forces after all this time in America. Maybe that's why she felt such a connection to him sometimes. They were both the same, both in-between people. Stuck in the middle of the river.

But tonight the currents were pulling her in a different direction.

"Nasser," she said. "There's something I have to talk to you about. That's why I finally returned your call."

He turned up the radio, trying to drown her out. "I carry a jimmy hat everywhere I go / I can do it like a man, so don't call me your ho," rapped a woman over what sounded like a syncopated car wreck.

"See, she says the women are as good as the men," Nasser said, shaking his head. "But it's not enough to say you are a man. You have to be a man."

"Nasser." Elizabeth turned the radio down. "I need to ask you something."

He stole a glance at her. "So what is it?"

"A policeman named Calloway came by the house today. He wanted to talk about you."

He accidentally hit the horn. "Yes, I know," he said, straightening up. "I talked to him. Everything's perfectly okay."

"It's not okay." She turned to him, staring hard at his profile. "He wanted to know where you were when the bomb went off."

"So you told him I was with you." A bead of sweat slid down his cheek. "No problem. Okay? I was buying you the helmet."

"*Nasser*, that's not true." Her sharp tone made him flinch. "I was waiting for you when I saw smoke down at the beach. You were late to pick me up."

"Did you tell him this?"

He suddenly veered onto the shoulder of the road and parked over by the piers. He sat in silence at the wheel for a moment, in the shadow of an old decommissioned battleship.

"Nasser, look at me," she said.

He turned his eyes to her and then turned them away, as if he was scared.

"I said, look at me."

"*I looked.*" His voice squeaked. "Do I have to keep looking all the time?"

"Did you have anything to do with what happened to that bus outside school?"

"This was your teacher, who did this." He flexed his fingers on the wheel. "They said it on the radio and the television."

"But now I'm asking you. I know you don't like to lie to me. I know the Koran is against lying. So I'm asking: was that your bomb?"

He put on his emergency flashers and the signal made a steady pleasant tick-tock sound on the dashboard.

Several minutes passed before he spoke again.

"Well, whoever does this—you don't know—they have the reasons. They have terrible pressure. Terrible choices. Not like where they go to college or what clothes to wear. Like the Americans. You can't understand these terrible choices. This is something different from what you know. This is an experience from a different world."

He stopped talking and she listened to the continuing tick-tock of the blinker, her pulse falling into its rhythm. She felt as if all the air had been sucked out of her lungs.

"So you did it," she said quietly.

"I don't say nothing about anything."

"But how could you do it? You killed Sam. You could've killed all of them. It's against the Koran."

He bowed his head for a second and then suddenly began to pound and scream at the steering wheel. She'd never seen him like this. At first, it seemed like an animal eruption, but then she realized he was more like a small frightened boy losing control. He pulled at the steering wheel this way and that with both hands, trying to yank it out of its column, and then beat the dashboard with his fists.

"All right!" he said. "You want to be a man? Be a man then! You want to be a Muslim? Be a good Muslim! Be a soldier! Don't be a coward, like your father, building houses for the Jews and taking their money. Do your duty. Fight like a man. Be a soldier for God. You say it's against the Holy Book. But this is a war, not a book."

Somehow, she sensed his argument was not really with her; he was trying to talk himself into something.

"I don't think our father is a coward," she said softly. "He survived the refugee camp and managed to make a new life here. To me, that makes him a hero."

"And he left his family behind." Nasser grimaced. "What kind of a hero does that?"

He turned off the blinker, took the car out of park and started down the West Side Highway again. "For you, it's a new life," he muttered.

Her mind was empty, her mouth was empty. What were the

words he used before? Terrible choices. That's what he'd just given her. Terrible choices.

He stepped on the gas and all the downtown buildings seemed to come rushing at her. A red neon umbrella glowing on the side of an office tower.

"So," he said, "did you tell him you were with me when the bomb goes off?"

"I did." She sank down in her seat, feeling caught up in thorns. "What else could I do? You're my brother."

"Exactly, right." He pulled himself up at the wheel. "This is for the family."

52

"Your students refer to you as an eccentric," said the talk show host. "Are you?"

Not if you use John Wilkes Booth and the Unabomber as your standards, *bucko*, thought David. No, scratch that. You're on television. Never practice irony in an underdeveloped country.

"I use any means necessary to get my students to use the equipment in their heads." David sat up straight and faced the camera, realizing it probably didn't help to quote Malcolm X now either. "If that makes me an eccentric, fine."

"Did you bomb the school bus?" asked the host, Lindsay Paul, a formerly dashing young newsman in the twilight of his good looks, undergoing a certain Fred Flintstone-ishness of the features.

"No, I did not."

David was back on the air, live and going national on America's second most popular cable news network. He'd sworn he wouldn't do this again, but circumstances had conspired. He had no choice, he told himself. None of his other frantic efforts—working the phones, talking to the kids, and trying a second time without success to read students' disciplinary files—were yielding any results.

"Then why have you become a suspect in this case?" asked Lindsay, gray-suited, dark-haired, and earnest in a two-dimensional way. "Come on, you must have done something."

"Well, then, somebody should step up and tell me what it is," said David. "I don't have a clue otherwise."

Behind the camera, Ralph Marcovicci was giving him an enthusiastic thumbs-up. *Piece of cake*, Ralph kept telling him before the show began. *Piece of fuckin' cake*. Lindsay was one of Ralph's oldest and dearest, as Donna would say. "He'll throw you one friggin' softball after another right down the middle of the plate," Ralph assured him.

"So the obvious question is"—Lindsay leaned forward, Flintstone brow knit in concern—"if you didn't do it, who did?"

"That's the point of my coming on tonight," said David. "My lawyers and I believe that someone out there knows something. And they haven't come forward." He thought of O. J. Simpson on the golf course.

"Why not?" Lindsay tucked in his drooping chin, trying to remind viewers he'd once been a serious journalist. "Why hasn't the FBI found them?"

"I don't know." David shifted in his chair, and tried to avoid looking at himself in the monitor, lest it turn him to stone like Medusa's severed head. "Maybe they're scared or just don't want to get involved. But I'm hoping they'll hear me speaking tonight, look into their hearts, and decide to do the right thing."

He looked over and saw Ralph next to a cameraman, silently applauding. Judah Rosenbloom was elsewhere in the studio, manning the phone lines in case a useful tip came in.

"And as far as everyone else goes, I just want people to see that I'm human, and not a monster after all."

"Fair enough, David Fitzgerald!" boomed Lindsay.

The cameraman moved forward a little and the host looked up, giving his rugged-integrity face.

In a million years, I'll never be able to do that. David glanced over at the studio clock, seeing he had another ten minutes to go in his segment. After this many appearances, he thought he'd start to relax and become more natural on television. But he still felt awkward and too aware of himself. And it was different now, appearing as the accused man fighting back, instead of being the hero justly celebrated. Before he'd been puffed up, full of himself; now he felt clenched and defiant, painfully aware of how every word counted.

"Let's throw open our phone lines and take some calls on the air," Lindsay said suddenly.

David stiffened. *Calls on the air?* Had he heard right? Off-camera, Ralph Marcovicci was flushing red and furiously giving Lindsay the finger. There'd been no mention of taking phone calls on the air. In fact, David's understanding was that Lindsay and Ralph had specifically agreed *not* to have them. But a new hum was coming over the studio speakers. The deal was off, the calls were starting. Storming off the show would only make him look guilty.

David stayed in his seat, remaining very still. By this point, he understood that any tightening of the jaw or shiftiness in the eyes would be multiplied a hundred times by the camera. *Of course*, the deal was off. He wasn't a real celebrity they were going to need again. They could afford to break their word to him. He should have expected it.

"We have Kevin, from Brooklyn," said Lindsay, checking an overhead monitor.

"Yo, Brownsville's in the house!" A voice falling off a cliff.

The line went dead and another caller came on.

"Yes, Emma Brown from Springfield Gardens, Queens!" said Lindsay, looking up at the new name in green letters on the monitor. "You're on the air!"

David's nostrils quivered and he realized the host sitting two feet away in a swivel chair had just passed gas.

"Good evening, Lindsay." A stately, older African-American woman's voice. A voice out of the church. "I am the younger sister of Mr. Sam Hall."

A little pistol shot of panic rang out in David's mind as he remembered the stories in the newspaper about her threatening a lawsuit. This was not going to be good.

"I'm sorry for your loss, ma'am," Lindsay intoned. "He was a great man. I was a tremendous fan of his music."

"I just want to know how this man can sit here, asking people to help him, when my family couldn't even afford a proper burial for my brother until the mayor stepped in."

What do I say? What do I say? David rifled through his mental files of homilies and platitudes, searching for some appropriately diverting bit of wisdom.

"Well, ma'am, that is a separate issue, really," Lindsay cut in, with just a pinch of common sense.

But Ms. Brown was on a roll. She was ready to testify. "That's what you say! But my brother is dead and I want to know when the man responsible is going to be punished for this. Where's the justice for my brother? He was murdered for absolutely no reason. And this man's sitting there, talking to you on television, Lindsay. I just cannot understand."

The emotion in her voice easily overcame the lack of logic in her words. David knew that counted against him. People watching at home would only hear the emotion, the anger. The medium didn't encourage dispassionate analysis. It demanded unconditional empathy. He could either get crushed by the moment, or find a way to ride it.

He took a deep breath and tried the latter. "Emma," he said, as if he'd met her before. "I completely agree with everything you just said. Your brother was a good man, and I want to help find his killer and bring him to justice as quickly as possible. I'm more anxious than anyone to find out what really happened. My life's on the line too."

Off-camera, Ralph was silently urging him on, rotating his arms, mouthing, "Give me more."

"But you—" She started to come back at him.

"And once this matter is cleared up, I will probably be joining you in a civil suit against the city and the state," David improvised. "So that may be something we're better off discussing off the air. I wouldn't want to do or say anything to compromise our case."

It was all just blowing smoke at smoke, since there'd been no such discussions with Ralph and Judah, but Emma seemed to lose focus anyway.

"I . . . well . . ."

"And I believe my lawyers are developing information that may become very useful to you in the near future," David went on, seizing the momentum away from her. "We could help each other. *I didn't do this.*"

Perhaps after all this time, he *was* getting the hang of presenting himself. And who knew, maybe his lawyers would discover something to help Sam's family.

"Emma, is there anything else you want to say?" asked Lindsay.

"Uh. Well. I guess I'd like to speak with my lawyers first."

"Thank you." Lindsay turned, giving the cameraman another angle on his face, as he checked the monitor. "Sioux City, Iowa. Glen. You're on the air."

"Yes." A slow young white man's drawl came over the speakers. "I'm a former student of Mr. Fitzgerald."

"Okay." Lindsay sat up and smiled, sincere and telegenic.

David tensed up again, having another moment of roller-coaster vertigo. Every time he thought he'd survived one of these treacherous drops, here came an even steeper and scarier hump.

"I just would like to say this man is a pervert." Even the boy's voice made David think of ascending the Cyclone. "He bought me beer when I was a sophomore. Then he got me drunk and took me down to the boys' locker-room, where he . . . attempted to touch me in an improper manner."

So here they were again, at the top of the ride. There was a pause and Glen exhaled on his end, as if he'd been keeping this in for a long time. His calm matter-of-fact tone made the call seem both surreal and utterly authentic at the same time. Ralph Marcovicci had his hands over his head as if he was about to get hit by an incoming Scud missile.

This was worse than disaster. It was annihilation. What if the judge was watching? David felt like he was suspended in mid-air. How do I get down without crashing?

He decided to try to do it slowly. "Excuse me, Lindsay?" He cleared his throat. "May I ask this caller a couple of questions?"

"Be my guest."

"Glen?" David looked up earnestly at the camera, as if the caller's image had appeared there. "Would you mind telling me your last name?"

He was desperately trying to come up with a face to match to the voice. How would one of his former students end up in Iowa?

"Sir, I'd prefer not to give my full name for obvious reasons. I'm trying to protect my parents."

"I see." David was careful to avoid sarcasm or obvious defensiveness. "Then would you mind telling me what year you graduated?"

"Recently."

It was a crank call. He was sure of it. But if he tried to brush it off too quickly, he knew it would appear suspicious. He was still on top of the Cyclone, his cart rocking slightly in the wind.

"Glen, which of my classes were you in?"

"English."

"Which English class? I teach several."

Glen hesitated for just a moment. "First period."

"Well, I haven't taught first period for several years." The cart started to descend gradually. "That's a matter of record. Anyone could look that up."

"Sir, I know what you did to me. And I know it was wrong."

A nervous, snapping tone had crept into the boy's voice. He knew he was getting backed into a corner. But again, David worried that the sound of righteous indignation would trump common sense. Not too fast. Let's bring it down slowly. The boy might come across as more believable if he was attacked too vigorously.

"Let me just ask you one more question," David said cautiously. "What books did you read when you were in my class?"

The phone line crackled and the boy didn't speak for a few seconds. *I'm going to make it*, David thought. *I'm on my way down. Easy now, baby.* Lindsay Paul looked over, confused, at the darkened room toward the back of the studio, where the calls were supposedly being screened. Finally, a high-pitched voice came over the speaker, muffled and stifling a giggle.

"Fuck you, faggot!"

Lindsay Paul looked huffy and bemused, like a society matron who'd just discovered all the guests nude and drunk in the library. "Thank God for the seven-second delay," he said, forcing a smile. "Sorry about that, folks. We have time for two more calls."

But David was on the ground and through with this torture. For once, he decided to take advantage of the silence. "You know, Lindsay, I have something else I want to say before you take those calls."

"What is it?"

He turned and faced the camera straight on. "Just that I guess the irony here is that I'm going back on the air to fight the image that's been presented of me in the media. Which is a bit like going to a cathouse to get rid of the clap."

He saw Ralph bury his face in his hands, but decided to press on. "So it's okay, some of the things that have been said tonight." He glanced over at Lindsay in wary amusement. "As we say in Coney Island, you pays your money and you takes your chances."

He shrugged and gave his full gaze back to the lens. "But all I'm asking is, let's be fair. I don't care how many high-speed, multichannel, digitized systems you have. I always tell my students, make your case or get outta my face. No one can say they saw me with bomb components. No one can say I had a timer. And certainly no one in their right mind can say I ever laid a hand on my wife or my child. And the reason is: None of these things are true. I didn't kill Sam Hall and I didn't make the bomb. I may not be perfect, but I am who I am. So don't convict me on a whisper. My kids have a saying: If you got a beef, *then step to it*. So that's all I have to say: if you know what really happened, step to it. You know what you have to do."

He sat back and took a deep breath, not at all sure he'd made his point. Lindsay Paul wasn't offering any acknowledgment. He was too busy grinning at the camera as his director stepped in front of Ralph and made the cut sign.

53

For the last twenty-four hours, Nasser had been on a tear: getting his sister to rent the storage locker on the West Side, going back to the garage in Sunset Park to mix chemicals in the middle of the night, returning to his job at six in the morning to work a double shift, and then coming back to the little apartment behind the cab stand to get some rest.

Youssef and Dr. Ahmed were waiting for him when he walked in, exhausted, his vision blurring.

"What's the matter?" said Youssef. "My wife gave me a message that you needed to speak to me."

"Yes, sheik, I called." Nasser flopped down on the moth-eaten mattress he'd laid out on the lumpy floor next to the kitchen.

God, how he hated living in this wretched little space with the doctor. The narrow thin-walled rooms, the blue paint peeling, the mice scurrying in the oven, the constant noise outside, the tobacco in the air, and the salsa pounding from upstairs. It was not much better than living in Deheisha. Why didn't more Americans revolt?

"A police officer came to see me the other day," he told the two older men. "And then he questioned my sister about what she was doing the day of the *hadduta* under the school bus."

The doctor hissed and began pulling on his beard again. "*Ya habela!*" he said loudly. "Why didn't you tell us this before?! *Yin an a bouk!* Do you want us all to go to jail?"

"No, sheik." Nasser tried to hold his hand up, but he was too tired. "I wanted to tell you before, but I couldn't reach you. So instead I just kept working. I felt time was running short."

Youssef leaned against the oven, trying to remain calm and magisterial. "So what did you tell him? What did your sister tell him?"

"We didn't tell him nothing." Nasser began to untie his boots and then gave up. "She said she was with me and I said I was with her. So there's no problem. But I thought you should know."

Youssef and the doctor glared at each other in silence. From behind the front wall, Nasser could hear the taxi dispatcher taking calls and sending out transmissions. Circuits of the city connecting and firing.

"I think we have to make a change in our plan," Dr. Ahmed said quickly and quietly, starting to limp in a circle around the mattress.

Nasser followed him with his eyes, noticing the doctor had begun to do things not just twice as fast, but three times as fast as necessary, as if he was completely out of patience with the world.

"This is something I've been thinking all along," the doctor said, cracking his knuckles and rubbing his nose with his handkerchief. "Because what this is about is *jihad*, *jiHAD*, *JIHAD*, *JIHAD!* Okay?!"

His voice reached a crescendo and then he abruptly stopped in front of Nasser, staring down through him with burning eyes.

"Okay," said Nasser, vaguely aware he was about to be taken on some kind of journey.

"It's not enough to say you are for *jihad* in your heart." The doctor began circling him again, weaving the words together with his hands. "*Jihad* is something that must be implemented. You must take a step for *jihad*, for the love of Allah, blessed be his name. He doesn't care about your prayers. He doesn't care about the *haj*. These are the lowest levels of faith. Allah respects actions. You have to take risks for God, to show that you truly believe."

"*Allahu akbar!*" Youssef sagged against the stove and slipped a nitroglycerin pill under his tongue. He'd been looking sluggish and unhealthy since their last meeting with the imam, Nasser noticed, with dark circles under his eyes.

But Dr. Ahmed was just getting warmed up. "Should I tell you when I felt closest to God?" He stopped again and bent down in front of Nasser, pointing in his face. "It was when I was in the Holy War in Afghanistan, riding on the back of a donkey with my leg half blown off by a land mine. Yes!" He rolled up his pant leg, showing Nasser a hideous red scar from his ankle to his knee. "Every time we hit a ditch and the pain was like teeth sinking into my heart, I thanked Allah the giver and taker of life for sparing me."

"*Insh'allah.*" Youssef touched his own heart scar.

Dr. Ahmed leaned closer to Nasser. "The Holy Book teaches us to doubt the existence of miracles. You know this, right?"

"Of course," said Nasser, knowing he was being maneuvered but powerless to stop it.

"We learn that God's will is not made manifest by magic tricks like turning water into wine, but by the sun and the moon and the cows in the fields and the birds singing in the trees." The doctor took him by the shoulders, only looking past him for a moment. "The child laughing in the nursery. These are the signs of Allah's grace."

"*Allahu akbar*," Youssef called out, but his voice sounded faint, as if he were in another country.

It was all the doctor now. On one knee in front of Nasser, no longer looking past him or through him but staring deeply into his eyes, reaching into his skull with carefully chosen words. "But death is a sign of God's power, also," he said. "I learned this in the war. All the things I studied at the University of Cairo, my doctorate in psychology, all the protests I made against the shah in Tehran, they were as nothing compared with the first time I saw a man killed. I stood over him and I shot him through the heart and I watched his life go away. He was a Russian soldier, you know. And I spoke with him. I asked him how many children he had and then I watched him go from being a living thing to a nonliving thing. And you know what? As the life left his body and he became gray, I truly felt the power of God. Because only God could take so much away. This was a sign of His grace as much as the birds, or the cows, or the babies. If it was not so, He wouldn't allow it. Do you understand this?"

"Yes. Yes, I do."

Nasser found himself swaying back and forth on the mattress, shaking, remembering his mother with her hands folded. He didn't know if it was the fatigue or the tension of the last few days, but he felt like he was being hollowed out and filled up by the doctor's words.

"This is why we make the change in our plans." The doctor stood up slowly and steadied himself with a broken metal chair. "The targets will stay the same. You'll still go back to your school with the *hadduta*. But you'll use dynamite instead of the fuel bombs we're going to use for the other larger *haddutas*. And there won't be any timer."

"I don't understand."

All at once, the room went quiet, the taxi dispatcher ceased his transmissions, the air around them became heavy. Youssef coughed into his fist and Dr. Ahmed looked away. This was the last stop on the journey. In his heart, Nasser had always known this time would come.

"We're going to have a martyr, my friend," said the doctor. He touched his beard, eyes, nose, and ears. "You're the one."

Youssef came over and knelt beside Nasser, putting a hand on his back and whispering in his ear. "This is a great opportunity, my friend. You will be rewarded in heaven with seventy virgin brides and you will be a hero back home. They will hold a great funeral for you in your village with thousands of people coming and they'll distribute pictures of you to the children, so they'll always know of your heroism."

"*Allahu akbar!*" the doctor said, leaning in so close he was practically nose-to-nose with Nasser. "And everyone will chant in your memory: *'With our blood! With our souls! We will redeem you!'* You will be *shaheen*. Because this is what will frighten the infidels the most. Even more than a bridge or a tunnel blowing up. The idea that there are suicide bombers in this country. Men who are willing to blow themselves up and die and take hundreds of others with them. This they cannot stop, no matter how hard they try. It will steal their peace of mind."

They were on either side of him, closing in. The doctor leaning down and Youssef still kneeling, still whispering insistently into his ear. "You will make your family proud. In heaven, your mother will smile on you forever."

The back of Nasser's throat cracked and he felt himself slump forward, worn down and overpowered by what they'd evoked. Yes, Mother would be proud. Always, she was saying, a man must be ready to submit to God's will, to die for what he believes, or else he is nothing. *The life of this world is but a sport and a pastime*. All earthly riches are transitory. Hadn't he seen her crying and tearing at her clothes at the funerals of martyrs? Hadn't she chosen to end her own life? Hadn't his friend Hamid made just as great a sacrifice at Ashkelon prison?

"This is a special duty you've been chosen for," Youssef was saying. "No one else has ever done this here. You'll be the first. I truly envy you . . ."

Yes, Nasser realized, he'd been set up for this all along. Youssef and the doctor knew exactly what to say to him, what pictures to put in his mind. But at the same time, Nasser understood it was useless to resist. This was his destiny, this was what he was made for. Everything had converged and forced him toward this point: the rusty key, the bag over his face, his mother, his father, the fact that never in his life had he experienced a single moment's pleasure without the shadow of misery falling over it.

One hour on the battlefield is worth a hundred years of prayer.

"You're not afraid, are you?" asked the doctor.

"No, of course not."

But in fact, he was afraid. A part of him didn't want this at all. He couldn't truly imagine the seventy virgin brides or the rivers running under the Garden. It didn't seem real. The city seemed real. The women, the cars, the red numbers, the bright lights and easy sentimentality, the throbbing music and endless grid of the streets.

Perhaps this was all a final test to see if he was worthy, to see if he could be a true hero, a *shaheen*, a martyr for God. Maybe the fact that he didn't want to die was what made this a true sacrifice. *Insh'allah*. These mysteries were beyond him and he could only pretend to understand. All he could do was act.

"So," he said, slowly rising and clutching his mother's key, still hanging from the chain around his neck. "What do I do now?"

54

David took the next morning off from school for the lie detector test and then went immediately to his lawyers' office on lower Broadway to discuss the results. When he came out at eleven o'clock, Judy Mandel was waiting for him on the sidewalk, notebook in hand, her mouth slightly open.

"Oh, um, hi, David." Her voice was young and tentative, as if she might be selling church raffle tickets. "Remember me?"

His mind split off in two different directions. Mandel, as a name, was eye poison. Mandel was the byline that had unraveled his life, equaling accusations of bomb planting, murder, wife-beating, and child abuse. But here once again he was faced with this winsome black-haired girl in brown lipstick. She looked like a student.

"You know, it's a funny thing," he said with a weary sigh. "Every time I see you I forget what you look like right afterwards. Why is that, I wonder?"

"I don't know." Her lower lip came up as if he'd hurt her feelings. "Maybe you're distracted."

"You put all those things Renee told you in the newspaper."

"Well, then you know I didn't make any of it up myself."

His chest heaved with mighty impatience. "My wife is sick. Anybody who talks to her for five minutes could figure that out." He stood before her, looking down, with his chin as hard as a fist. "You took advantage of her. So I don't think I have anything else to say to you. Go ruin somebody else's life."

He started to turn away, trying to remember where the nearest stop for the D train was.

"But I had one more question!" From the corner of his eye, he saw her actually raise her hand, as if they were in a classroom.

"What?"

Against his better judgment, he came back to her.

"I heard you failed your polygraph this morning."

He tried not to flinch. The official results were "inconclusive." *Squeeze your asshole*, Ralph Marcovicci kept telling him on the way in. *The machine measures stress, so if you squeeze your asshole on every question, it'll look like you're being consistent.* "I can't get my arms around you, Ralph," David had said. That was probably the last joke he'd be making for a while.

"I'm not going to have any comment on that," David told Judy Mandel.

How had she found out about it so quickly? Ralph and Judah had warned him that the feds would be leaking stories like crazy, trying to pressure him into making a deal, but this was ridiculous. The electrodes came off his fingers less than two hours ago. It was probably the examiner himself, a tubby, ruined-looking ex-cop called Cardio, who'd leaked the results.

"So there's a rumor the FBI is finally going to arrest you in the next day or two," she said.

He spread out his arms. "Then let them come and get me. I'm not going anywhere."

But inside, panic was eating him up like a raging infection. He knew he couldn't let this girl see it, though. He had to *take it*.

He hitched up his belt and tried to keep up the brave face. "So," he said, "I guess I'm supposed to fall on my knees and admit everything to you. Is that it?"

"No." She exhaled, twitched her shoulders a little. "I just want to get it right."

"Whatever that means."

People kept walking by, each locked in their own self-justifying interior monologues.

"Let me ask you something," David said. "Doesn't it bother you that everything you've done is completely speculative?"

"What do you mean?"

"You've made this cottage industry of writing about me and you don't even know me. What if you're wrong? I mean, I try to teach my students the value of critical thinking when they write their papers. I tell them: flip it around, consider the alternative, try it the other way. So did that ever occur to you? Have you considered the alternative? *What if he didn't do it?* Your whole world would collapse, wouldn't it?"

Her rouged little mouth opened, but nothing came out.

"Maybe you're the one I should feel sorry for," he said.

As he abruptly turned and started to walk away, Judy felt a heavy stone falling inside her chest. *What if he didn't do it?* She'd kept that thought at bay for days now. But it was no good. "In the pursuit of a story, everything must fall," Bill Ryan once told her. "Including the previous day's story." She began to chase after Fitzgerald, seeing the back of his head bobbing just a little bit above the crowd heading downtown.

She was angry with him. He should've been a gawky, strange man, cowering in his father's shadow. But his gaze had been too forthright, his presence too solid. Why couldn't he stay fixed on the page? Why couldn't he be more like the person she'd written about?

The great institutions always lie, Bill said; that's why you had to be ruthless in dealing with them. But here she realized she'd gotten it all backward. David Fitzgerald wasn't an institution, he was just a man. While she suddenly found herself becoming part of a massive unstoppable engine.

She came up behind him and tapped him on the shoulder. "David," she said.

"What?" He turned around, exasperated. "What is it now?"

"I was thinking about what you said on television last night. I just want you to know I'm human too."

He kept walking and looked once over his shoulder. "I guess I'll have to take your word for it."

55

"Excuse me, sir. Who are you here to see?"

Four days before he was supposed to bring the *hadduta* into the school, Nasser was sent on a practice run by Youssef and Dr. Ahmed. There could be no mistakes this time.

So just before one o'clock he stood before the school's metal detector, allowing the black security officer with the sharp-creased trousers to check his old I.D.

"I am reapplying," said Nasser. "I would like for to talk to the principal."

The guard turned the laminated card this way and that, catching the light at different angles on its shiny surface. Naked. Nasser felt completely naked standing there with all the students passing by on the way to the lunchroom. He hoped he wouldn't see Elizabeth among them. That would be more complication than he could possibly handle. His intestines had turned into wrestling serpents since last night. And sleep was out of the question.

He saw there was now a conveyor-belt scanner next to the metal detector, so the guard could look inside each bag coming in. Maybe he'd have to strap the *hadduta* to his body when he returned.

He tried to imagine what it would feel like. The cardboard rolls of dynamite taped around his midsection. Would the adhesive sting and pull on his skin? How baggy a shirt should he wear? And what would it feel like when the *hadduta* went off? Would it be over right away or would there be lingering death agony?

"Okay, you know where the principal's office is?" The guard handed his I.D. back.

"Yes, I'm thinking I remember."

"Well, good luck to you." The guard's voice was friendly but his eyes were cold and searching, as if he were memorizing Nasser's features.

Nasser moved away from him quickly and headed down the hall toward the principal's office. He could hear his heart beating loudly, just from imagining what it would be like when the time came. I'm a coward. I don't want to die. I'm not worthy. The words repeated over and over in his mind. He passed the wooden plaques with the names of past top students written in gold paint, going back as far as 1902. He tried to picture his name among them. Nasser Hamdy, valedictorian. Nasser Hamdy, school athlete. Nasser, with friends. When he reached the principal's office he kept walking and headed down a flight of stairs to the cafeteria in the basement, looking over his shoulder to see if anyone was coming to stop him.

Excuse me, are you supposed to be here? What would he say if he was stopped? *Yes, this is exactly where I'm supposed to be. God himself has willed it.*

He took the steps two at a time and reached the bottom in less than a half minute. He'd have to go much more slowly and carefully when he next did this. He was struck once again by the impossibility of this plan. Something had to happen that would change the course. Youssef and Ahmed kept telling him he would stop thinking and worrying at a certain point and just be able to act, to turn himself into an automatic trigger. But it wasn't happening. He was filled with awful apprehension every waking minute.

He stood in the basement corridor, staring straight at the double-doored entrance to the cafeteria. When he reached this point in four days, he would have less than a minute to live. What would be going through his mind? Would he be thinking about his mother? His father? Elizabeth? God, he still hadn't made plans to get her out of school that day, and the time was drawing close.

Their talk the other night hadn't resolved anything. Yes, she'd rented the storage room for him, but he felt very uneasy about her. He wondered how long he could trust her not to tell anyone what she now knew. Of course, she was still his sister, but she was also an American. He wasn't sure where her loyalties lay or how far he could push her. There was a quiet resistance in her that frightened him.

He began to walk toward the cafeteria, hearing the dull roar of student voices behind the closed doors. Getting louder as he approached. Each step dragging his stomach down into his bowels and making his bones ache from within. A little scream beginning at the back of his skull. What would it be like next time?

He could picture the lunchroom, the gruesome steam-table food behind glass, the ammonia smells, the soda machines, the boys and girls leaning so far across the wooden tables that their heads touched. He could see himself walking in with the *hadduta* as they all looked up. Wondering what he was doing back here and what he wanted from them.

And then . . . what? The *hadduta* detonates and the dimensions change. The dimensions of the room, the dimensions of life. Trays go flying, glass shatters, nails tear into flesh. There are bodies and blood all over the cafeteria floor. Clothes soaked in blood. Faces torn. Fingers missing. Hands reaching for the tables, people yelling for ambulances. The will of God exploding.

He tried to imagine himself, motionless and disfigured, lying on the floor with the other mangled corpses.

God, please find a way not to let this happen. Or give me the strength to do it without fear.

He turned his head just as he passed an open doorway on the right and saw a familiar figure. Mr. Fitzgerald was leaning over a little desk in a tiny office, holding his head and rocking slightly with his eyes shut. He looked ridiculous, cramped in there, with his long legs and big shoulders. Like a troubled, overgrown child hiding in a cardboard box.

Nasser found himself standing in the doorway, staring at him in horror. Before he could move on, Mr. Fitzgerald looked up. "Oh, it's you. What are you doing back here?"

Nasser thought of backing away, but now that he'd been spotted, he realized running off would only make his presence more conspicuous. The violent feeling between them was almost more than he could bear. He could see Mr. Fitzgerald rearranging himself in his chair, trying to decide what attitude to take. Was he frightened, about to call Security?

"I'm just here for another visit," Nasser said, trying to sound casual.

"Checking up on your sister again?"

The suspicion in his voice made Nasser's guts tighten. "No," he said. "I'm coming back as a student."

He would kill this Mr. Fitzgerald. That was the one part of his destiny that he could accept. The thought of this man touching his sister made his mind boil.

"That's good," said Mr. Fitzgerald, standing up and coming over to him. "You know, we really haven't gotten a chance to talk since our little run-in in the parking lot."

Nasser shrank back a little, not sure how the big man was going to challenge him. "Yes, I'm sorry about this stupidity," he said. "I don't know what happened. I got very emotional. Thank you for not reporting on me."

"It's all right. Things happen. We had a misunderstanding." Mr. Fitzgerald looked him up and down. "But you have to understand I would never do anything improper with your sister. I was only trying to help her. I think both of us just want what's best for her."

"Yes. Of course. It's so."

They shook hands. Nasser wished he'd had a knife with him. He'd stab this bastard right now and keep him from dishonoring Elizabeth.

"And we've all been under a lot of stress, I know," said Mr. Fitzgerald, letting go of Nasser's hand and forcing himself to smile. "I guess you've heard about some of the problems *I've* been having."

"Yes, I am very sorry about this too."

"Well, I'm sure it's going to be okay." Fitzgerald peered out into the hall for a second, making sure no one was listening. "It's just the crazy twentieth century . . . You haven't heard anything by any chance, have you?"

"About what?"

"About who might have done the bombing. You never know when somebody might have noticed something."

Nasser swayed back and forth a little. God, what was he doing here, talking to this man? This was madness. He had to get away. "No, I don't know nothing."

"Okay. Let me know if that changes."

"Of course."

He felt Mr. Fitzgerald looking at him in the way that made him uncomfortable again, like when he was a student. Checking the positions of Nasser's hands, the look on his face. Seeing things Nasser didn't want to show him.

"It's good, your coming back to school," the teacher finally said. "You've got a brain. You should use it. You should make a future for yourself."

Nasser smiled miserably, at a complete loss for words. God, this devil was playing with him, trying to coax him over the threshold and dissuade him from doing his holy duty.

"So I guess I'll be seeing you around school." Mr. Fitzgerald sat down at his desk again and tried to cross his legs, but he didn't have enough room. "Do they want you to take a test to see what reading level you're at?"

"Maybe. I don't know."

Nasser found himself touching his stomach, where he'd strap on the *hadduta*. *You should make a future for yourself*. It was tempting, this alternate version of the way things could be. Maybe he could get out of this and have another kind of life. But no, he wouldn't be deterred.

Mr. Fitzgerald looked confused. "They haven't told you they want you to take a reading test?"

"Everything is in the air. You know."

"If you say so."

Mr. Fitzgerald looked down at a row of perfectly lined pencils on top of his desk. Obviously he had too much time on his hands. But that would end soon.

"Well, I have to go," said Nasser.

"Okay. I'll see you around. Though with the way things are going, you'll probably still be here long after I'm gone. Let me know if you need any help preparing for the test."

"I can handle the test." Nasser nodded and moved on down the hall, glad to escape the grip of his old teacher's attention. "Don't worry about me."

56

When Judy Mandel got back to the newsroom, she was surprised to find Renee Fitzgerald waiting at her desk.

"You called me, so I came," Renee said a little too quickly, smiling and then not smiling. "I mean, first I called you back and then when I got your voice mail, I decided to show up . . ."

"Whoa, whoa, whoa." Judy threw up her hands.

This was a little too much neurosis being thrown at her too fast. Yes, she had called Renee from her cell phone right after her conversation with David, but she'd expected to have a few minutes to get her questions together.

Her faith in the bomber story, the signal achievement of her career so far, had been shaken a little by the things he'd said, and she needed some assurance she'd gotten at least part of it right. Across the newsroom, she could see Robert in his glass-enclosed office talking to Mr. Hampton, the newspaper's visiting owner. He was smaller than she'd imagined, Mr. Hampton, with a deep tan and wide, slightly simian nostrils. On another occasion, she might have tried sauntering in there in a micro-mini and saying something juicy and provocative to get the owner's attention. But there was no time for that today.

"So what's going on?" she asked Renee, quickly clearing files from her chair so her guest could sit.

Renee remained standing. "I need to talk to you about the article you wrote."

"Which one?"

Judy was aware of other reporters and editors staring at her from across the newsroom. The massive rainstorm clatter of ten thousand computer keys slowed down to a tentative tap-tap-tap drizzle.

"The interview you did with me." Renee clawed at a worn black Coach bag at her side. Judy saw the nails were bitten down to bloody nubs. Why hadn't she noticed that before? Was she so preoccupied with getting the bigger story that she'd missed the most obvious little details?

"Well, why are you coming to me now?" said Judy, taking a seat and lowering her voice. "That story's been out for days."

"I know." Renee licked at the dark indentation in the middle of her lower lip. "It's just that . . . Look, Judy, the truth is, I really don't have my act together. I haven't for a really long time."

Judy turned her head slowly and saw Nazi and Mr. Hampton watching her through the glass window of the editor's office. Even without hearing the words or knowing the details, they clearly sensed some career-immolating disaster unfolding in the newsroom.

"I don't know why I told you all those things," Renee was saying, her green eyes sweeping back and forth frantically. "David never hit me. He never hurt Arthur. He's a good man . . ."

"Look, Renee." Judy cut her off, desperate to salvage some little piece of the story. "If you're just saying this because David and his lawyers are pressuring you and threatening to sue, you're not doing anybody any favors."

Maybe that's what was going on here, Judy told herself. They'd all conspired to twist this poor woman's arm and make her take her story back.

But without another word, Renee reached into her bag and started lining up little orange prescription bottles along the edge of Judy's desk.

"You see?" she said.

"What am I supposed to be seeing?" Judy studied the prescription labels, the names of the drugs vaguely familiar from science articles: Lithium. Zoloft, Clozaril, Paxil.

"They don't give you these for these cramps," Renee said, bending gracefully and sweeping the bottles back into her bag. "This is who I am. This is what I'm up against. I want you to understand that."

Judy looked around for Bill Ryan, to give her moral support, but again he wasn't there. She felt a flash of resentment at him. It was all his fault, setting her up with all that hype about the good old days, integrity, and sticking your chin out. Didn't he know all that went out with Sinatra's fedora and Toots Shor's restaurant? Now look what she'd done. Had she really gone and ruined an innocent man's life?

"So what are you saying?" she asked Renee defensively. "I'm not supposed to believe anything you said before because you were taking pills and seeing a doctor?"

"No!" Renee grabbed Judy's shoulder for emphasis. "I'm saying I need David around to raise our son. He can't go to jail. Look at me, Judy. This is me. This is real. I'm a mess, but I'm trying to do the right thing. We won't make it if he goes away."

Judy tried to return her look but found herself quickly turning away. From the corner of her eye, she saw the green cursor on her computer screen blinking over and over, as if asking her, *now what are you going to do?* She politely excused herself, went into the ladies' room, and threw up.

57

As he sat on the elevated platform of the Stillwell Avenue station—the last stop in the city for some trains—David felt he'd finally reached the breaking point.

His eyes surveyed the gaudy and wrecked Coney Island skyline. This morning, a woman had called him a "child killer" on the train coming in, mixing up two unfounded allegations. Then shortly after he arrived at school, Larry Simonetti had come down to his office even whiter than usual with fury, having gotten wind of David's questioning students about the bombing instead of helping them with their essays. "I'll have you bounced by the end of the day if it happens again," he'd threatened. And worst of all, the story of the inconclusive lie detector test was in all the morning papers.

David laced his fingers on top of his head, feeling the full accumulated weight of the last two weeks descend on him. The interrogations, the raids, Renee's breakdown, Arthur's asthma, the lawyers, the talk shows. He was almost too tired to prioritize his worries. Up in the sky, seagulls looked like eraser marks against the clouds.

He didn't notice Elizabeth Hamdy until she was standing right in front of him.

"So I saw you on television the other night," she said, sucking in her cheeks.

A D train roared by on the other side of the tracks, sounding like a hundred trash cans rolling down a flight of concrete stairs.

"Great, huh?" He started to roll his eyes. "They ought to give me my own show."

"It got me thinking," she said.

" 'Bout what?"

"About things we've talked about in class. Things you've said to me." She looked away, raised her shoulders and then dropped them. "They keep going around in my head. Like what you read from the Stephen Crane book a few weeks ago."

"What was that?" He felt like he was pushing through waves of fatigue, trying to hear her.

"About what you would do in a war," she said. "Would you stay or would you run away?"

"I don't really see the connection, but then again I'm pretty fried."

Her eyes strayed, following a seagull walking by on the platform with a cigarette butt in its mouth. "You asked me something the other day and I didn't really answer it honestly."

"Oh yeah?"

He looked up at her, scratching his chin. She was transmitting, but he wasn't set up to receive her yet. Something was happening here. He forced himself to focus. "Why don't you sit down?" He patted the seat next to him.

She glanced around, as if she was thinking of bolting, and then gradually, reluctantly, lowered herself to his side, not daring to look at him directly. "It's hard, what I have to tell you. I feel like I'm coming apart."

"Then just say it already," he said, feeling pressure moving around inside of him. "Come on, we've known each other a long time, Elizabeth. If you don't trust me by now, then you're never going to."

"All right. Okay." She tried out three different expressions, before settling on a tight-mouthed determination. "You were asking me before about the day of the bombing," she said finally. "Right?"

"Right." He swatted a fly away. "And you reminded me you weren't there." Another in the classic series of frustrating dead-end conversations.

She took a deep breath as an out-of-service train pulled into the station. "There's a little more to it."

"Okay." He felt like he was cautiously peering around a half-opened door.

"My brother asked me to stay home that day. That's what I've been trying to tell you." She turned her feet at the ankles and contemplated them, avoiding his eyes. "He said he was going to take me shopping. And then he showed up late."

"And this is significant *why* exactly?" He noticed her eyes were sunken and her cheeks were drawn, like she hadn't gotten much sleep lately. "Come on, Elizabeth. Just tell me what you want to tell me. I'm no good at reading between the lines anymore."

The out-of-service train pulled out of the station and she squinted, making little asterisks appear near the corners of her eyes. "He showed up right after the bomb went off," she said. "Because he was the one who put it there."

The train was gone, but the station was still reverberating. "How do you know that?" said David.

"He told me."

David sat very still. Wide awake now. Not wanting to disturb the moment.

"Your brother planted the bomb." David coughed and replayed the last five seconds of conversation in his mind, trying to make sure he hadn't imagined it.

She turned away, pressing the heels of her hands against her eyes to keep from crying. "You see? That's what I mean. It's like the things we've talked about. Do you stay or run away when you're in trouble? All this time, I've wanted to tell you, but I've been afraid. I've gone back and forth on it a hundred times. It's like a hand over my heart."

David held himself in check, trying not to overreact. But in his mind, he heard a crowd starting to cheer. It sounded like long-dead fans at Ebbets Field, rising in the stands again.

He looked at Elizabeth. She was a beautiful doorway between one part of his life and another.

"Have you told anyone else about this?" he asked cautiously.

"I haven't said anything to anyone."

David closed his eyes and pictured the after-image of a train disappearing down the tracks on his inner lids. No, no, he wouldn't believe this. He wouldn't let his guard down so easily. There had to be a catch.

"So what are we going to do about this?" he said.

He had to go slowly and carefully here. It was like walking on thin ice in baseball cleats.

"I don't know," Elizabeth murmured. "I don't know what I'm going to do."

"Have you thought about going to the police?"

She looked up, hurt, worried that he was about to betray her. "A detective already came to our house. He said my brother would get the death penalty if it turned out he had anything to do with what happened. So I lied to him too."

"Okay."

David glanced down the platform at a pay phone, wanting to call his lawyers immediately. But then he stopped himself, realizing she was still like a bird on a railing. If he moved too quickly to grab her, she'd fly away.

"It's not just him, you know," she said in a choked voice. "It's what he's been through and the people he's with. The political situation. The terrible choices."

Yeah, *yeah*, *yeah*, thought David. And if pigs had wings and your aunt had a mustache and all the other Hall of Fame rationalizations. To understand isn't always to forgive. Sometimes, to understand is just to understand.

"Do you think he's capable of doing it again?"

She sniffed and wiped her face with the side of her arm. "I don't know. He asked me to rent him a storage space in the city. He told me he was going to put some material there. Compressors. So I don't know."

David sucked on his teeth and thought of Nasser. Their fight in the parking lot, their conversation in the office yesterday, his flickering, edgy presence in class. It's always the quiet ones.

"We gotta deal with this, Elizabeth," he said. "If your brother killed somebody in another bombing and you hadn't told the FBI about this, you could go to jail. Okay?"

"I know, I know." She doubled over on the bench, arms against her stomach. "But if I tell anyone, he could have me killed. You don't know what they're like, the people I think he's hooked up with. My father's told me about them, the fanatics from back home. Their whole lives are about killing."

David listened for a minute, to the sound of car alarms and seagulls crying in the distance. What could he tell her? What possible relevant experience could he offer to advise her? Come on. You're supposed to be a teacher. Teach.

"So which way are you leaning?" he asked, taking off his glasses and trying to give her some space.

"I don't know, I don't know." She moved against him and rested her head lightly against his shoulder. "It's going to kill my father to find out about this. It's against everything he ever wanted for us."

The weight of her head on his shoulder stirred him a little, even though he knew it shouldn't.

"You have to make a choice, Elizabeth." He tried to move and subtly shift his weight. "You know, it's like what we've talked about in class. Sometimes, you gotta step to it and see what you can live with."

"*No.* I don't want you to give me choices." She began crying and burrowing into the folds of his jacket. "I want you to tell me what to do."

He thought about putting an arm around her, but stopped himself. What if one of her classmates or another teacher saw them? The train they'd both been waiting for finally pulled in, but he ignored it.

"You know, I know what you've been going through. I'm not just this stupid girl." She pulled away, suddenly, so she could see him whole. "I know you have a wife and a child and they're blaming you for something you didn't do."

"There is that," he said.

"Well, I *can't* live with that. I just *can't*." She started to touch his knee and then took her hand away. "It's not the right thing. It's *haram*."

He looked over, surprised to hear her using her brother's word. But she'd moved on.

"Maybe it'd be different if you were somebody I didn't know or care about." She took out a Kleenex and blew her nose. "Then I could just side with my family and hope no one would find out. But this is *you*. Right? This is you."

For a few seconds, he couldn't respond. He felt like she'd dropped her raw, bleeding heart into his lap.

"We gotta work this out," he said.

"Oh God, I am not ready for this. I am not." She balled up the Kleenex and kicked at her book bag, threatening to send it tumbling over the edge of the platform. "Okay," she said, sighing and straightening up. "Just help me with this. Help me think it through. What will happen if I do tell the police about Nasser? Would he get the death penalty?"

"I don't know. You could probably plead mercy on his behalf."

"And what about his friends? They'd kill me if they found out about this. How would you protect me from them?"

"How would *I* protect you?" A good practical question that had never occurred to him. David put his glasses back on. "Um, well, you know, they have witness protection programs they could put you in, the FBI. They can change your name, give you a new place to live, a new school . . ."

The more he talked, the farther Elizabeth leaned away from him. She looked seasick and pale.

"You mean, I could never see my family again?"

"Well, I don't know, maybe you could all go in . . ."

"Then I can't do it," she said. "My father couldn't handle this. To take away everything he's worked for and make him live like a criminal and ruin my sisters' lives . . . It would kill him."

The train closed its doors and pulled away with a jolt. David watched the last car disappear down the tracks and knew he shouldn't miss the next one.

"Well, maybe they won't have to play it that way," he said. "Maybe they could use your information without making you testify in court. That's something you could talk to my lawyers about. Making sure you're protected."

That's right. Fob it off on the experts. Don't take any responsibility yourself. Manipulate this poor girl against her brother. Maybe you're not such a big man after all. She's the one taking the real risk here. Self-preservation wrestled with self-disgust. Self-preservation had the natural weight advantage, but self-disgust was pretty good in the clinches, David remembered.

"You sure this is the right thing to do?" Elizabeth asked. "I need you to tell me."

All of a sudden, she wasn't just a doorway anymore. He could see what was going on inside of her, and it made him unhappy. The vulnerable brown eyes, the mouth trying to be strong, the delicate shoulders. Why couldn't she be harder, more self-centered, like an American girl? Yes, he'd jarred a little information out of her by his questioning, but she'd come all the way across on her own, looking to do the right thing and help him. So could he let her just go ahead and risk her life for him? Self-disgust said: *Think about it*. Self-preservation said: *Go for it, dude!*

"Yeah, I think it's the right thing," said David.

Besides, said self-preservation, *other people's lives are at stake here*. This wasn't just selfish thinking. *Yeah, sure*, said self-disgust. *And here's a little stomach acid for your trouble*.

David grimaced. "So do you want me to pass on the information to my lawyers and see what they can work out?"

"I don't know, maybe. I'm not sure." Elizabeth raised her chin. "Yes. I guess that's what I need to do."

Another train pulled in. *A hero one day a week and a bum the other six*, said David's self-disgust. You never were worth anything anyway. *Kiss my ass*, said self-preservation. *I'm going to Disneyland.*

58

Ever since the decision had been made about the suicide bombing, Youssef and Dr. Ahmed had put Nasser under almost constant watch. They mixed chemicals for both dynamite and the fuel bombs with him at the garage, with nitric acid scorching his hands and burning his clothes as he tried to funnel it into little cardboard boxes. They took him to various mosques and prayed with him five times a day, making sure he did at least three full *rakas* on each occasion. They ate all his meals with him, they went with him to move the car, slept in the same room with him and, most important, they forbade him to have any further contact with his family.

Of course, this was to be expected. He'd always heard that the leaders cut the suicide bombers off from their friends and family in the days just before they were "activated." This was as it should be, he'd thought. Isolation was the best way to maintain the purity of purpose, especially so close to the end, when one's faith could wobble. But now he felt overwhelmed by terrifying loneliness and uncertainty. He longed to reach out to someone, anyone. About once every two minutes, he found himself wavering in his decision. It complicated everything. At meals, he couldn't choose between meat and vegetables; when walking into rooms, he couldn't make up his mind whether to go left or right.

Finally, he couldn't take it anymore. He waited until Dr. Ahmed collapsed from exhaustion and fell asleep early on Tuesday night and then sneaked out of their little behind-the-cab-stand hovel, seeking solace.

The time had come to see his old cell mate Professor Bin-Khaled. He'd carefully checked the City University class schedules again, and at ten o'clock, just as a gray drizzle began to fall on the city, he pulled up outside the building on West 42nd Street again and waited in his Lincoln Town Car. After a few minutes, the professor came out, talking to several students. Again, it struck Nasser how much Ibrahim had aged since the last time they'd talked.

"*Asalam allakem*, brother," Nasser called out the window. "You need a ride?"

Ibrahim approached cautiously, but his face broke into a hard-earned smile as he recognized Nasser. "Many years, little brother." He climbed into the car and they briefly embraced. "Many years."

The professor smelled of old tobacco and Turkish coffee. Nothing of the old prison stink remained with him. It was funny. When they shared a cell, they'd only been allowed one shower a week, and for years after his release, Nasser made a point of bathing twice a day. He sometimes thought he saw people wrinkling their noses as if they could still smell the jail on him.

"So can I take you somewhere?"

The professor used the moment to look at Nasser. His deep brown eyes refracted the light, as if he were measuring some distance between them. "Yes," he said finally. "Yes, that would be good. I am staying with a professor from Columbia."

He gave Nasser an address on the Upper West Side.

"Do you like to sit in the back, like a real passenger?" Nasser turned to make sure he hadn't left any newspapers or rags lying in the backseat.

"No, my friend. I am fine being in front with you."

Nasser studied the side of the older man's face as he got into the car. Seven years had brought new lines and crags and for a moment, Nasser felt a surge of gladness that he would never have a son of his own to lose, and therefore would never know such deep sorrow.

"So, my little brother," said the professor as they started up Sixth Avenue. "You have been in the city all this time, and you've never come to see me. Why is this?"

"I'm sorry, sheik. I've been busy, very, very busy."

"Sheik?" The professor looked bemused as they approached the diamond district. "I am not a sheik. I'm just a teacher. What have you been up to, my friend?"

"I am studying more the religion these days. I'm trying to understand God."

"Oh yes?" The professor looked through the briefcase on his lap, making sure he had all the papers he needed. "This is good, to study the Koran. This can be a great comfort in life. And what else have you been doing?"

"Politics." This was the euphemism Nasser had settled on when he tried to imagine this conversation several hours before. "I've been getting more involved in the politics."

"Oh, yes, the politics." The professor sighed, as they passed Radio City Music Hall. "I am afraid I don't have much time for politics anymore."

"Yes, there have been so many lies and disappointments." Nasser gripped the wheel, noticing once again it seemed loose since his conversation with his sister the other night. "Sometimes I think maybe the time for talking with the Jews is over. There is no point to this anymore. Now is the time for action."

"Actually, I don't have time for any of the politicians anymore." The professor wearily pulled on his seat belt and buckled it. "Not the Jews or the Arabs. Not since Abu died."

"Yes, I was sad to hear about this." The hum and pitch of traffic noise rose in Nasser's ears as he made a left on Central Park South. "I should have written to you."

Abu was the professor's firstborn son. Nasser remembered him coming to visit at the jail once or twice. A big-eyed boy with a haystack of black hair and an infectious laugh. Even the Israeli guards were nice to him, letting him wear their hats and not getting too upset when he asked to hold their guns. The circumstances of his death were still vague to Nasser. There'd been a stone-throwing incident between some local children and the Jewish settlers in Hebron, and then a confrontation in a schoolyard, and in the gunfire that followed, Abu was killed protecting a friend. He was sixteen years old. The age Nasser was when he first met the professor in prison.

"They should all die, the ones that did this," said Nasser, stopping at a red light near Columbus Circle. "When I think about the way these things happen, I think a bomb should come and blow all of them up. And there should be no remorse about this."

The professor grimaced. "I don't think this is the answer, the violence," he said quietly.

"But how can you say this?" Nasser was indignant. "After they put you in prison and killed your son? How can you not want them all dead?"

The professor raised a wry eyebrow. "Nasser, did I ever tell you the story of how they first tortured me?"

"No. I'm not sure. I don't know."

After all these years, the torture stories had begun to flow together and meld in his mind, mixed in with lies and exaggerations from the younger prisoners.

"Well," said the professor. "You know they jailed me for this ridiculous reason, for 'resisting the occupation' and suspicion of being a terrorist. There was nothing to it, but anyway, they were trying to get me to confess before I went to trial. So every day for a month, they would take me to see this same man, Avi, to answer the same questions over and over in his office, until one day, he said, 'I'm sorry, you're not giving us what we want. And now we're going to have to get physical with you.' So they handcuffed me behind my back, laid me down on the floor faceup, put a chair between my legs, and then this man, this Avi, reached down and squeezed my balls as hard as he could."

"Oh." Nasser stepped too hard on the gas and the car shot out into the busy intersection, near that monstrous Trump hotel, a black-and-gold whore of a building. He had to swerve to avoid getting hit by a truck. "This must have been agony."

"It was," said the professor. "It was terrible. The most pain I've ever felt in my life, physically. And there was only one way I could get through it."

"You became numb," said Nasser, remembering the stinking bag over his face.

"No," said the professor. "While he was squeezing me, I started telling myself, *He is getting weaker and I am getting stronger*. And then I looked up and I said to him, 'Didn't you tell me you got a degree in developmental psychiatry in the United States?' And he said, 'Yes.' So I said, 'And now you are squeezing my balls?' "

"So what happened?"

"He let go and never tortured me again." The professor allowed himself just a brief chuckle.

Nasser looked out over the dashboard, and the patterns of traffic didn't make sense to him for a few seconds. They were just red lights flashing and blinking in the night.

"I don't understand," he said, heading up Broadway. "How can you not want to hurt such people the way they've hurt you?"

The professor took some cigarette rolling papers and a tobacco pouch out of his briefcase. "Nasser, I don't think I ever mentioned it to you, but before I went to prison I was in favor of the peace process."

"No, you never said this."

"Well, probably it never seemed appropriate, after what happened with Hamid and all of us getting thrown in solitary confinement and kept away from our families. I mean, to be angry about such things is only human. I don't claim the Israelis are any friends to me. But to give in to the violence?" He raised his hands, as if considering the idea, and then dropped them. "This doesn't do anything. This doesn't help anyone, except the people who make the violence and can't imagine any other life for themselves. Violence can't make a state by itself. Violence can only make more violence. It's like a law of physics."

"So you are still for making peace?" Nasser looked over at the sideview mirror, trying to conceal his disgust. "After what they've done to you? After they killed your son?"

The car hit a pothole and was jolted, but the professor remained steady and focused on the task of laying tobacco onto the flattened rolling paper on the dashboard.

"I have to be bigger than that," he said. "The Jews have suffered too, at least as much. They lost six million. And I still have five more children. How does it help them to make a war so they can be killed? I don't want them to live like slaves, it's true. But every day when I go home in Hebron, I drive past the schoolyard where Abu was killed, and every night I look out my window and I see where the settlers live. I have to find a way to live like this. I cannot go around poisoned by hate forever. I have lost too much already. Life will never have the same taste again, the same joy. You understand? I cannot stand to lose any more."

For the next few minutes, Nasser was silent. He'd hoped that seeing the professor tonight would strengthen his resolve and give him a sense of clarity about his mission. He'd wanted to fuel himself with the older man's righteous anger, remember the dead, and rededicate himself to the cause. But instead he just felt more confused than ever.

They stopped in front of a sand-colored prewar apartment building on West 106th Street. A stiff wind made a play of shivering tree shadows and streetlights across Nasser's hood. The professor offered to roll him a cigarette, but he turned it down.

"You are good, my friend?"

"I am good." Nasser rested his chin on top of the wheel.

"I'm glad you came to see me tonight." The professor touched his shoulder. "It makes me think of the old days. When my son was still alive. I wonder if he would have turned out like you."

Nasser started to reply, wanting to say it was a tragedy, everything was a tragedy, but his throat was too parched and the words wouldn't come out.

In the meantime, the professor lowered his window and lit the cigarette he'd rolled for himself. "You know, it's a funny thing," he said wistfully. "I used to have a little private moment for myself, before I went to sleep most nights. A little daydream of something I hoped for. It would give me a little thrill of delight, just to think about it. A house I'd like to build for my mother. A college I'd want my son to go to. A rich and decent husband for my daughters. But then after Abu died, the dreams stopped. And I keep waiting for them to come back. Every night, I ask myself, 'What will I dream about tonight?' Sometimes I wonder if I can still dream."

"What's the answer?" Nasser asked.

"I don't know." The older man blew a long white line of smoke into the air and then watched it curl and dissipate as he opened the passenger-side door. "So, do you still dream, Nasser?"

59

"Let's set some ground rules here," said Jim Lefferts, the FBI's assistant director for the New York office. "Immunity is not on the table."

"Then we're not *at* the table." Ralph Marcovicci tapped David on the shoulder, rose slowly to his full six feet and three hundred pounds and began to amble toward the door of the conference room. "Come on, you guys, let's go get some whitefish at Greengrass."

His co-counsel, Judah Rosenbloom, hastily put his papers back into his battered overstuffed briefcase and scrambled after Ralph. David just sat there, stunned that his chance for redemption could be slipping away so easily.

"Really, boys, let's not go getting our panties in a twist." Lefferts, an ex–football player with a desk covered with Marine Corps mementos, smiled tolerantly. "We both have interests to protect here. Nobody wants any more shit splattered on their shoes."

David looked up and smiled encouragingly at his lawyers, like an overanxious parent trying to get the kids to play nice in the sandbox. But Ralph remained by the door and Judah stood stiffly with his jaw grinding and his ponytail swaying.

"As far as I can tell, Agent Lefferts, our client is the only one whose shoes have been splattered," Judah said with well-practiced indignation. "But now that David's attempting to bring forward information that could lead to a successful conclusion to this investigation, you're trying to splatter him some more. I think it's just outrageous!"

Lefferts's eyelids drooped, as if he was already bored with this little playlet. "I'm just saying, it's still not clear to me how we know your client is not an accomplice in this bombing. It seems awfully suspicious, the way he came into possession of this information. How do we know he's not a co-conspirator with these Arab gentlemen?"

"Oh come on, Jim, he's not a fuckin' co-conspirator." Ralph came back and sat down again, his chair giving a loud, alarming squeak. "He's a fuckin' schoolteacher. The bomber's the brother of one of the girls in his class. The girl likes him and gives up the brother, who she's got some problems with. What's so hard to believe about that?"

"Well, I'm still not entirely comfortable." Lefferts pushed his chair back from the table and winced as if suffering from an old football injury. "How's it going to look if the Bureau gets bitten in the ass again because your guy did it with somebody else and then decided to rat them out? We don't need another public relations disaster."

David started to open his mouth and protest, but Judah put a firm hand on his shoulder.

"A public relations disaster?" Ralph smiled and hunched over the table, like a poker player finally getting a run of cards he liked. "What do you call Waco? What do you call Ruby Ridge? What about all the other terrorist bombings where you never caught the guys?"

Lefferts winced again. "Well, I don't see the specific analogy."

Even Judah Rosenbloom started laughing.

"Gimme a fuckin' break, Jim." Ralph put his hands behind his head. "We're giving you the names of the bombers and the location where they have the explosives stored. We'll even bring the girl in to talk to you once we have an agreement. You want us to make the arrest and call the press conference too?"

Lefferts's face turned red. "Who said anything about a press conference?"

"Come on, Jim, get real. Our guy is giving the case to you on a platter. The least you can to is put out a release clearing his name and apologizing."

Lefferts looked at David, as if he was reality-checking, and then he barked at Ralph: "That's ridiculous."

"Let's go, David." Judah turned and swung his briefcase toward the door, clearly expecting David to follow. "I don't think we have anything else to discuss here."

Ralph flashed Lefferts a "hey-what-can-I-do-I'm-working-with-a-lunatic?" look, as if he was suddenly the reasonable one, and started to stand again.

"Now, now, now." Lefferts patted the air like a minister settling the congregation. "Let's just take a mental minute here and come to our senses. If we end up arresting somebody else for this crime, doesn't it stand to reason that the public will know your client is innocent?"

"Not good enough." Ralph remained in an awkward half crouch above his chair. "We want *vindication*."

"Well, the Bureau is not going to hold a press conference announcing that a man who was never arrested is not a suspect. You can just forget that, right now. This isn't one of your Larchmont Lolita circuses. As far as I'm concerned, our agents didn't do anything wrong. We had a lead and we investigated it. End of story. We don't apologize to everyone we investigate. And it wasn't us who damaged your client's precious 'reputation' anyway. If you've got a problem with that, take it up with the newspapers and the television stations."

"Then we have nothing else to talk about." Ralph stood up all the way. "The girl doesn't come in. David, come on."

David started to rise, feeling sick and unstable. Lefferts looked at him irritably.

"David, sit down," he said.

They were playing with him. Or rather they were playing with each other, and he just happened to be in the middle.

Without waiting for any further signal from his lawyers, he stood up with hands on the edge of the conference table as if he was about to overturn it.

"Just shut up," he said, feeling the blood rush to his face. "Okay? Can everyone just shut up a minute?"

The three of them were looking up at him as though he was a great building on the verge of collapse. But he stared down at a little paperweight shaped like the soldiers raising the flag at Iwo Jima. *My father's war.*

"I've had it with all the strategies and counterstrategies," he said quietly. "I'm fed up with all the surveillance and scrutiny. My students think I've betrayed them. My son has heard his father called a murderer. And my wife is ready for Bellevue. All *I* want is for this to be over. *Now.* I want you guys out of my life. Is that clear to you?"

Lefferts and the two lawyers looked at one another slightly aghast, as if to say, *What's his problem?* But David no longer cared about their good opinion. He just wanted to be made whole again.

"Ball's in your court, Jim." Ralph smiled, nervously watching David from the corner of his eye. "You need our client to bring the girl in, because your agents failed to find the real bombers. You need her to testify. And my client's the only one who can deliver her. Otherwise, she doesn't cooperate."

"Yes, well." Lefferts cleared his throat and looked at Ralph sideways. "Is that something you want publicized too? Him deserving credit?"

A part of David wanted to say yes. The same part that sat in the lifeguard chair, looking for someone to save, and stood in the outfield, waiting for a fly ball to come his way.

But all he said was: "Over. That's what I want."

Jim Lefferts shook his head, half sad and half amused, as if somehow he knew this would all end in tears. "Well, all right," he said. "You want your precious name back, you can have it back. But no official press conference apology. Word leaked out once, I guess it can happen again the same way."

60

Judy Mandel was humming again. That low ominous sound from just under the breastbone.

"When you do that, it reminds me of '*This has been a test of the Emergency Broadcast System*,' " said John LeVecque. " '*Had this been a real emergency you would have been asked to report to a fallout shelter . . .*' "

"Do I make you that nervous?"

They were sitting in a brown-paneled restaurant near City Hall called Spaghetti Western. Ceiling fans turned slowly, doing nothing to the air. A young lawyer in a double-breasted Italian suit was standing at the bar near the front, bragging to friends about how much money he'd just won in a civil case. "Three point seven mil! That judge loves my ass!"

In the booth opposite LeVecque and Judy, a middle-aged white woman with the face of a time-ravaged Botticelli model sat stirring her drink and staring into space, as though still trying to come to terms with a broken date from years before.

"So what's doing with the Fitzgerald case?" Judy said.

"Is that why you asked me out?" LeVecque played the mopey teenager, rearranging rolls in the bread basket.

"How do you mean?"

"I mean, is that the only basis we have for a relationship? You ask me about this case and I try to avoid answering you?"

"John!"

A waitress walked by. "Can I get a Bass ale and a shot of tequila?" he asked.

"I didn't know you drank like that," said Judy.

"I've changed. A lot of things have changed these last few weeks. Things haven't been . . . all that great at home."

"Oh?"

"Well, how would you know anyway? You never really ask me about myself. It's just work, work, work with you."

She smiled uncomfortably. She'd had a vague sense he'd been leading up to this the last couple of times they'd had lunch, but she'd ignored the signals.

"I'm crazy about you," he said. "You know that, don't you?"

The waitress brought him the beer and the shot. Outside it was getting dark and the neon signs in the window bled their light into the street. A gate roared down in front of a discount shoe store across the way.

Off-balance and tongue-tied, Judy tried to change the subject. "So I heard they were about to arrest somebody else for the bombing."

But LeVecque kept after her. "You know I've thought about leaving my wife for you and I've never even kissed you. Isn't that crazy?"

Judy felt her insides gather into a tight ball. This wasn't right. This wasn't meant to happen at all. They'd been sparring partners. Didn't he know flirting was just part of the game? This was a man with a family. Another responsibility she didn't want.

"Did you hear what I said?"

He leaned hard on the table and it began to tip over. She caught it just in time.

"John, I'm feeling very awkward about this. Could we talk about something else for a minute? I need to get my thoughts in order."

"Sure, sure, of course. I know I'm putting you on the spot." He reached out to cover her hand with his, but she moved it slightly, without being obvious.

She started humming again. "So. David Fitzgerald."

"What about him?" LeVecque asked glumly.

"So he wasn't the bomber, after all. His lawyers are saying he's about to be cleared."

"*You* were the one who wrote he was the guy in the first place." He pulled his lips back from his teeth.

"*You* were the one who told me that."

"That was supposed to be off-the-record." He paused and emotions whirled across his face; it was like watching a carousel turn. "You pulled it out of me. You betrayed me. I don't even know why I'm so attracted to you." He finished both the shot and the beer and ordered another round. "There must be something wrong with me."

Judy looked down into her wine glass. Come on. Get through it. Get what you need to write this story. Don't make this too personal. Don't let him suck you in.

"So now they know who did it?" she asked.

"Now *we* know," LeVecque said defensively.

"And is an arrest going to be made?"

"Yes. Maybe. Soon. Very soon." More spins of the carousel. "Look, I don't want to get into all this," he said. "I'm not going to let you do this to me again."

"Just confirm one last thing for me. Okay? The lawyers say he's cooperating?"

"Yeah, all right. I heard that too."

"What does it mean?"

"I don't know." LeVecque's thin blond hair was standing up a little. He patted it and looked distracted. "It means he's not giving anybody a problem."

"So he's helping with the investigation. Can I say that?"

Having taken a sledgehammer to the teacher these past couple of weeks, Judy was anxious to redeem herself and get it right. She was finding it difficult to sleep at night, thinking of some of the things she'd written about David Fitzgerald. So if she gave him a little too much credit in the process, then that was all right with her.

"Say whatever you want." LeVecque took his new drinks from the waitress. Judy noticed his hands were shaking. "I don't know anything about anything anymore, Judy. You got me hanging upside down. I probably shouldn't tell you anything. I probably shouldn't even talk to you anymore, because you'll just betray me. But I can't help myself. I know I'm drunk, but I have to try for the Hail Mary pass. Can you understand that?"

"No."

"Well I don't give a damn. I'm diving into the sidewalk anyway."

He gulped the shot and started on his beer. In the brooding silence, she could hear the bartender stacking glasses.

"I'm crazy about you," LeVecque said, putting the glass down, unaware of his foam mustache.

"I know, John," she said quietly. "But don't do this."

He didn't seem to hear her. "I mean, I know you look at me and you see I'm this middle-aged white guy working for the city and losing his hair. But there's more to me than that. I'm still alive inside. Inside I'm still soaring." He stopped to catch his breath. "So I guess what I'm saying is if you'd give me the chance, Judy, I could soar with you. I could still be better than what I am."

"Oh, John." She finally touched his hand, lightly. "You don't even know me."

The hope in his eyes began to fade. "No chance, huh?"

"I'm getting married in December."

She was doing nothing of the kind. And now that she'd lied about it, she felt she never would. She'd cursed her own future. A melancholy old Smokey Robinson song started playing on the jukebox. Something about love and mirages. She was beginning to think she would never have a child either; she didn't have enough trust to pass on. John LeVecque sat up a little and tried to straighten his tie.

"Well, I guess that's that." He took his hand back. "I hope you got what you needed."

"John, I don't know what to say to you."

She stared at the sweaty palm print he'd left on the tabletop. It was as if she'd run down a drunk who'd stumbled in front of her car. She felt guilty and mad at him at the same time. Yes, she'd teased and played with him to get this story, but he'd been complicit in all that. And now he was laying all this misery on her that was probably older than she was. It wasn't right. Yes, she felt guilty about it, but she felt a lot more guilty about David Fitzgerald. She looked at her watch and tried to calculate how long it would take her to get back to the office and write this story for tomorrow's paper. Almost six o'clock. She'd have to call Nazi and get him to hold the front page for her.

"We could have soared," LeVecque was saying. "I'm still so crazy about you."

She suddenly had a vision of him as a man caught in a long, elaborate dream. And here he was trying to catch her in it too. All this talk about soaring and being alive inside. It didn't have that much to do with her, she realized. It was the dream of a sad middle-aged man. In fact, once she moved on, there'd be another girl reporter in a short skirt for him to torture himself with and he wouldn't even remember her.

This was a very old game, she was finally realizing. And it was someone else's turn to play.

"John, let's get the check," she said. "It's late and I have to make a call."

61

Early the next morning, Nasser sat behind the wheel of the Lincoln Town Car, with Youssef and Dr. Ahmed in the backseat. The day seemed stunned and not quite ready to begin. Clouds like brains and old socks floated in the sky. A brown UPS truck was parked across the street. And a stumpy little Hispanic man in a white shirt and a tie hauled up the corrugated gate in front of West Side Storage.

"We wait ten minutes before we go in to get the material," said Dr. Ahmed, reading the top half of a folded-up newspaper. "Make sure no one's watching us."

"Blessings of Allah," said Youssef, eating a powdered sugar donut beside him. "I know we will have success."

"*Insh'allah*, if God is willing." The doctor straightened the paper three times in rapid succession and flashed an angry look in Nasser's rearview mirror.

The feeling between them had been coarse and volatile since Nasser sneaked out to see the professor the night before last. Dr. Ahmed had instantly accused him of being a *khan al-'ahad*—a sellout—and going to see the police, to alert them of the bombing plans. He'd demanded that Nasser show them exactly where he'd driven and tell them everything he'd discussed with Ibrahim. "*Yin an a bouk,*" he'd said. "I'll kill your whole family if I find out you've betrayed us."

And what made it worse was that inside his heart Nasser knew the doctor was half right about him. Doubts had been eating away at him since his conversation with Professor Bin-Khaled. Was the doctor pushing the suicide bombing plan to compete with his old friend Mehdi? Was it something other than a sacrifice for God? And now that he'd had time to think about it, what made it worse was finding out that Ahmed was in fact not a medical doctor or a doctor of chemistry, but a doctor of psychology. Someone perhaps capable of manipulating a young man's mind.

Nasser looked down at his door handle and was seized by the urge to pull it back, throw the door open, and go fleeing into traffic down Tenth Avenue. Away from Dr. Ahmed and Youssef. Away from the imam with his vague pronouncements. He didn't want to be a martyr. Forget the past, the wars, the bombs, the dead bus driver, the intimations of everlasting glory. He wanted to start all over again. Change his name. Reinvent himself. People in America did it all the time.

"Here, look at this." Dr. Ahmed thrust the newspaper at Youssef. "It's a good thing we go soon. We're running out of time."

"What is it?" Nasser checked them in the rearview.

Youssef wiped his beard and studied the paper intently while the doctor glanced once over his shoulder and then suddenly craned his neck to look out the back window.

"Your teacher is not in trouble anymore." Youssef adjusted his aviator glasses as he read. "They say he's no longer a suspect. He's a cooperator. What this means, I don't know. How could he cooperate if he doesn't know nothing?"

"Maybe he knows something." Dr. Ahmed turned back around and faced front.

For once, he wasn't fidgeting, blowing his nose, pulling on his beard, or doing any of his other rapid movements. He'd become rigid with tension.

"What's the matter, sheik?" asked Nasser. "You seem nervous."

The doctor's tongue slid around under his lips. "They are watching us," he said quietly.

"Who?"

"The ones in the van behind us. Don't turn around too quickly."

Without even looking in the mirror, Nasser knew which vehicle he was talking about. A white Dodge van with blackout windows, New Jersey license plates, and a bumper sticker, just added for today, that read DON'T LAUGH, YOUR DAUGHTER MAY BE IN HERE. He'd noticed the van before when they'd first driven up the block and thought it looked familiar. Now he was almost positive when he'd seen it before: yesterday afternoon, when they were buying twelve gallons of diesel fuel for the *haddutas* on Foster Avenue in Brooklyn.

"You think this is the police?" he asked Dr. Ahmed.

There was a long stomach-churning beat of silence.

"By the Prophet, we have to get out of here," said Youssef. "Drive, my friend. Drive." He grimaced and bent forward slightly in his seat, as if he was having a heart attack.

"Don't panic," Dr. Ahmed said evenly. "Just start the car and circle the block. See if they follow us."

Nasser turned the key in the ignition, stepped on the gas, and pulled out cautiously as a strong wind blew dirt into the street and moved clouds in front of the sun.

In the rearview mirror, the white van started to pull out after them and then stopped, as if someone had just given an order. Nasser could almost feel the eyes behind the blacked-out glass, watching them, waiting for them to act.

"Maybe it's okay, sheik." Youssef stuck his head out and looked back. "They don't seem to be following us."

"Come around the corner again. We'll see."

Nasser drove slowly around the block, feeling veins constrict in the side of his neck. In the rearview, he saw Dr. Ahmed whispering in the Great Bear's ear and then leaning forward to pull something out of his own waistband. A gun. He remembered the doctor was holding the one gun they had with them. A .38-caliber revolver that Youssef had bought from a Dominican drug dealer over the summer.

"*T'awa kaf*," said the doctor, as they approached West Side Storage again. "Pull over."

They parked on the opposite side of the street this time. The UPS truck was gone. Yellow cabs and motorcycles whipped by, like an urban hurricane, all senseless noise and fury. But the white van was still there, pulled up a little closer to the West Side Storage entrance.

"For sure, this is them," said Dr. Ahmed.

His hands were where Nasser couldn't see them. But his shoulders were jerking slightly, as if he was busy with some fine-motor control task, like tying his shoe or loading the gun.

Nasser found he was afraid to drop his eyes away from the mirror and turn around.

"Who would have told them we were going to be here?" asked Youssef, wheezing and swallowing another pill. "I don't understand."

"Why don't we ask our driver?" The doctor gritted his teeth, performing some last complicated bit of business. "He's the one who's been out and around."

Nasser stared at the lock on his door. A little black button pushed all the way down. Why had he let the moment pass when he could have run away? Why had he let so many moments pass? It was this indecisiveness that had cost him everything. If he'd still had that hard core of inner resolution, he could have just acted without thinking. He could either have run away or gone ahead with this plan to blow himself up and been done with it. But instead he was just trapped in between again.

"Sheik, I didn't talk to nobody except my friend," he said, turning around to face Dr. Ahmed and Youssef. "And I didn't tell him anything."

"That's what you said before." The doctor had the gun in plain sight now, lying sideways in his lap. Any passerby looking in the window would have seen it.

"I don't betray anybody," Nasser protested. "My heart is true! I cut my own hand off first! You know, I was tortured . . ."

He was going to die now, he knew it. Either the doctor would shoot him right here or they'd all be killed in a gunfight with the police in the white van.

"How else would they know to find us here?" asked Youssef.

His old friend, the Great Bear. The father figure turning his back on him once more.

"I don't know," said Nasser, pleading with his eyes, feeling his heart beat wildly. "Maybe they followed us from somewhere."

"No one followed us." The doctor put his hand over the gun. "They were waiting when we came here."

"Hold on." Youssef raised his chin. "Your sister is the one who rents the room for us. Right?"

To Nasser, it seemed the sky had just darkened. "You asked me to have her do this," he said. "My sister would not call the police."

"Then how else would they know?" The doctor breathed on the back of his neck. "There's no other way they'd have the information. Either she told someone or you did. Which is it?"

Nasser, speechless, looked out the passenger side window at the white van. DON'T LAUGH, YOUR DAUGHTER MAY BE IN HERE, said the sticker on its side. In his mind, the words were transformed into: Don't Laugh, Your Sister May Be In Here. Could Elizabeth have told anyone? It didn't seem possible, but there had always been a part of her that seemed remote and foreign to him. Had something wild grown there?

"Who would she tell?" he managed to choke out.

"Maybe this teacher they say is cooperating in the newspaper." Youssef rolled up the *Tribune* and held it like a baton. "*You said* you were worried he was getting too close to her."

"Exactly," said the doctor. "Maybe he is having the sex with her and it's made her weak in the mind."

Nasser felt as if he'd just been plunged under water. He was looking up at the surface, not hearing the words anymore. Something was rippling between him and the world.

"This is not possible," he said.

"It's you or her." Dr. Ahmed shrugged in the rearview mirror, fussing with the gun. "And if it's her, that means she's dishonored her family and she should die."

"It's not her," said Nasser numbly.

His emotions were bundled up like barbed wire inside of him: he was afraid to try to pull them apart. The idea of his sister having sex with Mr. Fitzgerald was too much to take in. He tried to shut himself down.

"If it's not her, then it's you." The doctor kept pressing. "And then you should die like a dog and burn in hell forever. And shame should be brought on your family. They should die like dogs too."

"It's not me," said Nasser.

"Then prove it!" the doctor yelled. "Let's go right now! Drive. To the school. No more waiting."

"What about the material inside there?" Youssef gestured lamely out the window, toward West Side Storage. "We've spent almost three thousand dollars."

"Leave it." The doctor sat back and gave a little annoyed wave with the gun. "We have no time to make the fuel bombs. But we have enough dynamite left over at the apartment for one time. We can rig up a toggle switch in a couple of hours and be ready to go. Let's not waste any more time here."

"But sheik," Youssef protested. "I never said I wanted to be a *shaheen*. I have a wife and children."

"It's the will of Allah!" The doctor shouted at him. "He alone guides us. Whatever will be is already determined. Are you great enough to question him? Is this what you're telling me?"

"No," said the Great Bear meekly.

Hearing this, Nasser began to panic. He realized there would be no way for him to get Elizabeth out of the school before he brought the bomb in. But if he protested or tried to created another delay, the doctor would surely shoot him on the spot and then perhaps do away with her anyway. Elizabeth. He tried to remember the way she'd looked at Mr. Fitzgerald before he'd driven up in the school parking lot that day. All he could recall, though, was how her face and body were turned to him. As if she were a flower, opening to the sun.

If she'd let him in, probably she deserved to die.

"Drive the car," said Dr. Ahmed. "Uptown, downtown, but not too fast. We want to lose the van. But don't break any laws so we get stopped. We've come too far now to make another stupid mistake."

"What about God protecting us?" said Nasser, trying to reconcile himself to this fate. "What if it's His will that we get stopped?"

"Just drive the car," said the doctor.

62

David came by the West 98th Street apartment early that morning intending to drop off the weekly $400 support check and walk Arthur to school, if possible. On the subway downtown, he'd noticed people were no longer moving away from him or leaving the car when he entered. Either he'd been redeemed by the story in the morning newspaper, or they'd just forgotten about him. Above ground, the air seemed cleaner, finer, more full of possibilities.

But inside the apartment, the atmosphere was dimmed. Renee was still in her bathrobe, and a stack of cardboard boxes sat by the front door. The living room curtains were half-drawn, draining most of the color from the room. Big-band music played on the kitchen radio.

"What's going on?" David asked. "Somebody die?"

"The world is lit by lightning," Renee answered in a distant voice. "I am more faithful than I intended to be."

"What?"

"Nowadays the world is lit by lightning." She sat down under Margot Fonteyn. "It's time to blow your candles out."

"*Glass Menagerie*," said David, drawing closer as he recognized the speech. "Except isn't it the son who says that, not one of the women in the play?"

"What does it matter?" Renee touched a finger to her lips. "Words are words."

David looked around, noticing all the furniture had been moved back into place, but something still seemed wrong. There wasn't enough clutter in the living room. There was too much open space. The rug looked too vacuumed. It was as if she'd cleaned the apartment from top to bottom in one manic burst and then collapsed, not trusting herself to do any more. He spotted two small canvas suitcases next to the boxes by the front door.

"Going somewhere?" he said, the thought flashing in his mind that she might be about to leave town with Arthur.

"Not me," she said. "I'm not going anywhere."

"Renee, what's the matter?" David sat down beside her. "Today should be a great day for us. Didn't you read the newspaper? It's all over. I'm not a suspect anymore."

"Congratulations," she said, without looking at him. "I should be happy for you."

"In theory, you should."

"Reporters have been calling all morning, wanting to ask about you," she said, drawing her fingers away from and toward her lips as if she were sewing her mouth shut. "A couple of them wanted to know if I was really retracting what I said before, about the way you were with me and Arthur."

"And what'd you say?"

"I said it had all been a terrible mistake." She rubbed her leg and took a pack of cigarettes out of her robe pocket. "And I wished I'd never spoken."

"That was kind of you."

"I'm not kind." She stood up and lit one of the cigarettes, folding one arm across her chest. "I'm not cruel either. I just can't help myself."

Not an apology. Just a statement of fact.

He looked around, noticing a smell like dead roses under the smoke. Maybe it was just him, he decided. He hadn't relaxed into joining the rest of the human race yet. He didn't trust the relief. He still had the metabolism of a man expecting to get hit by lightning.

"Where's Anton?" he asked.

"He's not here."

"I never heard of a musician who got up this early."

"He doesn't." The side of her mouth twitched. "He just packed his bags and he's moving out on Friday. He's staying with a friend until then."

"Oh?" He looked over at the bags and boxes by the door.

She took a long while inhaling, as if the smoke was giving her solace.

"He's decided to go on to L.A. without us," Renee said. "He figured that Judge Nemerson would postpone our custody hearing because you've been cleared, and that was it for him. He's had enough. He said this would never be over."

"Our divorce case?"

"I think he meant the way I am."

Her words drifted off into the smoke and silence of the room. She sat back down on the couch next to him.

"So what do you think he meant by that?" David asked.

"I think maybe he figured out there would never be a happy ending with me," she said flatly, finding herself an ashtray. "If you solved all my problems, I'd just have more problems." She looked up at him with red-rimmed eyes through the tangles of her hair. "I guess you probably noticed it a long time ago."

He took out the check and laid it on the coffee table for her.

"I'm sorry," he said.

"You wouldn't consider moving back in, would you?" She started shaking her head no before he even had a chance to answer.

"I'm not so sure it would be a good idea."

It was hard to believe that just a few weeks ago, he'd still held out hope that their lives could be mended and somehow they could get back together. But now that dream was over. She was right, there would be no upbeat endings for her. She was just on fire with unhappiness, and she burned anyone who got near her without even meaning to.

"I'd like to walk Arthur to school this morning," he said. "I know it's not technically part of our deal, but . . ."

"It's all right." She gestured limply with her cigarette, letting a dragon of smoke rise through the air. "Maybe you'll have better luck than me getting him out of his room today."

He left her on the couch and went down the little hall to knock on Arthur's bedroom door.

The morning wasn't supposed to go this way. This should've been his day back in the sun. He'd had a vision of carrying Arthur on his shoulders down Broadway, with the camera crews chasing them. The hard part would come later when he had to take Elizabeth in to talk to the FBI.

"Hey, buddy, come on out." David tried the doorknob when there wasn't any answer to his persistent knocks. "I'm here for the victory lap."

"Run away, Daddy," said the voice behind the closed door. "They're still after you."

"Arthur, it's all right." He turned the knob again, vexed and bewildered. "The bad time is over."

When there was no answer, he pushed against the door and was surprised by its stiff resistance. He pushed again a little harder and realized Arthur had one of his little two-foot-high wooden chairs wedged against it.

David's heart fell just a little. Please, God, not another one. Don't let my son go crazy like my wife. We've come too far for this.

"Arthur, no one's going to come for you. I swear. The bad guys have all gone away."

There was a wiggly little nervous pause, with thumps on the floor, boards creaking, and uncomfortable wheezing. Was he going to barricade himself in there? David put his head against the door, thinking this would be the final kick-in-the-teeth irony. That he'd been so busy trying to save his own neck these past few days that he hadn't seen his own son drifting away from him.

"Arthur, please," he said. "I did all this for you. None of it means anything if I can't be with you. I know it's hard to understand. But I just want . . ." He stopped and took a breath, not wanting to burden the child but not wanting to lose the connection either. "I just want to walk you to school. Trust me. It'll be all right."

The door opened a crack. "You promise?" A small green eye peeked out.

"If anyone tries to follow us, I'll run 'im through with a sword."

The door flew open the rest of the way to reveal Arthur fully dressed in backward khaki pants, red flannel shirt, and sneakers on the wrong feet. His room was in a shambles behind him, as if there'd been some kind of drunken, frenzied Lego festival during the night.

"Where's your sword?" he demanded.

"We'll have to look for it." David took his hand and pulled him toward the living room.

There would be time downstairs to fix Arthur's clothes and make sure he'd had breakfast. Right now, all he wanted to do was get the boy out of the apartment. There was something here that would swallow him if he stayed too long. The bad cloud.

"Here's your bag, sweetie." Renee teetered toward them with Arthur's backpack hanging off her arm. "I put your inhaler in so you wouldn't forget it."

She bent down and hugged Arthur for what seemed like a very long time. Then she stood up on tiptoe and kissed David on the cheek.

"I'm glad you're going to be all right to take care of our son," she whispered in his ear.

He rested a hand on her shoulder and studied her a moment as she pulled away. Smoking and worrying were starting to give her face new lines and shadows. And whatever pills she was taking had dulled the shine in her eyes. He suddenly had a vision of the next few years of her life: the frantic mood swings slowing down and giving way to inertia and long, sad days smoking on the couch. He hoped she wouldn't end up on the street, but he felt powerless to change her trajectory, whatever it would be.

"I'm not going to get better, am I?" she said quietly.

"I don't know."

He kept hold of Arthur's hand as she went to open the door for them. This one I'm saving, he thought. Okay, you're not going to be the guy who hits it out of the ballpark or saves the beautiful girl from drowning. You're going to be the guy who gets his kid to school in the morning.

"Be good to yourself, Renee."

He moved out into the hall with his son and let the door close behind them.

63

As she sat by herself in the cafeteria, watching Mr. Fitzgerald walk around the room accepting congratulations from other teachers and students, Elizabeth thought again of the story about her father and the Jordan. The water moving over the stones and his childhood disappearing over his shoulder. That was how she felt today. Like there was a river separating her from everyone else.

Later on this afternoon, Mr. Fitzgerald would be taking her across another river and into the city to meet the FBI men. The agents had wanted her to come in right away, but Mr. Fitzgerald's lawyers had advised her to wait until they worked out a plea agreement guaranteeing her immunity.

She got a high sweet ache in her chest thinking about what all this would do to her father. She'd meant to say something to him last night but couldn't find the nerve. His only son was a terrorist and his daughter was going to turn him in. Her father. All he'd ever wanted out of life was to work hard and provide a home for his family, a place where they could all live together. Many times her father had told her of his dream, that if he worked hard enough and God smiled his way in His beneficence, he might even build another home outside Bethlehem, where he might return one day, and die under the shade of a tangerine tree, surrounded by all his children and grandchildren.

But now that vision was dying and he didn't even know it. She looked around the basketball court–sized lunch room, watching some five hundred other students laughing, joking, sharing easy confidences. Another world she would never be part of again. This was supposed to be Blue Day in her class. Silly, really. It wasn't even an official theme day, like at the end of the year. It was just a fad. Everyone was supposed to wear at least one blue item because of something a DJ on WBLS said. Merry Tyrone had blue laces on her white Nikes and Seniqua Rollins was filling out a navy hooded Georgetown sweatshirt. But Elizabeth had chosen just to wear her usual black T-shirt and green fatigue pants. To put on anything else seemed too frivolous for what was about to happen.

She opened up her book and tried to lose herself in *A Tale of Two Cities* once more, but the words wouldn't come alive for her. There was too much electricity in her mind. Why was it in most books women had to make the quiet sacrifices no one noticed, while the men got to stand on the gallows and make great speeches?

"How's it going?" Mr. Fitzgerald had circled the cafeteria and was now standing over her.

"Okay, I guess." She licked her lips and fumbled with her book. "I'm kind of nervous. I'm hungry, but I can't eat anything."

A piece of undercooked chicken and a starchy mound of mashed potatoes sat untouched on her plate.

"Look." He knelt beside her. "We probably shouldn't talk here for too long, in case people get suspicious. The FBI guys are outside and they're taking us to the city in a couple of hours. So I just want to make sure you're still okay about this."

"I don't know." She pulled at the end of her shirt.

"You don't know?"

"Well, I've been thinking about it, and I've decided I *do* want the authorities to put me up in a hotel in Manhattan until my brother gets arrested. I can't bear to look at him and lie in the meantime. Do you think that makes me a coward?"

He looked at her plate and hung his head. "No," he said.

"I think it makes me a coward." She sniffled.

"Look, if anyone's a coward, it's me," he said, focusing with sudden heat.

"What do you mean?"

They both looked around, noticing that amid the daily ruckus more and more eyes were turning toward them, taking in their intimacy.

"Never mind," he said, standing. "We should talk about it later in the car. I want to make sure we both understand the consequences of what's about to happen here. I don't want to be the one responsible for ruining your whole future."

She looked past him, hearing something building in the distance, like the gathering of the sea.

"Then maybe you're not," she said, turning back to her book.

Nasser arrived at the school just before one o'clock with Youssef and Dr. Ahmed. At some point in the last few hours, with all the fussing with wires and strapping on of dynamite, the throb in his ears had become so loud that he could hardly hear anything else.

His thoughts were becoming disordered. He stood on the front steps of the school, thinking about traffic and honor and the end of the century. The dynamite sticks felt rough against his stomach and the masking tape pulled at the skin on his back. Wasn't there a better way to do things at the end of the century?

Dr. Ahmed pulled open the front door of the school and went in ahead of the other two. The black guard with the sharp-creased pants was gone and instead two white men stood by the metal detectors, as if they were waiting for this confrontation. FBI men. Nasser recognized them right away. They had the same clean-cut barbaric look as Calloway, the one who'd questioned him at the car service. The one on the left had sandy-colored hair and blue eyes like the Israeli soldier in the story Nasser's father used to tell about the coffee beans. As soon as he saw Nasser and the others, he began tugging at the side of his windbreaker, as if he was about to pull out a gun.

The throb in Nasser's head got louder, pounding against the base of his skull.

"Please," he made himself say. "I'm dropping off my application for the principal. He said it's okay."

Yes, this was right, what he was about to do. It was a heroic act.

Blue Eyes looked at his partner, a bald, modest-looking man with light-colored eyebrows.

"Hey, Don." Blue Eyes's voice was barely an insect twitter beneath all the throbbing. "You wanna get on the walkie-talkie, tell them we have some visitors?"

There was a shimmering trail of tension in the air. Blue Eyes's hand disappeared into his jacket, as he came down the steps, his heels making a deliberate click-clack in perfect time with the blood beating in Nasser's head.

"Excuse me, gentlemen," he said with the kind of exaggerated official politeness that gives way to brute force in a split second. "Do you have some kind of I.D.?"

Standing next to Nasser in the doorway, Dr. Ahmed and Youssef looked at each other. These men who'd expected so much of him. Who'd risked their own lives in *jihad*. The life of this world is nothing but a sport and a pastime. The true reward comes later. Nasser tried to force himself once again to believe that. Maybe in acting right now he would finally come to believe. A hero sacrifices. That's what he does. Everyone learned that in school.

"Yes, of course," said Dr. Ahmed. "Here is our I.D."

He reached into his waistband, pulled out the .38, and before either of the agents could react, he shot each of them once in the head and once in the chest for good measure.

David was standing in the middle of the cafeteria, talking with guarded friendliness to Henry Rosenthal, when the three outsiders came into the room. And immediately, he knew not just the circumstances but the very texture of his life was about to change.

The first one in was a big bald man with a heavy gut and a

graying beard. He walked the length of the cafeteria and took up a position in front of the emergency exit at the eastern end of the room, like a volunteer fire warden. The second one also had a beard, but was smaller, with a long horse face and a cheap dark suit without a tie. He seemed utterly impatient, as if he'd been kept waiting in a doctor's office for half a day. And the last to enter was Nasser Hamdy, back in school again, looking ferocious and distracted, a man with a mission.

He walked right by David, marched up to his sister sitting at an empty table nearby, and stared at her. Not a loving brother-sister look. It was something less forgiving, less comprehending. Then he seemed to make a decision. He stepped onto the seat next to her, climbed on top of the picnic-style table, and ripped open his shirt with both hands.

For a few seconds, he stood there over her, surveying the vast, stunned lunchroom, with his arms outstretched and his skinny torso bare except for a key hanging from his neck on a chain and five brown sticks of dynamite taped around his middle. Displaying himself as if to say: Step right up, come see the Incredible Exploding Boy of Coney Island.

A wave of panic went through the cafeteria. Five hundred–odd kids standing up, screaming and ready to bolt.

"Ho shit!"

"Oh my Gawwwd!"

"Get the fuck down from there, niggah!!"

David felt like the back of his head had been yanked off and his mind was empting out. *What do I do here?* He looked to the main entrance and saw the horse-faced man pull out a small handgun and hit Tisha Cornwall full in the face with it when she tried to elbow past him. She sank to the floor, stunned, with her nose and mouth bloodied, while he held up the pistol proudly, ready to shoot anyone else who tried. At the other end of the room, the big bear-like man was bracing himself against the emergency exit, not showing a gun, but clearly implying he had one just by his implacable stance.

Fear pressing down hard on his bowels, David began to run through the possibilities for tragedy. If anyone tried to rush Nasser, he'd likely set off the dynamite with the toggle switch hanging on his belt, killing everyone in the vicinity. However, if the kids all attempted to run out the door at once, the horse-faced man would surely shoot several of them, the rest would trample one another, and the bomb might go off anyway.

"Come on, you sissy-ass terrorist motherfucker!" Seniqua was screaming taunts at Nasser, her pregnant belly waggling. "Get on down, so I can kick your faggot-ass!"

Merry Tyrone had her by the shoulders, weeping as she tried to hold Seniqua back. Kevin Hardison kept bobbing up behind the two of them, yelling: "Step to it, niggah! Step to it!" Nydia Colone was on her knees nearby, praying loudly. Obstreperous Q, Ray-Za, and five other boys were huddled in a corner, clearly formulating some testosterone-crazed plan to try rushing all the terrorists at once.

Lungs tightening, David realized he had to take control of the situation somehow. No one else would. He clambered unsteadily up onto one of the tables next to Nasser's, raised his hands, and shouted at the top of his voice.

"AWWWRIIIGHT, PEOPLE!! CHILL!!!!"

Everything seemed to stop at once. Kids froze and fell silent. Nasser lowered his arms a fraction. Even the two older men at the opposite ends of the room looked up, interested in what he might have to announce.

But David, already streaming with sweat and pumping adrenaline, had *no idea* what to say next. His storehouse of comparable experiences was barren. All he had were his father's words: *Nothing happens and then everything happens.*

"What is going on here?" he yelled at Nasser.

The little man with the gun answered instead. "We are here because there is no other way to get your attention!" he called out in slightly stilted foreign-university English. "You are all too busy watching television! Muslim peoples are suffering all over the world and you do not care! You support our oppressors, because you are cowards and hypocrites! And you think you are heroes!"

His eyes searched the crowd of students, looking for someone who was following his message. Sensing he was throwing it over their heads, he tried to make adjustments.

"If you had a city here where only white people are allowed to work and own properties, you would call this racism!" the little man shouted out, trying to enunciate carefully. "But you are supporting it! You are supporting it because this country itself was based on racism and on the slavery of black people and the confiscation of land from the Indians. And then *you* invent terrorism by dropping the atom bomb in Japan and killing hundreds of thousands of women and childrens! So this is the only kind of language you understand."

It was useless trying to talk to this one, David realized. The little man was clearly one of those people who are born hot and have no identity without a war going on.

Nasser was a better bet. He was young, David reminded himself, and still a little unformed. Perhaps he hadn't turned himself into an absolute monolith of unappeasable rage yet.

"Nasser, why are you doing this?" he asked, turning and facing the boy as they both stood on tabletops some ten feet apart. "This is your sister here. These are your friends. Why would you do anything to hurt them?"

"These are not my friends!" Nasser spat out. "And my sister is a whore. You've made her that way!"

David saw Elizabeth shut her eyes as if to deny this was really happening. Seniqua shook a fist at Nasser and the rest of the kids in the room quietly seethed, ready to tear the visitors apart at the first opportunity. David glanced around the room, doing the simmer-down pat with his hands, hoping no one would jump up and do anything foolish that might get them all killed immediately.

"I'm not a whore, Nasser," Elizabeth finally spoke up in a wounded voice. "My heart is as true as yours."

"Then why?" Nasser stared down at her, his frail chest heaving over the dynamite. "Why, why, why?! Why do you act this way? Why do you betray me? Why is everything like this?"

For a second, hearing him sound so hurt and inarticulate made David feel a kind of fearful tenderness toward the boy. But the dynamite sticks were still wrapped around him.

"All right, enough." The little man with the gun was trying to reassert control over the situation. "All Muslim children out of the room, except the sister. You take the message with you and tell everyone what we're saying. Everyone else stays."

There was a flurry of movement and about two dozen kids lined up by the door near the little man. There was Ibrahim Yassin, an eleventh-grader from Egypt. And Fatima Fayyad, a Lebanese freshman, and Mohammed Azzam, a junior from Iraq. And sneaking onto the end of the line, Amal Lincoln and Yuri Ehrlich.

Seeing them standing there, David felt hope drying up in his chest. Everyone else in the room was supposed to die. The knowledge came over him suddenly like a rush of wind. No, you had it wrong before. You weren't supposed to die on a burning bus. That was just to get you ready. You're supposed to die *here*. This is the last room you'll ever see.

David clenched his fists in frustration. Come on, do something. A fighter fights. A writer writes. A teacher teaches.

He turned and looked over at Elizabeth's brother, who stood on top of the next table, shoulders hunched, shivering slightly against the prospect of his own imminent dismemberment.

"Nasser," David said, trying to appeal to him. "It doesn't have to be this way. You don't have to go along with this. Think for yourself."

"Think for yourself! Think for yourself!" The little man by the main entrance mocked him as he ushered the Muslim kids out. "That's the difference between us. You only think for yourself. But we think about the peoples. We think about God. This is what you cannot understand, I know. To you, this is just crazy Arabs who blow themselves up. You don't know what it is to make a sacrifice for something that's bigger—"

"Okay, okay. I get it." David put his hand up, hearing him, but not really acknowledging him.

He looked over at the big bearded man by the emergency exit, who was shifting slightly as if all this talk of Arabs blowing themselves up made him uncomfortable. Maybe this was more than he'd bargained for. But he wasn't moving.

So David turned back to Nasser and reached down into himself for what felt like the last bit of courage he had left. "You know, I've got my people here too."

Could he do this? He wasn't sure. His eyes swept around the room, taking in all the students. Seniqua in her belligerent pregnancy, Kevin in his striped Gatsby shirt, Elizabeth without her skates. Kids who in one way or another had entrusted a part of themselves to him. Yes, he was supposed to look out for them.

"I'm willing to make a sacrifice too," he said slowly.

In the gym upstairs, someone was bouncing a basketball.

Nasser looked over at him, not wanting the connection, but getting it anyway.

"Let everybody else go. I'll stay," David said wearily. "So there's my sacrifice." He waved his hand at the room. "These guys are my people."

"*Yin an deen nekk!*" the small man shouted, pointing the gun at David from some fifty-five feet away. "He's not going to listen to you. He knows you play with his mind."

"You got the power," said David, playing out the gambit and not taking his eyes off Nasser's. "You call the game. You'll get just as much press coverage if everybody else leaves and it's just you and me who get blown up when the building comes down. Come on. Let the rest of them go. Don't make it about anybody else."

But, of course, it was about somebody else. Not five hours ago, David had coaxed his son out of the bedroom, held his puffy little white hand, and promised him that everything would be okay from here on out.

And now he was throwing that promise away and it tore him up inside. Big man—so what? There was no such thing as a selfless sacrifice, he realized. In the end, someone else always got hurt.

"My life for their lives," he said, struggling not to be overpowered by emotions. "Come on. I'm ready to go. Are you?"

The little man with the gun and the big bald man both started hollering at Nasser in Arabic at once. "*Wala al noor! Wala al noor!*"

Nasser was starting to do a little worried-man shuffle on top of his table. Not knowing where to put his eyes. He glanced once down at Elizabeth and then back at the little man and then over at David.

"Come on, Nasser," David persisted. "Let your sister out of here. She hasn't done anything wrong. Just make it about you and me. I'm ready to go. *Are you?*"

Just saying the words was wrenching. How would Arthur and Renee make it without him?

"*Wala al noor! Wala al noor!*" The little man was frantically gesturing for Nasser to throw the switch. "*Ya habela!*"

"Come on." David stretched out his hand to Nasser and edged toward the end of the table, like a pirate getting ready to board an enemy ship. "I'll even stand next to you and we can hold hands when we go up together. *I'm ready to go when you are*. Just let everybody else out."

His heart was jackhammering against the walls of his chest.

"*Askat!*" The little man's neck veins were popping. "*Wala al noor!*"

Nasser was trying not to look at him. Trying to focus on anything else; the ugly green walls, the other students, the wretched, indigestible food on the plates. But his eyes kept slipping back to Elizabeth's and then David's. He was terrified himself, David realized. Not in any way ready to carry this out. What he needed was a way to step down.

The pressure inside Nasser's head was getting to be too much. The teacher yelling, Think for yourself, *are you ready to go?* And Dr.

Ahmed screaming, *Turn on the light, throw the switch!* His temples were bursting and he felt like his skull was going to explode and rain bloody bits on his shoulders. His eyes went down to Elizabeth once more, as if drawn by magnets. Seeing her again, but seeing her in a new way.

All this time, all these years, he realized he'd only been seeing parts of her. But now it all came together and it frightened him to the depths of his soul. He saw his mother, his father, his half sisters, the baby who died before he was born, ancestors from the Monastery of Branches, and grandchildren who would never exist. He saw himself and he saw the future exploding. And all at once, it seemed unbearable and unholy to destroy this, to wipe out every last trace of the family. It was like disturbing the universe, to do this. Blotting out the stars. Drying up the land, so nothing would ever grow again. Do you dream anymore, Nasser?

Was this truly God's will?

"Come on, Nasser." David tried to remember the word he'd heard both brother and sister use. "Isn't this really . . . *haram?*"

He saw Nasser arch his shoulders and then reach around behind his back, as if he had another detonator switch there. All together, the kids in the cafeteria started hollering and throwing themselves on the floor in terror and disgust.

And then time seemed to slow down and the noise seemed to die away again. Nasser's arm began to circle back toward his front and David heard the unmistakable sound of adhesive being peeled off, a little bit at a time. Several bands of masking tape were clinging to Nasser's fingers and as he pulled them away from his body, the dynamite sticks began to pull away with them.

Reacting out of instinct, David jumped off the table, came over, and stood beside Elizabeth, ready to receive the dynamite. The jackhammer in his chest had subsided, replaced by one tremendous thud every few seconds.

Here was a thing of moment. His heart was squeezed blue. He

reached up to Nasser, beckoning to him, staring, forcing him to look down and make that connection again. For a few seconds, everything depended on maintaining the connection. Easy there, steady now. The dynamite was halfway stripped off with its red and green wires hanging out. Nasser finally lowered his eyes to David's, locking in on him. Completing the circuit. Only this time, instead of looking angry or confused as David half-expected, the kid looked *relieved*. He didn't want to handle this thing either.

David put one foot up on the bench and stretched out his hands. The tape, the dynamite, and the wires were just barely attached to Nasser's body, a little over two feet away. David was already thinking about what he would do once he had them; what if one of the wires was loose and the device got tripped off anyway? Shouldn't they just sit down at this point and call the bomb squad?

But then the connection was broken. A little firecracker snap echoed across the lunchroom and the light in Nasser's eyes went dim. He turned in on himself and fell to one knee in front of his sister, blood spurting wildly from the side of his head.

Elizabeth let out a scream—a shriek heard across the desert—as Nasser collapsed sideways on the tabletop and blood sprayed onto the floor. The students all rose together and started to stampede toward the eastern end of the cafeteria, away from the little man who'd just fired the gun.

David tried to stand his ground as students went running by him going the other way, knocking into his arms and shoulders. Fifty-five feet away, at the main entrance, the little man with the gun was looking exasperated and furious.

He started to limp toward David with his chin lowered and the gun raised. His eyes were looking off to the side a little, though, as if his real objective were elsewhere.

David glanced over his shoulder and saw kids trampling each other brutally, trying to get out the emergency exit. The big bearded man had disappeared in the pack, but was obviously trying to hold the door and keep them back. And in the resulting gridlock, kids were falling and getting stomped. A ninth-grader named Cheryl Smith crawled away, spitting blood.

In the meantime, the little man kept coming—limping and grunting in outrage. From the corner of his eye, David saw Elizabeth trying to kneel on the bench and cover her brother's body with her own. Clearly she'd figured out what was just dawning on David—that the little man was coming for the bomb, to find the switch and finish the job.

David tried to stand in his way, even as the metallic taste of fear filled up his mouth.

The little man raised the gun and pointed at David's face. Warning him to get out of the way. David didn't budge. He didn't want to do this. He didn't want to play the hero anymore. He only wanted his ordinary life back again, but it was too late.

From twelve feet away, the little man fired.

David felt stinging just under his left eye and then a spider's web of pain spread back through his skull. He staggered backward and the little man brushed past him on his way to Elizabeth and her brother. The pain was more than enormous. It was a world in and of itself with no outside reference points. It turned into a horn boring into his head. Unbearable. It was impossible to remember not being in this much pain. But somehow David managed to break free of it for just one second and with a last furious burst of strength, like a mother lifting a car off a child, he reached out and grabbed the little man by the collar, spun him around, and punched him in the face.

More from the force of surprise than anything else, the man stumbled and started to lose his balance. Knowing he was about to black out, David threw himself forward, plowing into the little man with his shoulder, knocking him down and pinning him to the greasy floor. For a second, he was aware he was covering the man like a heavy rug and then he wasn't aware of anything.

When he came to, he heard a thousand feet running his way, a mad horde, the kids reversing field to come help him. Someone pulled him off the little man, and as he rolled over, he saw what looked like a forest come to life—hundreds of flailing limbs and branches closing in on the shooter, crashing down wild angry blows.

"Call my son. Call my son. Somebody please call my wife and my son and tell them I'm all right."

In the parking lot some twenty-five minutes later, David was beginning to collapse into a kind of delirium. He'd lost a great deal of blood and he kept hearing paramedics talking worriedly about the discharge coming out of his ears. There were ambulances, cop cars, bomb trucks, emergency service vehicles, helicopters circling, reporters swarming, broadcast trucks, satellite dishes and oh, who cared anymore?

"Somebody please call my son."

Camera shutters went off in his face. Sirens screamed in the distance. He was on a stretcher, being worked on by strong purposeful men in blue jackets and white shirts. One of them, a young black guy with kind eyes, kept holding his hand and smiling at him.

"Don't worry, man. We're not gonna let you die."

David tried to sit up. "Who said anything about me dying?"

"Never mind." The young guy gently pushed him back down and made sure David's IV line was still firmly attached.

More bodies materialized around him. More FBI agents, more reporters, more cameras, more noise. He was aware of other bodies on stretchers nearby. The little man and the big bearded man, looking badly beaten. He hoped they wouldn't go in the same ambulance with him. A black bag was carried by, and he knew Nasser was inside it.

"Who killed you?" somebody called out to him. He vaguely recognized Judy Mandel's voice.

Who killed me? But I'm not dead yet. Somebody started to put an inflatable sleeve over his leg and he mumbled that it wasn't broken. In spite of all the drugs they were giving him, pain still kept flashing through the inside of his head. He turned and saw Elizabeth Hamdy being led away by Jim Lefferts from the FBI.

"Somebody please call my boy . . ."

Donna Vitale suddenly appeared before him. She must have been in another part of the building when everything happened in the cafeteria.

"What is it?" she asked.

"Somebody please call my son. Tell him I'm all right." He could barely get any other words out, it was so hard to focus in all this agony.

"It's all right. I'll call your son for you."

She started to reach for his hand, but then Detective Noonan grabbed her by the elbow and pulled her off into the crowd.

Flashbulbs went off, leaving a blinding white light when he closed his eyes. But why would anybody be using flashbulbs? It was still daytime.

He wanted to cry out after her. She didn't have the number for Arthur. And she didn't know what he'd meant by "I'm all right." He wasn't sure if he was going to be all right, physically. In fact, with flashbulbs going off inside his head, it was gradually dawning on him that he might not be. But he wanted his son to know that his father was *all right* in the larger sense, meaning that he was no one to be ashamed of.

He tried to push up on an elbow and call out to her, so she'd come back and he could explain it to her. But it was too late. The drugs were finally beginning to wrap him up in a thick, warm, drowsy blanket. Somehow, she'd figure it all out anyway.

"Think we should move him now?" one of the medical technicians was asking.

"Better late than never."

Then he was being hoisted up and carried aloft. As in a dream. More bulbs were going off in his head. He was shuttling between there and not there. He was going, going, and people were still taking his picture. In the last flashes of consciousness, he saw a microphone suspended before his face and heard Sara Kidreaux's familiar voice.

"David, do you have any comment about what happened here today?"

"Noooooooo . . ."

He was shoved into the back of the ambulance and the door slammed. Then all at once, they were moving and the texture was changing again. Past the lights, the sound, the gyrating chaos of the city around him. Through the sound waves, microwaves, fiber-optics, high-definition pixels, and bouncing satellite signals. Toward a vast black empty space.

He closed his eyes and saw himself again as a skinny awkward boy, tracking the arc of a scuffed ball against a setting late afternoon sun, running, running, running hard for the love of his family and friends; diving in among the champagne-colored weeds, catching it just at the very tip of his mitt, and holding it aloft, triumphant in the gathering dusk for everyone to see.

64

Dear Mr. Fitzgerald,

Thank you for your kind note, which Agent Lefferts had passed on to me at my new location, which of course I am not allowed to disclose to you.

I am glad to hear you are feeling better. I prayed for you every day that you were in a coma, along with performing my traditional Muslim prayers.

I am not sure what to say about all the terrible things that happened with you and my brother at school. My father tells me there is no God but God and everything that occurs on earth is subject to His will, so we must accept it. Even if it means the destruction of a part of our family. On the other hand, you always taught me to think as an individual, and take responsibility into my own hands. So now I am not sure what I believe. Perhaps it was God's will that Nasser was killed and you got shot and my family has to live in hiding. Or perhaps everything is my fault because I am a bad person. I keep thinking there must be something I could have done or said that would have made things come out differently. Either way, I feel a sense of sadness about the way everything ended, like that hand is still over my heart, and it will probably take me the rest of my life to figure it all out.

I don't know what I'm going to do about college. The circumstances of my life make it complicated now. But I also know it's something you very much wanted me to do. So Insh'allah, *who can say how things will work out?*

I may be back in Brooklyn in time for the holidays, though the contact agents have asked me not to say when or where exactly because of the trial coming up with my brother's friends. If it is God's will, perhaps I will see you again. If it is not, know that you have a special place in my heart and may God smile upon you in His beneficence.

Yours very truly,
Elizabeth Hamdy

On a warm April day, David Fitzgerald sat on the sofa outside his physical therapist's office, still struggling for the tenth time to make sense of the perfectly drawn blue words on the white page.

God's will. My brother. A hand over my heart. The bullet in his head had afflicted him in unpredictable ways since he came out of the coma just before Thanksgiving. Words could float around in his head for a few minutes before he'd find the right order for them.

But the part about her sense of sadness kept coming back to him. His own life hadn't been easy these last few months. He'd lost part of the use of his right arm and needed a cane to walk. And even worse, the blinding headaches made him a liability as a teacher. The two visits he'd made to the school since starting therapy in December were grotesque humiliations. He wanted people to remember him as strong, incisive, an educator. Not an oversized cripple slurring his words. Everyone acted glad to see him—Larry Simonetti shook his good hand and Michelle the secretary gave him a discreet peck on the cheek—but David could tell they were also a little afraid of him. It wasn't just the limp or the bullet hole in his face, a small light-colored scar under his left eye. It was what he made them think of: disruption, violence, and death. They wanted him to go away, but they didn't want to admit it. And they resented him for making them so confused.

On the upside, he had a more-than-decent settlement from the city and he was seeing Donna. But Renee had continued her disintegration. She was in and out of hospitals and had been on and off a half dozen medications since the year started. So Arthur's child care had to be patched together on a day-to-day basis. David lived for the time he spent with the boy—the days at the museum, the nights at the apartment—but something still haunted him when he went to sleep at night, listening for the sound of his son snoring in his sleeping bag next to his bed.

That same sense of sadness Elizabeth wrote to him about. He'd had a hand over his own heart these last few months. He decided he needed to see her again, if only to thank her and let her know that what happened wasn't her fault. He needed one last connection.

He began plotting to find her again as he went through therapy sessions bouncing rubber balls and walking on balance beams. It wasn't going to be easy. He hadn't seen her since that last day in the cafeteria. She and her family had been put in the FBI's witness protection program immediately. He'd tried writing to her through the Bureau, to let her know he was okay and to ask what she was going to do with her life. But her reply had left him confused and unsatisfied.

God's will. How would he make contact again? She said she might be in Brooklyn for the holidays, but he didn't understand why she'd be coming back for Easter. A week after reading her letter at the therapist's office, though, he heard a news story on the radio that said there would be a festival celebrating the Muslim holiday Id al-Adha, "the feast of the sacrifice," on the Coney Island boardwalk next week and thousands of Muslim-Americans from all over the city were expected to attend.

God's will. Maybe it was a signal that she would be there. But it was up to him, having the guts to go look for her. He hesitated, and not just out of the obvious fear of running into one or two militant friends of the men who'd been arrested among the thousands of devout, law-abiding Muslims. He was afraid of what the trip down to Brooklyn would reveal about himself, about his own limitations.

Just getting on the subway alone would require a kind of courage. What if he got lost and disoriented? What if he fell down in the middle of a car and found he couldn't stand up? On the other hand, if he could make it all the way out to Coney Island on his own to find Elizabeth, it might mean he had the guts he needed to get on with his life.

So, early on a crisp Tuesday afternoon, he put on an old tweed jacket, found his cane, and started the long complex transfer of trains required to get him from the Upper West Side to the last stop in Brooklyn.

At the Stillwell Avenue station, he came down from the elevated platform slowly, already hearing the booming voice of the muezzin coming from loudspeakers near Steeplechase Pier.

"*Allahu akbar! Allahu akbar!*"

He approached what looked like a scene from someone else's dream. Thousands of shoeless Muslim men knelt on prayer mats with the rotting old Parachute Drop at their backs and the Atlantic Ocean rolling and pitching, sunlight in front of them.

Some small cowardly part of David shrank back, remembering it was a Muslim who'd shot him in the face and crippled him for life. But then again, it was a Muslim who'd saved him. Was he going to spend his life hiding behind prejudices and hopping off trains every time he saw someone with a head scarf?

The prayers ended and he followed the throng going into the Astroland amusement park nearby. There were enough people going in to fill a small stadium: old women in veils who looked like they'd just come off the road to Damascus, young men in ties ready for Wall Street, family men with heavy, tired faces, peppery little girls in head scarves. Apparently the group had rented out the park for the day and there were no angry militants in sight. Traditional Arab music wailed from the public address system, replacing the usual cavalcade of '70s and '80s disco hits. Workers had covered up the pictures of naked women adorning the Dante's Inferno haunted house. The Muslims dispersed onto the rides. Women in veils smashed into each other with bumper cars. Children shrieked with delight on the Cyclone roller coaster. Swarthy bearded men in *keffiyehs* rode carousel horses and spun around on the Break Dancer ride. Just ordinary people taking a day off and having fun.

David saw no sign of Elizabeth, but he sensed her presence nearby. A kind of springish radiance in the air. He stumbled through the crowd, slowly feeling himself becoming part of a surging life force again. He was determined to find her. It was a matter of honor not to give up looking, since he'd come this far. He had to connect with her just one last time and let her know everything was all right.

After twenty minutes of searching, he finally spotted a girl who looked like her waiting in line for the Wonder Wheel. But she was thirty yards away, and with his blurry vision he couldn't be sure. She was wearing a dark sack-like skirt and a white *hijab*. And she was in a separate line for girls. David called out to her, but she didn't hear him through the milling crowd and ride noises. He was feeling dizzy and weak from the warmth of the day and the crowd closing in on him. He tried to maneuver through with his cane, but his progress was slow and painful. He hoped he wouldn't collapse.

He made his way past a souvenir stand and saw the girl smooth down the back of her *hijab*, leaving a little handprint. Was it Elizabeth or wasn't it? He stopped and called out to her, and then suddenly realized that if it was her she might have changed radically these past few months. The *hijab* and the sack of a skirt. The separate line for girls. It dawned on him that she might be doing penance for everything that had gone wrong.

He wanted to tell her it was all right, that she shouldn't blame herself. But maybe he couldn't reach her anymore. Religion had come into her life. Something else was pushing her forward. The Wonder Wheel stopped and the line of girls waiting to get on it moved.

And then without warning, she turned and looked right at him. As if she'd known he was there all along. Slowly, a smile spread across her face and he knew he didn't have to come any closer. She was seeing him from across the river and it was okay. This was something more than penance. The hand over her heart had lifted. And now he knew he could go home too.

He started to wave to her, but she had already turned back and started to climb into one of the gondolas for the Wonder Wheel.

And so he just stood there by the ticket booth and watched her go up on the turning wheel, a smudged angel rising above the hot dog stands, mattress stores, and housing projects, into the fierce brightness of a Coney Island afternoon.

ACKNOWLEDGMENTS

This is a work of fiction. As most New Yorkers know, there is no Coney Island High School.

I would like to acknowledge the following books as invaluable research sources: Thomas W. Lippman's *Understanding Islam*, second revised edition (Meridian, New York, 1995); *Two Seconds Under the World* by Jim Dwyer, David Kocieniewski, Diedre Murphy, and Peg Tyre (Crown, New York, 1994); *Cry Palestine: Inside the West Bank* by Said K. Aburish (Westview Press, Boulder, Colorado, 1993). I'm also deeply indebted to Izzat al-Ghazzawi, head of the Palestinian Writers Union, who generously gave of his time and insights during my stay in the Middle East; Jennifer Goldberg from Edward R. Murrow High School; and of course, my uncle Arthur. Any errors in fact or interpretation are the author's original creations.

In addition, I'd like to thank the following people: Marcy Rutterman, Sandra Abrams, Don Roth, Jim Murphy, Midge Herz Kosner, Ken Wasserman, Hubert Selby, Jr., Lenore Braverman, Nasser Ahmed, Jeffrey Goldberg, Alyson Lurie, Kim Bonheim, Gail Reisin, Jarek Ali, David Ignatius, Dan Ingram, Dr. Charles Stone, Bart Gelmann, Dr. Bernard Sabella, Carol Storey, Daniel Max, Doug Pooley, Eric Pooley, Sonny Mehta, Alice Farkouh, Larry Joseph, Allen Leibowitz, Joe Gallagher, Fatima Shama, Guy Renzi, Donald Sadowy, J. J. Goldberg, Jim Yardley, Joyce London, Sarah Piel, Lori Andiman, Mel Glenn, Ari Mientkovich, Chiara Colletti, Michael Siegel, Larry Schoenbach, Naomi Shore, Caroline Upcher, and Joanne Gruber.

And finally, I want to thank my friend and agent, Richard Pine, and my editor, Michael Pietsch, for first helping me write this book and then making me write a better one.